R. H. Patterson

The Economy of Capital or Gold and Trade

SALZWASSER
VERLAG

R. H. Patterson

The Economy of Capital or Gold and Trade

Reprint of the original, first published in 1865.

1st Edition 2022 | ISBN: 978-3-75259-007-4

Verlag (Publisher): Salzwasser Verlag GmbH, Zeilweg 44, 60439 Frankfurt, Deutschland
Vertretungsberechtigt (Authorized to represent): E. Roepke, Zeilweg 44, 60439 Frankfurt, Deutschland
Druck (Print): Books on Demand GmbH, In de Tarpen 42, 22848 Norderstedt, Deutschland

THE ECONOMY OF CAPITAL

OR

GOLD AND TRADE

THE

ECONOMY OF CAPITAL

OR

GOLD AND TRADE

BY

R. H. PATTERSON

AUTHOR OF

MDCCCLXV

PREFACE

A PORTION of this work consists of a series of articles recently contributed to *Blackwood's Magazine*. The articles have been revised and re-cast, in order to obtain the symmetry requisite in a book. And in order to give completeness to the work, the concluding portion of the essay on the Economy of Capital (as originally published) has been withdrawn; and in lieu there is given a new chapter, on the Bank of England,—containing a full exposition of our Monetary System, and of the reforms which are requisite in order to bring it into harmony with the spirit of the age, and the requirements of the community.

The immediate cause of publication is the desire that has been expressed in many quarters for a reprint of those articles—particularly the "Economy of Capital" and the "City of Gold."

The subject of which this volume treats, has long been to me an interesting study; and, as a journalist, I have had a good opportunity of collecting facts, and of forming my opinions, from a watchful observation of the course of events during the last fifteen years.

R. H. P.

LONDON, *November* 8, 1864.

CONTENTS

CHAPTER I.

CHAPTER II.

CHAPTER III.

CHAPTER IV.

CHAPTER V.

CHAPTER VI.

CHAPTER VII.

APPENDIX.

A.

B.

C.

D.

ERRATA.

P. 55. *For* "the non-producers at the expense of the producing classes,"—*read* "the producing classes at the expense of the non-producers."

P. 133, 16th line from top, *for* "Finch," *read* "Birchin."

P. 226, 11th line from foot, *for* "one-fifteenth," *read* "one-tenth."

ERRATA.

Page 233, eighteenth line from top, *delete* " a sum equal to double the annual ngs of the nation in 1857."

Page 236, sixth line from top, *for* "bonus" *read* "loans."

THE

ECONOMY OF CAPITAL

THOUGHTS ON GOLD

In the spring of 1854 there was discovered in Australia one of the richest "placers," or gold-beds, even of that most auriferous country. The spot was a deep ravine, formed by the Buckland River, enclosed by steep mountain-sides which excluded every breath of wind. It was autumn in Australia, though spring here. The air in the ravine was stagnant, and the scorching sun made it intensely hot during the day, while at night the temperature fell to a piercing cold; so that the sojourners in the ravine were alternately in an oven and an ice-house. Moreover, as the gold-beds lay in the channel of the river, the miners worked up to their waists in water. To this gold-field of surpassing richness hundreds of adventurers flocked in feverish haste; but disease, like the fabled dragons and griffins of old, kept horrid sentry over the buried treasures. A peculiar fever, of the typhoid character, was the natural denizen of the spot; besides which, the gold-seekers suffered severely from eye-blight, owing to the concentrated blaze of the sunshine reflected from the steep sides of the ravine, and they were at all times grievously tormented by clouds of flies. Bad diet and want of vegetables aggravated the diseases natural to the place and to the kind of work. In the strangely interesting accounts which then reached us, we read of onions selling at six shillings a pound; and cabbages, which we buy here for a penny, were so precious that they were cut up and sold by weight—from half-a-crown to four shillings the pound being readily paid for them. Physic, or what passed for it, rose in price in a still more startling manner—Holloway's pills selling at one shilling each, or a guinea per box! It was a Valley of Death. "Constitutions that had borne the hardships of other fields broke down here," wrote an eyewitness of the scene; "and hundreds have perished, dying unattended and unknown. The little levels between the stream and the base of the mountain-wall, for ten miles along the valley, are so thickly studded with graves that the river appears to run through a churchyard." One new-comer, wiser than the rest, having counted eleven corpses carried past his tent during the dinner-hour of his first working day, and thinking that even gold may be purchased too dearly, left the place instantly. Many abandoned it after a somewhat longer trial. But the greater number, fascinated by the unusual richness of the gold-beds, remained in defiance of disease, and "took their chance," —with what result the numerous graves of the valley testify to this day.

It was a scene "to point a moral or adorn a tale." Had some wandering Spirit from another planet looked down upon that valley of death, or upon the many other striking incidents of the gold-fever of the last fifteen years; if he had seen men in myriads rushing across oceans and continents to the gold-fields of California and Australia, waste places in the uttermost parts of the earth; if he had beheld them toiling in the gulches of the mountains amidst all manner of hardships and disease, beset with extremes of weather, exhausting work, exorbitant prices, and lawless society, —he must have said to himself, "Surely mankind have some mighty end in view, when so many myriads come here to toil and suffer with such feverish energy and extraordinary endurance." Yet the yellow substance which these crowds so eagerly seek after, what could it do for them? They could not eat it or drink it,—it was neither food, medicine, nor clothing: it was simply a metal of unusual weight and ductility, and exhibiting a yellow lustre. And were this wandering Spirit to show a piece of the yellow metal to one of the natives of the country, and ask its use, the savage would tell him that it served to make rings for wearing in the nose and ears, or on other parts of the body, by way of ornament, but otherwise was of no account,—it could neither head an axe for him nor point a spear. In fine, were this planetary Sage, following the track of the gold-ships, to proceed to Europe and the abodes of civilisation, to see what is made of the metal which men seek for with so great eagerness, he would find that the getting of it is so expensive that (unlike iron and lead) it is of no use in the necessary commodities of life, and only figures as a costly means of ornament and decoration. He would find it, in fact—so far as the arts of life are concerned—closely allied in character to gems and precious stones, the exorbitant prices given for which show how much barbarism still lurks under the cloak of civilisation.

But this inquiring Spirit would also see another side to the question. Were he to go into our banks, our marketplaces, our counting-houses, he would speedily comprehend the object for which we mortals seek gold, and prize it so much. If he were to visit the great monetary emporium in Threadneedle Street, with its busy throng of customers ceaselessly depositing or withdrawing the yellow metal, and thereafter were to watch for half an hour the gay crowds who go a-shopping in Regent Street, he would see that this metal is the recognised symbol of property into which we can convert our wealth—whether it be of land, houses, or merchandise—storing it up in little space, and which we can reconvert into any kind of property at pleasure. He would see that by common consent nearly one-half of the entire civilised population of the earth take this view of the matter, and have made the yellow metal indispensable to them, by decreeing it to be the substance out of which shall be made the counters with which men buy and sell, and reckon up the gains of material existence. But what of the other half of the civilised world? Here the doubts of our planetary Sage would begin anew: for he would see that this enthroning of gold as a special and almost sacred metal is, after all, a purely arbitrary proceeding, and that civilised mankind are divided on this question into two rival and hostile camps. Six hundred millions of the human race (constituting fully two-thirds of the civilised population of the globe), in China, India, and Japan, and in Asia generally, repudiate the peculiar value attached to the yellow metal by their Western brethren, and exalt a shining white metal into a like conventional importance. If gold reigns in the West, silver rules in the East. And what of that outer world, those regions beyond the pale of civilisation which still occupy so large a portion of the earth's surface? There, among the uncivilised races of the world—in Africa, in parts of America, and among the multitudinous islands of the Pacific—we find that the counters in which men condense their gains and carry on the commerce of life are little shells picked up on the sea-shore; or else, that counters are dispensed with altogether, and trade is managed by simple barter.

Barter is the fundamental basis of commercial transactions; bullion is an accessory—most convenient, but very costly. In countries which have not the advantage of wealth and civilisation, an ox is bartered for so many sheep, a gun for so many skins of the beaver or tusks of the elephant, &c. But, among wealthy and civilised nations, the consumers have so many various wants, and, owing to the division of labour, each worker produces so little that is of use to himself, that simple barter becomes too cumbrous a process in wholesale transactions, and utterly impracticable in shopping, and other forms of retail business. Civilisation, therefore, has to pay for the infinite luxuries of life and subdivision of labour, which are its boast and enjoyment, by introducing a class of objects—counters or "currency"—the only use of which is to facilitate the exchange of commodities in buying and selling; and, secondarily, by representing value in little bulk, to admit of the gains of life being reckoned and possessed in less cumbrous form than houses and land, herds of cattle, or ships and merchandise. It is a form of wealth established for the purpose of representing all the other forms; and which, almost worthless of itself, derives its value from the other kinds of property of which it is the acknowledged representative. Gold and silver are the articles which civilised mankind have chosen as the prime materials out of which these counters of commerce and of life's gains shall be made. And in order to procure the material for these counters, hundreds of thousands of human beings proceed to the uttermost parts of the earth, encamp in the wilderness, and suffer in an aggravated form hardships, privations, and death,—toiling, as in that valley of the Buckland River, in pursuit of the yellow dross in which civilised man insists upon counting up his gains. The cost of the conveyance of these men to the distant gold-countries, the cost of their living in a region where everything is very dear, owing to the distance from which it must be brought, and the extra profit which is needed before men will go so far and suffer so much — these constitute the price which civilisation pays for its money-counters. It is a heavy price: and each ounce of gold represents so much labour withdrawn from agriculture and other industrial pursuits, which minister directly to the necessities and comforts of mankind.

It would be a curious inquiry to trace the mode in which gold, at first esteemed only for its ornamental qualities, was gradually invested with a wider value, until it came to be recognised as the most stable form of wealth, as the most negotiable of all kinds of property. The world, in its present temper, must have gold to carry on its grand game of buying and selling, and of condensing its ever-accumulating wealth; but it is well to remember the cost of this convenience. When a farmer purchases his neighbour's ox with half a score of his own sheep, or when the English merchant exchanges his printed calicoes for the rice of India, the sugar of Brazil, the tea of China, or the wool of Australia, he conducts his business in a way which for cheapness cannot be equalled. One useful commodity is given for another,—that is all. But introduce gold or silver money into the transaction,—elevate a barbaric ornament into a symbol of universal value, and consequently into a medium of purchase,—and then you have an artificial element introduced, and a very costly one. Gold is of itself an article of produce: it is obtained from the diggings in the same way as coal is quarried, sugar grown, or calico manufactured—namely, at the expense of labour; and the expense of labour is just the expense of the articles given in exchange for labour. And unlike most other commodities, this metal is intrinsically of little use to mankind; it is almost useless, save as money—as counters by which wealth is reckoned and purchases are made. A purchase by money is still a process of barter, but it is in an artificial form. It is no longer one useful article exchanged for another; but an intrinsically useless and most expensive article is kept up by the public simply for the purpose of symbolising wealth, and of facilitating the transfer of the really useful commodities.

Mankind have slid so insensibly into this state of things—the canonisation of gold as a peculiar metal and universal representative of property has taken place so gradually, that the remarkable character of the fact is little considered. Is it not a striking fact that mankind should have agreed among themselves, without any deliberation, and as if by instinct, that it was advantageous to have some medium in which wealth could be accumulated in a condensed form—in a form widely acknowledged, and therefore negotiable; and that they should have selected for this purpose a material which, though prized in barbaric times as an ornament, intrinsically is almost worthless;—that they should, without thinking, have established a means by which the wealth of every one, or his claims upon the labour not only of his own community but of mankind at large, should be correctly represented—a means by which the relative wealth of every one is measured and registered, as it were, in the Domesday Book of Civilisation, and made available for the instant purchase of whatever he wants?

All the world is busy playing the game of life: men's natural talents are the cards in hand, and Money is the counters in which their gains are reckoned and their respective wealth embodied. Money serves the same purpose in the stern game of life that counters do in games of amusement—and no more. Money, as regards its material, is of as little use to those who possess it as the bone or ivory or mother-of-pearl out of which are made the counters of the card-table. But what a difference in the cost! Men with infinite labour ransack the world for the rare material out of which they chiefly make their counters for the game of life; whereas counters for the card-table can be made in a moment out of any material—paper, wood, leather—that comes first to hand, and which the players agree amongst themselves to adopt. Yet, after all, does not the value of all kinds of counters, whether they be made of gold, or bone, or paper, depend upon such an agreement? And is it not probable that some day it will become a question whether we do not pay too dear a price for the convenience of money; and that future generations, enjoying a more advanced civilisation, will look back with pity on our "barbarism" in wasting so much wealth for the mere purpose of registering our wealth, and in employing such an infinitude of labour upon what could be accomplished without any?

The European nations are in the van of the world—they are the chiefs of civilisation; and if grand old Milton in his day spoke disdainfully of the pomp which delights in "*barbaric* pearl and gold," regarding it as a foible of the East, it is not to be thought that any sensible man of our time will ascribe the great value of gold to its mere attractiveness as an ornament. Doubtless it was its fitness for ornamentation which first, in the world's infancy, led men to attach value to gold. But this cause of the value of gold has long ago become quite subsidiary: indeed, its value is now maintained only in consequence of the metal having acquired a new and greater repute from an entirely different source. To have imparted a conventional value to an article for the sake of making it a medium of exchange, would have been very difficult in early times (though it was accomplished at Carthage), and quite impossible beyond the limits of a single community. Instinctively, therefore, and perhaps unconsciously, Civilisation availed itself of the high value which earlier times had attached to gold as an ornament, as a basis for giving to that metal an equal value of a civilised and really useful kind. Civilisation found that gold, from its wide acceptance or negotiability, its scarcity, portability, and divisibility, would make an excellent material for supplying counters for trade; and these counters, of course, became thereafter condensed wealth —a convenient form in which wealth might be compactly stored and easily carried about.

The great value, therefore, now ascribed to gold, and which makes men seek for it all over the world, arises from the fact that it constitutes Money.

WHAT IS MONEY?

But what is Money? What is the characteristic of this something which imparts a peculiar value to gold, and which disperses civilised mankind into the wildernesses of the world to search for the yellow metal? Every one knows that money is a good thing to have, and that there is no doing without it,—that it is used in buying and selling,—that men get it by giving for it labour or goods, and in exchange for it supply themselves with the comforts or luxuries of life. But what constitutes Money? Is money, like the pearl and the diamond, and some other prized articles, a thing which man must necessarily take from the hand of Nature? Or can he not make it for himself? And if so, what conditions are necessary for its production and circulation? Of what substances can money be made? and how do these substances come to be recognised as symbols of value?

The Currency of the world includes many kinds of

Money. Gold, silver, copper, iron, in coins, or by weight—stamped leather, stamped paper, wooden tallies—shells of various kinds—pieces of silk, or strips of cotton-cloth, of a fixed size and quality—are, or have been, all in use among mankind as forms of currency, as convenient and negotiable forms or representatives of property. Many of these kinds of money are simultaneously in use in the same country. Gold, silver, copper, and stamped paper coexist as different forms of money in the currency of Europe and America; gold, silver, paper, copper, and shells, in India; silver, copper, and pieces of silk, in China; copper, cotton-strips, shells, and the silver dollar, in various parts of Africa. Sparta had a currency of iron—Carthage of stamped leather, like our paper-money. There is ample variety in the substances out of which money is made,—metals, shells, cloth, leather, paper. Moreover, every country shapes these substances, or such of them as it uses for currency, in a different form from the others.

What, then, is Money? It is obvious that we need not seek a definition in the intrinsic qualities of the substances out of which money is made; for there is not a single intrinsic quality which is common to them all. The generic quality which constitutes money is manifestly something extrinsic to those substances—some quality superimposed upon or attributed to them, or at least to the shape which they assume as currency.

If English merchants send out sovereigns to China,

the Chinese will not receive these coins as money—nor any other kind of gold coins. Gold is not money in the Celestial Empire: one-third of the human race (nearly one-half of the civilised population of the globe) there refuse to accept the yellow metal as currency. Even in India, where gold-coins have been in use from the earliest times, the value of gold is greatly diminished owing simply to the fact that it is not recognised as money by the Government.* In like manner, if the Chinese or Hindoo merchant were to send payment of a large sum in his silver coins to this country, it would be extremely embarrassing to the English merchant. Not only will the coins not pass current in this country, but even as bullion they are of little use in making payments. If a man in this country seek to discharge a debt even in our own silver coins, the creditor is entitled to refuse payment in such a form. Silver is not money—is not a legal tender—in this country, save to the extent of forty shillings. Above that amount, it is simply bul-

* In December last, during the dearth of money at Calcutta, merchants who took £20,000 in gold to the Bank, could not get a single bank-note or rupee advanced upon it. The gold was of no use to them as money, nor could they get money in exchange for it. "The price of gold in Calcutta," said the *Bombay Times* of January 29, 1864, "sunk early in this month so low, that it could have been *reshipped to London at 3 per cent profit.*" In other words, although gold is the standard-money of Europe and America, and although it has been used for centuries as money in India, the mere fact of its not being a *legal* tender in that country sufficed to lessen its value to the extent of 4½ per cent.

lion: it is no more money than brass or tin or platinum is. Again, we laugh when a semi-civilised people propose to pay us for our manufactures in sea-shells, or some other form of non-metallic currency; but we find some of those people not less averse to receive our gold and silver coins which we regard as the perfection of currency. They do not see the use of them. Barbarous tribes will sell to us their produce for coloured glass beads and suchlike valueless trinkets, in preference to money or other articles which in our estimation are infinitely more valuable. We see, then, that the substances which some civilised nations regard as the best, if not as the only standard form of money, other nations, although civilised, refuse to acknowledge or accept as money at all. Moreover, even when different nations use the same substances as money, it sometimes happens that they differ widely in the relative value which they attach to these substances.

A few years ago, when the trade with Japan was opened by Lord Elgin's mission, our merchants were surprised to find that the Japanese appraised gold and silver very differently from us; so that a sovereign, a napoleon, or any other piece of gold, whether in coin or as bullion, was esteemed by the Japanese equal to only about one-fourth of the quantity of silver which the same amount of gold represents in Europe. A not less curious monetary fact may be cited from China. Half-a-dozen kinds of silver coin are current at Shanghai—five kinds of the dollar, and the Indian rupee; but a few years ago only one of these coins, the old Spanish Carolus dollar, was a legal tender. In consequence of this, although the intrinsic value of all the dollars was nearly alike, the old Carolus dollar (which is becoming scarce) was worth 7s., whereas the others were barely worth 5s. A difference of 40 per cent! The only reason for the preference was, that the Carolus dollar was the one which was best known to the Chinese merchants, and in which, accordingly, they had most confidence. This state of matters was remedied in the autumn of 1855, when, after duly assaying the different coins, the Chinese Superintendent of Customs published a proclamation informing the people of the true state of the case, and ordering that after a certain date all the six different coins should pass current, according to their respective intrinsic values, which he announced.

Such are some of the differences of value, and limitations of circulation, which Opinion, or Law as the expression of opinion, imposes upon the various forms of money. But the case is wider than this. The States of Europe have in some respects almost become a commonwealth, but the currency of one State will not circulate in another. The English sovereign, indeed, is readily taken in payment in most parts of the Continent; but it does not *circulate*—no more than napoleons will circulate in

England. They are strange to the people, who are suspicious of them, and (as foreign coins are never a legal tender in any country) refuse to receive them as money. Still more so is this the case with paper-money. Although the coins of one country will not circulate in another, gold and silver are recognised as the raw material of money all over Europe and America, and are valued accordingly; but paper-money, out of its own country, in many cases carries no value at all. Bank of England notes, indeed, which have the same prestige over other kinds of paper-money which the sovereign has over other coins, may be cashed without difficulty in Paris, Vienna, and other large cities, and at no greater charge than is made for converting sovereigns or half-crowns into French money. Indeed, as neither sovereigns nor Bank of England notes will circulate abroad, and have to be sent back to England before the foreign holder receives value for them, the notes are fully more acceptable than the sovereigns, seeing that they can be transmitted to England for the mere cost of postage. Convince a Continental money-changer that the English bank-note is genuine, and he will give you cash for it as readily as for our metallic money: although, of course, there is this difference, that coins can be tested anywhere, whereas bank-notes cannot, and in foreign countries can only be received as genuine out of confidence in the person who presents or endorses them.

Moreover, even in the same country there is often

a limitation to the circulation of some kinds of money. The sovereign—though a legal tender, and (save in some sequestered parts of the Highlands) readily accepted when offered in payment—hardly circulates in Scotland,—the Scotch preferring paper-money, as the best known to them, as in their opinion the more safe and convenient form of currency, and also as the cheapest. Scotch bank-notes, again, do not circulate in the other parts of the kingdom. In England, too, there are many provincial banks, the notes of each of which circulate readily in the district where the issuing bank is situate, but are looked upon with suspicion elsewhere. They will not circulate widely, simply because they are a kind of money with which the public at large are not familiar, and accordingly have not confidence in.

Of all forms of money Silver is the most widely recognised, and therefore holds the first place in the currency of the world. It is the standard money of China, with a population of 400,000,000, and of India, with a population of 160,000,000. It is also recognised as money all over Europe and America. Indeed, until recent times, it was the standard money of Europe—the English pound and the French livre originally consisting of a certain amount of silver. To this day silver still constitutes the greater portion of the currency of the Continent; and in many of the outlying and half-barbarous parts of the world silver will be accepted where gold coins would be refused. Gold at present holds the second place in the currency of the world. But it is rising in monetary importance, owing to its greater portability; and unless new silver-mines are found, the recent discovery of the gold-beds in California and Australia will, by making gold more abundant and more cheap, tend to wrest the supremacy from silver and give it to gold,—by inducing the European and American States to make all the necessary additions to the metallic portion of their currency in the latter metal. Next in amount of circulation to gold and silver money comes paper-money. In this country, the paper-money issued under legal restrictions by the banks amounts to about £40,000,000 sterling (the gold and silver money, whether in circulation or kept in reserve by the banks, amounting to about twice as much). In France, although banking is much less developed than in this country, the amount of paper-money is nearly as great as it is here. In Russia and Austria it is also very large—not owing to banking, which in both countries is still in its infancy, but owing to an actual dearth of the precious metals. Paper-money has the widest range in value of all kinds of money. It is also the cheapest and most portable. One could carry twenty or thirty £1000 Bank of England notes in one's waistcoat pocket; whereas a couple of the strongest porters could not even lift a bag containing such a sum in gold from the ground. At the same time, as is seen in Russia, Austria, and America, you may have paper notes in circulation of as small amount as the smallest silver coin. The gamut of paper-money, if we may so speak, goes far higher than that of gold-money, and ranges down to the lowest reach of silver-money. In fact, in the form of bills of exchange —which, however, are not Money in the strict sense of the word—paper-money plays the most important part of all in carrying on the trade and commerce of the world. It may also be used as a substitute for all the other kinds of money—if under proper restrictions, with perfect safety and great economy. And in modern times it has always been had recourse to, with more or less prudence and advantage, by nations who, in exceptional times, find themselves in a temporary deficiency of metallic money.

Coming back, then, to our starting point, "What is Money?" let us observe what is the one quality which all these kinds of money have in common, and which suffices to exalt each of them into a more or less widely recognised representative of wealth. Between gold, cowrie-shells, and paper, there is not a single point of resemblance. But the quality which gives to these and other substances their circulating power as money is one and the same: it is simply the agreement on the part of nations, or parts of nations, to recognise those substances, either of themselves or when presented in certain forms, as representatives of wealth.

It is an agreement on the part of communities, or of large sections of the population of the globe, to regard these substances or articles as a medium in which wealth can be condensed, and to make of them counters with which the game of life may be carried on, and property be transmuted at pleasure from one form into any other. The quality which constitutes Currency, therefore, is extrinsic to the material of which currency is made, and becomes imparted to any articles which a nation or nations may agree to recognise as tokens of value.

That paper notes or stamped leather possess no intrinsic value will at once be admitted; but, almost universally, it will be asserted that gold is money entirely because of its intrinsic value. Now—passing over the important fact that one-half of the civilised population of the globe do not attach to gold the value which we do—let us ask, How does gold acquire the peculiar value which we attach to it? It will be answered, "Owing to the great amount of labour required for its production." But how is it that so costly an amount of labour is devoted to its production? An article may be rare, yet valueless: it must be *scarce* before it becomes valuable. There are many things as difficult to find or produce as gold, which nevertheless are but little sought for, because for the finding or production of them no one will give sufficiently high wages. Before a thing can become valuable, there must not only be a difficulty in its production, but a great demand for it: because, unless there be a great demand for it, the price offered for it will be inadequate to induce men to encounter the difficulties or undergo the hardships inseparable from its production. What, then, causes the great demand for gold? *Because so many nations require it for Currency.* And thus the circle of reasoning comes back to our starting position, that the peculiar value of gold arises from its having been so widely adopted as Money.

Demonetise gold, and what would follow? Probably two-thirds of all the gold in use among mankind is employed as money; and if the Western world were, for the sake of uniformity, to adopt the currency of the East, and resolve that gold should not be received as money any longer, would not the value of gold fall immensely? The moment the news reached California and Australia, would not the mines be abandoned, and the workers betake themselves to other occupations;—feeling of a surety that, now gold was demonetised, the world had already more than enough of the yellow dross, and that henceforth no man would give a dollar for a whole ounce of it. Silver would be immensely increased in value, and gold would descend from its high estate to the rank of an ordinary metal. Thenceforth gold would only be used for ornaments, plate, and gilding—if, indeed, the comparative abundance of the metal for those purposes, owing to its demonetisation, would not make it too common to be a fitting ornament of the wealthy. It is the value, not the beauty, of the yellow metal that makes it so much prized nowadays in ornaments. It is not merely as barbaric toys and gewgaws that people wear it in chains and rings and other personal ornaments, and load their tables with it as plate; but because it is condensed wealth. It is the display of *wealth* which constitutes the chief charm of golden plate and ornaments; and if gold were no longer to be condensed wealth, but simply a metal like the others, it is probable that its dethronement as money would tend rather to diminish than to increase the demand for it as an ornamental luxury. Hence the two causes for the present great demand for gold being, one of them extinguished, and the other lessened, by its demonetisation, the value of gold would be immensely diminished.

Money is the expression of wealth—the voucher of accumulated gains—a "universal language" of property all over the civilised world. It is an *Open Sesame* which everywhere admits us into the enjoyment of other men's goods or labour. Unlike houses or horses or hounds, or food and clothing, or works of art, or articles of merchandise, money is of no use in itself—only as a means of getting other things. To borrow the language of the Schoolmen, the value of money is *in posse*—that of other articles *in esse:* the one is potential, the other is essential. Money is a useless thing for ever doing useful things. A valueless thing for ever purchasing things of value. Like the electric fluid, money is undynamic when at rest: it is only when in motion, passing in payments from one owner to another, that its great power is manifested. But that power, we repeat, is merely imputed to it, in order to facilitate the business of life: and if all the world could act together as easily as a single community can, we might say of every form of money, "A breath can make it, as a breath has made."

Money is not wealth, but a right to wealth—an established conventional equivalent for goods and labour. Apart from the command which it gives its possessor over the goods and labour of other men, money is valueless; but the goods and labour would be as valuable as ever though (as was the case in ancient Peru) there were no money at all. Money is but the counters which (apart from the property held in other forms) show the relative position of the players in the great game of life. It confers no power or property upon one man without taking these in equal amount from others. Abolish all the Money in the world, and mankind at large would be as wealthy as before. All the produce of the earth and of human labour would exist as before. The title which a certain class (the money-holders) have acquired to that produce would be extinguished, but the produce would remain as abundant as formerly. Certain established rights would be annulled, but not a particle of existing property. As regards paper-money, the effect would be the same as if a fire were to destroy a building in which were deposited all the bonds which certain members of a community hold over the property of others. What the creditors lost in wealth the debtors would gain. As regards gold and silver, indeed, these metals, when demonetised, would still reremain in the possession of those who had them, but their value would be immensely lessened. In this case, the material of the counters would remain, but the rights which they represented would be gone. Each player would still have his bits of mother-of-pearl or metal, but the value of those articles would be as nothing compared to the stakes which they previously represented. Demonetise the precious metals, and a labourer would no longer give a week's work for a bit of gold or silver which he could do nothing with except to give to his wife as an ornament. Men would no longer consent to be paid in bits of metal which no grocer or butcher or tailor would accept in exchange for his goods. And of what benefit would gold be even to the foreign trader, if the metal were to lose its present value of being recognised as money over half the world? Suppose some great man, of eccentric or barbaric taste, were to accumulate the demonetised metal, would not his golden pyramid be essentially as much a product of barbarism as the Pyramids of the Pharaohs, in which a maximum of labour is combined with a minimum of usefulness? It is only as Money that gold possesses a value such as civilisation endorses: and the demand for gold as an ornament is now mainly dependent upon the high value which attaches to it as money.

Let any one fairly think out the question, and he cannot help coming to this conclusion. And if, instead of starting with gold, he start with paper-money, he will arrive by the other side of the circle of reasoning at the same conclusion: namely, that all the various forms of currency depend for their peculiar value upon Opinion, or conventional agreement; that their value is (chiefly in some cases, entirely in others) extrinsic, not intrinsic,—a something imparted to them by the consent of the people among whom they circulate. In short, Currency of every kind is essentially dependent upon Credit—using that word in its amplest sense. Negotiability, *i.e.* acceptability, is the grand point—and that depends upon a common agreement. Accordingly, the more widely the credit of any coin or note is recognised, the more extensive will be its circulation, the greater its acceptability, and the higher its rank as a form of money.

These considerations, of course, render it doubtful whether mankind are right in the value which they continue to attach to the precious metals as the prime form of money, seeing that their place could be supplied by cheaper materials. We shall leave Posterity, with its superior advantages, to answer that question: content to believe that, in the actual circumstances of the world, the monetary system which has been established could not have been very different from that which exists. High as is the price which civilisation pays for the convenience of money, the investment, on the whole, has been a good and profitable one. The invention of Money lies at the base of all material civilisation. Division of labour is the grand characteristic of material civilisation; but there could not be any great subdivision of labour without money. Before the industrial classes of a community will devote themselves each to a separate pursuit, a means must have been found by which the produce of each is made readily exchangeable for the goods of any of the others. Money does this. A man who has only an ox to barter, will find it difficult to supply his wants. He will find it difficult to apportion it correctly among his various tradespeople—grocer, baker, tailor, shoemaker, landlord, &c.—even supposing that all these dealers need beef at once. But let him first convert the ox into money, and thereafter he can purchase all that he wants with rapidity and ease. Money is a reservoir of power, immediately available, and for any purpose. It is wealth condensed and mobilised. Its effective force is as much superior to an equal amount of property in other forms, as a mobilised and concentrated army is to an equally numerous crowd of common men. If there were no money—no conventional means of storing up accumulated gains in an instantaneously negotiable form—how long would be the time, and how cumbrous the preparations, requisite to prepare an expedition, to get up a railway-company, or to accomplish any great project? What would require the co-operation of thousands, and consequently great preliminary delay, in times of pure barter, can with money be accomplished at once. Secure the aid of a single great capitalist, and forthwith the streams of power flow in all directions simultaneously, each becoming transmuted into different objects—labour, stores, implements, raw material, or directing genius. The conversion of power is direct and instantaneous. By means of money, human power can strike its *coups* on the instant. Prove an object desirable, an enterprise profitable, and the man who holds his property in the form of money can accomplish the object or engage in the enterprise with the speed of the telegraph.

But if we would see the world-wide results of the invention of Money in facilitating all the branches of human industry, and in promoting friendly intercommunication between different nations and countries, we shall find these exhibited in their most striking form by the events which have accompanied and by the consequences which have flowed from the recent gold-discoveries.

THE GOLDEN AGE

EFFECTS OF THE GOLD-DISCOVERIES ON THE WORLD

THE first phenomenon attendant upon the gold-discoveries has been the great Emigration—the transfer of large masses of population from their old seats to new ones,—the vast and sudden spread of civilised mankind over the earth, making deserts and waste places to bloom, cities to rise amid the solitude, and seas, whose virgin waters had hardly been stirred by a single prow, to grow white with the sails of golden argosies.

EMIGRATION.

The countries where these gold-beds have been found are in the utmost ends of the earth—regions the most secluded, the most isolated from the seats of civilisation. The region of California seemed the last in the world that would be peopled by civilised men. Of all spots on the globe, it was the furthest removed from the highways of enterprise. Not a road to it was to be found on the map of the traveller, not a route to it was laid down in the charts of the mariner: the deserts and woods and mountain-ranges by land, the rocks and shoals and currents by sea, were known to not one in a million of earth's inhabitants. The Pacific Ocean rolled between it and Asia; the snow-capped chain of the Rocky Mountains, impassable save in a few places, and only at certain seasons—the deserts of the Salt Lake, and the pathless wastes of the prairies, traversed by hostile tribes of Indians—cut it off from communication with the eastern States of America. In this secluded region, extending some five hundred miles along the shores of the Pacific, and sloping from the margin of the sea to the summit of the Snowy Range, a few stragglers were the only signs of human life that appeared amid a primeval solitude. Six years before, when the French frigate Venus (in the course of its voyage round the world) put into the port of Monterey, then the chief town of California, they found the place "composed of forty or fifty whitewashed habitations—veritable huts, roofed only with rushes and boughs of trees. The frigate was in want of biscuit, and the country had to be laid under contribution; they went even to distant farms in search of flour, and, after all, could only procure an imperfect revictualment." * All at once gold was discovered—gold in abundance, gold

* *Revue des Deux Mondes*, 1843.

everywhere. In the beds of the rivers, in the sands of the hill-torrents, in the seams of the rocks, the precious ore appeared—nay, the very soil seemed impregnated with the glittering dust; and forthwith settlers came hurtling thither like clouds of locusts. Every wind of heaven seemed to blow them to the golden land. The love of gold soon peopled the solitude; the sparkle of the precious ore drew myriads from afar. Within eighteen months a hundred thousand men arrived from the other side of America; nine thousand waggons, bearing five times that number of persons, came through the passes of the Rocky Mountains, and four thousand immigrants came on horseback by the same route. Crowds poured in eager haste across the Isthmus of Panama, converting the neck of the New World, for the first time, into a highway between the two great oceans of the globe. Others made a sea voyage of 17,000 miles round Cape Horn, intrusting themselves for the stormy passage to leaky and shattered barks, resembling that in which Columbus made his last voyage from America to Spain. From the ships, they beheld a land without fruits, without cities, almost without inhabitants; but gold was in the mountains that rose in the distance; and, heedless of hunger and thirst, heat and cold, raiment and lodging, they plunged eagerly into solitudes where the wolf and the buffalo, the squirrel and the bear, had lived undisturbed since the Deluge.

What an assemblage was there gathered together! Men from all quarters of the globe—of every kindred and tongue, of every hue and dress and feature. Emigrants from every country of Europe—English, German, Swiss, Pole, French, Spaniard—worked side by side with the aboriginal Indians and Anglo-Saxon intruders of northern America, and with the native Chilians and half-breeds of its southern portion. The Australian joined them from his Antarctic continent; the Malay and Polynesian from the isles of the Pacific; and even the Chinaman came forth, like an anchorite from his cell, to join in this varied mass of golden speculators. Such a concourse of human tribes the world never before witnessed. Through the once solitary channel of the Golden Gate, clusters of sails began to enter the land-locked bay, on whose shores was rising the future capital of the region; and, like the magic seed of the Indian juggler, which grows, blossoms, and bears fruit while the spectators are looking on, San Francisco seemed to accomplish in a day the growth of half a century.

Australia was, if possible, a still more isolated quarter of the globe, and, if no new attraction had come into play, it would have remained for generations a slow-moving cityless country of pastoral settlers. But the attraction of gold rapidly changed the scene, and has opened a brilliant future for that vast island-continent, of whose glories we only see the beginning. Already the European race is making a new world for itself at the Antipodes.

Nor do the triumphs of gold, as an agent affecting the destinies of the world, stop here. Hardly noticed as yet, but certain to attract another rush of emigration in the future, is the auriferous region of Siberia, which Humboldt affirmed to stretch right across northern Asia, from the Ural Mountains to Kamtschatka and the bleak solitudes of "Oonalaska's shore." Here again is one of the vast solitudes of the earth; yet, ere many years have passed, we shall see the wizard Gold drawing all men after him, peopling with civilised men the heart of Upper Asia,—establishing cities and peaceful communities where once roamed the ruthless cavalry of the Golden Horde,—and bringing back mankind, after long and devious wanderings, to settle in maturity in the region that was the cradle of our race. The corresponding region of the New World — the American Siberia — the desolate zone which intervenes like an unbridged chasm between Canada and British Columbia, already begins to be affected from a similar cause; and the discovery of gold on the eastern side of the Rocky Mountains, on the head-waters of the Saskatchewan river, will mightily contribute to people that solitude also, and to extend British settlements in unbroken line from the Atlantic to the Pacific. Lastly, but not less surely, the passion for gold will, at no distant time, carry bands of adventurers into the heart of Africa, that greatest waste place of the earth. If famous in old times as "the fierce mother of lions," she was not less famous as a gold country; and we believe that the *auri sacra fames* will be the first agency that will give a great impulse to the invasion of that continent by the European race—leading bands of daring adventurers up the watery highways of the Nile and the Niger, to search for gold-beds beneath the Equator, and pitch their tents at the foot of the shadowless Mountains of the Moon.

Such is the mighty influence which gold is exerting upon the condition of the Earth. Let us now mark the chain of effects, and the nature of those effects, which the gold-discoveries are producing upon the condition of Mankind. The demand for gold, as the prime material of money, is so great that the wages of the gold-diggers in California and Australia are, on the average, four times greater than the class of skilled workmen can make at home. In consequence they spend four times as much. In other words, for every £1 of goods which they consumed at home, they now consume £4. Their consuming power has been quadrupled, and the result is, that they give four times as much employment to other men. Hence, not only are those emigrants benefited by the gold-diggings, but the population which they have left at home is likewise benefited. Not only is the labour-market at home thinned, but there

INCREASE OF COMMERCE.

is more employment than before. The profits of the gold-diggers keep more ships on the sea, and give more employment to the producers alike of the luxuries and of the necessaries of life. Nor is this all. For not only is a new and lucrative trade created between the gold-countries and the old seats of civilisation, but commerce in all directions obtains a mighty impulse, increasing the area of Employment, and the comforts of mankind all over the world. Extended commerce means more profits for our merchants and manufacturers, more employment for our working-classes, and a general bettering of the condition of our population and of the population of every country which comes within the sphere of these operations. It also means increased intercommunication among the nations of the earth; and by establishing among them a mutual knowledge and bonds of common interest, it prepares the way for the coming of better times upon the earth—morally not less than materially—than mankind has yet known.

Next in point of time, then, to their effects upon Emigration, and first in point of importance, the peculiar benefit arising to the world from the gold-discoveries is that they have given a great extension to Commerce. California and Australia, instead of desert places, have become countries which trade largely; and at the same time the produce of their mines enables us greatly to extend our commerce with other countries, such as India and China, which as yet take little of our goods, and with which no great trade is possible unless we have an abundance of the precious metals in which to discharge our trade balances. The principle of exchange is simply this, that goods which bring a trifle more in other countries than at home are sent thither. An increased trade with France, for example, means that we import more of her wines and silks, and send her more of our iron and cotton goods. An increased trade with India or China means that we import a larger portion of their produce, either in the form of food or luxuries or as raw material for our manufactures, and that we send in return a considerable portion of our manufactured goods and a large portion of the precious metals. In short, the primary benefit which commerce confers upon mankind is, that each country gets a portion of its produce exchanged for other commodities of which it has a greater need. Commerce adds to the comforts of life, and also it gives to each country new means of developing its industry. It is a branch of industry by itself: every extension of commerce implies a corresponding increase of employment. And an increase of employment is equivalent, (1) to a bettering of the condition of all the industrious classes; and (2) to a draft upon the mass of idleness and pauperism, or unproductive energy, which every community contains. No other branch of industry could have produced these effects to the same extent as that opened up by the discovery of the gold-mines. It is evident from what has taken place that gold is more needed by the world at large—it has a wider and better market—than any other produce; hence, the labour of the emigrants has been more profitably employed in the gold-countries than it would have been at home. The difference is in effect the same as if a good soil had suddenly taken the place of a bad one. Moreover, the novelty and profitableness of the trade of gold-seeking tempted not a few idle hands to emigrate and become busy; and the drafting away of many myriads of industrious hands from the labour-market at home likewise acted as a means of securing employment for men who, but for this opening, might have remained a burden upon the community.

EUROPE RELIEVED.

These are happy effects of the gold-discoveries. And they are political as well as social. When nations are prosperous, they are contented. Suffering is the great parent of revolution. Seldom, if ever, has a country been convulsed by political revolution, save when the outbreak had been preceded by a period of general distress. The distress, so widespread and apparently mysterious, which overspread our own country for twenty years before the passing of the Reform Bill, as well as for several years afterwards, was the agency which gave to that long crisis its exasperation and serious political perils;

and (if this were the place for such a discussion) it could be shown that the most potent cause of that widespread distress was the continuously increasing scarcity of gold, in conseqnence of the great decrease in the produce of the American mines. Now, happily, the position is reversed. Gold is abundant, wages are rising, employment has increased, and the people are contented. Nor is this benefit confined to our own country. All Europe feels the happy change. Look at the state of Europe in 1820, 1830, and 1848, and in a lesser degree in the intervals of troubled peace which lay between those crises of discontent; and say whether the last twelve years, in regard to political contentment, do not appear to belong to a wholly different epoch. The social discontent, the bitter war of classes, has almost disappeared. The old seats of civilisation, which appeared to be sinking under the weight of over-population, were suddenly thinned of their swarms; room was made for a new growth of population, and that new increase is growing up under circumstances of unexampled prosperity. France under a military despotism has benefited in this respect (considering the lesser action of the gold-discoveries upon her) as much as England under freedom and free-trade. Let neither Government boast itself overmuch, by attributing to mere legislative measures a happy result, in which future ages will see clearly the hand of overruling Providence. We are proud of our country and of our statesmen and of our Queen; but for the height of this great blessing let us give God the glory.

The remarkable increase which has of late years taken place in the commerce of the world is generally attributed to the adoption of the principles of free-trade in this country, and to the relaxation of tariffs which is slowly taking place abroad. Unquestionably there is truth in this view; but it is very far from being the whole truth. Every great movement of mankind is due to a concurrence of influences, rather than to a single one. Whatever may have been the initial cause of the great increase of international trade during the last fifteen years, it is important to observe that the commencement of the increase was contemporaneous with the discovery of the Californian gold-mines. That discovery at once, and even before its material effects began to operate, gave a moral impetus, an impulse of excitement and hope, to the trading world. And it is abundantly evident that the great expansion of trade which has since occurred could not possibly have taken place if the new gold-mines had not been discovered.

The most prominent feature of that expansion has been the increase of trade between Europe and America on the one hand, and the East on the other. That trade has in all ages been a peculiar one. The constant absorption of the precious

TRADE WITH THE EAST.

metals by the East has attracted attention, and given rise to much speculation, for at least a century and a half. The explanation is, that India and China have been non-importing countries. And to this day the exports from these countries are largely in excess of their imports. We yearly consume a large portion of their produce, while they take comparatively little of our goods. Such a trade can only be carried on when Europe possesses an abundant supply of the precious metals; and the trade could never have been carried on to the extent which has been witnessed of late years, if the new gold-mines had not rendered the precious metals in Europe not only abundant, but superabundant. In 1851, after free-trade had been for several years established in this country, and when the produce of the Californian gold-mines had just begun to operate, the exports of silver to the East from Great Britain and the Mediterranean ports only amounted to £1,716,000. But from that time our trade with, and investments in, the East increased rapidly, and the amount which Europe had to pay in the precious metals underwent a corresponding increase. So much so, that in the thirteen years which have since elapsed, the payments which have been made to the East in the precious metals have amounted to about £130,000,000, showing an average of £10,000,000 a-year. But for the new gold-mines such payments on our part would have been impossible;

yet without such payments our Eastern trade and in-vestments could not have been carried on. Before the gold-discoveries came to our aid, to have attempted to export even half the present average amount of bullion to the East would have so tightened the money market (in other words, would have so reduced the amount of loanable money) as speedily to stop the trade. The rate of discount would have risen to such a height as to leave no adequate margin of profits on the articles exported: indeed, we should have been fortunate if our whole trade had not been involved in the calamities of a monetary crisis.

ITS HAPPY RESULTS.

In present circumstances, on the contrary, this drain of bullion is of itself an advantage. Our increase of trade with the East, while adding to our wealth, is relieving Europe of a portion of the precious metals of which we have no need, and which it is advantageous to get rid of. Had all this bullion remained in Europe, the value of gold would have already fallen greatly: in consequence, the mines would be less resorted to, emigration would be already declining, the expansion of commerce and increase of employment would be checked, and the prosperity of the Golden Age—instead of continuing, as we trust, for several generations—would be all over in a few years. The prosperity of the world depends upon the continuance of this drain of bullion to the East. Without it, the effect of the gold-discoveries would be but local and evanescent; with it, the whole world will be partakers of the blessing. If this drain continues, the Golden Age may last for a hundred years; and, as the result of the ever-widening commerce, all nations both of East and West will be drawn together in bonds of mutual interest and sympathy, which will remain as a happy legacy after the Angel of Gold has again withdrawn from the scene.

Such are the effects upon the world at large which the new gold-mines are producing, and are calculated to produce. They constitute the most powerful lever by the action of which the world can be moved, human progress hastened, and human prosperity increased.

Let us now consider these gold-discoveries in another and narrower aspect. Let us ask, as a question

MONETARY QUESTION.

of purely monetary science, what good do we derive from the new mines? It is obvious that an addition to the currency of a country is not necessarily a benefit. If the country be already adequately supplied with money, every addition is a positive loss. If the currency of a country be increased from £50,000,000 to £100,000,000, while the productions of that country and the demand for money remain as they were, the hundred millions will do no more than the fifty millions,—only, all prices, wages, rents, &c., will be doubled in amount. The prices which a farmer or manufacturer gets for his goods will be increased; but so also, and in similar proportion, will be the amount of his outlay in rents and taxes, &c. It is like adding equally to both sides of an equation. It would be a sheer waste of money. The labour which produced these extra fifty millions would be as much lost as if that amount of gold had been sunk in the sea. A case like this, however, never occurs in the actual world. It would only be possible if the country in question were absolutely isolated from the rest of the world,—and hardly even then: for the mere influx of increased supplies of gold is found to give an impulse of hopefulness and energy which of itself tends to create more trade, and consequently more need for money.

Any sudden derangement of prices, whether caused by a rise or by a fall in the value of the precious metals, is bad; for it involves a transference of wealth from one section of the community to another, without any fault on the one side or merit on the other. A farmer, for example, who has taken his farm on a twenty years' lease, at a time when the ordinary price of wheat is 60s. a quarter, would lose greatly if prices (owing to a change in the value of money) were suddenly to fall to 40s., and would gain greatly if they were to rise to 80s.; while the landlord would equally gain in the first event, and lose in the second. True, there would be no loss to the community at large; what one man lost another would gain: but it would be a taking from those who rightfully had, and giving to those who had no claim to get. Moreover, it generally happens (on the principle of "lightly come, lightly go") that those who get money in such a way squander it, or at least do not turn it to so good account as those to whom it belonged.

So far as experience goes, however, it is doubtful whether any great change of value ever can take place suddenly. It is as gradual operations that these alterations in the value of money fall to be regarded and discussed; and this limitation at once strips such movements of their necessarily injurious character. Nevertheless such movements exercise a mighty influence upon the fortunes of States, or of mankind at large; and their social effects vary immensely according as they are produced by a Rise in the value of the precious metals, or by a Fall.

During the last eighteen hundred years we have had experience of monetary changes of both kinds.

GOLD AND POLITICS.

For fifteen centuries after the Christian era, the precious metals became gradually more scarce; chiefly, doubtless, owing to the widening-area of civilisation, and the consequent increase of trade. In the sixteenth century, a mighty change took place, owing to the enormous amount of the precious metals obtained by ruthless conquest in the New World, and by the discovery and working of the gold and silver mines in Peru and Mexico. All Europe was then astir with excitement: the epoch was one of unparalleled enthusiasm and enterprise; and in a single generation commerce experienced an expansion greater than had been accomplished during the previous ten centuries. By-and-by, however, as population and trade increased, the opposite tendency again commenced. The pendulum, whose operation is so visible in human affairs, began to swing backwards. A season of ebb ensued. Money gradually became scarce, and, despite the alleviation caused by the invention of banking and paper-money, hard times set in. After 1809, the annual supply of the precious metals declined fully one-half, owing to the stoppage of the Mexican mines, consequent upon the war between Spain and her American colonies. The period when the precious metals was most scarce was between 1810 and 1840; and this, as every one knows, was precisely the period when national distress and political agitation were most rife amongst us. The masses suffered, and clamoured for Reform; the middle classes groaned under the taxation, and cried for Retrenchment; and in Parliament there arose the policy of Peace, to lessen the burdens of a nation which could not afford to go to war. The discovery of the Ural mines of Russia thereafter began to mitigate, though not to remove, the dearth. But now, once more, a change has taken place; and the discovery of the rich mines of California, Columbia, and Australia, together with (let us hope) the impending regeneration of Mexico, has commenced a period when money will again become not only plentiful but redundant.

It is important to note the social effects which take place during these different epochs.

RISE OF PRICES.

In times like the present, when the value of the precious metals is falling, the effect of the change is (speaking roughly) to benefit the many at the expense of the few. Mortgages and all money-contracts which extend over a long period, are lessened in value; for in the course of twenty years, £1000 may become worth no more than (say) £800 was at first. Such creditors, who are necessarily capitalists or wealthy men, lose, and their debtors gain. But it is on the Government expenditure of a country that the change is most felt. The pressure of the Government debt is lightened, and the taxation necessary to provide for it is virtually reduced. The same amount of taxation may be raised, but that amount represents a much smaller value than before, and accordingly is less felt by the people. A large portion of the Government expenditure in all countries, including Government salaries and the interest on the Debt, are fixed payments—money-contracts which extend over a considerable period; and as these decline in value, the national burdens are lightened in this way also. Such effects, of course, are mainly confined to the actual period of transition. Government salaries will be gradually raised, and other measures will be taken to meet the altered circumstances. But still, as long as prices continue to rise, fixed payments, money-contracts, and annuities will tend to decline in value. What is most important of all, Trade increases with the increased facilities for carrying it on which an abundance of the precious metals affords; and with more trade there is more employment, and consequently increased prosperity among the working classes. Nor among these only: for even annuitants, and others who derive a portion of their income from fixed payments, benefit likewise—as regards themselves, and still more as regards their families—from the increasing abundance of employment; so much so that in most cases this cause will actually compensate them for the loss which they experience on the fixed portion of their income.

On the other hand, in periods when the precious metals are becoming scarce—in other words, when the value of money is rising—the mass of the community suffer severely. Trade, if not checked, is conducted under greater difficulties. Mortgages, long leaseholds, and money-contracts of all kinds, weigh more heavily upon those whom they affect; and the pressure of taxation—though no more taxes be raised than before—is seriously augmented. It was this pressure of Government taxation which wrought such havoc in Italy and some other provinces

FALL OF PRICES.

of the Roman empire under some of the emperors. The value of money was rising, yet the Imperial expenditure could not be reduced so as to comport with the altered state of affairs; and towns and provinces were called upon to pay their old amount of taxation, although the value of that amount had largely increased. Under the pressure of this taxation whole districts became depopulated, and large masses of the population became pauperised. Periods when the precious metals are becoming scarce are always times of more or less national distress and discontent.* This, as we have said, was notably the case in our own country in the period between 1810 and 1830, though the cause was never suspected. Had the real source of the national distress been perceived, there would doubtless have been more moderation and discretion on the part of the people, and the crisis would certainly have been met by wiser measures on the part of the Government.

Now, the first effect of the recent gold-discoveries was to save us, and Europe at large, from the hard times which had been in operation, and which, but for these discoveries, must have gone on increasing in

* In a partial degree, this is sometimes the case also when prices are rising: "strikes" being necessary in some cases to obtain a corresponding rise of wages. Still, in good times, masters are seldom reluctant to do justice to their workmen. And a strike in bad times is a much more serious affair than such a conflict in times of prosperity.

severity. The recent enormous expansion of trade, indeed, could never have taken place at all, if the new mines had not come into play; but even the ordinary increase of population and trade would soon have made money so scarce as to land the working-classes in this country, as well as in the States of the Continent, in profound distress, productive, it is to be feared, of wide-spread political discontent.

ARE PRICES RISING?

These benefits—alike the negative and the positive—arising from the gold-discoveries, are so manifest that no reasonable man can call them in question. It is considered doubtful by some authorities, whether the new gold-supplies have as yet produced any alteration in the value of money, as indicated by a rise of prices. For our own part, we entertain no doubt that this change of value, though slight, is perceptible, and that the effects consequent upon such a change are already in operation. Whether the value of money in this country has been depreciated to the extent of ten or fifteen per cent, as Mr Jevons maintains, we cannot assert with much confidence in the correctness of our opinion. But a change is certainly taking place; and it is all the better for us that the change is slow and gradual. At present we are experiencing all the advantages of an increase of the precious metals, with a minimum of disadvantages—in fact, with no perceptible drawback at all. In the fullest sense of the word, we may be said to be *enjoying* a rise of prices: the rise is so gentle, and the benefits of the new gold-supplies so widespread and substantial.

THE WASTE-PIPE.

Our fears have been disappointed, and our best hopes have been more than realised. A sudden change, even in a good direction, is an evil in monetary affairs. And such a change was fully expected and predicted by some of the best authorities in those matters. The circumstance which has falsified those predictions is of itself one of the happiest features of the times. The great increase of commerce which has taken place was not foreseen, nor its consequences calculated; yet it is to that increase that we owe our escape from a sudden change in the value of money. That increase has not only created more employment for money in Europe, but it has drained off the surplus of precious metals in payment of the large sums which necessarily accumulate against us in the course of extended dealings with the East. These payments, it is true, could not be made in gold—what the East wants, and will alone accept, is silver: but silver in sufficient amount was easily procured in Europe (especially from the currency of France), and its place was supplied by gold, of which we were obtaining such large supplies, and which is the superior metal of the two for coinage. As gold flows into Europe, silver flows out; and thus our increased commerce with the East proves to us a double blessing,—at once increasing employment, and averting any great change in the value of money. It is a waste-pipe by which nothing is wasted. It is a channel by which we not only rid ourselves of a surplus of the precious metals, but turn them to most profitable account.

THE GOLDEN AGE.

All present indications, therefore, are against the supposition that there will be any sudden fall in the value of gold. Demand treads closely upon the heels of supply—indeed, seems actually to keep pace with it. Apart from increase of population, which is facilitated by the means of emigration, there never was a time when the circumstances of mankind were so favourable for an increase in the demand for currency. We stand on the threshold, indeed we have already entered the vestibule, of an epoch when commerce and international relations will obtain an expansion undreamt of before. During the last thirty years, steam-navigation, railwavs. and telegraphs have given to mankind facilities of locomotion and communication which have immensely extended the sphere of human action, and have made each man a denizen of the world rather than merely of his own country. And now Gold comes to give wings to those inventions, and to carry them, and commerce along with them, into every civilised region of the earth. The flood of the precious metals which came across the Atlantic in the sixteenth century was poured only into Europe—or, rather, merely into part of Europe—into Spain, France, England, Italy, and part of Germany. But now the flood pours into every part of Europe and of America, and the surplus flows off rapidly to the other regions of the globe.

Not even yet has gold the whole world for a market. A large portion of mankind still remain in a state of barbarism which dispenses with the money required for international trade. And if we restrict our view merely to India and China, we find in the vast population of those countries, numbering nearly six hundred millions, a field for the absorption of the precious metals greater than all Europe presented in the sixteenth century. With India we may almost say that we had no commerce at all, till the new gold-mines gave us the means of prosecuting that commerce in earnest; and with the far vaster population of China our commerce is only in its infancy. We have been making railways in India, and we shall make many more; and every such enterprise sends the cost of it, in the form of specie, out of Europe to the scene of operations. Tea-planting, also, and many other kinds of investment opened to Europeans by the recent Act for the sale of waste lands, are attracting capital from this country to our empire in the East. And our native fellow-subjects in India, stimulated by the increase of employment, and by the contagion of English spirit and ideas, will soon follow in our path, and by their increased energy and trade will cause an increased absorption of the precious metals to supply their deficiency of currency. In China the field is still vaster: in sober truth, it would require the imagination of a poet to do justice to the triumphs which there await civilisation. Amongst the Chinese, as much as amongst any nation in the world, the people are industrious, and every man is anxious to better his condition. Every man in those four hundred million souls has an eye to business, a love for trade; they but wait for the quickening touch of European energy and science to enter upon a new career of livelier and more expansive action. Before long, ere ten years are over, the ships of the West will be whitening with their sails or darkening with their smoke the broad stream of the Yangtse-kiang, the noblest river-highway in the world, and the great artery of China; and from its banks the commerce and money of Europe will penetrate into the heart of the Celestial Empire. At present, metallic money is very scarce in China—so much so that the opium-trade was opposed by the Imperial Government chiefly on account of the export of silver which it occasioned. Domestic trade in that vast empire is shackled by the cumbrous process of barter; and foreign trade on an extensive scale is impossible till the nation has provided itself with a larger stock of the precious metals. Australia, also, has to be provided with railways, spanning the island-continent from Melbourne and Sydney to the Gulf of Carpentaria; and South America is still an undeveloped continent.

Or, turning from those wide fields for the absorption of the precious metals as money, and looking only at our own Continent, do we not find even here a growth of civilisation which will require no small amount of metallic currency to aid its development? Even in Germany, to this day, payments in kind are in use to a considerable extent. Austria, with her vast undeveloped resources, is very deficient in the sinews of trade. And the whole of Russia, with her sixty millions of people, is virtually an undeveloped region. All these countries have yet to provide themselves with an adequate metallic currency; and even in the most advanced countries, such as England and France, the increase of trade and employment will continue to absorb some of the new supplies of gold without any serious decline, being produced in the value of money.

We attach importance to these considerations as indicating that no great and sudden fall in the value of money is to be expected. But that a fall will come, steadily and surely, we firmly believe. Let it but be gradual and slow, and no well-wisher to humanity, and to the masses of our own people, will have reason to complain. We cannot expect to have the stimulus of the gold-discoveries, and the great facilities which they supply for an expansion of commerce, without experiencing an alteration in the value of money. A rise in the value of money crushes the many to the benefit of the few—and, speaking generally, the non-producers at the expense of the producing classes. A fall in the value of money does the reverse: and now the bees are benefiting at the expense of the drones. The more slow and unfelt the change, the better. In truth, if a fall in the value of money be spread over a long period, the loss is little felt by any particular owner of money. Government stock, railway debentures, and suchlike investments, are constantly changing hands; and if their fall in value be gradual, the loss of each holder of them is merely fractional. Leases, in like manner, are being constantly renewed. And unless the change in the value of gold prove much more rapid than there is at present any reason to expect, the hardships which the change will inflict on money-holders will hardly be appreciable,—especially since, as we have said, they will share like the rest of the community in the advantages arising from new or enlarged fields of employment. As a national concern, and as affecting the world at large, the new gold-supplies cannot but be regarded as a great benefit. By producing increased trade and employment, they are improving the condition of the masses of the population in every country which they affect; and by breaking down the barriers of isolation, and drawing all nations into mutual relationship, they are elevating the condition of mankind at large, and speeding the progress of civilisation in every quarter of the globe.

GOLD AND SILVER.

One interesting point remains to be noticed with respect to the extraordinary supplies of gold which are now pouring into the world; and that is, the small effect which is thereby produced in the value of gold in relation to silver. This will always be the case as long as both of these metals are alike employed as Money. During the three centuries and a half subsequent to the discovery of the New World, the addition to the stock of silver was four times greater than the addition made to the stock of gold: nevertheless silver, during that period, diminished in relative value only one-fifth. In 1500 the value of gold in relation to silver was as 12½ to 1,—in 1848 it stood at 15 to 1. After 1848 the tide turned: the supply of gold became in excess of that of silver—it is at present three times greater; but the change produced thereby in the value of silver is almost imperceptible. Silver is only 2 or 3 per cent dearer than it used to be in relation to gold. It has only been affected to the extent of 1-40th—while Money (we think) has been affected to the extent of 1-10th of its previous value.

In truth, an addition to the quantity of gold, or of silver, does not so much affect the relative value of these metals as the value of gold and silver taken together. In the case of two commodities which are employed or available for similar purposes, and either of which may be substituted for the other, it is obvious that an increase in the quantity of one will affect the value of both. An unusually large crop of wheat will lower the price of all the other cereals; and, in a lesser degree, an abundance of cotton will lower the price of flax and wool. Moreover, an abundance of wheat will lower the price of wheat to a lesser extent than an abundance of barley will lower the price of barley: because wheat is more prized for food and other purposes. In like manner an abundance of gold will depreciate the value of gold to a lesser degree than an abundance of silver will depreciate the value of silver: because gold is the superior metal for currency and for ornaments. Hence, since a fourfold excess in the supply of silver only lessened its value in relation to gold to the extent of one-fifth, it may be inferred that a still smaller change would be effected in the value of gold if a similar excess were to take place in the supply of that metal. It is not unlikely, however, that the world's supply of silver will ere long be largely increased—by an extended working of the Mexican mines, and by the exploration and mining of the immense silver-bearing regions of the Andes. In this case the balance between gold and silver would be fully maintained.

In any case, no change can take place in the relative value of gold and silver such as to produce injury to the community. In countries where a double standard exists—in other words, where both gold and silver are equally money—any depreciation of the one metal, or (which is the same thing) any appreciation of the other, will only be sufficient to create a preference, on the part of bullion-dealers, to export the one metal rather than the other. When one of the precious metals is rising in value, and is tending to become more valuable as bullion than as coin, then, of course, when a man has to export bullion, he prefers to do so in this metal. But in reality such operations do not yield a profit, in a monetary sense. It is only on perfectly new coins, and frequently not even on them, that an agio is obtainable, during the periods when the relative value of gold and silver is altering. The profit, in short, on such operations is only sufficient to give the dealer a *preference* for exporting the one metal rather than the other. And then, each successive export of this rising metal—say silver—by reducing the currency of the country from which it is exported, raises the value of that currency,—so that people cannot afford to part with either of its elements, whether gold or silver; while at the same time the exports of silver lessen the special demand for that metal by supplying it. Like water in a cistern, every excess of gold or of silver poured into a currency immediately occasions an overflow, so that the level is preserved. Hence silver, although ever tending for the last dozen years towards a rise in value compared with gold, has not established it to any degree appreciable by the community.

THE DOUBLE STANDARD.

It appears evident, then, that the formidable objections which theorists make to the existence of a double standard of value in a country, are unsupported by facts. They conjure up a vision of "hydras, gorgons, and chimeras dire," for which we feel no apprehension. If a country has enough of gold, or of silver, to make its coinage entirely of that metal, good and well. But if not—as is the case in India—by all means let it employ both metals. The correctness of this opinion is abundantly shown in the case of France. In that most logical of countries, the double standard has long been established, and no one there has any desire to abolish it. During the last dozen years, this double standard has been subjected to the severest test that could be applied, and yet every one is satisfied with its working. Gold is pouring in, silver is pouring out—a revolution is being effected in the currency of France,—yet no one complains. Evidently, practical or appreciable disadvantage of any kind is quite unknown. Theoretically, as we have shown, a double standard cannot do much harm; practically, we find, it does none at all. And since it works under the most trying circumstances without the least injury in France, it may safely be introduced without any apprehension, and with great advantage, into India.

There is also a political consequence of the gold-discoveries which is deserving of especial notice. These gold-discoveries will of themselves produce an extension of the franchise, on an important scale. If, as we believe, a rise of prices is in progress—producing alike a rise of wages and an increase of house-rents—it is easy to see that this change will elevate a new class into the possession of the franchise. Houses which were rented at £8 in 1848, as a general rule are now rented at £10, which secures the franchise for the occupiers; and this rise of rents, we believe, will steadily progress. Indeed, in an old and rich country like ours, where population, trade, and wealth are steadily increasing, there is a tendency even in ordinary times for rents to advance,—producing, of course, a corresponding extension of the franchise. Taking the case of England, in the nineteen years before the new gold-supplies came into play, we find (from Dod's *Electoral Facts*) that between 1832 and 1851 the registered electors for burghs increased one-half, and those for counties more than one-third, while the total population increased less than one-third. The figures stand thus:—

NATURE'S REFORM BILL.

	1832.	1851.
Total registered electors, .	619,213	874,101
Total population, .	13,091,005	16,819,017

These figures show that in England, in the nineteen years subsequent to the Reform Bill, the electors increased in numbers one-sixth faster than the population. The case of Ireland, owing to the great social and political changes which took place in that country in the same period, is valueless: nevertheless, as a matter of fact, we may state that between 1832 and 1851, while the population had decreased about one-seventh, the registered electors had more than doubled in number. Scotland in many respects furnishes a safer test than either England or Ireland, as there has been no disturbance as regards the increase of its population, and also inasmuch as it has no forty-shilling freehold franchise, by means of which factitious additions can be so easily made to the constituencies. And the statistics for Scotland show that whereas population in the nineteen years subsequent to 1832 increased less than one-fourth, the electors increased more than one-half. The following are the figures:—

	1832.	1851.
Population, . . .	2,365,114	2,870,784
Electors, . . .	64,444	97,777

Electoral returns, it is true, are very unsafe data to employ in a question of this kind, for the number of householders placed upon the roll is greatly influenced by periods of political agitation or apathy, and still more by the laxity or strictness observed in purging the roll. But if we exclude these data altogether, it will nevertheless be obvious that the vast increase of commerce, employment, and wealth, consequent upon the gold-discoveries, by gradually raising house-rents and the condition of the people, will steadily carry on this natural extension of the Parliamentary franchise. We think, then, that the small minority of "advanced" Liberals, who bewail the failure of Lord Russell's projects of Parliamentary Reform, may take comfort, seeing that, gradually and surely, a virtual lowering of the franchise is taking place sufficient to satisfy the desires even of the most ardent believer in the wisdom of the masses.

THE GOOD TIMES.

Halcyon periods of unbroken quiet and prosperity are of rare occurrence and of brief duration in the history of any country. There is always a shadow—always a drawback. Wars and calamities we may expect in the future, as we have met them in the past. Nevertheless there are times when the social condition of a people improves with a rapidity and to an extent which are exceptional in its history. Such a period, we believe, this country—and in some degree the whole civilised world—has now entered upon; and the chief agent (though of course not the only one) in producing this period of prosperity is the new and great supply of the precious metals, which enables every country to extend its foreign commerce to a degree impossible before, and, by means of that commerce, to obtain more employment for its people, and increased profits for its traders and capitalists. Every one has been surprised that so great a calamity as the Cotton Famine has weighed upon us so lightly; but if we look into the case thoughtfully, we shall see that the great mitigator of the calamity has been that increase of our trade with foreign countries, which but for the gold-discoveries we had not the means of carrying out. Providence sends hard times upon the world occasionally; now it sends prosperity. A prosperity, indeed, not uncheckered, but apparently more full of promise and of social advantages than any which the world at large has yet witnessed.

THE ECONOMY OF CAPITAL

Of all the inventions of which Necessity is the stern mother, the inventions of Economy are the most prominent at the present day. Many new forces have recently been discovered and placed under the control of man, but it is the utilisation of hitherto useless things which still more peculiarly characterises our times. What our forefathers neglected or despised, we have learnt to appreciate; what they threw away we carefully gather up. Nothing is too small or too mean to be disregarded by our scientific economy. The seeming rubbish and fag-ends of creation, which our ancestors would gladly have thrown over the garden-wall of the world into the limbo of chaos or of space, are now converted to profitable purposes, conducive to the greater comfort and prosperity of life. "Waste nothing" is the key-note of our material industry. In the farm and in the manufactory, and not least among the vast hives of population in our great cities, the word "refuse," in its old sense, is well-nigh exploded. We now see that everything is of use, if we take it to the right place, and put it to its right purpose. Just as the farmer turns even the weeds to account, as a manure for the fields which they encumbered, so is it in all the other branches of industry. The making of many small gains is now considered a safer and more profitable mode of business than aiming at a few large ones. It is the utilisation of neglected resources, the accumulation and concentrated appliance of a thousand forces or savings, each trifling of itself, which is the basis of our extending power. We are economising our Money, like everything else: and this economy of capital, almost as much as the new gold-mines, is the agency which is giving to commerce its enormous expansion.

The first gold-seekers in California, we are told, did their work so rudely and imperfectly that their successors, when they came into the field with new and better appliances, found it a profitable business to occupy the old diggings, and extracted from the despised heaps of refuse about as much of the precious metal as had been obtained by the first workers. The first comers thought only of nuggets and large prizes; the later ones sought their chief gain in concentrating and extracting the invisible grains of precious ore from over a wide and apparently unpromising field.

The appliances of Banking have a similar effect in our social system. They have economised enormously the wealth of every country in which, like our own, they have been well developed.

BANKING.

Even in England, until lately, banking was in a rudimentary state. The private banks of London, indeed, were perfect of their kind: their proprietary possesses the wealth which is requisite to insure confidence, and the practised ability (in most cases an hereditary experience) which insures efficient administration. The private banks throughout the country, on the other hand, could not be relied on as possessing either of those requisites, and were especially deficient as regards their amount of capital. The introduction of the joint-stock system—only recently adopted in England, though it has existed for more than a century and a half with marked success in Scotland—has given an immense expansion to banking, and has proportionally increased the available capital of the nation.

It is to Scotland that we must still look to see the economy of capital in the most perfect form that has yet been devised. There, every little country town has its bank or banks, branches of the parent institutions in the capital. Each of those branch-banks becomes a reservoir for the spare money of the surrounding district. The sheep-farmer, as he returns with heavy purse from the fair, and the grain-farmer, as month by month he receives payment for his sales, hasten to deposit their money in the bank,—where it is not only kept securely and at call, but where a moderate rate of interest is paid on the amount deposited. The country shopkeeper, in like manner, and even the cottar, take thither their small gains, to be ready for the payment of wages or of rent; and the great landowners of the district receive their rents through the same channel. The managers of these branch-banks, living in the midst of each district, and knowing well the character and circumstances of those who deal with the bank, are ever ready to lend timely aid to any of their customers who are in need of it, and who are deserving of confidence. In this way two great objects are gained. Each man in the district, instead of (as formerly) keeping his savings in a strong chest, or hid in an old stocking, is now richer by receiving interest on his money from the bank; and the industry of the district is at the same time fostered by the advances (in the shape of cash-credits) which the bank-managers are ever ready to make upon moderate terms to worthy customers. While the district is thus benefited, the greater part of its surplus money is transferred to the central banking establishments, where it is profitably employed in the discount of mercantile bills, and in other ways which are all more or less conducive to the development of industry and the expansion of commerce. The spare money of the country, the accumulation of hundreds of petty savings, is transferred to the chief seats of industry, and is made to quicken the wheels of trade and manufacture, and thereby increases employment and profits throughout the whole country. In short, the general commerce and prosperity of the country is immensely increased, at the same time that each district is separately benefited. Hence it is that a country so poor and so thinly peopled as Scotland has, during the last hundred years, made such rapid advances.

England, in proportion to her population, still more in proportion to her wealth, lagged far behind Scotland in her progress in the appliances of banking. Nevertheless, her progress in this line during the last fifteen years has been remarkable. Irrespective of private banks, the joint-stock banks already established, along with their branches, amount to about 1600—spread over the country, and forming so many centres for receiving and utilising the spare money of the nation. So successful have been the joint-stock banks of London (of which there are now twelve), that the amount of deposits intrusted to them is at present upwards of £80,000,000. The following statement of the deposits, paid-up capital, and the rate of profit during the last twelve months, demonstrates the success which has attended the leading establishments of this kind in the metropolis :—

* Six Months.	Paid-up Capital.	Deposits.	Net Profits on the Six Months.	Percentage of Profit per Annum.
July—Dec. 1863 :				
London and Westminster, .	£1,000,000	£15,629,095	£147,816	29½
Union Bank, .	720,000	16,472,279	114,324	32
London Joint-Stock,	600,000	14,056,731	80,573	26¾
Bank of London,	300,000	4,179,294	34,924	23⅓
City Bank, .	400,000	3,525,975	33,030	16½
Jan.—June 1864 :				
London and Westminster, .	1,000,000	18,516,083	284,032	47
Union Bank, .	780,000	19,518,765	154,370	39½
London Joint-Stock,	600,000	14,959,649	124,476	41½
London and Country,	692,000	12,167,884	109,501	31½
Alliance Bank, .	692,725	6,065,889	62,397	18

In the English provinces, the introduction of the system of joint-stock banks has proved equally successful—especially in the great seats of manufacturing industry. For example, for the first six months of 1863, the Birmingham Joint-Stock Bank paid a dividend at the rate of 10 per cent per annum; the Sheffield Union Bank, 10 per cent; the Sheffield and Rotherham Bank, 12½ per cent; the Bradford Banking Company, 17½ per cent; the Huddersfield Banking Company, 26 per cent; the Yorkshire Banking Company, 29½ per cent; and the West Riding Union Banking Company, 47½ per cent. For the subsequent twelve months these rates have doubtless been still greater. For it appears from the returns of the London joint-stock banks that, owing to the high rate of discount, the profits of banking were one-fourth larger in the

* See also Appendix A.

last six months of 1863 than in the previous half-year; and during the first half of the present year, as is shown in the preceding table, the profits of banking have been still greater. In fact, every rise in the Bank of England's rate of discount is tantamount to an increase in the profits of banking.

In the United Kingdom the number of existing banks and branch-banks is said to be about five thousand; and the amount of money deposited with those establishments cannot be less than three hundred millions sterling. We may add that, on the 30th January last, the capital deposited in Savings-banks—in other words, the spare money of the lower classes, concentrated and economised—amounted in the United Kingdom to £43,615,000. Of this amount $3\frac{2}{3}$ millions were deposited in the recently established Post-office Savings-banks.

BANKS OF ISSUE.

In Scotland there are thirteen banks (five of which are minor and provincial), with 615 branches; and all of these banks issue notes of their own, of the value of £1 and upwards. The currency of Scotland consists entirely of paper-money—gold-money, which the English people prize so much, being regarded by the Scotch as alike cumbrous and expensive. The paper-money issued by the Scotch banks amounts to four and a half millions sterling: against which they hold nearly two and a half millions of specie. Indeed, so thoroughly secured are not only the issues, but also the deposits, of the Scotch banks, that in no case has any one of them failed to discharge every farthing of its liabilities. In Ireland there are six banks of issue, with a note-circulation of about six millions,—of which amount about two and a half millions belong to the Bank of Ireland. In England there are 204 banks of issue, and the amount of their notes in actual circulation averages about twenty-seven millions. Of this amount, fully twenty millions belong to the Bank of England,—three millions to joint-stock banks of issue, of which there are 61,—and three and a quarter millions to private banks of issue, of which there are 142.

Since 1844-5, the expansion of the use of paper-money in this country has been checked. By the Acts then passed, no new bank of issue was allowed to be established; and for all additional issues of notes on the part of existing banks, it was made imperative that they should keep on hand an equal amount of gold. In England, where there are no notes of less value than £5, and where consequently cheques serve almost all the purposes of bank-notes, this restriction is of little moment. But in Scotland, where the greater part of the currency consists of £1 notes, the restriction is felt as a hardship, and as an uncalled-for interference on the part of the Government. It was an interference with the freedom of issue which had previously prevailed in Scotland, and it has also produced a waste of capital in the

Scottish currency. For every addition to the note-circulation of Scotland, the banks have had to purchase and keep on hand an equal amount of specie—a condition which neutralises the economy of capital which it is the sole use of bank-notes to effect. Moreover, by the failure of the Western Bank in 1857, a portion of the Scotch note-issues against which it was not necessary to hold specie, amounting to £337,000, lapsed, and has not yet been restored. The present Chancellor of the Exchequer acknowledges the justice of the demand for the restoration of these lapsed issues; and probably the existing banks will ere long be empowered to replace them.

It is only the portion of a nation's capital which exists in an available form that adds to the power and resources of a State. Twenty million pounds sterling lying in the strong-boxes of half a million little tradesmen and farmers, is so much money lost to the national industry; but the same sum concentrated and lent out in the form of discounts, and other commercial advances, would give additional employment to the working-classes, increased wealth to the trading community, and greater power to the State. Banking is the agency by which this desirable end is accomplished; and we are not surprised that, both in this country and on the Continent, banks and credit companies should stand high in public favour. Within the last dozen years, France has done wonders in supplying her defects in this respect. The shares of the Credit Foncier (250 francs paid) are now at 1210 francs; those of the Credit Agricole (100 francs paid) are at 740 francs; those of the Credit Industriel et Commercial (125 francs paid) are at 755 francs; and those of the Credit Mobilier (500 francs paid) are selling at 1000 francs: and before the present tightness of the money market, their value was very much higher. France has only one bank of issue, the Bank of France, although it is a controverted point whether it be legally endowed with a monopoly of the right to issue notes. It is an admirably managed institution, and has rendered important services alike to the State and to the country. Indeed, looking at the many seasons of difficulty which it has successfully surmounted, without occasioning any of those fearful panics and crises which are the bane alike of this country and of the United States, we think the Bank of France is fairly entitled to be considered the best managed bank in the world. It has fifty-three branches, and the number is being increased every year—the Bank being bound by law to establish a branch in each of the eighty-nine Departments within a given period. The number of "bankers" in France is 2300 or 2400; but the term bankers in France often—in fact generally in the provinces—means only bill-discounters. The use of cheques is still very limited; and, chiefly in consequence of this, there is a great waste of capital, owing to the amount of metallic money in use. The metallic currency of France has been estimated at from £200,000,000 to £280,000,000; but doubtless it has been considerably on the decrease of late years; and the last estimate of its amount which we have seen states it at from £160,000,000 to £200,000,000.*

In Turkey, British and French capital is reaping great profits by the establishment of banks. But of all the countries of the Continent, Austria (bating the political shocks by which she is menaced) is the one which presents the finest field for banking. So unavailed of hitherto have been the appliances of banking in that country, that the Austrian Government has kept its balances (about five or six millions sterling) locked up in its own vaults: thereby losing interest on the money, and keeping idle and useless a large sum which, if confided to a bank, would be employed in giving direct support and expansion to the commerce and industry of the empire. In India, also, new banks are being rapidly established. In Australia, New Zealand, the Cape, British Columbia, Mexico, and among the States of South America—indeed, all over the world—English capital is seeking investment in the formation of banking establishments. In truth, it is a remarkable fact that the Age of Gold is becom-

* Speech of the Duke de Morny, in the Corps Legislatif, on the 25th of May 1864.

ing also the age of Banks,—and that the extraordinary increase in the supply of the precious metals has been accompanied by a not less extraordinary increase in the means for economising them.

In no country in the world does the economy of capital approach to the comparative perfection which has been attained in the British Isles. But there are improvements yet to be made; and in London itself a change is at work which ere long will effect a revolution in our banking-system. The day of the private banks is drawing to a close. They are still as sound and as ably managed as ever, but it is easy to see that they are destined to wane before the new rivals that are taking the field. The great private banks will last, indeed, for many a day, and will continue to yield large profits,—but no new private banks will be started.

PRIVATE BANKS.

The private banks in London, like the Bank of England, used to pay no interest to their depositors, however large the amount deposited, or however long it might lie in the bank. This was a great drawback on their popularity, after the joint-stock banks started; and recently some of the private banks have begun to give interest on nearly the same terms as their new rivals. On the other hand, they have certain advantages peculiar to themselves. From having a narrower and more select range of business, and consequently knowing their customers unusually well, they are more ready to make advances to their customers, and (which is a great point with men in business) do so more privately, than is the case with the joint-stock banks—which are necessarily fettered by rules, and where the managing power is a board of directors. Men who are engaged in an extensive business, not seldom require a temporary advance in order to enable them to execute some large order, but, most naturally, they are reluctant to make a statement of their affairs which will be brought under the notice of a board of directors; whereas they need have no such delicacy in applying to the head of a private banking establishment. Again, as regards efficiency of management, the private banks of London cannot be surpassed—we may say, cannot be equalled; for they are managed by the proprietors themselves, who have a deeper interest in the welfare of the establishment than a salaried manager can have, and who also, in most cases, have an hereditary experience in banking.

JOINT-STOCK BANKS.

Nevertheless it is found that, as a rule, the joint-stock system of banking is the more popular and advantageous: and this in the end will decide the question between the rival systems. A board of directors, elected by the shareholders, and each having a separate business of his own to attend to, certainly does not constitute a beau-ideal of management; although the defect is partially redeemed by the appointment of a permanent manager. But it is found that the immense sums at the disposal of joint-stock companies, compared with those at the command of private bankers, gives them an advantage which enables a moderately good management to realise greater profits than can be attained by the most talented management of lesser sums. The large amount of subscribed capital which joint-stock banks offer as security, the publicity given to their balance-sheets, and, most of all, the interest which they allow upon money deposited with them, render them more popular than the private banks; their system of branches, and their large number of shareholders, give them a wider sphere of operations; and the high profits which they generally pay render them attractive to capitalists who desire to engage in banking. Joint-stock banks will continue to increase, and the private banks will slowly die out.* The private banks of London, indeed, as was suggested some years ago by Mr M'Leod, might themselves unite together, and form

* In 1840, Lord Overstone, in his evidence before the Parliamentary Committee on the Bank Charter, condemned the joint-stock system as quite inapplicable to banking. "I think joint-stock banks," he said, "are deficient in everything requisite for the conduct of banking business, except extended responsibility." And this opinion is quoted with approbation by Mr M'Culloch in his *Commercial Dictionary* so late as 1859. Yet only a few months ago, the great private banking firm, of which Lord Overstone was so long the head, gave up business; and, with the express approval of his lordship, transferred their business to the London and Westminster *Joint-Stock* Bank!

a joint-stock bank of unequalled prestige and resources; but so many private questions of punctilio and precedence would have to be overcome before such a corporation could be established, that such a project is not capable of realisation. Nevertheless, that the private bankers of London are not blind to the tendency of affairs, is evidenced by the union which has recently taken place between two of these banks (Messrs Heywood & Kennards' and Messrs Hankey's) and the Bank of Manchester—which three banks, uniting the advantages of both systems, now form a joint-stock company under the name of the "Consolidated Bank." *

PROFITS OF BANKING.

That banking is a highly profitable business is evidenced by the statement which we have given of the profits yielded by some of the leading banking companies. A successful bank in England, it appears, pays a dividend ranging from 15 to 25 per cent, with no trouble whatever on the part of its shareholders. Sometimes the dividend reaches the enormous rate of 50 per cent. How comes it, it

* Since this was written (Feb. '64), such banking amalgamations have proceeded on a large scale, viz.:—Jones, Lloyd, & Co.'s bank with the London and Westminster; Barnett, Hoares, & Co. with Hanbury's and Lloyd's; Currie's with Glyn's; Robarts' with Lubbock's; Masterman's with Bank of Agra; A. Spielman & Co. with the London, Hamburg, & Continental Exchange Bank. Some joint-stock banks have likewise amalgamated, viz.:—the English & Irish with the European, and the Bank of Hindostan with the Bank of China.

will naturally be asked, that banking yields such very large profits? The essential requirement of good banking is security for the depositors. Individual traders, whose failure or success affects only themselves, may apply their money in any way that appears to them most likely to yield the largest profits. But a Bank trades with other people's money; and the paramount consideration with the public, when placing their money in bank, is *security*. The science of banking consists not in employing money at the highest rates, but in the safest manner. And this is generally done. The explanation of the large dividends paid by successful banking companies is, that they obtain a profit on their depositors' money as well as on their own. The capital of a banking company may be two or three millions sterling—that amount being liable to be called up, if necessary, to meet the engagements of the bank; but only a part of that sum is paid up. The larger the capital, the greater is the security for depositors; and the greater the security, the greater is likely to be the amount of money intrusted to the bank's keeping. On the other hand, the smaller the amount of capital *paid up*, the greater (*cæteris paribus*) will be the percentage of profits to the shareholders. Say that a bank (which may have a subscribed capital of two or three millions) has £1,000,000 paid up, and that its deposits amount to £15,000,000—then it can deal with sixteen times the amount of money invested by its shareholders; and thus, instead of (say) 5 per cent, its gross receipts will amount to 80 per cent. The net receipts or profits, of course, are much less,—because the interest paid to depositors,* costs of management, &c., have to be deducted: nevertheless, it is easy to see how such a bank will pay 25 per cent. This, then, is the secret of the high dividends paid by the English banking companies. In Scotland, however, the banks rarely pay a dividend above 9 or 10 per cent: a much larger portion of their profits being given to their customers in the shape of interest, and their reserves also being larger in proportion to their liabilities than is the case with the English joint-stock banks. It seems to us, indeed, that the present high profits derived from banking in England are quite abnormal: they cannot, and ought not, to last.

The English joint-stock banks are still, we think, defective in some of their arrangements. These lack simplicity—and simplicity, as has been proved abundantly, is a matter of first-rate importance in the promotion of business. Most of them pay interest only

* The proportion which the amount of interest paid to depositors bears to the net profits of a bank is dependent partly on the skill of the management and partly on the state of the money market. In the case of the Union Bank of London, during the last six months of 1863, the proportion was one of equality,—the interest paid and due to depositors being £112,000, and the net profits, after making ample provision for bad and doubtful debts, being £114,000. See also Appendix A.

on such current-accounts as never fall below a certain amount (generally £500); and they vary their rates according to the length of time the money is placed at their disposal.* This is a great improvement on the system of the Bank of England, which gives no interest at all,—but it is still defective. The immemorial practice of the Scotch banks has been to pay a uniform rate of interest on every sum deposited with them, however small, and for however short a time. Recently, in November 1863, the Scotch banks resolved to allow their customers the option of having interest calculated as before—*i. e.*, on the daily balance—or on the minimum monthly balance of their accounts; the banks allowing

SCOTCH AND ENGLISH BANKING.

* There is a great and perplexing diversity in the practice of the London joint-stock banks in this respect. Some of them pay no interest at all upon current-accounts which at any time during the year happen to fall below £500. Of the more liberal class of banks we may take the case of the recently-established Alliance Bank, the custom of which is as follows:—If the balance shall not at any time during the half-year have been below £500, interest at the rate of 2 per cent per annum will be allowed on the minimum monthly balances; if not below £200, 1 per cent will be allowed; if below £200, no interest. It is obvious that, under the general system of these banks, a current-account which may average £500 on the whole year may yield no interest at all, owing to a temporary fall below the limit of £200; and on accounts which keep above this limit, as interest is paid only on the lowest sum at which the account may stand during the month, the depositor will in general receive interest on little more than two-thirds of the average amount which he has in bank throughout the month. Upon these current-accounts, too, the interest never exceeds 2 per cent. Upon sums received *in deposit*, the Alliance Bank pays interest at the current rates.

in the latter case, and also on deposit-receipts, one per cent higher interest. But this change is only nominal, and the rate of interest substantially remains the same on all sums: for it is obvious that, though the interest given in the latter case is higher than in the former, it is paid upon a lesser amount. The practice of the Scotch banks is entirely opposed to the peculiar feature of the English joint-stock banks—namely, the non-payment of interest except upon comparatively large sums. The English practice has these advantages, that it saves the bank a little trouble, and adds greatly to its profits; it also enables it to pay a higher rate of interest upon deposit-accounts, by paying little or none upon current-accounts. Its great defect, in a national point of view, is that it holds out no temptation to small capitalists,—the average cash-balance of each of whom may be only £100 or £200, but whose capital in the aggregate would amount to a very large sum. Too large to be received by the savings-banks, too small to obtain interest from the banks, these little capitals have not yet been looked after in England. In Scotland, on the other hand, they are attracted into the common reservoir, and constitute no insignificant portion of the motive power which drives the wheels of industry and commerce. England is so enormously wealthy, and the habits and ideas of the English are so much in accordance with their condition, that they are still careless of this portion of the national resources; but the Scotch, in the school of necessity, have become more careful in economical science, and in this matter their example may be followed with advantage by their English brethren. If the English joint-stock banks are to establish branches throughout the country in the manner of the Scotch banks (as we hope will be done in course of time), they will find it indispensable to alter their practice, and frame their rules so as to suit the wants of the small capitalists, farmers and shopkeepers, who form the bulk of the population in the country districts.

The heart of this great system of banking, which now overspreads the whole country, is the Bank of England. It was founded in 1694, and the Bank of Scotland in the year following. Both of these banks owed their origin to the same man—William Paterson, M.P. for Dumfries. The project of the Bank of England was ultimately taken out of his hands; but he had his own way in the establishment of the Bank of Scotland. And the issue in the two countries was very different—fraught with great benefit to the one, and with repeated disaster to the other. In Scotland the first established bank claimed no monopoly: banking was made a free trade. In England the Bank soon claimed and obtained a monopoly. No other joint-stock bank (no banking company having more than six partners) was allowed to be established in England. In 1826, after more than a century of complete restriction, this monopoly was narrowed to the district within sixty-five miles of London; in 1844 it was finally abolished, but the right of new banks to issue notes was taken away.

Mark the results on the welfare of the two countries. One by one, as they were needed, joint-stock banks were established in Scotland, having their head-offices in the capital, and gradually extending their operations by the establishment of branches throughout the provinces. In this way a small number of banks sufficed. Banking, free and unshackled, grew with the growth of Scotland. Each branch-bank had a local manager, and all were in perfect union with the head-office in the capital. The head-offices in Edinburgh, again—the parent-establishments—were all in connection with one another; each receiving the notes of the others; having a weekly "clearance," or balancing of mutual accounts; and each having a pretty good idea of the general business and position of the others. Thus banking in Scotland was (1) established in the best form—namely, almost entirely upon the joint-stock principle; and (2) the banks established in the capital, while ramifying through the country, can mutually support one another in times of temporary difficulty or panic. After lasting for a century and a half, free-trade in banking was brought to an end in Scotland by Sir R. Peel's Act of 1845, which propitiated the existing banks for the restrictions then imposed upon them, by conferring upon them a virtual monopoly. The Act, it is true, places no restrictions on simple banking—only on the right of issuing notes: but, owing to the peculiarity of the Scotch currency, no bank has an adequate chance of success which cannot issue its own notes. Such, at least, is the case at present. Happily, as the Scotch banks compete eagerly with one another in the establishment of branches, leaving no district unoccupied, the monopoly has not acted injuriously—unless it be in making the banks chime in too readily with any proposals of the Government for the sake of having their monopoly undisturbed. The principle is a bad one, but the fruits as yet have not been evil.

In England, the monopoly of the Bank prevented for more than a century the formation of any other joint-stock bank; neither did the Bank of England occupy the field itself by establishing branches throughout the country. But, as a want of banks was felt, private individuals came forward to do what would have been far better done by joint-stock companies. Private bankers started up in every town, receiving deposits and issuing notes of their own—many of them able and honest men, some of them not, but none of them possessing the extended resources of a joint-stock company. Moreover, by a sad fatality, even when the monopoly of the Bank began to be relaxed, in 1826, the provision that no joint-stock bank should be established within 65 miles of London was one of the most injurious that could possibly be devised. The consequence has been, that there is neither system nor connection among the English banks. The banking establishments do not ramify from London, as a centre; they exist, for the most part, independently of one another—head-banks being found all over the country, with few or no branches, and with no point of union with their neighbours. This is an expensive system, for head-banks are established sometimes where branch-banks would suffice; it is chaotic and without method; and it is needlessly perilous.

The Scotch banks can, and do, help one another most efficiently; the English banks can do so but imperfectly. The latter (until recently) have had to grow up everywhere except in the metropolis; and accordingly they lack central representatives, and find it difficult to combine for mutual support. All banks exist upon Credit: let that be broken, and not even the best and strongest of them can exist for a day. It is alike the duty and the interest of banks to support credit. If, for example, in times of panic, a run be made upon one of their number whose position they know to be sound, they ought at once to unite in support of that bank. This is the best, if not the only effectual, means of arresting a panic—that wild unreasoning fear which grows with every disaster which it

CO-OPERATION OF BANKS.

produces. The fall of one bank only increases the run upon the others: but united action upon the part of the banks (at least if the Bank of England were untrammelled by legislation) would be adequate to resist a greater panic than has yet arisen.

Without union, no banking system can resist the effects of a panic. A panic strikes at the root of all banking. The rules of banking are based upon the amount of money necessary to meet the ordinary demands of the public, whether in the cashing of notes or withdrawing of deposits. But if a run takes place for any considerable portion of deposits, the bank must close its doors. Banking was never designed to meet such emergencies. It is no slur upon a bank that it cannot sustain such an abnormal pressure. The Bank of England itself would break down at once under such a trial. Panic is a temporary collapse of public credit—a rupture of our whole fabric of material civilisation—a national epilepsy. To think that any legislation will suffice to render banks able to withstand such an abnormal pressure, is simply absurd. If banks had always to keep on hand resources adequate to meet a panic, this could only be done by keeping their deposits unemployed, in their vaults: in which case there would be no profit (only expense) to the bankers, no aid to commerce and employment—in fact, no banking at all. Nevertheless, strange to say, the banks themselves, by

PANICS.

their action, have frequently induced this most terrible of monetary tempests.

As this is a point of great importance, we shall illustrate it by referring to some cases where the facts are so clear as not to admit of dispute.

Let us take first the panics of 1793 and 1797. In 1792 trade had been unusually, if not excessively, brisk; and at the same time, as the year progressed, political agitation assumed formidable proportions. Acts of riot and insurrection took place, and when war with France was declared at the end of the year, the public inquietude almost amounted to panic. Bankruptcies had doubled in number before the close of the year, and "the declaration of war gave a shock to credit, which was already staggering." On the 15th February a house of considerable magnitude failed; and on the 19th the Bank of England refused the paper of Lane and Company, who stopped next morning with liabilities to the amount of nearly a million sterling. "In the mean time, the panic spread to the bankers." The run commenced on the banks in Newcastle, which were perfectly solvent, but which, in consequence of the run upon them, were obliged to stop payment. "The panic immediately spread throughout the country." In the west of Scotland, also, there was "the greatest distress from the total destruction of credit," which calamity was produced by "the refusal of the Glasgow,

OUR MONETARY CRISES.

Paisley, and Greenock banks to discount." The monetary pressure extended also to the London banks. "The extraordinary state of credit [to speak correctly, the total collapse of credit] had obliged every person connected with trade and money-transactions to gather in and husband every resource to meet all demands"—thereby, of course, greatly lessening the ordinary circulation. In these circumstances, "the Government urged the Bank to come forward and support credit, but they resolutely declined. When the Bank adopted this perverse course, universal failure seemed imminent." The Government, however, with Pitt at its head, wisely took the matter into its own hands; and, acting on the advice of Sir John Sinclair, made an issue of Exchequer bills, which acted like magic in sustaining public credit, and at once put an end to the crisis.*

The panic of 1797 was produced entirely by political causes. There had been no over-trading of any kind. In December '96 took place the French expedition under Hoche for the invasion of Ireland, and in the February following a French frigate landed 1200 men on the Welsh coast. "At this time the

* See M'Leod's *Theory and Practice of Banking*, vol. ii. p. 68-72. We prefer to make our quotations from this work, because it is the ablest on the subject of which it treats; and still more, because on this point Mr M'Leod's statement of facts is, to a considerable extent, that of an antagonist to the deductions which we make from them.

banks at Newcastle had a more than ordinary demand upon them for cash; because, in addition to the manufactories and collieries, the number of troops stationed in that part of the country had been considerably augmented. The banks had imported an extra supply of cash to meet their expenses, and were negotiating for more," when the panic broke upon them and compelled them to stop. ..." The news of the stoppage of the Newcastle banks spread like wildfire throughout the country, and soon reached the metropolis. The drain upon the Bank of England now became a run," till on the 25th the specie was reduced to £1,272,000. "Before this, the Directors, in a state of utter bewilderment at the state of the country, had used the most violent efforts to contract the issues. In five weeks they had reduced them by nearly £2,000,000. But even this gave no true idea of the curtailment of mercantile accommodation, for the private bankers were obliged, for their own security, to follow the example of the Bank." Next day (Sunday), to prevent the total stoppage of the Bank, an Order in Council was issued, authorising it to suspend cash-payments. And yet the position of the Bank was not only perfectly solvent, but such as to show a surplus of nearly £4,000,000 sterling—over and above the debt due by the Government to the Bank, which amounted to £11,686,000. So suicidal was the policy of restriction pursued by the Bank, that even the Bullion Committee of 1810, despite their morbid dread of "over-issues," explicitly condemned its conduct in this respect, both in 1793 and in 1797.*

The other case to which we shall refer, in illustration of this fatal but common error in banking, is that of the American crisis of 1857. The crisis began in the August of that year with the failure of the Ohio Life and Trust Company, which held deposits to the amount of £1,200,000, and of two or three other large firms. By this stoppage of payments great embarrassment and partial loss were occasioned to individuals, and also to the banks which had made advances to those firms; at the same time railway property and financial establishments of all kinds became greatly depreciated, chiefly owing to the efforts of an organised band of speculators.† Thereupon the American banks

* M'Leod's *Theory and Practice of Banking*, vol. ii. p. 88-92.

† "There is actually a powerful combination for the avowed purpose of bringing all the principal undertakings to ruin. Unlike those of any other country, the majority of the leading speculators of New York are devoted to the task of depreciating the national credit. Whether this arises from the extent to which American securities are held by foreigners, need not be discussed. A large body of active persons are known to be associated for the purpose; they influence the press, to work out their views, and are alleged not merely to operate with a joint capital, but to hold regular meetings, and permanently retain legal advisers, whose chief vocation it may be assumed is to discover points that may enable the validity of each kind of security to be called in question, and thus to create universal distrust."—*Times* City article, September 10, 1857. See also the City article for September 15 and 17; and the New York correspondence in the *Times* of September 14 and 24, 1857.

took alarm, and began to curtail their advances to the commercial community, by refusing to discount their bills,—the New York banks reducing their discounts to the amount of £5,000,000 sterling between the 8th of August and the 10th of October. Right and left they ruthlessly withdrew their customary advances, and commercial houses went down in dozens. By the middle of October, nine hundred failures were reported. What was the upshot? The banks sacrificed their customers with the view of strengthening their own position, but their conduct had quite the opposite effect. Seeing firms go down in dozens—the good as well as the bad, the strong as well as the weak,—and knowing that many of those firms were connected with the banks, either as shareholders or debtors, the public in turn caught the panic, and began a run upon the banks for their *deposits.* The banks, too late, now found that they could no more conduct their business without credit or faith than their customers the merchants could; and on the 14th October a general suspension of payments in specie had to take place throughout the Union.

The American banks were thus taught a sharp lesson. A week before they were forced to suspend, they announced that they would alter their policy, and meet the panic by its natural remedy—an expansion of credit to all solvent but embarrassed firms; and it was the publication of their returns in the week following, showing that instead of expanding they were carrying the work of contraction still further, which brought on the general run for deposits which compelled them to stop. It is important to observe that not only were the New York banks perfectly solvent, but their notes were never mistrusted: and even after the suspension of payments in specie, the notes continued to circulate at par.* It was a run for deposits which shut up the banks: and a similar run would shut up any and every bank in existence.

CONVERTIBILITY.

The sole object and advantage of paper-money is, that it economises gold. Paper-money, like banking, would be of no use at all, if it were requisite to keep an equal amount of gold in the banks. The proportion of specie requisite to maintain the convertibility of note-issues, varies with the credit of the issuer. The Bank of England's rule used to be that one-third of specie was amply sufficient to secure both notes and deposits. The common opinion

* The notes not only continued at par after the suspension of the banks, but actually, at one time, rose to a high premium compared with gold. "According to advices received to-day," said the *Times* of October 31, "good sight bills could still be purchased at an exchange of 101. The extraordinary fact is therefore exhibited of *the inconvertible currency of the New York suspended banks being actually at a high premium compared with the specie* currencies of other countries. That is to say, a bill on London could be purchased in the notes of the New York suspended banks at a price which, after allowing for interest and all charges, would bring back in gold a larger sum than had been paid for it."

which regards these note-issues as the great source of peril to banks is a mistake. The opinion has arisen from our monetary authorities having confounded two very different things. It is not a difficult matter to secure the convertibility of the note, but it is totally impossible to insure payment of any bank's deposits in gold. Banking deposits, in fact, are not made in gold, and cannot all be paid in gold. All the available gold in the country would hardly suffice to pay 5 per cent of their amount.* A suspension of cash-payments may become inevitable, although the notes of every bank were secured by an equal amount of specie in its vaults. It was not a run for gold in exchange for notes which caused the suspension of cash-payments in 1797. It was a demand for the payment of deposits in specie: the specie being wanted for export in payment of the loans which this country was then making to foreign Powers.

Now, in times of panic, the demand upon the banks is not, or is not merely, for gold for the notes: in fact, in this country, during the present century, the solidity of the notes has never been questioned. The run is for deposits. In truth

A RUN FOR DEPOSITS.

* The total amount of specie held by the banks of the United Kingdom, in ordinary times, is about £20,000,000; of which amount the Bank of England holds on the average 14½ millions, the Irish banks rather more than 2 millions, and the Scotch banks not quite 2½ millions. The deposits in bank probably amount to £400,000,000.

there never is, or can be, a run for gold apart from a run for deposits. If the holders of notes, who probably have not more than £5 or £10 on hand, lose faith in the bank, the depositors will still more surely take alarm. If a bank cannot pay its notes, how is it to pay its deposits? Hence the common idea which attributes such panics to a real or supposed unsoundness of the note-issues, is a great mistake. There would be panics and runs on the banks though they did not issue a single note. The demand for gold in exchange for notes is merely an accompaniment (and a comparatively trifling one) of the run for deposits. And such a run, if not promptly checked, must prove fatal: for no bank can pay up its deposits at once, whether in gold or in notes.

It is easy to see how this run for deposits is occasioned in times of monetary pressure and distrust.

REFUSAL OF DISCOUNTS. The ordinary business of banking consists in the discount of commercial bills—*i. e.*, in the purchase of the current debts of commerce. A manufacturer supplies a merchant with £1000 of goods, and receives from (or draws upon) him a bill for the same amount; and as the merchant's money is nearly all invested in his business, the bill is not made payable until after the lapse of such time (say three months) as may be required by him to sell at least a portion of the goods which he has purchased. The manufacturer, in like manner, having his capital invested in his business, and not being able to wait till the three months have expired, takes the bill to his banker and gets it cashed,—receiving the £1000 *minus* the interest for three months at the current rate. All commerce is carried on in this way, and in this way a great economy of capital is effected. What, then, is commerce to do when the banks refuse to discount? A general crash must follow. In ordinary times, when credit is good, a merchant may afford to wait a little before getting his bills cashed, for at such times he is not pressed by his fellow-merchants to whom he is indebted; but in times of a monetary or commercial crisis, he cannot wait. Every man, to secure himself, is then pressing his debtors for payment; and if the banks at such times refuse to discount bills as usual, nothing but bankruptcy can be the result, even for firms which are superabundantly solvent. The banks, when they take this course (which they generally do in a period of a crisis) doubtless act from a good and legitimate motive. They think of securing their own safety. They think of the convertibility of their notes, and the increasing scarcity of gold; and, by refusing to discount the ordinary amount of bills, they seek to lessen the amount of their own liabilities. In case a run upon them should arise, they seek to lessen the amount upon which the run can be made. But this is a fatal mistake, as experience abundantly demonstrates. It is impossible for any bank to reduce its liabilities to an amount which can be met by its available assets. The true policy of banks lies in preventing the occurrence of a run for deposits,—whereas they think only of trying to meet it. And the very measures which they take to prepare against a run, produce a run. These measures occasion a panic, and the panic produces a run; and quite reasonably. No other consequence is possible. When the commercial public find that it is becoming difficult or impossible for them to get their bills discounted, they call up every shilling of their deposits; or they sell their goods, and, taking the cheque which they receive in payment to the bank, withdraw the amount in cash. When they cannot get money the one way, they take it in another. The general public, catching the infection, join in the run on the banks; and the result is (if the panic be kept up by a continued curtailment of discounts), that the banks, after a feverish scramble among themselves for the possession of the small stock of gold, stop one after the other, or by agreement simultaneously—as was the case with the New York banks in 1857.

Banks exist for the community, not a community for the banks. And whenever banks forget this, and (like those in America) begin slaughtering a community from a false notion of strengthening themselves, it is not an evil, but a good, when they are pulled up in their course. The run for deposits which immediately arises in such circumstances is a natural and inevitable result of the banks curtailing their discounts. At the same time, it is a natural and most obvious means of retaliation; and as such, it was deliberately adopted by the commercial classes in New York in 1857. The language then used was this:—"If you, (the banks) think yourselves justified, in a time of crisis, in bringing down scores of good firms, as solvent and reputable as yourselves, the public are still more justified in checkmating *you*, by requesting you to fulfil your 'promises to pay.' Since it is on the plea of preserving the convertibility of the note (which we had no thought of questioning) that you produce this widespread suffering, the outraged community may well turn round upon you, and say, 'Very well, gentlemen, *let us see if you can do it.*' Moreover, since you will not lend us your money, give us back ours: give us our deposits." The banks, of course, *could not do it.* And thereupon, perceiving that they had been sacrificing the substance for the shadow, they reversed their policy, discounted freely, though they had hardly a dollar in their tills—and the crisis was at an end. What is more, from that instant gold began to flow back into the banks in abundance! Within three months after the 14th of October, when cash-payments were suspended, the stock of specie in the New York banks increased from £1,744,000 to £6,500,000—actually a million sterling higher than it had *ever* been before. And "in the five principal seaport cities of the Union, the stock of specie advanced from £3,400,000 to £10,000,000, although £3,200,000 were sent to Europe in the interval." *

This is a lesson and a danger to which all banks should give good heed. The American public is not likely to forget the experience which it acquired in 1857, of its power to checkmate the banks. It is also by no means improbable that the lesson has been observed and noted on this side of the Atlantic, and may be put in practice if ever our banks should foolishly challenge the commercial classes to a trial of strength.

HOW PANICS ARE STOPPED.

Having shown how monetary crises may be, and often are, aggravated into destructive panics by a mistaken policy upon the part of the banks, let us complete the lesson by showing the chief means by which panic and a run upon banks are stayed. In 1793 we have shown how the monetary panic was produced, or at least intensified, by the Bank of England curtailing its discounts, thereby aggravating the prevalent distrust; and how the Government wisely came to the rescue by making an issue of Exchequer bills. The amount authorised to be issued was £5,000,000 in sums of £100, £50, and £20; but not half of that amount (only £2,202,000) was needed, and the whole of this sum was punctually repaid. What was the effect of this aid to the com-

* *Times*' City article, Jan. 27, 1856.

mercial classes? "It operated like magic," we are told: "its success was perfect and complete. All contemporary writers bear witness to the extraordinary effects produced. Macpherson says that the *very intimation of the intention of the Legislature to support the merchants* operated like a charm all over the country, and in a great degree superseded the necessity of the relief by an almost instantaneous restoration of confidence."* In the crisis of 1797, when the Bank of England again took the course of enormously curtailing its discounts, the run upon it became so overwhelming that it was left almost without a sovereign in its coffers, and the Government had to come to its relief by ordering the total suspension of payments in specie. What followed? "The relief produced on the instant by the definite determination to *suspend cash-payments and extend their issues of paper* was very great: within one week the Bank increased its accommodation by nearly £2,000,000 sterling"—or nearly one-fourth! Here, then, we see plainly that the convertibility of the note—for the sake of which the Bank had curtailed its discounts so enormously (one-fourth during five weeks)—had never really been questioned by the public: for an issue of notes was the very thing that was desired, and which stopped the panic. The notes were taken as readily by every one when it was known that there was no

* M'Leod's *Theory and Practice of Banking*, vol. ii. p. 72-75.

gold to cash them, as when the Bank was abundantly supplied with specie.*

Let us next look at the great crisis of 1826. The crisis was at its height in London from Monday the 12th to Saturday the 17th December. For six months the Bank had been "violently contracting its issues" (*i.e.*, by curtailing its discounts), and it continued this policy down to the night of Tuesday the 14th. During the previous forty-eight hours, said Mr Huskisson afterwards, even the best Government securities could not to any extent be converted into money: other stock, of course, was still more unsaleable: and Mr Baring said that persons would not part with their *money* on any terms, nor for any security. The prevalent distrust, by invalidating the ordinary forms of commercial credit, had rendered a greater supply of money absolutely indispensable,—yet the Bank had been steadily doing its best to render money much scarcer than usual. At length it found that such measures were undermining its own position, and that, if continued for another day, they would involve the Bank as well as the country in a common ruin. Accordingly, "on Wednesday the 14th the Bank totally changed its policy, and discounted with the utmost profuseness." In the words of the Deputy Governor, "they had [at length!] taken a firm and deliberate resolution to make common cause with the country." Instead of refusing

* See M'Leod, vol. ii. p. 92-100.

to discount, they *forced out* their money in loans in all directions. "We lent it by every possible means," said Mr Harman, "and in modes we had never adopted before; . . . we were not on some occasions over-nice: seeing the dreadful state in which the public were, we rendered every assistance in our power." Between the Wednesday and Saturday, the Bank made issues of notes to the amount of £5,000,000. This policy, says Mr M'Leod, "was crowned with the most complete success: *the panic was stayed almost immediately.*" The mere sight of the bank-notes was enough. "At Norwich," said Mr Richards, "when the Gurneys showed upon their counter so many feet of bank-notes of such a thickness, it stopped the run in that part of the country." By the 24th of December the panic was completely allayed all over the country; and by the end of the month the credit of the banking world was completely restored.*

* M'Leod, vol. ii. p. 245-251. The immediate cause of the panic in London was the stoppage of Pole & Co., bankers, with whom forty country banks were connected, on Monday the 12th. "The fall of this great banking-house," says Mr M'Leod, "was the signal for a general run upon all the London bankers, and three or four more gave way — spreading universal consternation among the country banks, sixty-three of which succumbed to the crisis, though a considerable number paid 20s. in the pound, and eventually resumed business." Yet it was proved that Pole & Co., whose stoppage produced all this disaster, had a surplus of £170,000, after payment of all claims against them—besides large landed property belonging to Sir Peter Pole, and about £100,000, the private property of other members of the firm. Ought not such a firm to have been supported, instead of being pulled to the ground? Co-operation among bankers, we repeat, in a time of crisis, is everything.

The next great crisis was that of 1847; previous to which (by the Act of 1844) all liberty of action had been taken from the Bank in regard to its issues of notes, which were made entirely dependent upon the amount of specie in its possession. The extreme pressure in this crisis began on the 23d September, "when the Bank adopted more stringent measures for curtailing the demand upon its resources." On the 15th October it refused to make advances either on Government stock or on Exchequer bills: the consequence of which was that the other banks hastened to sell their public securities, and, for their own safety, hoarded the notes received in payment,—thus still further reducing the circulation. What they could not get from the Bank in advances on their securities, they got by the sale of them: so that the only effect of the Bank's restrictive policy was to create panic and hoarding, which immensely increased the difficulties of its position. Everything became worse day by day. Several large banks stopped payment in Liverpool, Manchester, Newcastle, and other towns; and the drain on the Bank of England became greater than ever. "As the whole of the commercial world knew that the resources of its banking department were being rapidly exhausted, a complete panic seized them. A complete cessation of private discounts took place. No one would part with the money or notes in his possession." On the 23d of October the terrible game was played out. The Bank Act had to be suspended; and the Government, with the view "to restore confidence to the mercantile community," recommended the Bank Directors to *enlarge the amount of their discounts and advances.* What followed? The Government letter "was made public about one o'clock on Monday the 25th, and no sooner was this done than the panic vanished like a dream.... Mr Gurney stated that it produced its effects in ten minutes! No sooner was it known that notes *might* be had, than the want of them ceased."

From the conduct as well as the statements of the Bank Directors on this occasion, it appears evident that they had no desire to contract their advances to the public, apart from the necessity to do so imposed upon them by the Act of 1844. They told the Chancellor of the Exchequer that "they could save themselves"—that is, they could comply with the law; "but that they could not do so without pressing more stringently on the commercial world." In how great a degree the crisis was artificial—how immensely it was aggravated by the restrictive policy imposed upon the Bank—cannot be better shown than in the following extracts from the speech of the Chancellor of the Exchequer (Sir C. Wood) on the subject:—

"Evidence was laid before the Government, which proved not only the existence of severe pressure, but also that it was aggravated in a very great degree by the hoarding of gold and bank-notes to a very large extent—in consequence of which an amount of circulation, which under ordinary circumstances would have been adequate, became insufficient for the wants of the community. . . . Parties of every description made application to us, with the observation, 'We do not want notes, but give us confidence.' They said, 'We have notes enough, but we have not confidence to use them: say you will stand by us, and we shall have all that we want: do anything, in short, that will give us confidence. If we think that we can get bank-notes, we shall not want them.' . . . . Parties said to me, 'Let us have notes—charge 10, 12 per cent for them—we don't care what the rate of interest is. We don't mean, indeed, to take the notes, because we shall not want them; only *tell us that we can get them*, and this will at once restore confidence.' . . . As soon as the letter of 25th October appeared, and the panic ceased, thousands and tens of thousands of pounds were taken from the hoards; some from boxes deposited with bankers, although the parties would not leave the notes in their bankers' hands. Large parcels of notes were returned to the Bank of England cut into halves, as they had been sent down into the country. And so small was the real demand for an additional quantity of notes, that the whole amount taken from the Bank, when the unlimited power of issue was given, was under £400,000. The restoration of confidence released notes from their hoards, and no more was wanted—for the trifling quantity of additional notes is hardly worth notice."*

Here, again, we see that the sufficiency of the Bank's notes was never questioned;—that the crisis was mainly due to the hoarding of notes and gold by the public, owing to the breakdown of credit and confidence;—that the restrictive policy of the Bank of England was the chief cause of this collapse of credit, aggravating a season of commercial difficulty into one of most destructive panic;—and finally that, immediately on the reversal of that policy, the panic and hoarding were at an end, and confidence returned.

CRISIS OF 1857.

The crisis of 1847 was the most severe which had occurred; but it was surpassed in disaster by that which followed ten years afterwards. In 1857 a wave from the American crisis crossed the Atlantic, and produced an equal crisis in our own islands. Towards the middle of October, the news from the United States assumed so sinister an aspect as to forebode some great monetary catastrophe; and, ere the month ended, came the announcement of a universal suspension of cash-payments throughout the Union. This naturally put a severe strain upon the British firms engaged in the American trade, and upon the banks connected with them. The position of these houses was simply this, that they had to lie

* Hansard, Third Series, vol. xcv. p. 383.

out of all the money due to them by American firms, and to lose a part of it. The actual loss so incurred was the least part of the embarrassment; for although the American firms, in consequence of the breakdown of credit, had suspended, the greater part of them were perfectly solvent, and able to resume as soon as the effects of the panic were over. The embarrassment of our trade, therefore, was essentially of a temporary character; and the true way to have tided over the difficulty would have been by supporting to the uttermost all the *sound* firms imperilled, until the monetary equilibrium should be restored in America, and the usual remittances reach this country. This course was adopted by the Bank of England *after* the Bank Act was suspended, but as long as the Act remained in force such a course was impracticable.

No crisis was ever so unexpected; none ever culminated so rapidly, or proved so destructive. Credit was shaken, and a run commenced upon several banks which were known or supposed to be connected with the suspended firms. The Liverpool Borough Bank, closely connected with the American trade, stopped payment. Dennistoun & Co., likewise closely connected with American trade, had also to suspend, with liabilities to the amount of £2,143,701; and after reeling for some time under the run made upon it, the Western Bank of Scotland likewise closed its doors. Great exertions were made in Glasgow by the authorities and leading merchants to arrest the panic; the other Scotch banks, alarmed at the aspect of affairs, and urged thereto by the community, at length came forward to check the distrust, and gave their united and most energetic support to some of their number which were run upon. Thursday the 12th was the last day of the panic in Scotland.

Meanwhile the crisis had spread to London. The Bank had raised its rate rapidly from 5 to 10 per cent; and as all the discount-houses in London ceased to make advances, the accommodation given (or which under the Act could be given) by the Bank was totally inadequate. The more tight became the money-market, the faster were gold and notes withdrawn from the Bank. Every bank or firm sold its securities, and kept beside it the gold or notes thus obtained. In order to meet the run upon them, the Scotch banks had ordered about £1,000,000 sterling in sovereigns from London,—which they obtained by selling a portion of their Government stock (which, being readily convertible, they always hold in reserve for such emergencies), and thereafter getting the notes received in payment cashed at the Bank of England. The English and Irish banks took similar precautions; and altogether, in consequence of the panic, the banks found it necessary to keep by them about three millions more than their ordinary amount of specie. On Wednesday the 11th the great discount-house of Sanderson & Co. was forced to suspend, with liabilities to the amount of £5,298,997 sterling. The great American firm of Peabody & Co. also was known to be *in extremis*—it was perfectly solvent, but, like other firms, it had for the time to lie out of its money, and thus was unable to meet its engagements. It was of the utmost importance to support this firm, as it was known that its fall would bring down many others, and establish a general panic in London. The firm required assistance to the extent of £800,000 sterling; and the Bank, as fettered by the Act, had not this sum to advance. But no sooner was the Act suspended (on the afternoon of the 12th) than the required sum was advanced to Peabody & Co.; and the Bank in like manner extended its aid to many other firms, and to some of the English banks. In London, Liverpool, Manchester, Birmingham, indeed all over the country—as every one will remember, and as is proved by the trade-reports now lying before us—the beneficial effect produced by the suspension of the Act, and the resolution of the Bank to extend its issues, was instantaneous.* But so tremendous had been the calamity, that Trade remained nervous and palpitating for several days; and four days after the suspension of the Act, the *Times* remarked, "The liability to an extension of panic has still been such, that the principal banking institutions would have incurred a grave responsibility if they had suffered any mischief to take

* See Note at end of Chapter.

place which was fairly preventible:" that is to say, if they had not freely made advances to all sound firms which needed assistance.

SUSPENSION OF SOLVENT FIRMS.

The number of solvent, indeed very wealthy, firms which had to suspend during this crisis was remarkably great; and the fact throws an important light upon the character of such crises, and upon the best means of averting them. The suspension of Dennistoun & Co., for example, which was one of the first houses that gave way, was so entirely artificial that, after providing for every shilling of their liabilities, "the accountant on the estate declared them possessed of a surplus of nearly three-quarters of a million." The suspension of Naylor, Vickers, & Co. was of a similar character,—the firm having assets to discharge all their debts, with a balance in their favour of £250,000. Messrs Sanderson & Co., with liabilities to the enormous amount of £5,298,997, paid in full, and resumed business; and a large portion of the other suspended firms were proved to be in like manner perfectly solvent.* If these firms

* For example, the accounts of Messrs Arthur & Co., of Glasgow, showed a *bona fide* surplus of £90,800. Messrs Sewell & Neck, engaged in the Norway trade, with liabilities to the amount of half a million, exhibited a surplus of £57,581, after paying their creditors 20s. in the pound, with 5 per cent interest. Messrs Pelly & Co., with liabilities to the amount of £36,316, showed a surplus of £49,425—"a result," justly observed the *Economist*, "which excites surprise that the house should have been allowed to succumb." In like manner, the assets of Mr

could have been assisted, as Peabody & Co. were after the suspension of the Bank Act, it is obvious that the crisis would have been greatly mitigated, and the run

Johnstone of Glasgow were proved by the accountant to be nearly double his liabilities (the assets being £21,580, and the liabilities £11,440), "after deducting all ascertained and probable losses." C. Waud & Co., with liabilities to the amount of £60,000, showed a surplus of £20,000. Rew, Prescott, & Co., with liabilities to the amount of £150,000, paid 20s. in the pound, with a surplus of £8000. T. & H. Elmenhorst paid 20s. in the pound, with a surplus of £3114. Mr Peter Brown, whose suspension was caused by the pressure of a single creditor, had a surplus of £7719. Heine, Simon, & Co., whose liabilities amounted to £700,000, after paying 20s. in the pound, with interest, had a surplus of £53,000. Crossley & Leeminge of Halifax, Craven & Harrop of Bradford, Woodhall & Smith of Dudley, T. Callender & Co., and others, paid 20s. in the pound and 5 per cent interest. Messrs Fernie Brothers & Co., also, whose suspension helped to bring down the Liverpool Borough Bank, were perfectly solvent, and have since paid all their liabilities, together with 5 per cent interest, amounting in all to £420,517.

This list of solvent or wealthy firms, who figured in the bankruptcies of 1857, could be greatly extended. But even among those who had to compound with their creditors, there were very many cases in which the apparent insolvency was produced purely by the stoppage and bankruptcy expenses. In Scotland, the expenses of winding up an estate under sequestration are about 18 per cent—in England, at least 45 per cent; and as the trade, and consequently the bankruptcies, in England are very much greater than in Scotland, 35 per cent is a low estimate of the average cost of each bankruptcy in the United Kingdom. In this way, a firm whose liabilities and assets balance one another—in other words, which is solvent—may, in a crisis like that of 1857, be not only forced to suspend, but have more than one-third of its assets swallowed up in bankruptcy expenses, and figure in the newspapers as paying only 12s. in the pound. Indeed, the magnitude of bankruptcy expenses is such, that the leading firms in the City seek to avoid driving their debtors into bankruptcy, and almost all the larger businesses are now wound up "under inspection," which is a less costly process.

upon the banks proportionately lessened, if not altogether prevented. The stoppage of any large firm not only gives a great shock to credit of itself, but a similar stoppage is produced of dozens of small firms in connection with the large one: and thus panic spreads over the country. Commerce cannot go on without credit,—still less can banking. Commerce, indeed, is the first to suffer in times of crisis; but no sooner do the merchants begin to reel, than the pressure is communicated to the banks. Every great failure, by the distrust and apprehension which it produces, is equivalent to a heavy draft upon the banks. The credit of commerce and of banking cannot be dissociated; and any policy on the part of the banks which seeks to strengthen themselves by sacrificing the merchants, is alike mistaken and injurious.

We have narrated the measures by which all the great commercial crises have been stayed during the last seventy years. It is curious to note some of the defensive manœuvres by which banks have occasionally met a run upon them. The rush for money at such times is frequently so great that ordinary means are of no avail to meet it. Even if gold were there in plenty, but uncoined, its presence would not ward off disaster.* In 1826, although "the Mint was

* The Mint, despite its admirable machinery, which is unique in the world, cannot coin above fifty thousand sovereigns in a day.

kept working night and day," money could not be coined with sufficient rapidity; and as notes were taken as readily as gold, a chest of old one-pound notes was made use of in the emergency. To gain time at such junctures is everything. During the run upon it in 1720, the Bank of England employed a number of clerks to tell out, coin by coin, the money which was demanded, as well as that which was brought in; so far as possible also, the Bank made payments in light shillings and sixpences, which took a great deal of time, and must have considerably disgusted the recipients; and finally, it paid large sums, all deliberately counted, to friends of its own, who went out with the bags of money at one door, and delivered them to persons placed at another, who thereupon were let in (in preference to the real customers, who thronged the doors) to pay the same money to the tellers, who once more took ample time to count it over. During the run upon the Bank in 1745—a purely political crisis, caused by the advance of the Pretender and his Highlanders into the heart of England—the expedient of paying in sixpences was again resorted to by the Bank, as successfully as before.

Such expedients are now out of date, they savour

And as the workmen employed in the Mint are a select body, whose numbers cannot suddenly be increased, the system of working both night and day cannot be much resorted to.

so much of dodges. But we can give an example in recent times of how banks may most legitimately meet the effects of a run. In 1857, after the fall of the Western Bank, the other banks which have their central establishments in Edinburgh, seeing that the panic was assuming a most destructive intensity, resolved to co-operate strenuously in the support of each other. Accordingly, as fast as gold was withdrawn from the Union Bank and deposited with some of the other establishments, it was immediately returned to the menaced bank. And thus, on that critical 12th of November, there was a double current of gold passing up and down Bank Street—anxious depositors carrying off their heavy bags in cabs, while steady bank-clerks with equal promptitude carried back the bags to the Union Company. There was a dash of the humorous in the operation, but no measure could have been more beneficial alike to the banks and to the public. The proceeding, we need hardly remark, was perfectly legitimate. The banks to which the customers of the Union Bank transferred their accounts, became responsible for the sums thus deposited with them. That was a terminated transaction. The lending of the gold by these banks to their menaced comrade was a separate affair—amply justified alike by the solvency of the establishment to which the loan was made, and by the advantage which

HOW BANKS SHOULD ACT.

resulted from it to all the banks, as well as to the community at large. Such united action on the part of the Scotch banks, if timeously commenced, is adequate to stop the heaviest run for gold which any panic can occasion. To withdraw money in gold is a cumbrous and anxious process. One would require a cab to carry away even £1000 in sovereigns. Moreover, no one is willing to run the risks attendant upon keeping a large sum of gold in his house or office. And hence, as happened in Scotland in 1857, money which is withdrawn from a bank, not for business purposes, but simply in consequence of distrust, is immediately deposited with another bank. Indeed it is a curious fact that the greatest transfer of accounts from the Union Bank in 1857 was made to the Bank of Scotland, which is only distant some two hundred yards: the panic-stricken bearers of gold evidently being anxious to be rid of their precious burden as soon as possible, and depositing it accordingly with the nearest of the other banks.*

* The Western Bank—which failed totally, although all its liabilities were discharged in full—had from the very outset of its career ignored the principles of Scotch banking. It advanced money upon securities which were either hazardous or not readily convertible—in this way obtaining higher rates than the other Scotch banks did; and latterly its advances of this kind became so large that it may almost be said to have engaged in trade in the fashion of a *Credit Mobilier*. It was in difficulties in 1847, but was then supported by the other banks on the condition that it should bring its management into accordance with the ordinary practice of banking,—a pledge which it never fulfilled. When its

This procedure on the part of the Scotch banks was a true economy of capital, at a time when such economy was peculiarly called for. Credit, as we have shown, is the only possible means of economising capital; and this operation of the Scotch banks was just an extension of credit, with a view to support a great establishment which was known to be perfectly solvent and prudently conducted. Such extension of credit to solvent firms is the true means of preventing or arresting a commercial crisis; and it is especially applicable to maintain the credit of the banks. It is a defect of the English system of banks (if that can be called a system which is totally unsystematic), that it

difficulties were renewed in 1857, it again solicited support from the Chartered banks, and obtained it to the extent of £500,000. But the banks, very properly, would not support it further. It was a mistake, however, on the part of the Chartered banks—a mistake which Mr Laurence Robertson, in his evidence before the Parliamentary Committee, seeks to palliate by alleging that "they were not precisely informed" of the position of the suspended banks—that they did not immediately offer to take the *notes* of the Western and City of Glasgow banks (the latter being a perfectly solvent establishment which for the moment only had to shut its doors); for they knew that the capital of the shareholders in these banks, every shilling of which was liable, was far more than sufficient to meet any uncovered liabilities. It was this temporary refusal on the part of the Chartered banks to take these notes, that converted the crisis into a panic: especially as it occurred at a season of the year when, according to the evidence of Sir George Clerk, the issues of the Scotch banks are for a day or two, owing to the requirements of the public, nearly 50 per cent above their usual amount. "After further consideration," said Mr L. Robertson, "the other banks resolved to take all the notes as they came forward; and when that was done, the thing [panic] subsided."

does not offer the facilities for co-operation and mutual support which are possessed by the Scotch banks. And hence, with all their immense resources, their machinery of resistance to a panic is clumsy and unreliable, compared with that of their northern rivals. In course of time, doubtless, order and system will arise out of the present chaos of English banking. The new joint-stock companies, with their headquarters in London, are gradually establishing branches in the provinces; and it is to be hoped that, by the offer of suitable terms, many of the private banks throughout the country will consent to change their character, and become branches of the great banks in the metropolis.

SYSTEM AND CO-OPERATION.

Not until this revolution is accomplished can an economy of capital be efficiently established among the English banks. All banking, undoubtedly, effects an economy of capital on the part of the public: what is now urgently called for is, that there should be a corresponding economy of capital effected among the banks themselves. When great banks are established in London, with branches throughout the country, all acting harmoniously together, the fabric of public credit will be rendered as nearly proof against the shocks of panic as need be desired. The great burden of sustaining credit, which, in times of panic, is at present thrown entirely upon the Bank of England, will then rest upon a wider basis; and a cordial co-operation among the banks will suffice to reduce to manageable proportions crises such as at present overwhelm the whole country with disaster. It is not more gold that is needed to fortify our banking system,—it is more System and Co-operation.

But if we do not need more gold, at least let us have the use of what we possess. A large stock of the precious metal at present lies useless in this country, withdrawn from the purposes of banking and from the support of trade. When we come to take a look at the Bank of England, we shall see both where this portion of our gold is, and why it is there.

NOTE.—Before concluding this chapter, it may be well to show, by extracts from the newspapers of the time, how the news of the suspension of the Bank Act, in November 1857, was received by the community—especially in the great centres of wealth and industry, *e.g.*, London, Liverpool, Manchester, Birmingham, Leeds, and Bristol:—

LONDON.—"The notification that the Directors had been empowered by Government to disregard the restrictions imposed on the issue of notes by the Act of 1844, immediately produced a powerful effect. The great discount-houses and other firms were enabled to procure a large supply of money from the Bank, and at once began to grant liberal accommodation to their customers, at some advance upon the Bank rate. The mercantile public, who had rushed to the Bank to procure large supplies of money, of which they had no actual need, have now become reassured, and hopes are entertained that the money market will assume a quieter appearance. On Friday the feeling in all commercial circles was decidedly better."—*Economist.*

"An immediate effect was visible—the Funds advanced, and the general remark was that the 'worst had passed.' So far as can be ascertained at present, the course adopted by the Government and the Bank has germinated a feeling of confidence, which, if developed, must soon insure a return of ease and prosperity. Increased confidence is apparent in most departments of business, and the letters received from the country show that the symptoms which have followed the temporary suspension of the Bank Act are as encouraging as could be desired."—*Globe.*

"The letters received on Friday from the country indicate an extent of monetary disturbance and commercial excitement almost if not altogether unparalleled, and it is fearful to contemplate the ruin which would have resulted from the postponement of the expected relief for even one or two days. On Friday money circulated much more freely in the discount market, and, in consequence, there was witnessed the expected and satisfactory circumstance of decided diminution in the demand at the Bank of England."—*London Express.*

LIVERPOOL.—"To such a dead-lock had business matters arrived on Thursday, that the Committee of the General Brokers' Association gave notice that they would be obliged to discontinue for the present the issue of their daily market receipts. The Council of the Chamber of Commerce met on Thursday, to take into consideration the present monetary crisis, and it was agreed that a deputation, consisting of the Mayor, Mr C. Bushell (President of the Chamber), and several other gentlemen, should go up and have an interview with Government on the present state of the monetary affairs of the country. Shortly before four o'clock in the afternoon, however, a rumour became current on 'Change, and spread like wildfire in every direction, that the Bank of England had been authorised by Government to suspend its Act. In place of features of the most gloomy despondency and forebodings, all is now exhilaration, and the panic is generally believed to be at an end."—*Times.*

MANCHESTER.—"The virtual suspension of the Bank Charter Act has calmed public feeling on commercial matters considerably, and we have had a more cheerful and hopeful feeling in the market."—*Times.*

BIRMINGHAM.—"A meeting of the merchants of Birmingham, for the purpose of supporting the views of the Glasgow merchants, was contemplated, but we presume that this communication from Government to the Bank Directors will render it unnecessary. There can be no doubt that the proposed measure will greatly relieve the manufacturing interests, and that in this respect the local trades of Birmingham will largely participate." —*Birmingham Mercury.*

BRISTOL.—"The intelligence that Government had authorised the Bank of England to extend its issue of notes upon securities was communicated on Thursday afternoon. The gloom which had been caused among commercial classes by the disastrous advices of the morning was at once dispelled, and the general feeling was that the right step had been taken at the right time for preventing the ruinous consequences of a monetary panic. The change in the aspect of commercial matters here within the last twenty-four hours is very gratifying."—*Times.*

LEEDS.—"The measure of relief afforded by the Government is approved both by the local press and the commercial community generally; and though the business transacted in the market this morning has shown no improvement, there has been greater firmness and a more hopeful feeling expressed."—*Times.*

THE CITY OF GOLD

London, as every one knows, contains a city within a city; and within that inner city there is yet another, the very heart of the metropolis. It is a small place. In a couple of minutes you may walk across it from side to side, from end to end. Yet it is the centre and citadel of our greatness—the heart whose pulsations are felt to the farthest extremities of the empire. There is to be found concentrated the spare capital of the nation; and from thence it flows forth, as from a fountainhead, in irrigating streams, to extend industry and increase employment and produce everywhere. There, our traders and producers obtain the loans and advances by means of which they carry on their immense business. There, lie concentrated the sinews of material strength alike in peace and in war. The occupants of the precinct have dealings with all the world; and from thence proceeds the power which helps on the civilisation of the globe. The railways which accompany the ceaseless advance of the White race into the prairies of the Far West of America—the companies which explore and develop the resources of California and Australia—the iron roads and irrigating canals which are maturing the prosperity of India—the enterprise which covers with tea-plantations the valleys and slopes of the Himalayas, and which carries our countrymen into new regions everywhere—are created or sustained by the ongoings in this little spot in London. The wastes of Hudson's Bay—trading companies for the Nile—the cotton-planting which is invading Africa—ocean-lines of steam-ships, submarine telegraphs connecting dissevered continents, water-works for Berlin, gas for Bombay — these and a hundred other matters and projects engage the thoughts and employ the capital which is at the command of this busy hive of operators. Almost every country is included in their operations, and almost every State is in debt to them. From gigantic Russia to petty Ecuador and Venezuela, they hold the bonds of every Government—Persia, China, and Japan alone being excepted.

Prosaic as the operations of the precinct are in detail, taken in the mass they constitute a grand work, and may be followed as a noble as well as an honourable profession. Daily and hourly it is the business of the occupants to scan in detail the condition of the world. They weigh the influence of the seasons, they investigate the produce of all manner of harvests—they know the condition of every mine, the prospects of every railway, the dividends of every company. They are ever feeling the pulse of Trade, and watching the course of Politics. They ponder the chances for the maintenance of peace or for the outburst of war; and when war is on foot, they follow the fluctuations of the contest with as keen an interest as either soldier or statesman. Everything concerns them that affects the condition of countries or the solvency of Governments. The very spirit and temper of nations, rebellious or loyal, warlike or industrious, is canvassed in that busy mart. It is no exaggeration to say that the progress of mankind is mirrored in the operations of this monetary metropolis. It is a city of money-dealers—a sanctuary of Plutus; a place where men think only of profits, and yet accomplish more good than all our philanthropists. Blot out that inner heart of London—paralyse the operations of that busy hive—and the whole world would feel the shock and suffer from the calamity.

London is best seen from the top of an omnibus. Hail one of those vehicles as they roll in ceaseless stream along the Strand and Fleet Street,—yield to the solicitations of the conductor who with uplifted finger calls out "Bank! Bank!"—and, mounted on the top, proceed eastwards to view the metropolis of

Gold. Passing under the shadow of St Paul's, which towers above you like a splendid mountain of stone, you enter Cheapside, and with slow and halting course your vehicle wends its way through the currents of human life seething and battling in the too narrow street. The din is so great that even the famed Bow Bells, as they ring out from the elegant spire overhead, hardly make themselves heard. At length you reach the Mansion House, the civic palace of London, whose festivities are known unto all men, and especially to aldermen,—and your omnibus stops on the very threshold of the City of Gold.

Magnificent buildings rising aloft on all sides show that you have reached a peculiar precinct. A wide open space is before you, which seems, as you look down from your elevated seat, as if paved with the tops of omnibuses, cabs, and vehicles of all kinds, making their way through a black mass of busy humanity. No longer pent up in the defile of Cheapside, the current of busy life here branches out into many channels. To your right it pours down Lombard Street, and towards London Bridge,—the entrance to which you see marked by the tall column of the Monument, rising against the blue sky of this sunny day in June. To the left, the current spreads through Princes Street—to or from Lothbury and Moorgate Street, which lie out of sight, hidden by the solid quadrangular mass of the Bank. In front, the busy throng is pouring along the wide channels of Cornhill and Threadneedle Street, leading eastward from where you stand; and in an island between these two channels rises aloft, like a rocky promontory, the pillared front of the Royal Exchange. Stretching out in front of the Exchange there projects, almost to where you are, a triangular expanse of pavement—like a spit of sand—over which the wavelets of human life, the spray of the deep currents which roll around, are ceaselessly washing and intercrossing. Watching a favourable moment, dart through the perilous stream of vehicles and foot-passengers which separates you from that haven of rest, and take your stand (getting the mud brushed from your boots the while by one of the red-coated members of the Shoe Brigade) beside the equestrian statue of the Great Duke. As you look up at the bronze figure of the old warrior, you remember his saying, that "High interest means bad security." You think, too, of the words once placarded all round where you stand, "To stop the Duke, run for Gold!" And you begin to think that, after all, the site of his statue is not so inappropriate as at first you felt it to be.

But *circumspice!* The Royal Exchange, with its high pillared portico, surmounted by an entablature in which symbolic figures are crowded together as densely as are the living crowds below—with its wide archways of entrance, and large inner court open to the sky—looks gay, affable, and accessible,—a place of easy and lively resort, savouring (as the Greek style of architecture usually does, whether in palace or in temple) of a sunny everyday world. As you look across Threadneedle Street, the low, heavy quadrangular structure of the Bank creates a very different impression. It has an imposing look; and the dead wall all round, scantily relieved by short pillars let into the front, almost windowless and doorless, bespeak a sombre, jealously-guarded sanctuary. It is the treasure-house of Plutus, the sovereign and deity of the precinct. You feel an awe and sombreness in the façade, very accordant with all our notions of the Old Lady of Threadneedle Street. While thinking of its wealth and power, you think also of dishonoured bills, and of the gloomy courts in Basinghall Street, —even as the Palace of the Doge reminds one of the Bridge of Sighs and the prisons beyond.

These two buildings, which far surpass in size any of the surrounding edifices, fitly represent respectively the two powers, or agencies, whose conjoint action constitutes the life of this busy little world. The Bank represents money—the Exchange represents trade. Generally they act in harmony—sometimes, however, in rivalry; but at all times they deeply affect one another. A panic on 'Change makes a crisis at the Bank—a crisis at the Bank makes a panic on 'Change. They are like brother and sister. But Money is the stronger; it is the male principle—sombre and powerful. Trade is the female—gay, lively, and various in its forms; but dependent for its fertility upon money, and at times subjected by it to a cruel bondage. You will not be long in the neighbourhood before you find what vast issues are dependent upon the presence of Gold in that solid building in Threadneedle Street.

The mightinesss of these two powers, which together hold sway in this little precinct, is evidenced to the eye by the stateliness of the capital which they have here built for themselves. All great phases of national life find expression in architecture. The present is peculiarly an age of money and of monetary trade; and Banks and financial companies adorn this sanctuary of money-dealers with conspicuous edifices. The place looks like an Acropolis—a civic citadel—a peculiar precinct, where palatial edifices, clustering together, rise in close contact, and in marked contrast with the ordinary buildings of the city. Brick and dinginess give place to Portland-stone, iron-palisading, and highly-burnished door-panels. Banks, credit-companies, discount-houses, insurance-offices, are yearly raising for themselves fine premises; and the area of the golden metropolis is gradually extending itself at the expense of the meaner districts which surround it. Stand at the north-east corner of the Royal Exchange, and you are in the centre of the precinct. From that point a radius of three hundred yards will include the whole locality. Princes Street and Lombard Street bound it on the west and south; Lothbury and Throgmorton Street on the north; while to the east, beyond Birchin Lane and Finch Lane, it gradually merges in the region of the produce-markets and shipping-offices. Such are the narrow limits of this City of Gold,—a precinct which rises like an oasis of commercial palaces in the heart of London, and in which is concentrated an amount of wealth and power unrivalled elsewhere in the world.

CITY MEN.

The Royal Exchange, with its wide expanse of pavement alike in front and in rear, forms an islet amidst the rushing thoroughfares around. On these paved open spaces groups may be seen standing engaged in absorbing conversation. But all around nothing is to be seen but motion and bustle. The streets are thronged with hurrying vehicles; the foot-pavement with bustling but steady-going passengers; the alleys, like Birchin Lane and Finch Lane, which connect the leading thoroughfares, are equally thronged; and hurrying steps are ever racing through those covered passages, lined with offices on either side, which form a peculiar feature in this part of London, and before whose entrances the stranger naturally halts, fearing to trespass on what seems, and indeed is, private ground. Young men and old men alike are seen hurrying to and fro, and all appear absorbed in their work. You may easily tell the office-clerks, racing on their errands to learn the latest price of some particular stock, from the less mobile but more absorbed seniors of this busy world. Engrossed as all are, you nevertheless see (in ordinary times at least) that theirs is not a sad work. The sight, in truth, is rather disappointing to a stranger who has heard of the cares of wealth and the deceitfulness of riches. As he looks upon the men who go past him, the sight does not realise the conception of "City" life which he has formed from books or from his own imaginings. He looks in vain for the haggard look and care-worn features which he has learnt to associate with City men, and especially with the dealers in money. Overburdened, no doubt, some of these men are occasionally—and in what trade or profession is it otherwise?—but, on the whole, they wear a more lively and cheerful look than any other set of business-men we have seen. They are intent on their work; they have no time to stand and parley with you; but they go about their business with liveliness and zest. You never hear the slow monotones of depression: their voices are quick and lively, and a laugh and a bit of badinage are seldom quite absent as they fly about in search of information or in execution of commissions. They dress well, in the substantial style—and a gold chain across the waistcoat, or a flower in the button-hole, are their favourite and not very conspicuous modes of personal decoration. Sometimes, indeed, you will see the gay-coloured neck-scarf, buttoned surtout, white waistcoat, and light gloves, familiar to you in Pall-Mall and Piccadilly; for even the West-end swell nowadays ventures into the vortex of financial speculation; but he looks a butterfly among the busy throng, and his air (as doubtless he wishes it to be) is quite different from that of the habitués of the precinct.

Nothing more conduces to preserve youthfulness than a considerable amount of mental activity. The alertness and vivacity of the mind transfer themselves to the personal appearance. And, despite all the worry and anxieties which these money-dealers and speculators are supposed to, and sometimes do, undergo, they wear better, and keep their youth longer, than the farmers and provincial classes generally. There is no sauntering here; and men of threescore and upwards step out as lightly as men of half their age in provincial places. In truth, it is the elderly gentlemen who show to most advantage in this monetary metropolis; and ever and anon you meet with the fresh clear complexion, pure white whiskers, and brisk look and movement, which characterise the best specimens of our elderly English gentlemen. It seems a healthy as well as exciting pursuit which men ply in this precinct of Mammon. Even the speculators *par excellence*—men who are rich to-day and poor to-morrow—as a class, live for the bright side of the picture, and look as if they did so.

It is curious to note how the tide of business and population ebbs and flows in this peculiar precinct. THE CITY AT NIGHT. The busiest and most crowded place in the world for half-a-dozen hours of the day, it thereafter becomes almost a solitude. Except in Cornhill, where shops have not yet been wholly supplanted by offices, the precinct after sunset relapses into darkness. At nine in the morning, the omnibuses begin to deposit load after load of passengers at the corner of Cheapside, opposite the Mansion House; while Hansom cabs and private broughams convey to business the grandees of the place. And during the next six or seven hours vehicles of all descriptions ply to and fro the precinct. But between five and six o'clock the daily exodus begins. Bankers, brokers, speculators, clerks, and directors alike, all rush off homeward, out of town it may be, or to distant suburbs; and the Golden City becomes wholly silent, dark, and solitary. In the moonlight, this solitude of palatial edifices looks even more grand and imposing than by day; but the currents of busy life no longer flow between the towering piles, and the streets seem like river-beds which have suddenly been left dry. On Sundays, the solitude and apparent desolation are still more conspicuous. Hardly any one lives in the precinct save the porters left in charge of the offices. The churches, accordingly, are almost empty. It is only when some highly-gifted preacher is appointed to the locality that the pews become filled—a rare occurrence—by persons drawn from other parts of London. Some of us can recollect the time when Dr Croly, in his heyday, drew crowds to the fine church of St Stephen's, Walbrook, at the back of the Mansion House, and when his noble oratory and high intellect converted the solitude of empty pews into a crowded and attentive audience. There, for years, he lifted up his voice like one preaching in a wilderness. The emptiness of the churches in the precinct, however, is simply the result of there being no parishioners of the class who ordinarily attend churches.

ITS EDIFICES.

Banks form the most conspicuous architectural feature of the precinct. And naturally so, for without them trade and financial operations could not acquire the remarkable development which is here to be witnessed. They are the reservoirs of the place, into which flows the spare money of the nation, and out of which flow the monetary streams which set agoing all the other operations of the place. Besides the Bank, which in external appearance, as well as in real power, throws into the shade all its compeers, we see conspicuous among the others the large building of the London and Westminster Bank, facing on the other side of Lothbury its old opponent the Bank of England,—the huge but unattractive fabrics of the Union and London Joint-Stock Banks in Princes Street,—the London and County Bank in Lombard Street,—and the handsome pile of the Oriental Bank. Next in importance, as architectural features of the place, are the Insurance Offices,—and chief among these, the Sun, the Imperial, and North British, all in good sites in Threadneedle Street. In the third rank—and soon likely to take a higher place—are the offices of the Discount-houses and new Credit companies: the massive and costly edifice of the National Discount Company in Cornhill, occupying the first place in point of architecture; while in Lombard Street, the great discount-house of Overend, Gurney, & Co. (familiarly called "the house at the corner") and Hanbury's bank, face each other at the foot of Finch Lane; and in Lothbury are the offices of the two giant credit-companies, the "General" and the "International Land Credit."

Every year some of the old establishments, banks or others, are building for themselves finer edifices. They feel a necessity not only to be prosperous, but to advertise their prosperity by architectural display. There is a rage for Portland stone and polished granite pillars; and the movement in favour of external display is proceeding to an extent which has excited considerable criticism and distrust among the older and more cautious grandees of the locality. Perhaps the "old fogies" are right, if we judge from a London point of view,—for

London architecture (we except the fine old churches) is a very poor affair compared with the wealth of the place. At the same time it is only truth to say, that none of the London banks, save the Bank of England, can compete in architectural beauty, whether internal or external, with the half-dozen leading banks in Edinburgh. The Modern Athens is a dream of beauty in stone: externally, at all events, it is a city of Fine Art,—a place where the marvellous picturesqueness of Nature has made the inhabitants intolerant of commonplace architecture in their street and public buildings.

The classification which we have made of the edifices of this monetary metropolis is likewise applicable to the population—to the busy crowds whom we see rushing to and fro—and to the pursuits which they follow. Let us see what is the style of business which each of these classes carries on. We shall find that they are all closely connected—integral parts of one great system of monetary trade,—and that the line of demarcation between some of them is not drawn with sufficient sharpness to be readily perceptible to the uninitiated.

Let us describe first, generically, the leading operations of the Banks. The fundamental part of their business is to receive deposits of money. They take money into safe keeping, and they manage it in such a way as to meet the require-

THE BANKS.

ments of the depositors. They give the depositors cheque-books, blank forms of drafts upon the bank; and whenever one of those cheques is presented, either by the depositor or by any one to whom he has made it payable, the bank hands the money across the counter, in notes or in gold as may be demanded. In some cases the banks give interest on the sums deposited, in others they do not: and the Bank of England does not pay interest in any case.* The next part of the business of banks is to recompense themselves for this management of their customers' money, by employing at usury the balance of the deposits which is not likely to be called for by the depositors. This balance amounts in ordinary circumstances to more than nine-tenths of the whole money deposited with the bank. When trade is stagnant, this balance is at its highest amount; when trade is brisk, or when credit is shaken, it is at its lowest. A bank, in short, must mark well the signs of the times in order to know the exact amount of the deposits which may be safely lent out. If too much be lent out, the bank is embarrassed in meeting the demands of the depositors; if too little be lent out, the bank loses its profit on the sum thus needlessly kept on hand. Having determined what portion of the deposits is not likely to be called for, the bank invests or lends out at interest this sum in various ways. First of all, it

* For other details connected with banking, see *supra*, pp. 66-88.

invests a portion in the purchase of Consols—a species of security which is of all others the most steady in value, and the most readily negotiable; in other words, which can be most readily sold and reconverted into money. Next, the bank makes advances to its customers. Any one who has an account with a bank may, in ordinary times, by tendering Government or other good stock, obtain a temporary loan on that security to the amount of three-fourths of its current value. But the most extensive kind of advances made by the banks is in the discount of commercial bills. A customer of the bank has a bill, or bills, falling due say three months hence; but by taking them to the bank he deals with, he can get cash for the full amount of these bills *at once*, minus three months' interest on that amount. In extraordinary cases, the banks—and especially the Bank of England, the great fountainhead of credit—will make advances to some large firm or company whose position is solvent, but which is in temporary embarrassment. In this case, an agent of the bank examines the books of the firm, sees what are its assets, and decides what amount may safely be lent to it. "The whole principle of banking," said Lord Overstone in 1840, "is to transfer capital from the inactive accumulator to the active and energetic person who wants capital,"—even though these persons "in some cases have no security to give, except that best form of security, their character, their energy, and their prudence." The advances made on these various forms of security—viz., stocks, commercial bills, or in aid of wealthy but temporarily embarrassed firms—are for considerable periods; say, on the average, three months. But there is a portion of the banks' deposits which it would not be prudent to lend for such periods, yet which may be safely lent for a week or a day. The great point in banking is to see that every pound which is not needed by the depositors is profitably employed. Each day there is a surplus available for short investments. What is done with it?

It is handed over to the bank-brokers, who may be called money-brokers pure and simple. This is another class of business. These men are the intermediaries between the banks and the various other institutions, companies, or individuals who flourish in this monetary precinct. It is the duty of these bank-brokers—whose position is most onerous, and who are few in number—to employ the sums at their disposal in loans at call, or for a week, or a single day. Their vigilance must be unceasing. They have to keep their eye on the expiry of each of those brief loans, renew it, or find a new investment for it; and when a change in the rate of discount takes place, they are on the trot the whole day, altering their terms and making new bargains on the footing of the change. To lend money *for a single day,* when the rate of interest is at (say) four per cent per

MONEY-BROKERS.

annum, may seem to an outsider a very infinitesimal operation—one which would not repay the cost and trouble connected with it. But sometimes these bank-brokers have three or four millions sterling to dispose of: and the interest on that sum for a single day amounts to £330 or £400. By neglecting these daily loans—by letting the amount which can be safely employed in this manner (the surplus on the day's proceedings) lie inactive in their coffers, the London banks would lose £100,000 or £150,000 a-year! The bank-brokers of course get a commission on their work—a small percentage; and as one of these brokers has been known to have had £2,000,000 pass through his hands in a single day, their business is as lucrative as it is onerous. But to whom, to what parties, are these very short loans made? Who is it that is ready to take money on loan for a single day?

DISCOUNT-HOUSES.

To some extent these loans are made to all the other sections of the community in this monetary precinct. It is only to its own customers that a bank discounts bills, or makes advances on stock, &c.; but the daily surplus which is distributed by the bank-brokers is lent to any suitable parties, without distinction, who may desire to have some of it. Nearly all of it, however, is taken up by the Stock Exchange and the Discount-houses—the latter of which establishments rank next in importance to the banks in this city of money-dealers. The discount-houses do not receive money in deposit as the banks do; they do not issue cheques, or undertake the management of money for customers. They receive money, not in deposit, but on loan. They take short loans, for a week or a fortnight, or "at call,"—paying interest, of course, on all sums thus received. In this way the discount-houses offer a good means of investment for sums which could not otherwise be employed to equal advantage—namely, for sums which the owner has on hand merely for a few days. For example, a man who has money invested in some particular kind of stock or shares, and who thinks it advisable to sell out at once, with the view of re-investing his money in some other form, may have that money on hand for a week or two, waiting for a favourable opportunity of re-investing it. Instead of keeping it on hand, he lends it to a discount-house, and receives a high rate of interest on it, till he is ready to use it again. The daily surplus of the banks, as we have said, is also employed to a great extent in this way.

The money thus obtained on loan, as well as the private capital of the discount-houses, is employed by these firms in discounting commercial bills. And as they do not require to keep money on hand, like the banks, to meet the wants of depositors—as all their money, in short, is fully employed at interest—the discount-houses can afford to discount bills at a rate slightly lower than that of the Bank. The cashing of bills is their special and only business, and they get a very large share of it. The main principle which they have to observe is this: They know the amount of their private capital, and the amount of money which they may reckon upon receiving on loan from the public, on the one hand, and, on the other, they know the average term of the bills which they discount (say three months); they then discount to the full amount of their resources, — taking care, thereafter, that the amount of bills which they discount shall be balanced by an equal amount of bills "running off," *i. e.*, falling due. If the state of the money market renders it advisable for them to increase their reserves, they have only to lessen the amount of the bills which they discount, and in a single week their cash on hand is increased, in consequence of the bills falling due to them being in excess of the amount which they are discounting.

To discount a bill is to purchase a debt falling due at a specified time. Ordinary commercial bills are as good as money: and the entire portion of what figures in the returns of the joint-stock banks as "deposits" is held by these banks in the form of commercial bills which they have discounted. The money deposited with a bank is employed in the purchase of these bills, and the rate of discount charged upon them is a chief source of bankers' profits. If a firm which has purchased a bill (by discounting it) is in need of ready cash, money can be obtained by re-discounting the bill—*i. e.*, selling it to a bank or other party which deals in that kind of business. And every time a bill is thus paid away, the more solid does its value become; because every party through whose hands it passes endorses it, and becomes security for its ultimate payment. In this way, bills to some extent become part of the currency, circulating from hand to hand in payments which would otherwise have to be made in cheques, notes, or gold.

As every discount-house keeps an account at a bank, it can (if in temporary need of money) take some of the bills which it has discounted, and get them re-discounted at the bank with which it deals. Some years ago, however, the Bank of England refused to treat the discount-houses on the same terms in this respect as its ordinary customers. They are rivals of the Bank in the discounting line, and manage to get the lion's share of the business; and the Bank, with considerable justice, said:—"We have to keep on hand reserves to meet all demands that can be made upon us, whereas you trade to the full extent of your resources: in this way you make larger profits in ordinary times than we can do; and it is rather too much, when you become embarrassed by so trading, to come upon us to help you." The discount-houses are the great rivals of the Bank; and whenever a monetary crisis takes place, a great deal of bitter feeling arises between them; and the Bank is seldom loth to see one of these rival establishments brought to the ground.

THE ROYAL EXCHANGE.

Let us now come to another important branch of business carried on in this precinct. Let us enter the Royal Exchange. For the greater part of every day a stranger will be at a loss to discover for what purpose so fine an edifice was erected. As he enters the central court, the place looks deserted—only a few loungers, looking neither very business-like nor respectable, sauntering or sitting beneath the verandah. One may guess that some of those people have met here by appointment, as a convenient rendezvous; and what the others are waiting for, it is not easy to see. On the afternoon of Tuesday and Friday, however, the scene is very different. All idlers are then excluded, but any one may enter who has business to transact. The Royal Exchange belongs to the City, as represented by the Gresham Committee, and the public has full right of entry on the simple condition that they come there on business and not as idlers. The business consists in the buying and selling of "bills of exchange," *i. e.*, orders for money payable in foreign countries,—bills on China, India, Egypt, Paris, Hamburg, New York—on all the chief seats of commerce. A merchant who has to pay a sum of £10,000 in Calcutta, instead of sending specie, goes on 'Change and buys bills to that amount, which he transmits at the mere expense of postage.

The price of these bills of exchange is regulated by two considerations. First, there is the length of time a bill has to run. If it is payable four months after date, it is of course less valuable than one at three months—the discount, or rate of interest, in each case having to be deducted. But the value of these bills is also affected, like everything else, by the amount of supply and demand. If the amount of bills upon Calcutta happens to be greater than the amount of money which requires to be sent thither, the bills may be purchased at a fraction below their normal value; but if the payments to be made in Calcutta exceed the amount of the bills, then a competition for the bills ensues, and their price is slightly enhanced. But the range of variation never exceeds the difference between the cost of postage on the one hand, and the expense and inconvenience of transmitting specie on the other. The normal price of a bill, as we have said, is simply the amount of the bill, *minus* the discount on the time it has to run. Accordingly, by means of these bills of exchange, the whole cost, risk, and inconvenience of collecting and transmitting specie from one country to another is saved. And this saving is really an immense one. If the payments of commerce had to be sent backward and forward from country to country, not all the specie in the world would suffice to carry on operations so vast. If the agency of bills were suspended for a few months even between England and

India, the drain of currency would speedily produce a deadlock in both countries. Such is the importance of the operations in the Royal Exchange; and there are no others, even in this Capitol of money and trade, which display in so remarkable a manner the immense extent of British commerce, as well as the skill and mutual good-faith with which its operations are carried on.*

THE STOCK EXCHANGE.

The operations on the Stock Exchange are of quite a different nature. The property there dealt in is stocks and shares of all kinds; Government securities, ranging in solidity from British consols, the steadiest of all, to Greek coupons and Spanish passives,—railway shares, mining shares, and shares and bonds of joint-stock companies of all kinds. In these the public invests its spare capital, and the transfer of these stocks from one hand to another, by buying and selling, is so great that the daily transactions frequently amount to several millions sterling. The commission upon these transactions—which varies from one-eighth of a per-cent on the sale or purchase of Consols, to one-fourth of a per-cent on the dealings in other and more variable kinds of stock—amounts to a large sum; and this sum constitutes the

* In the financial year 1862-3 the number of stamps used for bills of exchange was 5,501,498,—of which number 1,961,602 were for foreign bills. Of this number, 6740 of inland bills, and 4288 of foreign bills, were drawn for sums of upwards of £4000 each.

profits of the stock-brokers, who conduct these sales and purchases for the public. A stock-broker ought not to deal or speculate in stocks at all. He is simply the agent by which such sales and purchases are effected. And if he himself becomes a dealer (as not a few of the second and third rate brokers do), the persons who employ him have no security that their interests will be properly attended to. He may buy for himself the stock which they commission him to sell; and in such a case it is not to be expected that he will give for it the highest price that can be obtained. But the stock-brokers are not the only parties in the Stock Exchange. There are also the stock-jobbers—men who deal in stocks and shares, selling them at the highest price which they can get, and buying them at the lowest.

The entrance to the Stock Exchange—or Capel Court, as the large room is called where these operations are carried on—is through a pillared front, or portico, facing the east end of the Bank. But it has other entrances. We remember the first time we stumbled upon this sanctuary of jobbing—upon this forbidden ground to the public, or to any one who is not a member of the brotherhood who carry on their operations here. Seeking a short cut from the eastern part of Threadneedle Street into Throgmorton Street, we entered an alley not so private-looking as many which in this precinct connect one thoroughfare with another. Men were passing along it to and fro, and we did not doubt we should quickly emerge in Throgmorton Street. But suddenly it assumed the appearance of a *cul-de-sac,* and we found ourselves at the doors of a large hall, full of people and of a clamour of tongues. A porter was at the door to keep out the profane vulgar: and the room into which we were looking, both through door and window, was the Stock Exchange. This place of business is the property of a corporation; and, unlike the Royal Exchange, no one can come there to sell or buy unless he be a member of the corporation. It is for its own members that the Stock Exchange reserves all the profits on the traffic which goes on within its walls.

The business of the stock-broker is simple enough, and if he have good connections, it is as profitable as it is easy. When he gets an order to execute, all he has to do is to buy or sell at the current rate. He steps into Capel Court, and at once finds the dealers he wants. Every stock-*jobber* has a special line—one deals chiefly in Mexicans, another in Indian stock, and so on; and, moreover, there are places in the room where certain kinds of stock are specially dealt in. The broker finds the jobber, and, after ascertaining that the terms offered are in accordance with the ruling price, he makes the bargain, and in five minutes the business is over. The money, whether given to him to make a purchase, or received as the proceeds of a sale, passes through the hands of the broker, who deducts from it his commission, the cost of stamp or registry, &c.

The business of the jobber is a much more difficult one. He is, in fact, a speculator. He buys stock in the hope of selling it again at a higher price. It is therefore indispensable that he should carefully examine the character of the stock in which he deals, and the circumstances, whether political or commercial, which from day to day affect its value. He knows that the value of stock, although substantially dependent upon the soundness of guarantee and the rate of interest which it yields, is nevertheless affected from day to day by what may be called merely moral influences — by passing gleams or shadows, flitting prejudices it may be, which affect the popularity though not the permanent value of the stock—or merely from sympathy with the rise or fall in other stock of a similar character. The public has neither the leisure nor the knowledge sufficient to judge with confidence, and is generally more encouraged or depressed by the rumours or facts of the day than there is reason to be. All these things the jobber has to take into account; and as it is no easy matter to be a prophet, he must either be a lucky or a clever fellow if he does not sometimes come to grief. Great gains usually alternate with great losses in this kind of business. One would think these jobbers would soon die of worry and anxiety,—and often enough they are to be seen very down-in-the-mouth. But Nature is kind, and fits the back to the burden. Or rather, most of these men have been born with the peculiar temperament of the speculator: they have an extra amount of hopefulness, and get through life, with more excitement indeed, but hardly with less equanimity, on the whole, than any other men engaged in trade.

CREDIT COMPANIES.

The most novel feature in the economy of capital during the last year or two, has been the establishment of great credit companies. The special object of these companies is to provide money for carrying out industrial or financial enterprises which are worthy of support. The credit companies do not directly engage in these enterprises: they simply launch them, or at least provide the capital requisite for carrying them on,—charging a commission for their aid. One of these, the International Land Credit Company, is worthy of notice here, because its operations display in a remarkable manner the system of financial co-operation which is now being established throughout Europe, as well as the great amount of social good which may be effected on the mere principle of self-interest. There is no safer security than land; but the prime requirement in financial operations is, that the security should not only be perfectly safe, but readily negotiable. In other words, the bonds, representing the money advanced, should not only be certain to be paid when due, but the holders of them should be able to sell them easily, or get money advanced upon them. Not one, but several financial establishments are needed to accomplish these ends on a large scale; and the International is the last and crowning company of a series previously established. It will deal with land everywhere, but at present its field of operations is in Austria. In Austria there are estates of immense size, held by individual proprietors, many of them heavily burdened with mortgages contracted on the most usurious terms. Half-a-dozen years ago some foreign capitalists discerned the fine field that was here open to them; but before foreign capital to a large amount could be attracted, it was indispensable to establish the perfect soundness of the security and the negotiability of the mortgage-bonds. The first step towards this was the establishment at Vienna of the *Vindobona*—a joint-stock company which, on receiving a percentage or commission, guarantees the repayment of loans on estates, as well as the regular payment of the interest. In this way, the creditor acquired a double security: first, the land itself,—secondly, the capital of the Vindobona. Next, land-banks were established which advanced money on these bonds or mortgages to their full amount—thus rendering them negotiable. Next it was seen that a large and most profitable business might be carried on by the purchase and re-sale of estates—purchasing them in block, and re-selling them immediately in comparatively small portions, say of 100 to 500 acres. To accomplish this, the Banque de Credit Foncier et Industriel was established, which has agents all over Austria, who examine into titles and values, who find out proprietors ready to sell and small capitalists ready to buy, and in fact manage the whole of this part of the business, while the Bank furnished the funds. This business proved so profitable, and the field of operations was found to be so extensive, that it was resolved to invite the co-operation of capitalists all over Europe. Hence the establishment of the International Land Credit Company. The business of this company is simply to raise funds for carrying on the highly profitable operations above-mentioned: the money being obtained from the public upon bonds issued by the Company, bearing 5 per cent interest, and which are rendered more than usually negotiable, owing to the number of local land-banks and other financial establishments which are affiliated with the International. The credit of conceiving so remarkable a series of co-operative companies, and of successfully establishing it, is due to M. Langrand-Dumonceau, of Brussels. The security offered is the most complete that can be imagined:—1, the land; 2, the double amount for which the purchasers give their bond; 3, the capital of the Vindobona; 4, the capital of the Banque de Credit Foncier et Industriel; and lastly, the immense capital of the International. But what is chiefly remarkable, from our point of view, is the system of financial co-operation herein displayed—a system which is destined to be ere long immensely developed—until, in fact, Europe shall become but one country as regards industrial finance, the spare capital of each country being drawn to common centres, and seeking the best market wherever that may chance to be found.

THE CITY ARTICLE.

This wealthy and busy precinct has a literature of its own—journals whose special task it is to record its operations and set forth its condition. But it has more than this; for the whole country takes an interest in its bulletins. In all our daily newspapers there is a department of news, never omitted, which is scanned with devout attention by hundreds of thousands of readers, yet which is certainly not indebted for its popularity to any attractiveness of style or appearance. It is the driest column or columns in the paper. It is full of figures, and tables of figures (usually so repulsive to readers), preceded by a few paragraphs, seemingly of a very stereotyped aspect, and couched in language peculiar to itself. Therein we read of "Consols for delivery," "Reduced and New Threes," "Turkish Consolidés," "Danish Scrip," "Greek Coupons," "New Granada Deferred," "Spanish Passives," "Russian Threes," "Chilian Sixes," and other such things hard to be understood by the uninitiated, however conversant they may be with the grammar of Lindley Murray and the dictionary of Dr Johnson. We also read that "the market is easier,"—or that it "opened flat,"—that it "assumed a more lively appearance," or that it "showed a falling tendency," or "great depression." This never-omitted and much-studied portion of the paper is the City article, in which the health and spirits of the Money Market are described pathologically; and the price of stocks and shares, and the condition of all established companies quoted on 'Change, are carefully recorded. A single glance at this portion of the *Times* will show the magnitude and variety of the enterprises quoted on 'Change. Besides the loans to foreign governments, there are nearly 700 kinds of stock or shares in the official list, connected with railways, mines, docks, joint-stock banks, colonial government securities, and miscellaneous enterprises.*

The City article is no longer read merely by a particular class of the community. All classes, and all

* The British Funds (comprising Consols, Annuities, and Exchequer Bills), Indian Government Securities, and Bank of England Stock, are represented by 20 different kinds of stock; of Foreign Government Stocks there are 81; of Colonial Government Securities, 28; and of American State Securities, 5. The stocks and shares connected with Railways in all parts of the world are 430; with Banks, 90; with Mines, 74; with Docks, 6; and with Miscellaneous Joint-Stock Companies, 134.

places in the country, have a direct interest in the facts which it records. It is read with interest not merely in London, Liverpool, Manchester, Birmingham, Glasgow, and the other great centres of industry, but even in uncommercial cities like Edinburgh, where men live by the learned professions only, and who scorn trade in the old sense of the word. In truth, nearly all men in this country are traders now, though many of them trade as it were by proxy. The joint-stock system of enterprise has of late years drawn the whole community into its vortex. As a nation, we have grown very rich. It is computed that the annual savings of the nation amount to the enormous sum of £130,000,000. Like thrifty men, we desire to employ that sum, our spare money, in the most profitable manner. Nowadays, too, we have the whole world open to us as a field of commercial and financial enterprise. In commerce, at least, nations are now brethren. No nation objects to the introduction of foreign capital to develop its resources. These two facts—the vast increase of wealth in this country, and the magnitude of the field open for its employment—have given an extraordinary expansion to the joint-stock system; an expansion which has been greatly aided by the passing of the Limited Liability Act.

Previous to the passing of that Act, it had been proved by experience that business could be conducted as successfully by a board of directors as by a private firm. True, the management of a public company is never so economical as that of a private firm, and the supervision of a salaried board of directors is seldom so vigilant as that of private partners, whose whole fortune is at stake in the concern. But, on the other hand, a joint-stock company obtains the command of a larger amount of capital than private firms—which gives it a great advantage; and, moreover, in many cases, it is ensured of a large amount of business, in consequence of its shareholders being also its customers. Take, for example, the case of a joint-stock bank. It may have a thousand shareholders, and all these shareholders are its customers. They have not only subscribed the capital by which the business is carried on, but they intrust all their money to its keeping, and get all their loans and discounts from it. In this way they make business for it, and at the same time share in the profits of that business. They not only get from it the usual interest on their deposits, and the usual advantages of monetary accommodation, but they share in the profits which arise from this form of business.

THE JOINT-STOCK SYSTEM.

The Limited Liability Act has greatly lessened the risk incurred by shareholders, by limiting the liability of each to the amount of capital for which he has subscribed. Shareholders are now comparatively at their ease. They elect from their own number a Board of Directors, whom they pay for conducting or at least supervising the business of the company, and they know that at the worst they cannot lose more than the sum which they have chosen to subscribe. The system, on the whole, has worked remarkably well. It is also accomplishing a revolution in the ideas and financial habits of our people. It offers a higher rate of profit than the interest obtainable upon deposits in banks, and thereby more effectually puts an end to hoarding, extends the spirit of enterprise among all classes, and draws into active use the whole spare money of the people. Clergymen, lawyers, doctors, noblemen, and tradesmen alike, now become shareholders in joint-stock companies. Each, while pursuing his own calling, invests his reserve funds in some financial, trading, or industrial enterprise. He thus obtains the profits of another trade while following his own.

ERA OF CO-OPERATION.

We are at the outset of a new era in social progress, and one which is probably the highest to which material civilisation can attain. It is the era of Co-operation. Hitherto Competition has been regarded as the most efficient agent of social progress. But the principle of competition is one of rivalry and struggle—it is a system of beggar-my-neighbour—most useful in the earlier stages of civilisation, but one most unworthy of civilisation in its maturity. It is costly, for it requires many companies and establishments to do the work which would be more economically performed by one; and it is full of social unhappiness, and fruitful in the bitter feelings of rivalry and jealousy, because each establishment seeks its gains at the expense of the others. The new system of co-operation, on the other hand, seeks to unite and fuse into one the hitherto rival interests of the trader and his customers, of the consumer and the producer. Take for example the case of a company for the supply of gas, or water, or any other necessary or luxury of life, and there you find that a large portion of the customers are also shareholders. By-and-by the system will be more fully developed, and the social advantages will be commensurately increased. Say that a little town is desirous to supply itself with gas or water; then a company will be formed, with a capital apportioned in many small shares, so that nearly every householder may be a member. In this way the company will ensure for itself the largest possible number of customers—opposition and jealousy will disappear, and the little community will have but one interest in the matter. In like manner, a town may supply itself with bread, or groceries, or butcher-meat, or any other article for which there is a general demand. The employés, too, of the company, by holding shares in it, may be made to participate in its interests, and to discharge their duties with more scrupulous diligence than is usually to be found in a hireling or salaried agent. No doubt the time is still distant when the system of co-operation shall reach this development; nevertheless, its coming may be calculated upon. And thus, at the present hour, we are witnessing the initial stage of a principle which will revolutionise our system of industry, and accomplish results fraught with a vast increase of happiness and prosperity to the community.

Large as are the annual profits of our nation, it seems beyond doubt that a considerable portion of the immense capital recently invested in joint-stock companies has been drawn from little hoards, which previously lay dormant. But the peculiar feature of the new position is this—that instead of keeping their reserve funds in bank, men now invest them in joint-stock enterprises, for the sake of obtaining a higher rate of profits. Banks give a comparatively low rate of interest, for they have to pay themselves for taking charge of deposits, and for finding appropriate employment for their customers' money. But by becoming a shareholder in a joint-stock enterprise, a man employs and invests his money without the help of intermediate parties, and hence is entitled to and obtains the profits of trade subject to no abatement. It might be supposed that, owing to this change, the amount of deposits in the banks would be diminished; but it must be remembered that the money thus abstracted from the banks is in great part returned to them from another quarter. The decrease in the deposits of individuals is compensated by the deposits of the new companies. Each company opens an account with a bank, and deposits with it its spare funds; so that what the banks lose in one form they gain in another. This change, however, is important in one aspect. Banks do not speculate. They lend their money only on the best and most negotiable securities, and abstain from employing it in industrial enterprise. Hence, although they are of inestimable value in sustaining commerce, they do not take direct part in the establishment of new branches of industry, or in the development of new national resources. The joint-stock companies, on the other hand, do this as their general feature. They make railways, they open mines, they manufacture gas, and engage in all manner of reproductive enterprise. In fact, the distinction may be stated thus:—The companies *make* the securities upon which the banks *lend*.

Money on loan, we think, would have become cheap of late years but for the great growth of joint-stock companies. If the great and ever-increasing profits of our people had been deposited, as before, with the banks, these establishments would have had so much money to lend compared with the amount of securities upon which they make their advances, that the rate of interest must have fallen. But the new companies have immensely increased the aggregate of securities upon which banks are in the habit of lending. They have made almost every man a trader, and supply him with a form of property which banks will lend upon: and partly in consequence of this, the rate of money has not only maintained itself, but has greatly advanced. In fact, men nowadays keep their reserve funds, not in the banks in the form of money, but in the form of bonds, shares, and coupons—negotiable when necessary, and bearing a higher interest than the banks could give. To keep money in bank (save what is absolutely necessary for one's ordinary expenditure) is now an exploded custom. All that we think of commanding, or keeping in reserve, now is, not cash, but the paper representative of property, and the interest which comes to us as the holders of these symbols or title-deeds of wealth.

THE CITY'S CURRENCY.

Strange to say, in this City of Gold, gold cannot be seen. We know, from official returns, that so many millions of gold lie in the vaults of the Bank, and we infer that a few thousands of sovereigns are kept in each of the other banks, as small change for their customers' wants. But the precious metal makes no appearance in the business transactions of this City of Money. Bits of paper, with some writing on them, are the potent agents of the scene. Paper, paper everywhere; but no gold—not even bank-notes. Let a man go to buy some shares. He sees the rate they are quoted at, and, going into the dingy office of his broker, commissions him to buy. The broker runs out into the busy crowded room of the Stock Exchange, finds or calls out for some one who has shares of the kind to sell, makes a bargain at the current rate, and brings back either a cheque or a stamped agreement to purchase, which he hands to his client. Coupons or certificates are given on one side, and a cheque on the other. But no gold—not even notes! The same takes place in the Royal Exchange and Mincing Lane—only bills and produce are there dealt in, instead of stocks. If you pay a man, you give him a cheque. If you discount a bill, you get the produce in a cheque. If you obtain a loan from your banker on stock, the amount is placed to your credit, and you tell your creditor to draw on you, or give him a cheque. It is really a strange thing to contemplate—so much wealth changing hands: money ceaselessly *in transitu* —yet not a sovereign to be seen. It is but the ghost of money that occupies the city: or rather, it is money in its most civilised form—convenient and inexpensive. It is the cheque-system—the credit-system. And, after all, money itself is nothing else than a form of credit: a thing (whatever its substance) which men by common consent have agreed to recognise as a definite symbol of wealth—a representative of property.

The truth is, the whole operations of this monetary metropolis would come to a standstill if the payments and exchanges of property had to be carried on in gold. A single dealer sometimes lends, or pays, or receives a million sterling or more in a single day; and dealings to the extent of several hundred thousand pounds are by no means exceptional occurrences on the part of single individuals. Many millions of property are changing hands, in loan or purchase — in banks, discount-houses, on 'Change, or in Capel Court—every day. Fancy what it would be if men had to carry about with them such a mass of gold. A thousand sovereigns is a burden which few men would care to carry about with them for a single hour. What a sight, then, it would be if the busy hive had to trot about thus laden. Ants in their hive, carrying about their eggs as big as themselves, would be a joke to it. And consider, too, what insecurity there would be—what occasions for loss of the precious coins—what temptations to theft or robbery—if the transactions in this busy place were so conducted. It would be quite impossible to carry about such a mass of gold as is needed to liquidate the engagements which daily take place. Still more, even if it were possible to carry about these loads of gold, the gold itself in such quantities could not be procured. Happily the yellow metal is not wanted. Cheques, bills of exchange, and bank-notes are found to be equally valuable and negotiable: they represent property quite as reliably as gold, besides being infinitely more portable, safe, and convenient. And hence they —or rather, bills and cheques—constitute to all intents and purposes the only currency on 'Change and throughout the monetary city. By means of them, transactions to the extent of many millions take place daily, without a single sovereign or even bank-note being visible.

We have styled the narrow but all-important precinct of which we write the City of Gold. Yet we have had to say that no gold is visible there. If gold be regarded as an equivalent expression for wealth and property, our title is correct,—for the whole place abounds in wealth, and deals in it. Nevertheless it is the City of Gold even in the literal sense of the term, for its whole existence, all its operations, depend upon the presence of gold in one part of the locality,—in the Bank of England. The gold, it is true, is invisible. The thousands who operate there never see it. It lies hid in the strongest chambers of the Bank, and no one sees it or counts it but the officials who make out the weekly return. But, visible or invisible, its presence and amount regulate the operations of the Bank, and those operations regulate and affect all the other operations of the precinct. The value of stocks and shares rises or falls, panic or prosperity occur, according as much or little of the yellow dross is reported to be in the occult chambers of Threadneedle Street.

PERILS OF THE CITY.

Hence it is that the paragraph in the City Article which is most closely studied is that which relates to the supply of gold. The two brief lines which tell how much gold was taken to the Bank or withdrawn from it, are in reality the vital point of each day's monetary news. If gold is being deposited largely in the Bank, the dealers are all elate, and business and enterprise go ahead; if much gold is being withdrawn from the Bank, every one becomes uneasy; enterprise stands still. How is this momentous effect produced? The practical answer is, that the movements of the precious metal regulate the Bank's rate of discount, and the rate of discount affects the whole industry of the country. If traders can borrow, or get their customary advances, on easy terms, say at 4 per cent, they have every inducement to extend their business and employ as many men as possible; but if they have to pay 8 or 10 per cent, their margin of profit is seriously diminished, if not altogether swept away. Hence every fluctuation in the Bank-rate is watched with intense interest throughout the whole country, and most of all in this monetary metropolis. But in this precinct, as elsewhere, the community is divided into two classes which are very differently affected by the changes in the Bank rate. Trade and Money, we have said, are the great powers which together set agoing the whole business of the precinct; traders and money-dealers constitute its population. A high rate of discount is disadvantageous for the trading and commercial classes, but, on the other hand, it is very profitable to the banks and money-dealers. An increase in the rate is virtually a transfer of a portion of the profits of the former into the pockets of the latter. Bankers like a high rate of discount, the trading classes do not. But both of them are alike interested in watching the movements of gold, as productive of the changes in the rate of discount—or, in other words, in the value of money on loan.

But why, it may be asked, should a little more or less gold in the Bank of England produce such immense effects upon the trade and prosperity of the country? All the engagements which are contracted in this monetary metropolis, as well as throughout the country, although carried on solely by means of cheques and bills, are bound to be met, if required, by payment in the legal money of the country. This legal money is gold and Bank of England notes. Gold, in exceptional times, may not be easily procurable; but the other element of the legalised currency—namely, bank-notes—may be manufactured in any quantity. It may be asked, then,—When gold, at these rare times, becomes scarce, cannot its temporary deficiency be compensated by an increase in the issue of notes—which in the eye of the law, as well as in the estimation of the public, are as valid a tender as gold? It must be remembered, however, that these notes are a *legal**

* Scotch notes are not a legal tender at all,—they circulate simply from the confidence which the public have in the banks which issue them. Yet they are as readily received as if (like those of the Bank of England) their acceptance were made compulsory by Act of Parliament.

tender only so long as the Bank is ready to give gold for them on demand. The first duty of the Bank is to take care that it is at all times in a position to do this. It must insure the convertibility of the note. It must always be ready to give gold for its notes whenever such payment of gold is demanded. It is necessary, then, to observe to what extent such a demand for gold-payments is likely to arise, before we can decide as to the propriety of the measures which the Bank takes to meet such a contingency.

As gold becomes scarce, does the public lose faith in the notes, and rush to the Bank to have them converted into gold? By no means. Experience enables us to speak with perfect confidence upon this point. It is not a question of opinion, but a simple matter of fact. No such loss of confidence in the notes of the Bank has ever occurred, either in our own time, or in that of our fathers and grandfathers. The Bank of England note is a tender which no one mistrusts. People take the notes as readily when there is not a spare sovereign in the Bank, as when its coffers are overflowing with the precious metal. Even in times of the direst commercial crisis, of the worst monetary panic, the public ask only for notes. In 1826, when there was hardly a sovereign in the Bank, the public readily accepted even old £1-notes which had been withdrawn from circulation, and which had not been a legal tender for four years before. The notes serve their purpose as money quite as well as gold does, and the public greatly prefer them. The convertibility of the notes is never endangered, and people would much rather have the notes than an equivalent sum in gold. This is a fact beyond dispute. As a medium of internal circulation—as a means of settling accounts among ourselves—Bank of England notes are accepted everywhere and at all times as preferable to specie. Indeed, we may go further than this, and say that a cheque upon a good bank is preferable to either, although it is not a legal tender at all. Gold is quite unneeded in our monetary transactions with one another. And even if it were announced that the Bank could not give us gold for its notes for a twelvemonth to come, not one man in a hundred thousand would care. The public at large neither require the gold nor desire it.

Who, then, are the parties whose action at times produces a drain of gold from the Bank? They may be classed under the following heads. It may be the Bank of France, or any other great foreign bank, which buys up bills of exchange upon London, and sends them here to be cashed, in order to supply itself with gold from the stock kept on hand by the Bank of England. Or it may be our own Government, which, by making loans to a foreign State, necessitates a corresponding export of the precious metals—or which, in times of war, has to export specie to provide supplies for its army abroad. It may be our corn-merchants importing grain to compensate a deficient harvest; or our manufacturers who purchase abroad the raw materials of their industry. Or, finally, it is great capitalists, great money-dealers, who convert their money into gold or silver as best suits their purpose for the time, and who transfer it from one country to another, wherever they can make the largest profits upon it. It is these agencies, and not any mistrust of the notes, which produce the occasional heavy demands for gold upon the Bank of England.

It is extremely rare that such drains ever become so great as to be a *real and unavoidable* embarrassment for the Bank. In times of war, indeed—as, for example, during the long and gigantic contest with France under the First Napoleon—the Government may have to send its last sovereign abroad in order to sustain the military operations of itself and its allies. But, save in such extremely exceptional circumstances, which have occurred only once in our history, the drain of gold for export never assumes a magnitude such as really (that is to say, apart from the artificial restrictions of the Act of 1844) to imperil the position of the Bank. The export of three or four millions of specie generally produces such an effect upon the rate of exchange, as of itself to render any further exports of the kind unprofitable. Hence the drain ceases. And moreover, as experience amply shows, in two or three months all the gold thus exported returns to us. These, then, are the causes which produce the occasional drains of gold from the Bank, and such are the limits by which these drains are circumscribed. But never—not in a single instance—is gold demanded from the Bank owing to any loss of faith in its notes. No one doubts the value of the Bank of England's notes, and the power of converting them into gold is never desired save as a means of procuring gold for export, by the parties and for the purposes which we have specified.

The City of Gold is based upon gold: and the foundation is found to be pre-eminently unstable and perilous. The golden base perpetually oscillates to and fro, and each of its greater oscillations is felt like the shock of an earthquake. It rises and falls, expands and contracts, and sometimes seems to slip away from beneath the City altogether. Then goodly houses go down by the dozen,—not because they are ill-built—not from any fault of the architect or occupants, but simply because the foundation upon which they all stand has given way. Of late years these oscillations have become more frequent and more serious; and every ten years or so, a convulsion takes place—not of nature, but by Act of Parliament—which spreads terror and disaster through the Golden City, and para-

MONETARY EARTHQUAKES.

lyses the whole country as effectually as if an earthquake had strewed with ruins the great seats of our national industry. The merchant and the manufacturer, the shopkeeper and the day-labourer, alike find their trade stopped, and their gains swept away. Suffering and want spread over the land, as if there were a great famine. There is a paralysis of trade, a dearth of employment; and the hard times are felt by the mill-worker and the bricklayer, not less than by the magnates of the trading and commercial world.

Is there not something wrong here? Ought the presence or absence of a few millions of gold to make the vast difference between national prosperity on the one hand, and national disaster and widespread suffering on the other? How will posterity speak of us when it sees that we made the huge fabric of our national industry stand like an inverted pyramid, resting on a narrow apex formed of a chamberful of yellow dross? Will they not laugh at our folly, our barbarism? When the usual supply of gold is temporarily diminished, why should our usual credit-system be restricted in proportion, or totally suspended? Of what use is Credit but to take the place of payments in coin? Was it not for this purpose, and for this alone, that credit and paper-money were adopted? Why, then, not make use of our credit-system as a means of compensating the temporary absence of gold? Why not tide over the difficulty, instead of aggravating it? and so avoid the tremendous sufferings which are ever-recurrent under our present system of monetary legislation. Suffering thousands and starving myriads signalise each great monetary crisis. Even during the last twelve months, though the crisis of evil has been escaped, the Bank-rate of 9 or 10 per cent has swept away a large portion of the profits of trade into the pockets of bankers and capitalists. Parliament inflicts misery upon the country out of an antiquated deference to some bits of yellow dross. Is this wisdom,—is it humanity,—is it civilisation?

THE BANK OF ENGLAND

A GRAND and imposing place is the Bank of England. Its very exterior bespeaks its importance and its power. It rises in the midst of the City of Gold like a fortress, the Capitol of the precinct. The currents of traffic and of black-coated myriads of busy human beings flow around it, as sundered streams around a mountain-rock which they are powerless even to abrade. As you walk around its quadrangular mass, covering several acres of ground, each side presents the same feature of a front of solid stone, massive enough to be the face of a fortress. Yet it is a fortalice of Gold, and wealth as well as power is represented by its exterior. Its solid front is relieved by stately architectural decoration; and ornamental columns, supporting nothing, but simply let into the wall, present a display of opulence and grandeur which makes no sacrifice of strength. On all sides, the frontage is relieved by the framework of windows, but the decorative mouldings enclose only blank surfaces of solid wall. A few small upper windows, on the side which faces the Royal Exchange, are the only breaks in the solid front. The vast building is lighted entirely from the interior. There is so much of the fortress in the external appearance, that one almost expects to see the grim mouth of cannon peeping out somewhere in the recesses between the columns. At the time of the Chartist mob in 1848, the Bank was actually garrisoned by the troops; and much of its internal as well as external architecture has been planned with an eye to military defence. The building is a melange of many different styles: but the unity of general effect is well sustained, and the architecture of the vast edifice admirably suits the requirements, and symbolises the character, of this fortalice of Gold.

Conscious power is never nervous about petty dangers; and, solid and defiant as is the façade of the Bank, all may enter who please. The restrictions upon entrance common in minor establishments are here unknown. Strong and secure, the Bank lets strangers come and go as well as its own customers. Any one who summons courage to do so, will pass unchallenged through the solid portals, and past the grand-looking porters in their gold-laced cocked hats and gold-embroidered red mantles. On each front of the building there is an entrance. The largest of these, an arched carriage-way, is on the north side, facing Lothbury; where a solid gate studded with iron rivets, backed by inner gates of solid iron, guards the entrance to the Bullion Office; and through these portals vans laden with the precious metals daily come and go.

But the chief entrance to the Bank is in Threadneedle Street. Passing through it, we find ourselves in an open paved court. On either hand are the halls of the Banking department of the establishment, and in front is the Issue department. The portion of the Banking department to the right (forming the entire eastern end of the Bank) is devoted to the management of the National Debt,—where all transfers of Government Stock are registered, and where periodical payment is made of the dividends. In ordinary times these large halls are mere *vacua regna*, where a few clerks may be seen behind unfrequented counters, with old and musty-looking volumes of large size arranged in shelves on the wall. But at each quarterly term these rooms are crowded by people of nearly all ranks and classes (many of them from the country), who come to get payment of their dividends—which vary in amount from several thousands sterling down to a single pound or even less. The amount of work which this entails upon the Bank is greater than might be thought. Apart from the work of paying the dividends, the transfers of stock, which the Bank has to

THE BANKING DEPARTMENT.

register, amount in the aggregate to the enormous sum of about 230 millions sterling a-year.*

Leaving this generally empty part of the edifice, let us visit the other portion of the Banking department, lying to the left of the chief entrance. Here we find the Drawing Offices—a long range of counters, one portion of which is devoted to Public or Government business; and the other, and larger, to banks and private customers. In the former of these offices are paid in the moneys received by the Government in payment of revenue, while the Government salaries and other expenses are paid out. This portion of the Banking department forms two sides of an oblong court (once the little churchyard of St Christopher-le-Stocks), in which is an elegant parterre, with some healthy trees and shrubs, and an ever-flowing convolvulus-shaped fountain, which is supplied by a well. Looking into this elegant court from the north is the grand Court-room of the Bank, where the Directors meet in Council every Thursday, and publish those

* The amount of stock transferred at the Bank of England in 1860 was £196,282,526; in 1861, £268,900,776; in 1862, £228,453,050. In other words, one-third of the bonds connected with our National Debt changes hands every year. The number of holders of stock varies but slightly: in 1861 it was 261,367; in 1862, 264,696; in 1863, 264,011. The number of persons entitled to large dividends is increasing. In 1861 there were 529 persons entitled to dividends of £2000 a-year and upwards: in 1862 there were 569; and in 1863, 585. At the humbler end of the list are 92,190 persons whose year's dividends did not exceed £10 in 1861, 92,262 in 1862, and 81,870 in 1863.

announcements of change in the rate of discount which set a-palpitating the City of Gold, and sometimes also the whole country. Adjoining is the Committee-room, where three Directors attend daily to supervise the business of the Bank,—seldom alone; for other Directors generally drop in, animated by a love of business, and attracted also by the excellent lunch which daily makes its appearance at one o'clock.

A large portion of the Bank's business makes little show. The discounting of bills is the most important part of the daily operations, but very properly these operations are hidden from view. A man who has a "discount-account" with the Bank, and who wishes to cash certain bills in his possession, drops them in the morning into places like letter-boxes, and returns in the afternoon to learn the fate of his application. Ordinarily, the bills are discounted as a matter of course; but in ticklish times—and these are the very occasions when money is most needed by the trader—many a heart palpitates as its owner awaits the decision of the Bank-parlour. But still larger issues are occasionally at stake, when the representatives of great firms are ushered into the presence of the Court, and explain the state of their affairs with a view to obtain exceptional assistance in order to tide over some great but temporary embarrassment.

Let us now see the other great division of the Bank—the Issue department. Leaving behind us the first court which we entered from Threadneedle Street, with its red-mantled porters, and the Detective in plain clothes who seems to idle his time over a newspaper by the doorway,—we ascend half-a-dozen broad steps, and enter a hall where people are getting notes exchanged for gold, or gold for notes, or notes for others of equal value. This is a public office, open to all, whether customers of the Bank or strangers. The chief applicants here are persons who wish to exchange their notes for coin; and as these notes are handed in, their genuineness is carefully ascertained by an elaborate but rapid process of scrutiny. In the north-western corner of the building—if you are provided with an order—you may see the manufacture, or printing, of the notes; and in another room, you may inspect the stock of cancelled notes, which are preserved for ten years after being returned to the Bank. Thus—as in the printing-office there is always a stock of unfinished notes, still wanting the date, number, and signature—you may see the notes in embryo, as it were before they are born, and also after they have been long dead.

THE ISSUE DEPARTMENT.

In the centre of the Issue department, and in the very heart of the Bank, you come into a glass-roofed court; and standing on the landing-place of a flight of steps which leads down into it, you see below you men engaged in packing or unpacking the precious metals, conveying them

THE BULLION OFFICE.

into the vaults of the Bullion Office, or sending them away in vans. There you may see the precious ores in boxes as they come from the mines; or returning from the Bank-refiners in glittering ingots,—the silver in blocks almost as large as a common brick, and the gold of similar shape, but only about an inch in depth; or finally, you may see them returning from the Mint in the shape of coin, packed in strong boxes. The packers toss about the ingots, or fill with bags of coin the iron-bound boxes, with an equanimity or indifference which seems strange to onlookers who have never before seen the precious metals in quantity. The bullion-vaults, as might be expected, are exceedingly strong chambers, and a guard of soldiers and policemen nightly keep sentry over the golden treasure.

For the coin and bullion thus brought to it, the Bank pays—either in its notes, or, as is generally the case, simply by placing the amount to the account of the depositors. Thereafter the coin or bullion no longer belongs specially to the depositor, but equally to every one who keeps an account at the Bank, or who holds any of its notes. The Bank is bound to give gold for all its notes on demand,—and also (although this is utterly impossible) to pay all its deposits likewise in gold; but the persons who brought the gold have no other claim upon the Bank's stock of the precious metal than that which is common to all the noteholders and depositors alike. The gold has been sold to the Bank; and thereafter any one who has an account with the Bank, or who holds some of its notes, may draw upon its stock of gold at his pleasure.

As you lean over the brass-topped balustrade, looking at the coming and going of the precious ores, you witness operations which affect the whole business of the Bank, and, to a great extent also, the whole trade and industry of the country. Every van-load of gold which enters or leaves that court causes a rise or fall in the value of money, by increasing or diminishing the amount of currency available for the requirements of the community. The reason of this is not obvious, but it is easily explained. The Bank is authorised by Act of Parliament to issue notes to the amount of fourteen and a half millions sterling (£14,650,000) upon an equal amount of Government securities which it holds; besides this, it is entitled to issue an amount of notes corresponding to the value of the gold which happens to be in its vaults.* Hence the amount of Money in this country is constantly varying. When much gold is deposited in the Bank, the currency is increased; when little gold is deposited in the Bank, the currency is diminished. What is of

GOLD AND NOTES.

* All the specie is kept in the Issue department,—save a small portion (usually about £700,000), partly in gold and partly in silver coin, which is needed for the ordinary business of the Banking department. But it is the amount of gold in the Issue department alone which regulates the amount of the Bank's notes.

more consequence, the value of money on loan, the rate of discount, is affected to a still greater extent by every variation in the stock of gold in the Bank's vaults. It is this latter process which invests with such critical importance the entrance or exit of the gold-laden vans through the gates of the Bank of England.

HOW NOTES ARE PUT IN CIRCULATION.

Let us see the process by which these variations are accomplished. In the first place, how is this increase or decrease, this addition to or subtraction from the currency of the country, effected by the Bank? It is usually said that the Bank gets its notes into circulation by paying them away to the persons who bring the gold to it. It is supposed that the depositors of the gold ask for, and obtain in exchange, notes of the Bank equal in amount to the value of the gold so deposited. But this is a mistake. Suppose an individual take twenty or fifty thousand pounds' worth of gold to the Bank, what motive has he for carrying off a corresponding amount of bank-notes in his pocket? Save in exceptional cases, he does nothing of the sort. The amount is placed to his credit in the Bank, or a draft is given him upon some other bank where he keeps his account, and thereafter he can draw to that amount in larger or smaller sums as suits his convenience. It is a mistake, then, to suppose that every deposit of gold necessarily occasions, or does occasion, a corresponding increase of the note-circulation of the Bank.

When gold is brought to it, the Bank does not necessarily pay away an equal amount of notes: it merely becomes authorised to make an issue of notes to that amount. It makes a corresponding addition to its stock of notes in its Banking department,—that is all. And it may keep them there as long as it pleases.

The variations in the amount of notes in the Banking department are effected in this way. Every day a large amount of bills which the Bank has discounted are falling due, and are being paid to it in notes. The Bank never re-issues any of its notes; but, when its stock of gold remains unaltered, it places an amount of new notes in its Banking department equal to that of the old ones which it has received in payment of the lapsed bills. And if its stock of gold has altered, it places in its Banking department either a greater or lesser amount of notes than it has received in payment of these bills, according as its stock of gold has increased or diminished. For example, if a million's worth of bills which the Bank has discounted fall due and are paid to it on a certain day, and if its stock of gold has on that day diminished to the extent of £100,000 then instead of placing £1,000,000 of new notes in its Banking department, it places only £900,000. In like manner, if the same amount of discounted bills falls due, while its stock of gold has increased to the extent of £100,000, it places

£1,100,000 notes in its Banking department, instead of £1,000,000.

The notes thus kept in the Banking department are inactive,—they are not in circulation. They are currency,—but (if we may so phrase it) they are not part of "the currency." They are not in use,—only ready to be put in use. Gold may flow in increasing streams into the Bullion Office, but such influx has no power to put into circulation the notes in the Banking department. Another process must come into play before these inactive notes become active, by being transferred to the hands of the public.

This is effected chiefly by means of the discount operations. As the stock of gold in the Issue department increases, authorising a corresponding addition to the amount of notes in the Banking department, the Bank endeavours to get this increase of notes into circulation. It can only do this in one way—namely, by letting the public have its notes on easier terms than before. For example, suppose there are 15 millions of gold in the Bullion Office, and the rate of discount is 4 per cent: when the stock of gold increases to 20 millions, if the rate of discount be still kept at 4 per cent, there will be no increased demand for discounts, and accordingly no increase will take place in the note-circulation,—unless an expansion should simultaneously occur in the trade of the country and its monetary require-

VARIATIONS OF THE CURRENCY.

ments. If the Bank-rate remained steady at (say) 4 per cent, any exceptional increase in the amount of notes in the Issue department (owing to an exceptional increase in the Bank's stock of gold) would not get into circulation. The public, having already as much money as it wants at that rate, would not take this extra amount of notes off the Bank's hands. But in order to get these additional notes into circulation, the Bank at times reduces its charge for discounting bills to so low a point as 2 per cent. In other words, it announces to the public that it will lend its money at fully one-half below the usual rate of charge. Who would not have money on such easy terms? Every merchant and shopkeeper who has a bill in his possession (instead of keeping it beside him, as he might otherwise do, till it becomes due), takes it at once to his bank and gets it discounted. Moreover—as almost any kind of business will pay when it can be carried on with money borrowed at 2 per cent—people extend their business, and new enterprises are undertaken. And every increase of business augments the number of bills which have to be discounted. In this way the discount-business of the Bank is increased. And as the Bank pays the proceeds of many of those discounted bills to its customers in notes, it gets its surplus stock of paper-money off its hands, and proportionally increases the active currency of the country.

With these facts known, a very different feeling

from that of mere curiosity fills one, as he looks down upon the packers at work in the Bullion Court of the Bank. The ingots there tossed about are so many bricks added to or withdrawn from the foundations of our prosperity. They constitute the narrow basis upon which the vast fabric of our monetary system is made to rest. The variations produced in the superstructure by these ebbs and flows of gold are twofold in character: one affecting the amount of the Currency, the other affecting the rate of Interest.

EXPANSIONS.

The variations produced in the amount of the currency, by the operations of the Bank which we have just described, are by no means inconsiderable. In the autumn of 1853, for example, the amount of the Bank's notes in circulation was £24,500,000; in December 1855 it was only £18,142,000—less than three-fourths of what it was two years before. Such a variation unquestionably seems excessive; but, instructed by experience, we no longer attach to it the momentous importance attributed to it by the monetary authorities of the past generation. Prior to 1844—indeed until several years later—an expansion of the note-circulation such as occurred in 1852-3, would have occasioned, on the part of our authorities in monetary science, a great outcry about "over-issues." They would have protested loudly against the "depreciation of the currency;" and the direst evils would have been predicted as the inevitable consequence of the currency having been thus made "redundant." According to them, the public should have commenced a run upon the Bank in order to convert the "depreciated" notes into gold, and the precious metals should have immediately fled from our shores. No such dire results followed. As a simple matter of fact, we may state that when the currency was at its highest point (in 1852-3) there was no drain of gold at all, either from internal demand or for export; and the subsequent drain upon the Bank by the efflux of specie only assumed a critical magnitude in the latter months of 1855, when the note-circulation was at a lower point than it had been for several years before, or than it has ever been since. Two or three millions more of bank-notes in circulation (in 1853 the excess above the ordinary amount was about four millions) is found to make no impression upon the value of the general currency. In truth, the mere amount of the note-circulation (to which so much importance used to be attributed) is of no significance of itself,—*i. e.*, apart from the commercial position and monetary requirements of the country. A supply of money, as of any other commodity, which is simply adequate in ordinary circumstances, may become either excessive or inadequate owing to a change in the amount of demand. An expansion of trade — still more a panic, or paralysis of our ordinary credit-system—may render 24 millions less adequate for the monetary wants of the country than 21 millions in ordinary times.

Contractions of the currency, as well as expansions, are effected by means of the discount-operations of the Bank. If the Bank refuse to discount its ordinary amount of bills, its note-circulation will be correspondingly reduced. This used to be its practice in seasons of monetary difficulty. But, recently, it has altered its practice. It no longer contracts its note-issues below the average: indeed, in times of crisis, its issues now are always greater than in ordinary times. The Bank raises its rate of discount, but it does not seek to reduce the amount of the currency. When it greatly lowers its rate of discount, the trading classes may take an increased amount of its notes or not as they please. But as, when it greatly raises its rate, money is in unusual demand, the trading classes must take off its notes, whatever be the terms. Distrust of the ordinary forms of credit, such as bills, is then prevalent; the other banks and discount-houses greatly diminish their operations; and hence an unusual amount of discount-business goes to the Bank. In ordinary times, many persons who have a discount-account with the Bank prefer to get their bills discounted with other establishments, because these establishments generally charge somewhat less than the Bank-rate. But as, in times of crisis, these establishments contract or suspend their discount-

CONTRACTIONS.

operations, every one who has a discount-account with the Bank has to take his bills to it. So that, in times of monetary difficulty, the demand for discounts at the Bank is invariably much greater than usual, however high may be its charge. In fact, a very high Bank-rate, by depressing the markets and causing failures and distrust, of itself occasions an increased demand for its notes. A larger supply of money than usual is at such times indispensable to the community. And the Bank now supplies them with what they want, on condition that they pay the high terms which it exacts. Thus, although the Bank expands the currency, by an extra issue of notes, when a large stock of gold is in its Issue department, it does not seek to contract the currency below the ordinary amount at times when its stock of gold is unusually diminished.

These facts are worthy of attention, because they throw light upon a question which at present is not rightly understood. It is generally supposed that the system followed by the Bank is based upon the principle embodied in the Act of 1844. This is a mistake. The principle upon which that Act was based is now repudiated by the Bank Court; the means which Sir R. Peel, Mr Goulburn, and Mr Jones Lloyd (now Lord Overstone) desired should be adopted to meet a drain of gold, are not employed; and our monetary system is now regulated on a method which was not thought of by the

THE BANK ACT.

framers of the Bank Act. The system and the Act proceed on different principles. The Act was passed for the very purpose of securing a contraction of the currency, in proportion as the stock of gold in the Bank decreased. But the Bank, now, makes no such contraction,—nor even attempts it. How is this?

Let us examine the Act, and the motives of its framers.

In 1844, and for thirty years previous, the predominant idea with authorities in monetary science was a dread of "over-issues." That had been the current theory, in connection with Bank-crises, from 1810 downwards. It was a pair of coloured spectacles which the Bullion Committee left as a legacy to the subsequent generation, and which became the medium through which all our monetary difficulties were viewed. The increase of the Bank's issues to the extent of a million or two above the ordinary amount, was held capable of producing the most momentous consequences.* It "depreciated the

THEORY OF OVER-ISSUES.

* The expansion of the aggregate note-circulation of England, upon which Mr Jones Lloyd (now Lord Overstone), in his evidence before the Parliamentary Committee of 1840, founded his charges of "mismanagement" against the banks of issue, only amounted to two millions and a half. Moreover this expansion took place gradually, being spread over a period of five years,—the note-circulation (we take his own figures) being £28,368,000 on the 1st of January 1834, and £31,020,000 (its highest point) on the 18th September 1838. To this "over-issue" he attributed the severe crises which occurred between 1836 and 1839. What has his Lordship

currency," and was the parent of our recurrent monetary crises. The upholders of this theory, it is true, never demonstrated, by a reference to prices, that the currency *was* depreciated.* They took that for granted, and a good deal more besides. Upon this hypothesis they built a currency-system. They held that "over-issues" was the main cause of all the drains of gold from the Bank. The Bank, they said, from a love of gain, increases its notes to the extent of a million or two above its ordinary issues; thereupon the currency becomes redundant, the notes are depreciated, and an inflation of prices takes place. The public, finding the notes depreciated, make a run upon the Bank to get them exchanged for gold; and as the gold is of no more value than notes in this country, they send it abroad. If the Bank, in

to say to the much greater "over-issues" in 1852-3, which produced no crisis, or difficulty of any kind?

* So far from the currency being depreciated during the disastrous years ending with 1839, the case was the reverse. It was a period not of "inflated" but of very low prices. It appears from the published statement of Mr Smith, chairman of the Manchester Chamber of Commerce, that in the winter of 1836 and spring of 1837 (when "over-issues" were alleged to have been made by the country-banks) the fall in price upon the five great articles of "cotton, woollen, silk, linen, and hardware," amounted on the average to 37 per cent. He says—"The rates of depreciation on all these great articles of production may be gathered without difficulty from the prices-current of the spring and autumn of 1837,—the fall in price varying from 25 to 50 per cent:" the value of money, of course, having been temporarily enhanced to a corresponding extent.

order to fill up this gap in our currency, issues more notes, these notes are immediately brought back to it again in order to be exchanged for gold, which is in like manner sent abroad. And this goes on till the Bank is drained of its gold, and the country is involved in panic and disaster. "Over-issues," in short, in their opinion, was the chief cause of the recurrent drains of gold from the Bank, and all our woes.

Sir Robert Peel found this theory prevalent—so to speak, established. It was the orthodox creed of the day. He adopted it, and framed upon it his Bank Act of 1844,—by which he sought to secure a contraction of the currency whenever a drain of gold should commence upon the Bank. By contracting the currency at these times, he reckoned he should prevent the "depreciation" which (as then believed*) was the cause of the drain; and thus save the country from the dreadful disasters which such drains of gold had unquestionably produced.

It is a very neat theory. But it will not square with the facts. We, who have seen £300,000,000 added to the general currency within fifteen years, with so little

* Proceeding upon the hypothesis that our drains of gold were occasioned by "over-issues," which produced a "depreciation" of the currency, Lord Overstone, in 1840, said: "The influx and efflux of gold constitutes the only proper rule by which to regulate the variations of a paper-currency. . . . Upon the principle which I contend for, when an export of gold takes place from the country, there would be a cancelling of paper-notes to *an equal amount*."—See his evidence before the Parliamentary Committee of 1840.

effect that it is still doubted by many authorities whether there has been any depreciation of money at all, and when the loanable value of our currency has notably increased, may well be sceptical as to the doctrine of over-issues, even if we had not other and direct evidence to the contrary. Experience shows that the occasional expansions of the Bank's currency (although they may foster undue speculation, if accompanied by a low rate of discount), have no tendency whatever to make the currency redundant. Of course we speak of the actual, not of problematical, expansions. For example, in 1852-3 we had a greater expansion of the Bank's issues than used to occur under the Act of 1819, and twice as great as that to which Lord Overstone attributed the crises of 1836-9, —yet no drain of gold ensued, nor crisis of any kind. Take another recent case. In November and December 1857, the Bank was empowered to make additional issues to the amount of two millions sterling,—although its note-circulation was then greatly above the average. In fact, Lord Overstone maintained that the Bank on that occasion "exceeded its proper limits of issue by £6,000,000 or £7,000,000." *

* "The Bank has not only been compelled to avail itself of the permission accorded to it by the Government [to issue £2,000,000 beyond the fixed amount], but has actually exceeded its legitimate issue by some £6,000,000 or £7,000,000. I know exactly what I say, and I maintain its accuracy. . . . It has exceeded its proper limits of issue by £6,000,000 or £7,000,000."—*Speech of Lord*

Did any depreciation either of the notes or of the general currency ensue? Let facts answer. During these two months there was indeed a great alteration in prices—a vast change in the relative value of goods and money. But it was goods that were depreciated, not money. At that time prices were immensely reduced below their ordinary level, and the purchasing power of money was enormously increased. So far from the currency being depreciated, owing to a redundancy, money was then excessively scarce; and, in consequence, the prices of goods experienced a sudden fall to the extent of fully twenty-five per cent.*"

Overstone, 3d December 1857. If this was not "over-issue," what are we to understand by the term?

* This fact is proved by the subjoined comparison of prices of imports *before* and *during* the season of panic in November 1857, as given in the *Commercial Daily List*:—

	Averaged	Now	
"Tallow, which averaged	60s.	is now 50s.	per cwt.
Sugar, ...	55s.	... 35s.	per cwt.
Cotton, ...	7d.	... 6d.	per lb.
Scotch pig-iron, ...	60s.	... 50s.	per ton.
Saltpetre, ...	65s.	... 45s.	per cwt.
Rice, ...	15s.	... 10s.	per cwt.
Silk, ...	30s.	... 20s.	per lb.
Linseed, ...	70s.	... 58s.	per qr.
Do. oil, ...	40s.	... 32s.	per cwt.
Tin, ...	135s.	... 122s.	per cwt.
Tea (Congou), ...	1s. 3d.	... 1s.	per lb.
Pimento, ...	5d.	... 3d.	per lb.
Turmeric, ...	60s.	... 30s.	per cwt.
Shellac, ...	120s.	... 80s.	per cwt.
Jute, ...	28s.	... 20s.	per cwt.
Hemp, ...	36s.	... 30s.	per cwt.

Here is a fall of 27 per cent within a fortnight."—We select this statement on account of its precision, although it does not express the full extent of depreciation which sometimes takes place in seasons of monetary crisis.

So much for the theory of "over-issues" in regard to depreciation of the currency. Of course, if it be shown that the expansions of the Bank's note-circulation do not really produce depreciation, then the whole theory falls to the ground. If there be no depreciation, there can be no run for gold in exchange for notes, from this cause,—nor any export of the precious metal,—nor any consequent panic and crisis. But the whole theory is a piece of fancy. The most ordinary acquaintance with facts, with banking business during a time of drain and panic, suffices to show it is all moonshine. Since the drains of gold were supposed to be caused by the public losing faith in the notes and sending them into the Bank to be exchanged for gold, the supporters of the theory ought to have been puzzled by the fact that, despite this paying in of notes, the amount of the note-circulation remained undiminished. If the public would not have the notes, and returned them upon the Bank, there was at least no sign of this. Although seven or eight millions sterling of gold was supposed at times to be withdrawn from the Bank in this way, strangely enough, the amount of the Bank's notes in the hands of the public continued unaltered. The theorists, indeed, alleged that this was owing to the fact that the notes were no sooner sent into the Bank for gold than the Bank sent them into circulation again. How the Bank contrived to do so, the theorists did not explain. If the notes were so re-issued, there must have been a corresponding expansion of the discount-business of the Bank; whereas official statistics show that the discounts at these times of drain used always (until panic was created, and placed the Bank itself in jeopardy) to be reduced. But to clench the argument, let us say at once that the drains of the precious metals, the runs upon the Bank for gold, *are not made by means of notes at all.* They are made by means of cheques. To talk of a drain of gold upon the Bank being occasioned by people taking their notes to be exchanged for sovereigns is sheer illusion. No such thing takes place. It is the depositors, not the note-holders, who make the drain; and it is by the presenting of cheques, not by the cashing of notes, that the specie resources of the Bank are diminished.

Thus we see (1) that the Bank's issues, as a matter of fact, do not produce depreciation of the currency; (2) that the public at times of crisis do not return the notes upon the Bank in order to get them exchanged for gold; and (3) that the drain upon the Bank's stock of gold is made not by note-holders, but by depositors. Thus the theory fails at all points. Moreover, what are we to think of a theory which attributes our monetary crises to "over-issues," when it is a fact that, in every crisis during the last seventy years, the very thing which at length stopped the run upon the Bank has been a sudden, and sometimes a great, *increase of its note-circulation*, by an expansion of its discount-operations?*

It is a matter of importance that the actual provisions of the Act of 1844 should be clearly understood.

PROVISIONS OF THE ACT.

When we discuss the objects or merits of a measure, let us consider what its enactments really are. The opponents of the Act attribute to it faults, and its supporters see in it merits, which, whether they be faults or merits, do not belong to it. The provisions of the Act are very simple. It severed the Bank of England into two separate and independent departments. It placed the Issue department, which deals with the currency, wholly apart from the Banking department, which deals with the deposits intrusted to the Bank by the State and the public. It enacted that a certain amount of Government securities belonging to the Bank should be taken out of the banking department, and placed in the currency department, as security for an equal amount of the Bank's note-circulation; and also, that for all notes issued beyond this amount, the Bank should keep in the currency department an equal amount of gold. This was the whole scope of the Bill: the minor enactments of the measure being simply a carrying out of this leading provision.

It will be seen from this, that although the Act

* *Vide supra*, pp. 89, 99-104, and 109.

might necessitate contractions of the currency, it did not necessitate expansions beyond the ordinary amount —such as took place in 1852-3. It permitted the Bank to enlarge its note-circulation in proportion to any increase which might occur in its stock of gold; but it did not enact that such enlargement should take place. It conferred a power of issue, but the Bank was left free to make additional issues or not. When an unusual amount of gold is deposited with the Bank, the Act imposes no necessity upon the Directors to make an equally unusual issue of notes. Such enlargement of the note-circulation is not enjoined by the Act,*—it is wholly the doing of the Directors. The Act rendered compulsory the keeping of a certain amount of gold as a security for the notes. It fixed the limit beyond which notes should not be issued. But it did not enjoin that the note-issues should at any time be enlarged beyond the ordinary amount. Therefore, if at times the note-issues of the Bank are exceptionally increased, those augmentations are not rendered necessary by the Act of 1844. Hence one part of the variations in the amount of the currency, and one part of the still more important variations in the rate of discount, are not the consequence of the Act

DOES NOT NECESSITATE EXPANSIONS.

* "The House must be responsible, not the Government," said Sir R. Peel in June 1844, when the bill was making slow progress, "if the present measure failed and a period of *increased issues* again arrived."

at all. If the rate of discount is reduced at times to the extremely low point of 2 per cent, that is simply the doing of the Directors. It is a course which they take in order to get out the additional notes which they have the power to issue; although they are under no obligation to use that power. They are right to issue these additional notes if, from any cause, there is a spontaneous demand for them on the part of the public: but are they right in forcing them out, by means of an exceptionally low rate of discount, which creates an abnormal demand for them?

The object of the framers of the Act, we repeat, was to prevent "over-issues," and thereby—according to the theory then held—to render impossible that "depreciation of the currency" which was believed to be the cause of the recurrent drains of gold from the Bank, which occasioned such disasters to the country. This theory, as we have shown, has been exploded by facts. It lingered on until 1857, and possibly it may linger in some quarters yet. But the facts connected with the crises of 1847 and 1857 fully demonstrated its unsoundness, its utter baselessness. The Bank Directors found that, so far as it could be carried out, instead of being a preventive or alleviator of our monetary difficulties, it was only fitted to aggravate them. They also found that such contraction of issues was very unprofitable for the Bank. Prior to 1857, therefore, the Bank had abandoned the theory upon which the Act was founded. It had adopted a new system of action. And in 1858 we find the old doctrine of "over-issues" ignored by the Parliamentary Committee of that year, and another theory enthroned in its stead.

THEORY OF VARIATION.

"The main object of the Act of 1844," says the report of that Committee, "was undoubtedly to secure the *variation* of the paper-currency of the kingdom according to the same laws by which a metallic circulation would vary." Before considering the merits of this currency-doctrine, we feel bound to say that this is a view of the Act which certainly was *not* taken by its framers. Mr Goulburn stated explicitly in his letter to the Governor of the Bank of England (April 1844), that the main object of the Act was to "prevent fluctuations in the currency."* If it be said that the Chancellor of the Exchequer of the day was mistaken in so representing the purpose of the Act, it will at least be admitted that Sir Robert Peel is a good authority in regard to his own intentions. Speaking on the 3d of December 1847, Sir Robert Peel said: "The Bill of 1844 had a triple object. Its first object—that in

* Mr Goulburn, in that letter, explanatory of the Act, stated that the chief object of the measure was "to place the general circulation of the country on a sounder footing, and *prevent, as much as possible, fluctuations in the currency*, of the nature of those which have at different times occasioned hazard to the Bank and embarrassment to the country."

which I admit it has failed—was to *prevent severe and sudden contraction*, and the panic and confusion inseparable from it. But the Bill had two other objects,—the one, to maintain and guarantee the convertibility of the paper-currency into gold; the other, to prevent the difficulties which arise at all times from undue speculation being aggravated by the abuse of paper-credit in the form of promissory notes"—*i.e.*, bank-notes. As the Act was then upon its trial, and as he spoke after he had gained experience from the recent crisis, Sir R. Peel doubtless took care to represent his measure in the most favourable light. Nevertheless, in the three objects of the Act which he then carefully specified, that which the Parliamentary Committee ten years afterwards asserted to be the "main object" had no place. Again and again, in 1844, he stated explicitly that his grand object was to prevent sudden contraction of the currency on the one hand, and undue expansion on the other,—and to maintain the convertibility of the Bank's notes. And the measures were adopted by him simply as means to an end: not for the sake of carrying out any theory, but to accomplish a great practical result—namely, in his own words, "to ensure to industry its legitimate profits."

The doctrine that the paper-currency of a country ought to vary with the scarcity or abundance of gold, is a maxim which—with all deference to Lord Overstone—is not compatible with common sense. If the doctrine be right, paper-money should never have been invented. If it be right, we should cancel all our bank-notes at the very seasons when they are most needed—*i. e.*, when our metallic currency becomes diminished and inadequate. Sir R. Peel approved of a contraction of the note-circulation at times of a drain of gold, because he had been taught to believe that such drains are occasioned by a depreciation of the currency arising from over-issues. And, adopting this hypothesis, he thought that the prevention of such "depreciation" would suffice to keep an ample supply of gold at all times in the country. But he saw well, and in 1847 fully acknowledged, the evils which such contraction necessarily occasioned—namely, "panic and confusion inseparable from it." On principle, therefore, he was strongly opposed to "severe and sudden contraction"—even though he believed that contraction was indispensable at times when gold was ebbing from the Bank. Had he known—what subsequent experience and fuller investigation amply demonstrate—that "over-issues" on the part of the Bank are a bugbear, and that no expansion of the note-circulation, such as actually occurs, produces any depreciation of the currency, he would have seen still more reason to protest against great variations of the currency of either kind. Make the paper-currency vary in amount as gold varies! "When an export of gold takes place, cancel paper-notes to an equal amount!" No gold, no notes! What a *reductio ad absurdum!* Surely a doctrine which leads to such a conclusion is theory run mad. How would it have fared with the country if, instead of William Pitt, a Jones Lloyd had been at the head of affairs during the great war with Napoleon? For many years during that war, especially from 1808 to 1815, there was hardly a sovereign left in the country: we needed all our specie to send abroad to maintain our victorious army under Wellington, and to make those loans and subsidies to the Continental Powers without which they could not co-operate with us in the field. At such a time—and it may occur again—the supporters of the "variation" theory would have nothing left to vary. The gold being 0, the paper-currency should also be 0! To hold such a doctrine is to bid defiance to common sense.

The practice of the Bank, for some years past, has been regulated by a different principle from either the theory of "over-issues" adopted by Sir Robert Peel in 1844, or that of "variation" as propounded by the Committee of 1858. Had the Bank Directors adhered to the currency-hypothesis upon which the framers of the Act of 1844 proceeded, their practice would be as follows. The ordinary note-circulation of the Bank is about twenty-one millions; and, as the Directors now keep the rate of discount at 8 per cent when there are thirteen millions of gold in the Bank, they evidently regard sixteen millions of gold as requisite to justify a rate of 4 or 5 per cent, which may be regarded as a fair rate when the currency is in its ordinary condition. Accordingly, if they proceeded upon Sir R. Peel's theory, whenever the stock of gold in the Bank began to fall below sixteen millions, the Directors should take measures to reduce the amount of notes in circulation to a corresponding extent. Thus, when the stock of gold falls to thirteen millions, they should reduce the amount of their note-circulation from 21 millions to 18; when the stock of gold falls to ten millions, they should reduce their note-circulation to 15 millions.* Such a course is quite impracticable. The reduction would mainly† be effected by diminishing their discount-operations to a similar extent,—that is to say, by refusing to discount perfectly good bills which their customers desired to cash. It is needless to say that

* So far mistaken was Sir R. Peel in regard to the practical working of the system which he inaugurated in 1844, that he actually contemplated the possibility of the currency being diminished at times by the effect of this Bill to only £11,000,000. And in order to enable the Bank Directors to carry out this contraction, he specially provided that, at their pleasure, they might cancel 3 millions of the 14 millions of securities which were to be placed in the Issue department, and thereby enable themselves to reduce their note-circulation to 11 millions!

† The Bank can reduce its note-circulation in two ways,—either by selling a portion of its Government Stock, and cancelling the notes which it receives in payment; or by diminishing its discount-operations. The first course occasions a loss to the Bank, the second imposes a still greater loss upon Trade.

any such reduction of discounts on the part of the Bank (*i. e.*, to the extent of six millions) would bring our whole fabric of commerce to the ground, and would occasion a crisis unparalleled in severity, while there were still ten millions of gold in the Bank. The Bank, in point of fact, cannot reduce the national currency in this way—cannot reduce its note-circulation from 21 to 15 millions—even if it were to make the attempt. It would produce a condition of affairs which would require *more* notes, instead of less; and by attempting to withhold them, by contracting its discounts, it would occasion a fatal run upon its deposits. The Directors know this; and as men of sense they neither try to effect such a contraction, nor wish to do so.

It is also to be observed that they do not carry out the "variation" theory tacitly approved by the Parliamentary Committee of 1858. If they were to do so, they would act as follows. In 1852-3, when the stock of gold in the Bank amounted to 22 millions, they should have increased their note-circulation from 21 millions (its ordinary amount) to 36 millions: that being the amount they were then entitled to issue—namely, 14 millions* on Government securities, and

* This was the amount as it stood in 1852. But as the Act provided that the Bank (on an Order in Council being issued to that effect) should replace two-thirds of the note-issues of provincial banks which might lapse, the amount of the Bank's note-circulation issued against securities was increased to £14,475,000 in Decem-

22 millions on gold. This course could only have been carried out by means of the discount-operations of the Bank; and as the remarkably low discount-rate of 2 per cent barely sufficed to get 24½ millions of notes into circulation, it may safely be concluded that 36 millions of notes could not have been got into circulation even though the Bank had reduced its rate to 1 per cent! Hence to carry out this "variation" theory, and make the amount of the currency vary as the stock of gold in the Bank varies, is obviously as impracticable, and if effected would be as pernicious, as to carry out the contractions requisite to an observance of Sir R. Peel's theory of "over-issues."

Profiting by experience, the Bank Court have devised a new system of action,—and a much better one for the Bank than either of the two which in recent times have been stamped, the one formally and the other tacitly, with the approval of Parliament. This new system pays no regard to the *amount* of the currency. Let the gold in the Issue department decrease as it may, the Bank takes no measures to contract the amount of the currency, by withdrawing from circulation any portion of its notes. In like manner, let the gold in the Issue department increase as it may, there is a point beyond which the Bank will not go in its

THE NEW SYSTEM.

ber 1855, and, in consequence of a further addition, now amounts to £14,650,000.

measures calculated to produce an expansion of its note-circulation. The Directors carefully observe the positive provisions of the Bank Act, but within that limit they act as they please. When a certain amount of gold is in the bullion-vaults, they are empowered to keep an equal amount of notes in the Banking department. These notes constitute the reserve of loanable money. It is something apart from the ordinary circulation: it is a supply of money in excess of that which is employed in the Bank's ordinary discount-operations. It is, in fact, as we have said, the Bank's *reserve* of loanable money. The Act regulates the amount of this reserve, by compelling it to vary with every change in the Bank's stock of gold: but the Act leaves the Directors free to use this reserve as they please. Accordingly, when this reserve is very large, the Directors lower the Bank-rate, and invite the trading-classes to engage in new enterprises, and to bring more bills to be discounted at the Bank. They say at such times, "We have a great deal more notes in reserve than is usual or than is necessary: therefore let us reduce our rate for loans, and induce the public to take a portion of them off our hands." Again, when this reserve of notes is diminished, they say, "Let us charge the public a higher rate for the use of them." The Bank Act may be quite wrong in the limit, and in the fluctuations, which it imposes upon the amount of the Bank's reserve of notes: the Directors have nothing to do with that. It is also true that the Directors may, and we think do, err to some extent in the use which they make of their powers. But let us see, in the first place, how this new system is worked.

VARIATIONS OF THE BANK-RATE.

It certainly does not obviate those "fluctuations which (to use the words of Mr Goulburn) have at different times occasioned embarrassment to the country." On the contrary, fluctuation is now the order of the day. Fluctuations in the rate of interest are the peculiar feature of the new system. The rate of usage throughout the country, the charge for money on loan, varies with every million or half-million of gold deposited in or withdrawn from the Bank of England. Let us give a specimen of these fluctuations of the Bank-rate, taken from the years 1857-58:—

1857.	Oct. 1,	the Rate stood at	5½	per cent.
...	Oct. 8,	raised to	6	...
...	Oct. 12,	...	7	...
...	Oct. 22,	...	8	...
...	Nov. 5,	...	9	...
...	Nov. 9,	...	10	...
...	Dec. 24,	reduced to	8	...
1858.	Jan. 7,	...	6	...
...	Jan. 14,	...	5	...
...	Jan. 28,	...	4	...
...	Feb. 4,	...	3½	...
...	Feb. 11,	...	3	...

A series of eleven great changes, first upwards and then downwards, in four months! In a single month the Bank-rate was raised from 5½ to 10 per cent. Thereafter, in six weeks, it descended precipitately from 10 per cent to 3. During this period, the condition of our Trade resembled that of a traveller who has to cross a lofty pass of the Alps at midsummer, and who alternately shivers with cold and broils with heat within the space of twenty-four hours. Fortunately for the traveller, he usually suffers only a temporary inconvenience from these changes; but Trade, when compelled by the Bank to undergo such vicissitudes, becomes paralysed by the severity of the tortures inflicted upon it.

The whole commerce and industry of the country is affected by those changes; for—let it be distinctly kept

THEIR EFFECTS UPON TRADE.

in mind—all our trade is carried on by means of bills, which their holders have to get discounted in the ordinary course of business.* Every commercial enterprise, therefore, every industrial contract which extends over a considerable period, is liable to be vitiated by the alterations which are made in the Bank's rate of discount. For example, when a Company accepts a contract for the execution of some large work, if the Bank-rate is thereafter greatly lowered, the contractor gains at the cost of the Company. If, on the other hand, the rate is greatly raised, the contractor finds his expected profits swept away,—perhaps himself swept into the Gazette. His profits, unless he be a wealthy man, are all that he has to live

* *Vide supra*, pp. 95-96.

upon: and when these are swept away, he must either starve (an alternative which is not usually preferred) or, by withdrawing money from his business for his own support, become unable to meet his engagements. The effect is equally serious in the wider department of general trade. Our trading and manufacturing classes, in embarking on their enterprises, base their calculations upon the current rate at which bills can be discounted. But if the Bank of England raise its charge greatly and suddenly—as it has often done—they find that they have to pay double what they reasonably expected for the ordinary advances of trade. Or rather, as the discounting of bills is simply the transfer of a certain species of property (like the purchase of a house with entry into possession three months afterwards), they find their property of this kind—and, as we shall see presently, of all other kinds also—suddenly depreciated in value, from no fault of theirs, nor from any act of theirs of any kind.

When gold overflows in the Bank, all sorts of trading are promoted to the uttermost; when gold becomes scarce, they are remorselessly checked. The consequence is, that what is very moderate trading at one time is treated as over-trading at another. What was very slow trading in 1852, is set down as reckless speculation in 1857. In 1852, when the Bank had 22 millions of gold in its vaults, it reduced its rate of discount to 2 per cent, and, by offering money, on such easy terms, tempted all classes of traders to engage in new operations. There are very few kinds of speculation that will not pay when money can be borrowed at 2 per cent; and if the British public, in those years of low discounts, did not rush into all manner of rash and uncalled-for schemes, it was because they knew better what was good for them than the Bank did. In due course the wheel turned round; and, after various fluctuations, in the autumn of 1855 the Bank-rate was raised to 7 per cent,—nearly four times greater than it was two years before. In 1857 we had another series of embarrassing fluctuations: the rate passing from one extreme to the other in the course of a few months. In 1862, we once more had the rate at 2 per cent. And now—as a set-off to the previous very low rate—during the last twelve months we have had the Bank-rate standing at the extremely high point of 8 and 9 per cent.

In short, since 1844, there have been fluctuations in the amount of the currency, and, still more, ceaseless and excessive changes in the rate of discount, such as were unknown under the Act of 1819, and which have produced in a severer form those embarrassments to the country which Sir R. Peel and Mr Goulburn specially desired to prevent.*

* The feature of our present monetary system which has been described in the preceding paragraphs long ago attracted the attention of the author; and by a consideration of it, in connection with

Very low rates of discount—such as 2 per cent—are hardly to be desired even as a means of promoting trade; for this reason among others,* that as they are certain to be succeeded by much higher ones, they tempt traders to embark in enterprises

* See also pp. 277-80.

the political aspect of the times, he was enabled, in the spring of 1855, to predict the monetary difficulties which overtook this country in the concluding months of that year,—as well as the precise form in which the difficulty arose. In the middle of April, the Bank-rate, which had been falling for the previous twelve months, was reduced to 4 per cent—which the author regarded as a "low rate of discount for times of war," seeing that we had to export specie for our army abroad. And, in exposition of the policy of the Bank, and of the results which might be expected to ensue from it, he wrote as follows:—

"The recent reductions in the rate of discount have been made by the Directors of the Bank of England *in order to get off their reserve-notes;* and the process of reduction *will be continued until they succeed in their object.* [It was reduced to 3½ in eight weeks afterwards.] Thus tempted, the mercantile class will come forward and take off the notes of the Bank, for the sake of engaging in enterprises which, but for the low rate of monetary accommodation, they would not have ventured upon. . . . But suppose that a bad harvest comes, and we have to increase our imports by large purchases of grain, which we have to pay for in so many millions of bullion,—or suppose we have *to pay large subsidies to foreign Powers, or have to leave the provisioning, &c., of our army to be obtained by purchase in a foreign country,*—then, all those disbursements being made in *gold*, the amount of that metal in the Bank of England will be greatly diminished. The Directors (in order to comply with the Act of 1844, which requires that the paper-circulation shall be diminished as the gold diminishes) must then 'put on the screw,' by imposing a high rate of discount. [Between the 7th September and 20th October the Bank-rate was *doubled.*] The effect of this is, of course, to check mercantile enterprise. But it does more than this: it not only prevents new enterprises being undertaken, but it *will bring ruin upon many of the speculations which are going on.* These spec-

which will not pay in ordinary times, and which must end in failure should the Bank, before their completion, return to its ordinary rate. But there is a great distinction to be made in considering the practical effects of an exceptionally low rate, and of an excep-

ulations may be perfectly sound and justifiable; they may be such as, in ordinary circumstances, would have returned a handsome profit to their projectors; but the sudden and great rise in the rate of discount will at once blast them with disaster. It does so in two ways. Suppose that the speculation be a cargo of foreign goods for this country; and suppose that, before the ship conveying them reaches our shores, the scarcity of money produced by the Bank-regulations has lowered the price of such goods in the market; then it follows that the enterprise may prove wholly abortive, in consequence of the price obtained by the merchant falling far short of that which he had calculated on as sufficient to remunerate him for the speculation. Or, suppose the merchant not a millionaire (as comparatively few are), and suppose the banks put on the screw and urge him for repayment of [or rather, refuse to renew] their advances, or decline to discount his bills except at impossible rates, while his speculation is still in progress; then he may be forced into the bankrupt-list, although, but for those proceedings, he would have remained perfectly solvent. A speculation cut short in the midst, however good it may be, is necessarily unprofitable; and the procedure of the Bank in such cases is *like setting men to sow and not allowing them to reap*."—*Edinburgh Advertiser*, 17*th April* 1855.

Before the end of 1855, the scarcity of money became so great that an Order in Council was passed directing the Bank to issue nearly half a million of notes (£475,000), unsecured by coin—this being the amount of lapsed issues of country banks which the Bank was conditionally authorised by the Act of 1844 to replace. And in spite of this, the export of specie in Government loans and for the supply of our army, proved so embarrassing that it became a matter of discussion in the newspapers, and in political circles, whether an issue of £1-notes should not be had recourse to,—in order to allow our sovereigns to go abroad, and at the same time provide an adequate currency for domestic purposes.

tionally high one. The effects upon trade of a very low rate of discount are permissive; the effects of a very high one (such as the Bank adopts during a drain of gold) are, virtually, compulsory. Prudence on the part of our traders may, and to a great extent does, prevent any over-trading arising from the Bank's exceptionally low rates. But no prudence will suffice to prevent loss when the Bank resorts to the very high rates such as of late years it has frequently enforced.

DEPRESSION OF THE MARKETS.

These high rates have a double effect. They affect sales as well as loans. They alter prices, as well as the terms of monetary accommodation. Through them the markets are depressed; and the whole goods and property in the country are temporarily depreciated to a serious extent. The amount of sales which goes on, and must go on, at all times is very great; and upon all of these, when the Bank-rate is at 9 per cent, the holders of the goods lose heavily. It is upon the import-trade that these losses fall most heavily. It takes months before an order for cotton, for flax, for Australian wool, and foreign produce generally, can be executed; and when the Bank-rate is greatly raised in the period between the giving of the order and the arrival of the goods, the importer finds all his calculations falsified, and instead of a profit reaps only loss. Moreover, at such times merchants have to force sales. Very few of them, however wealthy, can afford to hold back, and wait for better times. Their whole capital (as the best means of employing it) is embarked in their business; and they must send their goods to market, in order to obtain means to pay for the produce which they have imported. On the other hand, their customers, having to pay high rates for the usual trade-accommodation (*i. e.*, for the discount of the bills by which trade is carried on), naturally curtail their business: they stop buying altogether, or only bid at extremely reduced prices. In this way, during a season of monetary pressure, the holders of stocks of goods have to force sales; while at the same time, and from the same cause, there are few buyers. In consequence, a great fall in prices takes place.

THE LOSSES OF TRADERS.

Thus the mercantile classes suffer in a twofold manner from a great rise in the Bank-rate. They have to pay, it may be, a double price in order to get their bills discounted; and also, in consequence of the depressed state of the markets, they lose 15, 20, or even 25 per cent on their sales of goods. As a considerable portion of the import-trade is conducted by means of large orders—a whole cargo of goods being sometimes ordered by a single firm,—a fall of 15 per cent in the home markets necessarily produces heavy embarrassment, and in some cases actual failure. Say that a firm sends out an order to India for £100,000 worth of cotton, or to the West Indies or Brazil for a like amount of sugar, and that, owing to a rise in the Bank-rate, the market price of these goods falls 15 per cent before they can be sold in this country; then the importing-merchant will suffer an unexpected loss of £15,000. It is not every firm that can stand such a loss; but in some cases the loss is still heavier. Instead of £15,000, the loss on this single transaction may be £25,000. In November 1857, as we have shown,* the depreciation of goods amounted to 27 per cent in the course of a single fortnight; in which case the loss of the importer on £100,000 worth of goods would be £27,000. And in some cases the depreciation of goods from this cause is even greater.

FAILURES AND THEIR CONSEQUENCE.

Hence it is that so many failures take place whenever the Bank-rate is raised to 9 or 10 per cent. Instead of profits, our importing firms reap crushing losses. These firms, in many cases, fall by no fault of their own; and each one, as it suspends payment, becomes the centre of fresh embarrassments to others. Failures and suspensions multiply; distrust spreads; no one is sure of his customer's bill; credit is contracted; notes are demanded in payment instead of bills; and to meet this new requirement the Bank's reserve of notes is largely drawn upon.——What follows? Under the present system, as the reserve of notes is diminished, the Bank still further raises its rate: the markets

* See footnote, p. 191.

become still further depressed; still greater losses are sustained by the merchants; distrust is swelled into panic; and, with the country strewed in ruins, the Bank itself becomes helpless. Then the Government has to come to its aid—by suspending the Act which arbitrarily limits its power of issue. Thereafter the public get the extra supply of notes which they want, and which are indispensable to them in seasons when distrust nullifies the ordinary forms of credit. The panic is stopped as if by magic: the evil goes no further. But so many firms have fallen—so many more have escaped only with heavy loss—that trade is paralysed for several months afterwards; and so many thousands of the working-classes are thrown out of employment, that all classes of the community have good reason to remember the calamity. This is a sadly different result from that contemplated by Sir Robert Peel, who, in his speech when introducing the Bank Act, expressed his desire thereby "to ensure the reward of industry, and the legitimate profit of commercial enterprise."

ON WHOM DO THE LOSSES FALL?

The startling doctrine has been held, that these great calamities entail no loss upon the country. "If the aggregate loss had reached £100,000,000," it was said in 1857, "the country would not be a single pound the poorer." To a certain extent this is true. Supposing (which is not correct*) that foreigners do not at such times

* *Vide infra*, pp. 232-3.

become purchasers of our depreciated goods and stocks, the losses of one portion of the community are balanced by the gains of another. What is lost by the sellers is gained by the buyers. So far, there is no national loss of wealth. Nevertheless there is a national calamity. Immense losses are experienced by certain classes; and it is poor comfort for those suffering classes to be told that another class has grown richer upon their spoils. Even if we look at the matter as a mere case of wealth transferred, the question arises, From whom, and to whom, does this transference of wealth take place? Is it not *from* the industrious producing classes, who have their all invested in business; and *to* the great capitalists, who have their funds lying ready to pick up the countless good bargains which every crisis forces into the market? It is simple truth to say, that, in every monetary crisis, the purchase of the depreciated goods and shares of the mercantile class goes to swell the fortunes of a few millionaires: of men who do not invest their capital in trade, but who, as money-dealers, keep it in hand on the outlook for good bargains. These "hard speculators," as the *Times* calls them, "prudently reserve their gold" when they see a season of difficulty approaching (thereby still further tightening the money-market), in order to secure great prizes amidst the general wreck. We make no objection to such conduct. The world moves on by every one attending to his own interests. At the same time, we think that every transference of wealth, occasioned by such monetary convulsions, is greatly to be deplored, —from whatever class it be taken, and to whatever class it be transferred. We have as little satisfaction in seeing the wealth of the trading-classes swept off into the hands of the great capitalists, as we would have in seeing the mills and machinery of Lancashire suddenly transferred, during some convulsion, from the manufacturers to the operatives.

But these monetary crises do inflict loss upon the country, and that to a most serious degree. In the year following the crisis of 1857, our trade, as evidenced by the aggregate of imports and exports, fell off to the extent of thirty millions sterling.* And as the average annual increase of our trade for the last ten years has been fully fifteen millions, the diminution caused by that crisis was nearly fifty millions —equal to 18 per cent of our amount of trade at that time. The loss thus occasioned to the country fell alike upon the employers and the employed: the former making less profits, and the latter getting less wages or employment.† So much wealth had been

PARALYSIS OF TRADE.

* See "Our Nilometer," given in next chapter.

† In December 1857, the return of the state of employment in 236 factories and workshops in Manchester, showed that, of the whole number of these establishments, only 54 were working full time with a full complement of hands,—50 were working full time with less than their full complement,—109 were on short time,—and 23 were stopped altogether. Of the workpeople usually employed

withdrawn from the trading-classes, their position had been so enfeebled by the crisis, that they were disabled from carrying on their business to the usual extent. And the amount of capital which they had lost, being for the most part invested by its new possessors in the stock and shares of Governments or established companies, gave no impetus to industry to compensate this enfeeblement of the trading and producing classes. Thus, then, it is evident that our monetary crises do inflict a heavy loss upon the country; and also, that the wealth transferred at such seasons is employed with less profit to the country by its new owners than by those from whom it has been taken.

Under the present system, the action of the Bank, by alternate fits, increases and diminishes the currency —expands and contracts credit. When the currency is abundant, the Bank increases it; when credit is easy, it expands it still more. Again, when money becomes scarce, the action of the Bank makes it scarcer; and when credit is contracted, it contracts it still further, and eventually destroys it.

To ordinary minds this seems a strange procedure. It seems a singularly perverse course that the Bank,

WHY IS THIS?

which has been constituted the great fountain and reservoir of the national currency, instead of regulating the flow in accordance with the

in these factories, only 15,498 were on full time,—21,766 were on short time,—and 9185 were wholly out of employment.

requirements of the country, should open its sluices widest when the supply is least needed, and should contract them in seasons when, from a temporary cause, a free supply is indispensable to the wellbeing of the community. It may seem strange that an establishment which was instituted at first for the very purpose of supplying, by means of its notes, a temporary deficiency of specie, should, whenever such a deficiency occurs nowadays, see in it a reason for withholding its usual supply of notes.* The first effect of the establishment of the Bank in 1694 was to bring down the rate of interest; why should it now reverse its character and functions, and, by means of its high rates, make England the dearest country in Europe for money?

* When William III. ascended the throne, the whole amount of metallic money in this country did not exceed £7,000,000. The war which followed with the Grand Monarque necessitated the export of a portion of this specie for the support of our army in the Netherlands, till in 1694 the Government found it impossible to obtain a further supply. Then it was that the Bank of England was established; and its first act, in compliance with its charter, was to lend £1,200,000 (nearly one-fifth of the entire specie then in the country) to the Government,—issuing its notes (convertible into coin on demand) to replace the amount of metallic money thus withdrawn. In regard to the effect of the new establishment upon the rate of interest, Mr Godfrey, Deputy-Governor of the Bank, stated, that whereas in the beginning of 1694 the Government tallies (a sort of exchequer bills) were at a discount of £25 to £30 per cent, in addition to the interest which they carried, the Bank took them at par, and from the former heavy discount they rose in 1694 to a premium. Mr Godfrey also entertained the hope that the establishment of the Bank would suffice, in the course of a few years, to reduce the rate of interest throughout the country to 3 per cent.

But there are two sides to every question; and the following are the grounds upon which the present system is supported.

In the first place—as a broad general basis for the present system—it is maintained in many quarters that an export of the precious metals is a loss of capital, a diminution of the country's wealth. And upon this hypothesis the following reasoning is based:—An export of gold being a loss of capital, the wealth of the country is thereby diminished; and therefore it is only reasonable that our merchants and others who require to obtain in loan a portion of that capital should pay a higher price for it—*i.e.*, by a rise in the rate of discount. Accepting for a moment this hypothesis, let us see what it is worth. The income of our upper and middle classes alone, as represented by the income-tax returns, amounts to 350 millions sterling a-year. And the actual *profits* of the nation—the increase made annually to the capital of the country—amounts to about 130 millions.* Compared to this, what is the 4 or 5 millions to which our occasional drains of gold for export† amount? Supposing

"LOSS OF CAPITAL" THEORY.

* This is the conclusion at which the *Economist* arrives, after a careful examination of the matter in a series of articles published at the end of last year. A very large deduction from this estimate may be made without in any way affecting our argument.

† Drains of gold from the Bank are not necessarily for export. On all occasions when a monetary crisis culminates in a panic, we

such exports did represent a loss of capital, what would it amount to? It would not be a diminution of the national wealth at all, but simply an insignificant deduction from its increase. At the end of the year in which such loss of four or five millions took place, the capital of the country would be £125,000,000 greater than at the beginning. In fact, before any diminution of the national wealth can take place, the country must experience a loss, not of four or five millions, but of upwards of a hundred millions.

CASE OF ENGLAND IN 1862.

For example, in 1862, when, in consequence of the extraordinarily bad harvest, we paid nearly twice as much as usual for foreign corn, this deduction from our annual profits produced no actual diminution of the national wealth, even though we had to encounter at the same time the dreadful calamity of the Cotton-dearth. Take 1859 as an average year by which, as a standard, we may test the relative loss (*i.e.*, diminution of profits) which the country underwent in 1862. In 1859 our imports of corn amounted to 18 millions,—in 1862 they amounted to 38 millions: an extra expenditure to the country of 20 millions sterling. In the former year the value of our exported cotton goods was 48 millions,—in the latter year it was only 36 millions. Moreover, as the profits of manufacture bear a nearly

may safely reckon that two or three millions are withdrawn from the Bank of England to meet the requirements of the other banks.

fixed proportion to the quantity of the work done, quite irrespective of the price of the raw material, the quantity of cotton spun or woven is a better test of these profits than the value of the manufactured goods, which necessarily includes the cost of the raw material (which in 1862 was treble what it was in 1859). Now, as the total quantity of cotton imported in 1862 was only one-half of what was imported in 1859, the profits on the manufacture of it must have fallen to a nearly similar extent. To this loss (which it is impossible to estimate with correctness) add the extra 20 millions sterling paid for foreign corn; and then the magnitude of the relative loss sustained by the country in 1862 will become abundantly evident. Nevertheless, even though that loss amounted to £40,000,000, the realised wealth at the end of the year must have been much greater than at the beginning. How absurd, then, to suppose that a drain of four or five millions of gold produces a diminution of the country's wealth, and makes capital scarce: when, in fact, such a sum is not a twentieth part of the new wealth that is every year being added to our capital.

So much for the hypothesis, even if it were well founded. But it is radically unsound. An export of gold is not necessarily, nor usually, a loss at all. It is like the paying of money in wages, or in purchase; comparatively seldom is it

WHY GOLD GOES ABROAD.

a payment of debt. In the case of a bad harvest, or of a great war, the export of gold requisite to meet such emergencies is unquestionably a loss of the national capital,—or at least a deduction from the yearly increase of that capital. But, more frequently, an export of the precious metals is produced by other causes than these. Generally such an export takes place simply for the purchase of raw materials,—the manufacture of which not merely sustains the industry, but adds to the profits, of the country. Frequently, also, it takes place for the purpose of employing a portion of our yearly gains in remunerative investments abroad,—for example, in the guaranteed stock of Indian railways, or suchlike undertakings: and in these cases likewise the country derives a profit from the transaction. Hence the hypothesis that an export of gold is a loss of national wealth is essentially unsound. We might as well call the export of our iron or cotton goods "a loss of capital." It is not a diminution of capital that is occasioned by exports of gold, but a diminution of currency. Or rather—merely of that portion of our currency which is needed for making payments abroad, in those exceptional cases when there is a lack of bills of exchange, and when, also, it is not profitable for our merchants to make such payments by an export of goods.*

* See further, pp. 237-8, and also our remarks on the movements of the precious metals in next chapter.

Hence, whatever be the reason for very high rates of discount, at seasons when there is a drain of gold from the Bank, they are not occasioned by any diminution of the national wealth or capital. Usually (as we have shown) an export of gold is simply a means of increasing the amount of the national wealth; and in absolutely no case does it diminish the amount of that capital. In fact, great gains may be accompanied by an export of the precious metals; and such an export may be indispensable to their realisation. An export of gold may be, and generally is, nothing more than a small portion of our yearly savings sent abroad in order to make new investments,—or to get the materials for more employment and trade, and more gains to all classes of our people.

Moreover, if a loss of capital were really the cause of these high rates, how did it happen that in 1862 the Bank-rate was so low? In that year, partly from a bad harvest, and partly from the calamitous Cotton-dearth, the country experienced a greater loss than in any year within the memory of the present generation. Nevertheless the Bank-rate in that year stood at the lowest point which has ever been witnessed—namely, at 2 per cent. During the first six months of 1862 it stood at 2½ per cent, and in the autumn it fell to 2. Or take another case of recent experience. At the close of last year there was a monetary crisis in India—so severe that

CASE OF INDIA IN 1863.

prices were reduced 27 per cent. The opium, which, according to a low estimate made by Sir Charles Trevelyan, ought to have sold at 1400 rupees a chest, only brought 879. We need not say that the wealth of India is rapidly on the increase,—that it was no "loss of capital" which occasioned this extraordinary fall of prices. We may add, it was still less a loss of capital produced by export of the precious metals (which the theory we are now considering regards as the cause of our high rates and low prices),—for at that very time, and for years before, the precious metals had been pouring into India in prodigious quantity.*

* The quantity of the precious metals which had been imported into India during the previous ten years (*i.e.*, since 1st July 1853), is stated by Sir Charles Trevelyan as follows:—

1853-54,	£4,871,956
1854-55,	2,028,258
1855-56,	11,301,288
1856-57,	14,413,698
1857-58,	15,814,359
1858-59,	12,817,070
1859-60,	16,356,963
1860-61,	10,679,350
1861-62,	14,809,350
1862-63,	20,523,459

So purely artificial was the late monetary crisis in India, that merchants in Calcutta who had large sums in gold in their possession could not get *money* (*i.e.*, legal currency) from the Bank, either in exchange for, or upon the security of, this gold. The same thing would happen during a monetary crisis in this country, to merchants who had large sums in silver. We may add, that during the crisis in Calcutta the Government had some fifteen millions of silver-money (the standard-money of India) lying in its Treasuries —furnishing the amplest security for the convertibility of the extra

We need not carry our exposure of this "loss of capital" theory any further. If the charge for money on loan depends simply (as this theory supposes) upon the amount of a country's capital, then surely in England—the wealthiest and most orderly of countries, and the most advanced in monetary economy—the Bank-rate should be lower than in any other place in the world.

"LOANABLE CAPITAL."

With less of error, but with equal unsoundness of data, it may be alleged that our high rates of discount are caused by a diminution of the "loanable" capital of the country,—which is but a small portion, a mere fraction, of our aggregate wealth. In one sense every kind of property is loanable. A man may lend his farm or his house, and get interest for it in the shape of rent. A carriage, or a horse, or a piano may be loaned, and interest received in the shape of hire. But by "loanable capital" is meant the spare wealth of our people which is deposited in the banks.* Let us see, then, if there are any fluctuations

note-issues which were then required, but which, in obedience to a legalised crotchet, were rigidly withheld. It is in this way that communities make miseries for themselves.

* These Deposits are a source of credit, but only a very small portion of them exists in the form of Money. They are a kind of ledger-wealth,—representing real property, but which cannot be all converted into money at once. Money is the instrument by which these bank-deposits are effected and accumulated; but the money, as soon as paid in, is sent on its travels again, and may be employed in succession to make new deposits. Cheques also are largely used for this purpose. It may safely be stated that

in the amount of this loanable capital which will account for the variations in the Bank-rate. The returns of the London joint-stock banks and of the Bank of England may be taken as a fair indication of the general increase or decrease of banking-deposits throughout the country; and we have compiled the following statement from the balance-sheets of these banks* during the last nine years:—

	Deposits.		Total of these Deposits.	Variations of the Bank-rate during the previous half-year.
	Joint-stock Banks.	Bank of England.		
	£	£	£	
1856 June 30.	34,491,000	15,514,000	50,005,000	6, 5, 4½
1856 Dec. 31.	33,408,000	17,633,000	51,041,000	4½, 6 & 7, 7, 6½, 7
1857 June	31,796,000	17,427,529	59,223,000	6, 6½, 6
1857 Dec.	40,809,000	23,116,000	63,925,000	6, 5½, 6, 7, 8, 9 & 10, 8
1858 June	38,253,000	20,597,000	58,850,000	8, 6, 5, 4, 3½, 3
1858 Dec.	37,254,000	22,709,000	59,963,000	3, 2½
1859 June	38,957,000	22,812,000	61,769,000	2½, 3½, 4½, 3½, 3
1859 Dec.	38,787,000	22,876,000	61,663,000	3, 2½
1860 June	40,789,000	21,081,000	61,870,000	2½, 3, 4, 4½, 5, 4½, 4
1860 Dec.	43,098,000	19,334,000	62,432,000	4, 4½, 5, 6, 5, 6
1861 June	46,855,000	19,670,000	66,525,000	6, 7, 8, 7, 6, 5, 6
1861 Dec.	50,606,000	20,400,000	71,006,000	6, 5, 4½, 4, 3½, 3
1862 June	50,478,000	23,028,000	73,506,000	3, 2½, 3
1862 Dec.	50,192,000	22,961,000	73,153,000	3, 2½, 2, 3
1863 June	59,042,000	24,089,000	74,131,000	3, 4, 5, 4, 3½, 3, 3½, 4
1863 Dec.	63,198,000	23,863,000	87,061,000	4, 5, 6, 7, 8, 7
1864 June	74,833,000	23,013,000	97,846,000	7, 8, 7, 6, 7, 8, 9, 8, 7, 6

the amount of Money, whether in the form of specie or of paper-money, actually existing in the banks of the United Kingdom (the Bank of England excepted), is not more than one-fifteenth part of their deposits. Of specie, whether in the form of coins or bullion, the aggregate stock held by the banks of the United Kingdom (the Bank of England included) is not more than £20,000,000; whereas the Deposits amount to about twenty times as much. The "loanable money" of the country, therefore, bears only a very small proportion to the amount of the "loanable capital." Money and Capital (however some theorists may confound them) are very different things: the use of the former being simply to transfer, and in a small degree to store up, the latter.

* Namely, the London and Westminster, the London Joint-Stock,

There is no indication of loss of capital, or diminution of loanable capital, here. On the contrary, these statistics show a steady and remarkable increase of the capital available for loans and discounts. Since June 1856, the amount of this capital has actually doubled. The only year in which there is a marked decrease is in 1858; and all through that year the Bank-rate, instead of rising, was steadily falling. The variations of the Bank-rate, as will be seen, do not correspond in any way with the variations of the amount of loanable capital. For example, in 1857, when the great monetary crisis occurred, the loanable capital in the possession of the banks was 20 per cent larger than in the previous year; and 3½ per cent larger than in the year following, when the rate was lowered to 3 and 2½ per cent. Again, during the last twelve months, for the greater part of which time the Bank-rate has been kept at 7, 8, and 9 per cent, the amount of loanable capital has been fully 25 per cent larger than in 1862, when the rate was only 2½ and 2 per cent.

The theory of "loss of capital," therefore, whether in its wider or its narrower form, is contradicted at all points by the testimony of experience and facts. Evidently there must be some other reason than this for the high rates of discount which are imposed by

the Union, the London and County, the City Bank, and the Bank of London—these being the only ones of the present joint-stock banks in the metropolis which were established prior to 1856.

the Bank at times when a portion of our gold is being exported.

SCARCITY OF MONEY.

The real explanation of these high rates is, not that there is less capital than before, but because there is a deficiency in the means of transferring it. It is not Capital that is diminished, but Money. Money is the chief medium by which loans of capital are made*—by which property of all kinds is transferred; and it is a deficiency of this medium which is occasioned (under Act of 1844) when the Bank's stock of gold is reduced. Nothing more. We do not here discuss whether the Bank, under the present system, does not unnecessarily aggravate this deficiency of money; or whether, but for the Bank Act, there need be any such deficiency at all. We need not observe that although a want of Capital cannot be supplied, a want of Money may. We simply desire clearly to point out that the cause of the high Bank-rate, at times when there is a drain of gold, is a temporary deficiency of Money,—a temporary lack of the medium by which Capital is transferred, whether in loan or in purchase, and one of the forms in which Credit is given. This point being established, a great

* It is not the *only* medium,—for bills and cheques are largely employed for this purpose in ordinary times. But in seasons of commercial failures and distrust, these latter instruments of exchange fall into temporary disrepute, and their place must be supplied to a considerable extent by an increased use of Money, in the form of Bank of England notes.

deal of irrelevant matter is at once eliminated from the discussion, and the subject begins to narrow to a definite and intelligible point.

High rates of discount, indeed, are also enforced by the Bank upon a different ground from this, and under quite different circumstances: *i.e.*, when there is no drain of gold at all, but simply an increase of the requirements of the public for notes—for the instrument of exchange which it is the special function of banks of issue to provide. This feature of our monetary system will be dealt with by-and-by. Meanwhile, for the sake of clearness, we shall pursue our exposition of the Bank's action during a drain of gold for export,—the object of that action—and the practical consequences of it.

Under the Bank Act, whenever a drain of gold occurs, a scarcity of Money is produced. How, then, are these occasional and temporary deficiencies of our currency treated? The principle adopted by the Bank in these cases has been briefly and clearly stated thus:—"To restrain the efflux of gold abroad, and to encourage its influx." To accomplish this object, the Bank raises its rate of discount. And the effect of this operation is as follows:—

HOW THE BANK RESTRAINS THE EXPORT OF GOLD.

There is always a large amount of bills of exchange payable in London, in the hands of foreign merchants; and there is also a large amount of bills payable in foreign countries held by our own merchants. These bills usually neutralise one another. That is to say, an English merchant who has to make payments in Paris and Calcutta, instead of sending specie, goes on 'Change, and purchases from other English merchants an amount of bills which they hold on those cities equal to the sum which he has to pay; and then forwards these bills to his creditors in Paris and Calcutta, who obtain payment from their fellow-merchants there, upon whom the bills are drawn. Foreign merchants in similar fashion discharge the payments which they have to make in England: that is to say, they purchase from their brother merchants a certain amount of bills payable in London, and forward these bills to their English creditor, who thereupon obtains the amount from the merchants by whom the bills are payable. This is the course followed in ordinary times. But, if it is more advantageous for him, an English merchant may forward to Paris and Calcutta the bills which he holds upon these cities, and order the amount to be sent to him in specie; and a foreign merchant, if it is advantageous for him to do so, may in like manner forward his bills upon London, get them discounted there, and withdraw the amount in specie. But if the rate of discount be very high in London, the foreign merchant is sometimes deterred from sending over his bills to be discounted, and, rather than pay so high a charge for the ready money, may prefer not to discount his bills at all, and wait till they fall due. When he does so, the object of the Bank of England in raising its rate is attained. The payment, it is true, must be made all the same. All that the Bank effects is to cause a postponement of the payment,—by deterring the foreign merchant from discounting his bills in the usual course. Thus "the efflux of gold is restrained," so far as foreigners are concerned. The English merchant is in like manner restrained. He never thinks of sending specie to make his payments abroad unless as a necessity or for a profit: that is to say, unless when he cannot get bills of exchange upon the particular place where his payment has to be made, —and when also, owing to a temporary depression in the markets of that place, it is more profitable for him (not having bills) to send gold than to send goods.* By raising its rate, the Bank seeks to destroy his advantage in sending specie, by making this mode of payment more unprofitable for him than the other—*i.e.*, by exporting goods. Thus the raising of the Bank-rate tends to "restrain the efflux of gold abroad."

It also tends to "encourage the influx of gold." But in accomplishing this part of its object, the rise of the

* If a merchant sends goods abroad, he at once becomes possessed of a bill of exchange, payable by the party to whom the goods are consigned, which he (the exporting merchant) can forward to his foreign creditor in the same place.

Bank-rate operates in a different way. It produces its effect by depressing the home market, and causing a fall of prices. It acts upon our produce-markets, upon the Funds, and upon English shares and stocks of all kinds.* By so doing, it induces foreign capitalists to make purchases of our temporarily depreciated goods. A French or American capitalist, for example, at such seasons finds he can purchase foreign produce cheaper in our markets than he can get it in the countries from which it has been brought. The produce of all countries is to be found in our markets. We have at all times on hand a large stock of sugar, of cotton, of flax, of tea, coffee, &c.; and when a great fall of prices takes place, foreign merchants supply themselves with these goods from our markets. In like manner, when the shares, bonds, and debentures of our railways and other joint-stock companies, and securities of all kinds, become similarly depreciated, foreign capitalists become purchasers of them at a corresponding profit. Say that foreigners make purchases of this kind to the amount of a million sterling. Then a million of their money comes to this country—of course, in the form of specie: and the object of the Bank is accomplished. But what does this operation amount to? We have got a million of money more, and have parted with a million's worth of property. So far

AND ENCOURAGES ITS IMPORT.

* See *supra*, pp. 211-12.

the exchange is even. But on what terms has the exchange been effected? That depends upon the extent to which our markets have been depressed. During the monetary crisis of 1857, as we have shown,* the fall of prices in our produce markets amounted to upwards of 25 per cent. In our share-market (consols and some other prime securities excepted) the depreciation amounted to about 15 per cent. At such a time, if foreign capitalists made purchases to the amount of a million sterling, say one-half in goods and the other half in shares, we should have experienced a loss of capital to the extent of £200,000.

This is a heavy price to pay for "encouraging the influx of gold." The Bank thereby obtains a million more of gold to place in its vaults; but the country, in paying for this gold with its goods, experiences a loss of two hundred thousand pounds,—a sum equal to double the annual savings of the nation in 1857. In short, for every sovereign that in this way is added to the Bank's stock of specie, the country pays twenty-four shillings. This is called "correcting the exchanges." Considering the many failures and widespread commercial embarrassment which attend such depreciations of the property of the country, it would really be much better for us to purchase gold abroad at this price—*i.e.*, giving 24s.

WHAT IT COSTS THE COUNTRY.

* *Vide supra*, footnote, p. 191; and also, for the depreciation in 1836-7, see footnote, p. 188.

for every £1—than to continue our present system. Yet what would be thought of the matter if it were put in this form?

This is a very costly method of upholding our monetary system. The Bank, indeed, loses nothing by it.

WHAT THE BANK GAINS.

On the contrary, every rise of the rate of discount increases the profits of the Bank. Its dividends, like those of our banks generally, are *now* largest when the country suffers most from monetary embarrassment. To the community, the injury is twofold. There is, first, the national injury—the loss of capital occasioned by a transference of a portion of our goods, when exceptionally depreciated, to foreign capitalists. Secondly, there is the injury to individuals,—to certain classes of our people to the profit of others: the sweeping away (what the late Sir Robert Peel respected so much) "the legitimate profits of industry,"—the loss of reputation to solvent firms which are forced to suspend,—and the bankruptcy of others who, but for the depreciation of their goods caused by the tightness of the money-market, would have been able to meet all their engagements, and to continue their business as usual.

These are great evils. How far is it necessary that the country should undergo them? Before answering this question, let us see how long the gold thus exported—either as a matter of State necessity, or as a means of obtaining profit and employment for our people—remains abroad. Is it lost to us?—or is it so long of returning that we must act as if it were lost to us?

TEMPORARY NATURE OF DRAINS.

Any one who has watched, either in his own experience or as recorded in our annals, the ebb and flow of the precious metals, must have been struck with the fact that the drains of specie which occasionally take place are very transitory. A few months, sometimes a few weeks, is the ordinary limit of their duration. In most cases, the gold simply does its work, and returns. In the great crisis of 1857, the whole amount of specie sent from this country to the United States, in the two months preceding the suspension of the Bank Act, was £1,125,000; and before the expiry of two months afterwards (during which time the Bank Act had been suspended, the note-issues enlarged, and the rate reduced to 5 per cent), we had not only got back from America all that we had sent thither, but nearly three times as much—namely, £3,200,000. In fact, an export of gold suffices to annihilate the causes which produce it. It is the very thing that is required to restore the temporarily-disturbed equilibrium, and it "rectifies the exchanges" of itself. Unless in the highly exceptional time of a great war, such as that which we waged with the first Napoleon,—when we had to make vast loans and subsidies to foreign Powers, and had to send abroad, year after year, large sums in specie for the support of our army in the field,—an export of five or six millions of gold suffices to stop any drain, by meeting all the requirements which occasion it. These requirements are occasioned simply by a temporary deficiency of bills,—owing to the payments (it may be *bonus*) which we have to make to some particular country being in excess of the ordinary amount, and also to the condition of the markets of that country being simultaneously such as renders it unprofitable for our merchants to export thither an extra quantity of goods. The export of gold at once puts an end to this exceptional deficiency of bills: it acts instead of bills of exchange—in supplement of our deficient supply of them,—and restores the normal equilibrium.

The cotton-crisis of 1862 was the most extensive derangement of our commercial relations which has ever occurred, and it is hardly possible to conceive a greater. Such a transference of a great branch of our trade from a country (the United States) with which we traded largely, to others which took from us little of our goods, necessitated payments in specie to an unusual extent in carrying on that branch of trade. Yet, after all—thanks to the energy and enterprise of our merchants,—the drain of specie which it occasioned never assumed really formidable proportions. As regards India, that sink of the precious metals—to which the greater part of our cotton trade was transferred,—although the specie which we send thither does not return to us, our trade with that country commensurately increases, yielding increased profits to our merchants. And moreover, by manufacturing the raw materials we obtain from thence, and exporting them, we obtain from other countries (notably from Australia) a supply of the precious metals equal to the amount which we have sent to India.

In the ordinary course of commerce, or of financial operations, the gold which we send to other countries quickly returns to us. We repeat,—it simply does its work (makes a payment) and comes back to us. The movements of gold, in fact, are like those of a cheque which is never cancelled. The man to whom gold is paid can make no profit by keeping it. He passes it on to another, who for the same reason acts likewise, and so on,—the gold sufficing to make payments, as a cheque does, and, like a cheque, having no other use. A man may, indeed, encrust the walls of his room with gold-coins, or he may paper it with a choice selection of bank-notes of different countries,—and it is hard to say which of these modes of decoration would be the better-looking, or the more insane. But the public votes him a lunatic, for employing the instruments of purchase in a way that purchases nothing. If a man pays another with a bill of exchange, the

MOVEMENTS OF SPECIE.

receiver may keep it for several months,—for it is equivalent to an interest-bearing security; but no one keeps gold or cheques, for they are sterile. Gold is profitless unless it circulate: to circulate is its grand use and its normal habit. And as it circulates, flitting from country to country, making payments or purchases, and circling back again, a momentary ebb of the precious metal may occur in one country while a plethora is produced in another. But this is merely transitory—a state of unstable equilibrium which is over in a few weeks' time. Why, then, should these temporary ebbs of gold put us in a flutter? And yet, when they occur, we actually allow them to shake down our whole fabric of trade and industry.

INTERNAL DRAINS.

In order to check these merely temporary ebbs of gold, the Bank adopts measures which not only (as we have shown) inflict serious injury upon the country, but also which in many cases imperil its own position. In trying to stop an external drain upon its resources, it produces an internal one. The means which the Bank employs to check a drain upon its gold for export, are such as inevitably create an increased demand for both gold and notes at home. It does so in this way. By raising the Bank-rate to 9 or 10 per cent, a great fall of prices is produced in the home markets, occasioning heavy losses to the holders of produce and goods of all kinds. Many failures take place; distrust spreads; notes in many cases are required in payment, instead of bills or cheques; and hence a drain of notes takes place upon the Bank. A drain for notes, under our present system, is as fatal to the Bank as a drain for gold.* And the more the Bank raises its rate, in order to check this demand for its notes, the more numerous become the failures, the more widespread becomes the distrust, and the greater the drain upon its reserve of notes. And also of gold,—because many of the banks, in order to meet the panic, have to provide themselves with a larger supply of specie—by cashing their securities, and withdrawing the amount in gold from the Bank. In this way, under the present system, *an external drain inevitably produces an internal drain also,*—which is like lighting a candle at both ends. Indeed, during the last crisis (1857), the amount of gold withdrawn from the Bank of England to meet the internal drain was twice as large as the amount which during the same period was sent abroad; while the Bank's reserve of notes was in like manner encroached upon, owing to the increased demand for money which the Bank's operations had produced in the country.

* As the amount of notes which the Bank is permitted to issue is limited by the amount of gold in its possession, it is all the same whether the demand is for notes or for specie. If the depositor calls for notes, the reserve of notes is, of course, correspondingly lessened; if he calls for gold, the Bank has to cancel notes to an equal amount.

Thus, the crises which ever and anon inflict widespread ruin and suffering amongst us, are mainly of our own making. Temporary difficulties we aggravate into stupendous calamities,—panics and bankruptcies by Act of Parliament. The recipe to produce monetary crises is very simple. They can be made at any time by the action of the Bank. Raise its rate to 8 per cent, and "uneasiness" is produced: markets droop and losses begin. Raise it to 9 per cent: the losses become heavy,—failures and suspensions multiply,—and distrust spreads. Raise it to 10 per cent, and we have a panic and a crash. Or if 10 per cent is not enough, another turn of the screw will do it. The Bank can always "correct the exchanges,"* and ensure a commercial crash, by raising its rate to 10 or 11 per cent.

The principle of restricting the export of the precious metals, which most Governments acted upon in

* The term "favourable" or "unfavourable," applied to the rate of exchange upon foreign countries, is a purely banking phrase. The state of the exchanges, as we have shown (pp. 221-2), has no necessary connection with either gains or losses on the part of a country; it simply indicates a fact—namely, whether more specie is coming in or going out. This is a matter which has nothing to do with the profits of Traders, but it is of great importance to Bankers,—who, when there is a demand for specie, must keep on hand a larger stock of it than usual to meet the requirements of their customers. This causes a temporary diminution of bankers' profits. And hence bankers term the exchanges "favourable" when specie is flowing into the country, and "unfavourable" when it is flowing out. This, and nothing more, is signified by the "state of the exchanges."

medieval times, has been condemned for the last two hundred years. No one would venture nowadays to propose an export-duty on the precious metals. Nevertheless it is only the truth to say that such a frank return to an exploded principle would be wiser, and more advantageous for the community, than the adoption of it in the form which is at present in use. Such an export-duty, rising and falling with the varying amount of specie in the Bank of England—as the rate of discount does at present—would "correct the exchanges" quite as effectually as the present system. And it would have this great advantage, that, without imposing any burden upon those who export the gold, save that to which they are at present subjected, it would relieve the internal currency of the country from the convulsions which now take place so frequently. The few individuals who for their own advantage export the gold, would have to pay for so doing, although not more than they do at present; while the community at large, who are quite content with bank-notes, would not be subjected to an artificial scarcity of these indispensable instruments of exchange. If country is to fight with country, in this barbarous fashion, for possession of the yellow ore, an export-duty is certainly the cheapest way in which we can wage the conflict:—

OPERATION OF AN EXPORT-DUTY.

"Let those who make the quarrel be the only ones who fight."

We say this for the purpose of bringing more clearly into view the real import and working of our monetary system.

SYSTEM OF THE BANK OF FRANCE.

It is worthy of notice that, in times of crisis, the Bank of France adopts a different system from that pursued by the Bank of England. The Bank of England seeks to obtain gold by raising its rate of discount: whereby our whole industry is checked and employment is restricted. The Bank of France, on the other hand, avoids raising its rate to a similar extent,—it refuses to check industry, and subject the community to such a strain; nevertheless, it obtains gold by a process quite as efficient as that adopted by the Bank of England. When the drain upon it is great, it purchases commercial bills upon other countries, as a trader might do, forwards them to be cashed—at London, Vienna, Hamburg—and gets the specie: or it contracts with some great capitalist to do this for it. The difference between the two methods is, that in supplying itself with specie, the one Bank gets high rates of discount, and the other gives them. The Bank of England, in times of crisis, makes a profit at the expense and to the detriment of the community; the Bank of France, at such times, incurs a loss in order to fortify its position and fulfil its engagements. When the Bank of France, keeping its own rate at 7 per cent, buys up bills upon London, where the rate of discount has been raised (we shall say) to 9 per cent,—then the Bank of France loses fully 2 per cent on the bullion which it thus obtains; but the inestimable advantage is attained of sustaining commercial credit, and preserving the national industry from the convulsions of panic and the pressure of exorbitant rates of discount. In either system the remedy is temporary: but so also (it must be remembered) is the drain. The Bank of England seeks to postpone payment by deterring foreigners from discounting their bills upon London. The Bank of France does not adopt this course to the same extent, but seeks to meet the demands that may be made upon it by taking means to obtain a supply of specie. The one Bank throws the burden upon the country; the other takes a large portion of it upon its own shoulders. The Bank of France assumes that those who profit by banking, and by the issue of notes, should bear the expenses incidental to banking. To provide a supply of gold or notes to meet the requirements of its customers, is regarded by the Bank of France as a duty incumbent on itself, and which it must observe, even though it be at a loss. The Bank of England holds the opposite doctrine: it takes no steps to obtain specie, but simply deters its customers (at what cost to the community we have shown) from asking for gold,—or for notes either.

In contemplating the features of our monetary

system which have been passed in review, it is manifest that its operation inflicts serious injury upon the country. This fact does not of itself justify a condemnation of the system. It may be that these losses are unavoidable,—that the sufferance of them is necessary in order to avoid still greater evils. Before determining this point, it must first be clearly understood what is the object which the public desire to attain. What are the great ends which Parliament and the country desire to accomplish by means of monetary legislation? Till this point is settled, all argument is aimless, and discussion is useless. It is impossible to judge of the means, unless we know with precision the end which they are meant to serve. What, then, is the definite object, or objects, of our monetary legislation?

WHAT DOES THE COUNTRY WANT?

There was no ambiguity on this point in the views of the late Sir Robert Peel. As a practical statesman, he had a practical object, a definite end, in view; and he clearly and repeatedly stated it. That object was,—"to ensure the just reward of Industry and the legitimate profit of commercial enterprise."* And we know no better definition of the true aim of monetary legislation. With a view to this end, he desired to prevent severe monetary contraction, because, in his own words, "panic and

PEEL'S OBJECT AND MISTAKE.

* *Vide* his speech on May 6, 1844.

confusion are inseparable from it,"—inflicting heavy losses upon the industrious classes; and, for the same purpose, he desired to prevent "over-issues,"—as these (according to the theory then prevalent), by producing a "depreciation of the currency," imperilled the convertibility of the note, by causing drains of gold for export. Thus, in brief, the object of Sir R. Peel was: to protect legitimate trade from losses inflicted upon it by monetary convulsions, and also to guard the convertibility of the note. The means which he took to ensure the first of these ends, being based upon an erroneous hypothesis, have totally failed. On the other hand, the convertibility of the note has been fully maintained. But when was it in danger? When has the public lost faith in the Bank's notes? Not, certainly, in the experience of this generation, nor of that which preceded it. We have no fear for the credit of these notes,—neither has any sane man in the country. These notes were as safe under the Act of 1819 as under that of 1844. Their value was as unquestioned in 1826 as in 1847. We may say more: the validity of the note was as unquestioned during the crises of 1793 and 1797, as it has been since the passing of the Acts of 1819 and 1844. In the worst monetary crises which have overtaken this country during the last hundred years, so far from the public mistrusting these notes, their great desire has been to get them. And the best proof of this is, that the moment the public got a free supply of these notes, the panic was at an end. These notes have been the very thing which people have made a run upon the Bank to get. It is not gold that is wanted, but discounts — the ordinary accommodation of commerce. Let the public have notes, and that is all they care for. This is proved by the evidence given before every Parliamentary Committee that has investigated the subject.* In disregard of this fact, the Act of 1844 took the most stringent precautions against a danger which never occurs, and totally overlooked a danger which is now more recurrent than ever. In securing the convertibility of the note, the Act only accomplished what was sufficiently effected before; and as regards the great end which its framer had in view, and to which the maintenance of convertibility is an accessory, the Act has failed entirely.

But if the illustrious framer of the Act was mistaken in the means which he employed, there was no mistake or ambiguity as to the object of his monetary legislation. And if we are to act in his spirit, and adhere to the great end which he had in view, we must resume the work where he left off, and profit by the light which subsequent experience has thrown upon the subject. We must ascertain what is the practical mistake which has caused the object of his measure to miscarry; and what are the means by which our mone-

* See "Our Monetary Crises," *supra*, pp. 88-91 and 99-110.

tary legislation may be brought into harmony with the interests of Trade, and be made conducive to ensure to Industry its legitimate profits.

IT IS NOT A CURRENCY DIFFICULTY.

Statesmen in this country are so engrossed by their Parliamentary duties that they have little time fully to study for themselves questions of economical science. They naturally avail themselves of the opinions and theories of others: and monetary science is, or has been made, so misty a subject, that it is not strange that mistakes should have occurred in applying its principles to practical affairs. The object of Sir Robert Peel was admirable; the means which he took to accomplish it were mistaken. Had the monetary crises which periodically overtake this country been caused by an unsafe Currency, his precautions would have been well-directed. As the fact stands, they have been wrong aimed. The currency was perfectly sound. But the precautions which he took to strengthen it have landed the Bank in a new dilemma, and created for the country greater embarrassments than before.

BUT A BANKING ONE.

It is not currency, but banking, embarrassments which occasion our recurrent disasters. No one loses faith in the note-circulation. A drain upon the Bank does not arise from the public demanding gold in payment of its notes. It is not the note-holders, but the depositors, who make the drain of gold. It is not the public, but the

Bank's own customers, who make the inroad upon its stock of bullion. This is obviously a purely banking difficulty,—a difficulty which the Bank itself ought to meet. The community is no more called upon, whether actively or passively, to provide means for the Bank's carrying on its banking business, than to do the same for other establishments. To meet the requirements of depositors by payments in gold is the ordinary condition upon which banking business is carried on.

BANKING RESERVES.

The banks of Ireland and Scotland, when an unusual demand for specie is made upon them, take active measures to provide themselves with the commodity which they are bound to supply. They sell the securities which they keep in hand for this purpose, and with the cheques received in payment they obtain the required amount of specie. Why should not the Bank of England, in similar circumstances, take similar steps? So far as profit is concerned, it does not matter to the Scotch and Irish banks whether their reserve of securities be payable in London or in Paris and Amsterdam. They draw the gold from London simply because they can provide themselves from that quarter more promptly than from the Continent. But Paris, Brussels, and Amsterdam are as near to London as London is to Dublin and Edinburgh. Why, then, should not the Bank of England keep in hand an amount of Continental securities, in order to provide specie to meet exceptional demands upon the part of its customers? Yet the Bank does nothing of the kind. Instead of this, it raises its rate of discount (which regulates the rate all over the country), and compels the whole community to suffer in order that specie may be brought to the Bank, or that the demand upon it (whether for gold or for notes) may be stopped. Because a few individuals—a very small section of its customers—whether Englishmen or foreigners, require payment of their deposits in specie, the Bank raises its rate to an exorbitant height upon the whole community,—thereby depressing our markets, sweeping away the "legitimate profits of industry," and sometimes covering the country with bankruptcies.

It is obvious that these evil results would to a great degree be obviated if the Bank were to make an adequate provision for its banking liabilities: say by keeping a portion of its reserve invested in the stock of foreign Governments,—just as the Scotch and Irish banks keep a portion of their reserves in the form of Consols. By making these investments at a time when gold is flowing into its vaults, and selling them at a time when gold is ebbing away from it, the Bank would lessen the effect of these fluctuations, and would meet its liabilities in the most natural and legitimate manner. Or, in lieu of this process, the Bank might adopt the system pursued by the Bank of

France,—*i.e.*, of buying foreign bills, when an exceptional demand for specie arises. It matters little in what form the object is attained. But that it ought to be attained—that the Bank ought to meet its banking liabilities (in other words, the legitimate demands of its depositors) is, we think, indisputable. The question is simply one of fair dealing.

THE BANK *versus* TRADE.

The Bank trades with other people's money,—it makes its profits by lending out the sums deposited with it, all except the small portion which in ordinary times is found sufficient to meet the demands of its depositors. When extraordinary times come, it is the Bank's duty to increase its stock of gold, that it may discharge the liabilities which it voluntarily accepted. All profit and no loss is a condition which is no more applicable to banking than to other kinds of business. Yet, looking at the present practice of the Bank, one would think that it is Trade alone that is to suffer in hard times,—that the profits of banking are sacred,—that it is all right that the community should suffer during a monetary crisis, but that the banks at such times should only reap increased profits. This is a strange state of things. We have shown to demonstration that the high rates which the Bank imposes, are not caused by any "loss of capital"—whether as represented by the aggregate wealth of the country, or by the "loanable capital" in the banks. Nor are they caused by any distrust of its notes. The high rates are imposed simply because the Bank has not enough of gold (or of notes, which it can get for gold) to meet the liabilities of its banking department. Instead of keeping a reserve of securities convertible into specie, in order to meet an exceptional increase in the demands of its customers—as the Scotch and Irish banks do,—the Bank not only shirks this obligation, but does so in a manner which adds greatly to its profits. And when it raises its rate of discount, all the other banks willingly follow its example. Thus, not content with their profits in fair-weather times, our banks now make still larger profits in times of difficulty. The "hard times" which should fall upon themselves, the banks shift on to the shoulders of the community. The very seasons which ought to entail upon them a diminution of gains are nowadays converted by them into their richest harvests. ...

WEAKNESS OF ITS BANKING DEPARTMENT.

Actually, however, this weakness of its Banking department is no fault of the Bank's. The weakness is purely artificial. The Bank would be amply provided to meet all its banking liabilities if it were allowed to have free use of the gold in its possession. This it has not. Nearly seven millions of its stock of specie are at all times, even in its hour of greatest need, wholly withdrawn from its use. This was the leading provision of the Act of 1844. Sir R. Peel believed that the main cause of all our monetary troubles was owing to the defective state of the currency,—to over-issues on the part of the Bank, and a loss of confidence in its notes on the part of the public. We now know that this idea was quite erroneous. But, acting upon it, he directed his attention entirely to the Issue department of the Bank. He enacted that all times and under all circumstances a large amount of gold should be kept in this department. By so doing, he crippled to a corresponding extent the Banking department: withdrawing from it seven millions of gold,—an amount almost equal to that which in previous times had been considered an adequate reserve for *both* departments (*i.e.*, to cover alike the note-issues and the banking liabilities of the establishment).* So imbued was he with the idea that it was the note-issues of the Bank that were the source of its weakness and the cause of our troubles, that on the 13th of June 1844 he said:—"The Bank can always *cover its notes,*—but by a tremendous sacrifice of the mercantile classes. That is what I wish to avoid." Yet experience has proved to demonstration that the "tremendous sacrifice of the mercantile classes," which he wished to avoid, now occurs in a

* The average-stock of gold held by the Bank of England during the twenty-two years previous to 1844 was £8,000,000. The Bank of France, which has a note-circulation of £31,000,000 (about one-half greater than the Bank of England's), sometimes sees its specie reduced to 6½ millions, without raising its rate beyond 7 per cent, and without the occurrence of panic or crisis of any kind.

worse degree than ever, not from any difficulty in maintaining the convertibility of the notes (which is never endangered), but from the weakness of the Bank in its banking department.

The want of elasticity in the Banking department is the real cause of the "sacrifice of the mercantile classes," which so repeatedly occurs under the Act of 1844, despite the earnest desire of its framer to the contrary. Sir R. Peel thought only of securing the convertibility of the notes: and he overlooked the enfeeblement which his enactments for this purpose inflicted on the banking department. His procedure was like that of an engineer who fortifies the part of a position which will not be attacked, by transferring to it the armaments which previously guarded the key of the position. Sir R. Peel did not perceive the weak point of his Act. He did not see that, under it, monetary crises, and the sacrifice of the mercantile classes, which he so sincerely deplored, would of necessity become more frequent and disastrous than ever. After the crisis of 1847, he saw and acknowledged that the "first object" of the Act—namely, "to prevent the occurrence of panics and crises, such as had occasionally before inflicted great injury upon the country"—had "failed:" but even then he failed to see the reason why.

Many seasons of monetary pressure, which would hardly have been felt as embarrassments under the Act of 1819, occasion panic and overwhelming disasters under that of 1844. A few words will show how this evil and unexpected result is produced. For every note issued beyond the arbitrarily fixed sum of £14,650,000, the Act requires that the Bank shall hold a corresponding amount of gold. As the ordinary amount of notes required for the wants of the public is £21,000,000, it follows that £6,500,000 is the lowest amount of gold that must be in the Issue department to allow of these twenty-one millions of notes being kept in circulation. And, taking into account the requirements of the branches of the Bank and other matters, this sum may be stated in round numbers at seven millions.

HOW THIS IS CAUSED.

Thus, when seven millions of specie are in its possession, and twenty-one millions of notes are in circulation, all the notes which the Bank is allowed to issue are in the hands of the public. When this point is reached—when the bullion in its possession has sunk to this level—the Bank cannot issue a single additional note. Neither can it part with a single sovereign. As discounted bills fall due, it may discount others to an equal amount; but that is the most it can do. However pressing be the emergency, it cannot extend its discount-accommodation one iota. What is more, when an actual crisis occurs, it cannot even continue

SEVEN MILLIONS NULLIFIED.

it. Its Issue department being literally shut up, it must withdraw from its discount-business whatever amount of notes may be called for by its depositors. Otherwise, if a depositor were to ask at such a time for even a £5-note, the Bank could not give it,—its legal power to issue notes being exhausted. And if the depositor were to say, "Then give it me in gold, of which you say you have seven millions," the Bank must reply that that form of issue is shut up too,—because every sovereign of these seven millions is needed in its own vaults, in order to avoid an infringement of the Act. And compliance with the Act is the condition of its existence: any violation of it involves a loss of the Bank's charter. Thus the Bank at such times cannot make payment of a single note or sovereign to any of its depositors, except it withdraw a similar amount from its discount-operations, which are the mainstay of trade and credit. And this artificial dilemma occurs at times when, as every one knows, there is a greatly increased demand for discounts at the Bank of England, owing to the curtailment of discounts on the part of the other banks and discount-houses.

THIS IS THE GRAND ERROR OF THE ACT OF 1844,—so far as that measure relates to the Bank of England.

ARTIFICIAL CRISES.

It is a strange spectacle to see nearly seven millions of gold thus condemned, by a legislative embargo, to inactivity in the vaults of the Bank at the very seasons when they are most needed. The effect of such an artificial curtailment of the resources of the Bank is obvious. It renders monetary crises more frequent and disastrous than formerly, or than they would be but for the Bank Act. By nullifying nearly seven millions of gold, the Act produces, when the bullion in the Bank has fallen to nine millions, a panic as violent as used to occur when the gold was reduced to two millions. The Bank has to stop when it has still nearly seven millions of gold, just as if the gold had fallen to zero.* In this way every trifling ebb of specie is converted into a serious catastrophe. The Bank Act, in fact, makes us sail in shallower waters than before. Although our commerce has now become a veritable "Leviathan"—achieving prodigious results, and only the more exposed on that account to great embarrass-

* The following is a return of the lowest amount of coin and bullion in the Bank of England, during critical seasons of our monetary affairs—from 1819 to the present time. As it was only in 1825, 1847, and 1857 that a regular crisis took place, it is the position of the Bank in these years that specially deserves attention.

Date.	Bullion.	Bank-rate.	
1825—Dec. 31,	£1,261,000	5 per cent.	Weathered the storm unaided.
1837—Feb. 7,	3,831,000	5 ,,	
1839—Sept. 3,	2,406,000	6 ,,	
1847—Oct. 23,	8,313,000	8 ,,	Bank Act suspended.
1857—Nov. 11,	7,170,000	10 ,,	
1864—Sept. 14,	12,905,511	9 ,,	

The rate of discount compared with the amount of gold, as will be seen, has been progressively increased. And thus, with thirteen millions of gold in the Bank, the mercantile classes suffer more hardships than fell to their lot under the Act of 1819, when the bullion had fallen to barely three millions.

ments—the Bank Act strikes nearly seven fathoms of water from beneath her keel, so that the least ebb of the tide now brings the huge fabric aground. The nullifying of these seven millions of gold is complete; yet what might they not effect if they remained available as formerly! Such an amount of gold might actually form the basis for an entire currency.* And judging from the history of past crises, we believe that the issue of notes to one-half of that amount, in timeous assistance to solvent but temporarily embarrassed firms, would suffice to have averted the worst panic that has yet arisen.†

* The stock of specie kept by the Bank of England under the Act of 1819, did not exceed on the average eight millions. And as shown by the published monthly statements, the amount of bullion in the Bank of France, during December and January last, averaged exactly £7,000,000. For several months at that time, the Bank of France, with equal liabilities to those of the Bank of England, had only half as much bullion; yet its rate of discount was only 7 per cent (which was fully higher than the average rate on the Continent), and more confidence prevailed in the commercial world of France than in ours. If the Bank of England, under its present management, were so circumstanced (as it actually was in 1847 and '57); our country would be covered with bankruptcies from end to end, and tens of thousands of our working-classes would be thrown out of employment. Why is this?

† The issue of 2½ millions in the form of Exchequer bills, bearing interest at 5 per cent, sufficed to stop the panic of 1793. An issue of 2 millions of *inconvertible* notes stopped the panic of 1797. An old chest of £1-notes stopped that of 1826. And the suspension of the Bank Act of itself sufficed to stop the panics of 1847 and of 1857,—although, even in the latter and more severe of these crises, the additional issue of the Bank's notes only amounted to £928,000, and though the exorbitant rate of 10 per cent was exacted as the minimum upon the Bank's advances.

Is it not a great mistake, then, to condemn such potent agents of good to virtual non-existence in the vaults of the Bank? Like some of the shadowy things shown to us in the world of metaphysics, these seven millions of gold at once *are, and are not.* They are a fixture in the Bank, which only one or two persons within that establishment, and not a soul beyond its pale, ever sees, and from which the public derive not the slightest advantage. If any one were to abscond with them, the public need not know anything of the loss, nor (so long as the Bank Act exists) would be a whit the worse for it. There is a tradition in the Bank that once upon a time the Directors received an anonymous letter informing them that the writer could enter the Bullion Office whenever he pleased, and that he would meet them there at any hour they should appoint. Incredulous, they gave him a rendezvous for midnight: and lo! exactly as the hour struck, they heard a subterraneous noise, part of the stone floor was raised, and the anonymous correspondent stood before them. He had made his entrance by means of an old drain which ran below the Bank. Now, if, even at a time of severest crisis under the present Act, such a subterranean explorer were to carry six or seven millions' worth of the glittering ingots down into the drain with him, the country would never feel—nor, if the Directors held

ABSURDITY OF THE SYSTEM.

their tongue, even know—of the loss. In fact, the best thing the Directors can do with these seven millions is to count them once for all, place them in a vault apart, and then close up the entrance with stone and lime. But perchance they have already done so.

This arrangement, we repeat, is the grand error of the Act of 1844. That the arrangement is eminently absurd may be of little consequence: but it is a matter of serious importance that it is the prolific parent of monetary crises and commercial crashes. We have shown that this is the case,—nor can it be otherwise. The nullification of seven millions of gold being complete, whenever the Bank's stock of specie is seen falling to this point, the consequences are the same as if there were no gold in the Bank at all. And in this way every little ebb of gold, which under a natural system would occasion no embarrassment, produces a monetary convulsion of the greatest magnitude. The nullification of these seven millions—this is the cause why monetary difficulties in this country are now more frequent and severe than ever. And until this arrangement be abolished, the country cannot hope to escape recurrent disasters.

ITS DISASTROUS EFFECTS.

Nor is this the full extent of the evil. The effect of the arrangement weighs upon the community at all times. It not only, at recurrent periods, produces panics and convulsions, but it permanently and artificially enhances the rate of discount — the loanable value of money—throughout the whole country. The Bank Directors now regard seven millions of their stock of specie as non-existent. When they have fourteen millions of gold, they act as if they had only seven. Seven millions form the zero-point in all their calculations: that is to say, one-half of the ordinary amount of bullion in the Bank is nullified, and a double price is charged for the other half. What would be thought if a similar arrangement were to be adopted in regard to our supplies of food? Suppose seven million quarters of wheat (fully one-half of our yearly produce) were placed in a huge granary in Cornhill, and that an Act of Parliament forbade the sale or giving away of any portion of that large stock of wheat, unless in exchange for another kind of food of equal value. The consequence would be that the slightest deficiency in the amount of our ordinary supply of food would subject the country to the horrors of famine. Wheat to the amount of one-half of our ordinary crop would be stored in Cornhill, but even when famine prevailed not a bushel of that corn would be available for the use of the community. The price of wheat, of course, would thereby be greatly enhanced. The marketable supply would be reduced one-half, and famine-prices would become the ordinary rate of charge. How long would such an arrangement be permitted to last? Not one day. The whole country would be in arms to resist such monstrous folly and injustice. Yet a system which would not be tolerated for an hour if applied to our supplies of Food, actually exists by Act of Parliament in regard to our supply of Money. And—if it be worth while to mark degrees in so monstrous a policy—with even less excuse than if the system were applied to wheat: for we can easily increase the supply of bank-notes (which is all that people want during our monetary crises), but we cannot in like manner augment our supply of corn.

Reason stands abashed when contemplating so absurd, and so frightfully injurious, an arrangement. The embargo upon these seven millions is not only an error, but an injustice. It is not only a defective currency arrangement, but a wrong to the community. It is an act of oppression committed upon trade by Act of Parliament. Not designedly, of course, but by mistake. It is the worst form of "Protection" that ever existed in our Statute-book. It is the chain which binds the Prometheus of trade, in order that the vultures of the moneyed interest may feed upon his vitals. We are told that unhappily for himself the liver of Prometheus ever grew as it was devoured, so that his torture was eternal; and in much the same way, Trade recovers itself and grows fat again, only to be subjected to fresh extortions. We pity the ignorant idolaters of India, when, of their free will, they throw themselves beneath the ponderous wheels of the car of Juggernaut. But here we have created an engine of destruction which periodically crushes Trade, and wrings the life's blood out of our commercial classes, whether they approve of the process or not. The high-priests of the idol, indeed, vaunt the system, and when firms go down in scores, and industry is robbed of its legitimate profits, regard these results with infinite complacency, if not with glee, as a "clearing of the commercial atmosphere." But the system cannot last much longer. The dilemma, so artificial in its cause, so disastrous in its effects, has been wholly occasioned by legislation; and legislation can — and we trust soon will—remove it.

APOLOGIES FOR IT.

As a journalist, and in the pages of *Blackwood's Magazine*, we have frequently, and in ample detail, exposed this extraordinary feature of our monetary legislation; and although we hear few voices publicly endorsing our opinions, we believe that these opinions are gaining ground. Even supporters of the Bank Act begin to hesitate in their approval of this its leading provision. The *Economist*, the ablest of our authorities on monetary affairs, the most sensible and practical in its views and judgments, seeks to palliate rather than to uphold this pernicious arrangement. It acknowledges that the theory upon which the framers of the Bank Act proceeded was quite erroneous; and also that the embargo laid upon these six or seven millions of gold in the Issue department is not needed to maintain the convertibility of the note. But, it says, although the object for which this embargo was imposed was a mistaken one, yet the result happens to be good; because this reserved stock of gold is useful as a general banking-reserve,—as a depot of specie for the use of all the banks in the country.

Now, if the Bank of England is to be compelled to keep on hand a stock of gold for the sake of all the other banking establishments, it is well that this fact should be fully known and plainly stated. Sir Robert Peel neither contemplated such an arrangement nor desired it. During the debates in 1844, he repeatedly stated that his bill was simply a currency-measure,—that it was not meant to apply to banking business at all,—and that it would be a great error, and an unjustifiable act, if the Government were to interfere in any way with the arrangements of banking. The soundness of this opinion, we think, will hardly be questioned.

But, whether this opinion be approved or not, the fact remains — that these millions locked up in the Issue department of the Bank of England are *not* a general banking reserve at all. They were consigned to the Issue department expressly in order that they might not be employed for banking purposes; and the provision of the Bank Act on this point is so explicit that, as long as the Act remains in force, these millions cannot be so employed. They are of no use whatever to the banking establishments of the country. They cannot even be used by the Bank itself. Not theoretically, indeed, yet as a matter of fact, the Act condemns them to absolute inactivity. It virtually nullifies them. They are utterly useless as a banking reserve of any kind. And this is precisely what the Act means them to be.

It is true, this arrangement is so unworkable, and so disastrous in its effects, that whenever the time comes for its actual enforcement, the Act must be suspended. The arrangement is acknowledged to be a failure in the very circumstances which it was designed to meet. No community will stand being strangled for the sake of a crotchet,—for the sake of an erroneous and impracticable theory, even though that theory has been approved by Parliament; and the Government has always to intervene, and suspend the Act, to prevent matters coming to a total dead-lock. Every one now knows, as he sees the Bank's reserve running down to seven millions, that next day the Act will be suspended. The Act remains in the Statute-book simply on the condition that it shall be suspended during the very seasons when this, its leading provision, should come into direct operation. Why, then, not abolish this provision altogether?

ABOLITION, NOT SUSPENSION, REQUIRED.

The *Economist* is now so shaken in its allegiance to the Bank Act that it proposes that a bill should be passed authorising the Government of the day to suspend the Act at pleasure.* At present, any Government which suspends the Act must summon Parliament immediately, in order to obtain from the Legislature a bill of indemnity for this arbitrary violation of the laws; and the object of the *Economist*, in proposing to give to the Government a permissive power to suspend the Act, is to diminish the heavy responsibility which at present attaches to the Government in violating the law,—so that the Act may be suspended more frequently, and at an earlier period of our seasons of crisis. The proposal is inspired by an excellent motive,—but it is objectionable on constitutional grounds, and the working of the proposed system would not be long tolerated by the community. No Ministry, we feel confident, would consent to have such arbitrary powers conferred upon it. Great practical injustice, immense individual hardships, are occasioned by the manner in which these suspensions of the Act are, and must be, made. For example, why should discount-houses

* "There ought to be, *within* the law, a power of doing, when necessary, precisely what was done without and *beyond* the law in 1847 and 1857. The Chancellor of the Exchequer and the First Lord of the Treasury should have the legal power of suspending the Act of 1847."—*Economist, Oct.* 1, 1864.

and mercantile firms be compelled to fail, at half-past two o'clock on the 12th of November 1857, when other firms in like circumstances at three o'clock are freely assisted, and go on as before? Why should dozens of highly-respectable and solvent firms be sacrificed—losing their good name, which is everything to a merchant, and having to lose also a heavy percentage of their capital in the shape of bankruptcy expenses,—merely because the Chancellor of the Exchequer did not suspend the Act of 1844 an hour or two sooner? It is not right that any man—be he who he may—should be allowed to exercise such a power. Although the Act were harmless in other respects, it were better that it should be blotted from the Statute-book than that any Minister should have such powers. And no English Minister, we feel assured, would desire to have so invidious a task imposed upon him.

Temporary suspensions of the Act, moreover, would leave uncured the greater part of the evils which this, its leading provision, inflicts upon the community. Artificial monetary difficulties would be created just as at present. The only difference would be, that they would not be permitted to attain the same magnitude. The golden cord around the neck of Trade would be relaxed before the strangling process was carried to the length it now is. That is all.

Besides, such temporary suspensions of this provision of the Act would leave wholly untouched a serious evil of the present arrangement. The nullification of so large a portion of the Bank's stock of specie, as we have pointed out, not only creates monetary difficulties which would not otherwise occur, but it artificially raises the rate of usage throughout the country.

GREAT RISE OF THE BANK-RATE.

We see the effects of this in the immense rise which has of late years taken place in the loanable value of money. The Bank now raises its rate of discount to 8 per cent in circumstances where formerly it charged 4 per cent. In other words, in similar circumstances, the Bank charges twice as much for its money as it used to do. This change, so little noticed, but so important to the commercial classes, has been introduced during the last half-dozen years. Previous to 1857, when the amount of bullion in the Bank was between thirteen and fourteen millions, the rate of discount usually stood at 4 or 4½ per cent; but now, when the bullion stands at a similar amount, the rate is raised to 8 or 9 per cent. In December last, when the Bank's rate was 8 per cent, its stock of bullion ranged from £13,048,000 to £13,673,000. At present (Nov. 8), the Bank-rate for the last two months has stood at 9 per cent, while the amount of coin and bullion in the Bank has ranged from £12,905,511 up to £13,313,441. An artificial crisis is thus produced—markets are depressed, mills are stopped, and failures multiply—while the Bank has fully thirteen millions of gold in its possession. At the same time the Bank exacts, and the community pays, double the rates that used to prevail, or which, but for the Act, could prevail. This is a highly profitable process for the Bank.

But there is another object, besides gain, which induces the Directors to act thus. Stung by their repeated failures to observe the Act, in 1847 and 1857—a result which was due to no fault on their part, but simply to the unworkable character of the measure—the Directors are now resolved to "save themselves" from another break-down, at whatever sacrifice to the commercial community. Hence they charge high rates even under ordinary circumstances; as a platform from which they can advance in extraordinary times to still higher rates. Whenever a crisis like that of 1857 recurs, we may expect to see the Directors raise the Bank-rate to 20 per cent where, in the former crisis, they charged 10. Perhaps they will ostensibly continue to discount all good bills, but their exorbitant charge will practically amount to a contraction of discounts. Fettered by the Act, and intent only on saving themselves, they will raise the rate remorselessly, leaving the commercial classes to pay a Shylock rate of usury or go into the Gazette.

To sum up. The characteristic features of our present monetary system, so far as they relate to the

Bank of England, are—(1) the withdrawal of nearly seven millions of gold from the use of the Banking department of that establishment; and (2) the high rates of discount which are a consequence, chiefly of this arrangement, and partly of the new system of action adopted by the Bank Court. We have shown alike the needlessness of these arrangements, and their evil effects. We have shown that this nullification of seven millions originated in a mistake on the part of the framers of the Act of 1844: that this legislative embargo is not needed to preserve the convertibility of the note-issues,—seeing that during our worst crises there never is any serious demand for gold in exchange for notes, and that the notes of the Bank maintained their credit as fully in 1826 when there was only a million of bullion in the Bank, as in 1857 when there was upwards of seven millions. During our monetary panics, in fact, it is notes only that are wanted by the public; and whenever the required supply of notes is obtained, the panic is at an end. We have also shown that, as long as the Act of 1844 remains in force, this large stock of gold is quite useless as a banking reserve of any kind.——So much for the needlessness of the embargo. As regards its practical effects, we have demonstrated, we hope with sufficient clearness, that this arrangement, by which one-half of the Bank's average stock of gold is virtually nullified, occasions severe monetary pressure

RECAPITULATION.

and commercial disasters at seasons when, but for it, the money-market would be buoyant and trade prosperous. And also, that the ordinary and permanent effect of the embargo placed upon this large stock of gold, is to enhance artificially the value of money, by doubling the rate of usage throughout the country.

This mistaken arrangement is the only ground upon which the Bank justifies the exorbitant rates which it now charges; and if this arrangement were at an end, the Bank-rate might fall to its natural level. But there is more than this to be said:—

Even as the matter stands, the Bank's practice of charging the very high rates which it now does whenever there occurs a greater demand for discounts than usual, is open to serious criticism.

HIGH RATES CREATE CRISES.

Professedly* the present minimum rate of 9 per cent is charged in order to prevent any serious diminution of the Bank's reserve of notes; but in many cases such a high rate produces the very opposite result. Our merchants, while paying this extreme rate for the monetary advances by which nearly all our trade is

* "The rate of discount is charged for one purpose only—the purpose of keeping the Reserve fund at a proper and safe limit." —Speech of Mr Hodgson, M.P., Governor of the Bank, at the recent quarterly meeting of the proprietors of the Bank on the 22d of September. What the Bank Court regards as "a proper and safe limit" for the Reserve was not stated; but as the Court now charges 9 per cent as their *minimum* rate when they have thirteen and a quarter millions of gold, it is difficult to imagine what their idea of safety and propriety is.

carried on, have at the same time to encounter a loss on their sales, owing to the fall of prices which these high rates occasion. It is admitted on all hands that these high rates are undesirable in themselves —that they are most injurious to the welfare of the country,—that, by abnormally depressing the markets and the value of property of all kinds, they cause heavy losses, especially to the mercantile classes, and that the employment of the people is correspondingly reduced. But, while thus injurious in their action, do they really accomplish the object for which they are had recourse to by the Bank? The numerous failures which occur whenever the Bank-rate is raised to 9 per cent—and still more when it is raised to 10—by spreading distrust, temporarily destroy our system of credit, and, by rendering a greater supply of notes necessary, tend to increase the inroad upon the Bank's reserve. Although these high rates crush Trade in the end, their immediate effect is to augment the demand which professedly they are meant to check. By imposing these high rates, the Bank temporarily creates a greater demand for its money; and, though it may thereby aggravate the crisis, the Bank at least gets higher rates for its advances. The Bank not only gets extraordinary profits by charging these high rates, but these rates become in turn a means of continuing themselves, by creating an artificial crisis.

AND CANNOT CURE THEM.

As a cure for a monetary panic, these high rates are not only worthless, but act as a positive aggravation of the difficulty. In fact they are a chief cause of such panics. They cause more failures, more distrust, and a greater inroad upon the Bank's reserve, than there would otherwise be. Every season of monetary pressure is a harvest-time to the banks and great money-dealers; and these high rates (whether meant to be so or not) are a means by which every crisis is aggravated, and the gains of the banks and money-dealers proportionately increased. We have shown abundantly, by reference to historical facts, that the special feature of monetary crises is a temporary paralysis of our ordinary credit-system—produced, it may be, by the action of the Bank itself—which necessitates a larger supply of bank-notes to take the place of less valid forms of credit; and that the true and only remedy for them is for the Bank to give this supply freely, by increasing its usual amount of monetary accommodation. It is not a want of good securities on the part of the public at such times that causes this dilemma, but an artificially-produced want of notes on the part of the Bank. An increase of discounts has stopped in succession every crisis which has occurred, from 1793 down to 1857; and no crisis can be stopped in any other way. In the great crisis of 1826, as in those of 1793 and 1797, as long as the Bank went on contracting its discounts, the crisis continued to increase, and the Bank's reserves continued to diminish; but the instant the Bank reversed its course and discounted freely, even "forcing out its notes in all directions" (though there was only a million of specie left in the establishment), the panic was at an end, and its gold began to increase. All monetary crises show the same features and are cured by the same means. Moreover, in 1826, as in 1793 and 1797, all this was accomplished without any raising of the Bank-rate. The panic was stopped as effectually in 1826, when there was only a million of specie in the Bank, and the rate of discount was only 5 per cent, as in 1857, when there were upwards of seven millions of gold in the Bank, and the rate of discount was 10 per cent. In truth, as we have said, high rates aggravate, and sometimes of themselves create, a crisis. That crisis is the death-struggle of Trade, during which it yields up its gains to the moneyed interest; and thereafter comes a collapse. By augmenting the losses of traders, through depression of the markets, &c., these high rates prostrate trade and diminish the employment of the working-classes to an extent and for a duration of time much greater than used to be when such rates were not imposed by the Bank. Every season during which the Bank-rate is unusually high, is followed by a period of mercantile depression. Merchants and manufacturers, crippled by their losses, and unable to pay the high charges exacted by the Bank, contract their ordinary amount of business, and discharge a portion of their hands. With diminished trade, there are fewer bills; and then, for lack of business, the Bank has to lower its rate. But if the Bank did not kill trade by raising its rate so high, it would not, from want of business, have afterwards to reduce its rate so low.

Such is the practical operation of exceptionally high rates of discount. And it is by its practical effects that any system is to be judged. But having shown the facts, let us consider the matter from another point of view.

THE RATE OF INTEREST.

As the peculiar feature of the New System adopted by the Bank is to operate upon the money-market by means of variations in the rate of discount, it is well to consider what are the normal causes which regulate the Rate of Interest. Looking at the facts of the case, the first thing that strikes one is the wide difference which exists between the present practice and that which formerly prevailed. In the twenty years which have elapsed since the passing of the Act of 1844, there have been 104 changes in the Bank-rate; while there were not more than a dozen in the hundred and forty years which elapsed between 1695 (the year after the Bank was established) and 1836.* Moreover, during

* See Appendix B, where the variations in the Bank's charge for discounting commercial bills are shown from 1795 down to the

the last twenty years the minimum rate has varied from 2 per cent up to 10; and as still higher rates have been occasionally charged, we may state the range of the variations in the Bank-rate since 1844 to have been from 2 per cent up to 12. On the other hand, with the exception of a few months in 1839 (when the new system was coming into vogue), the Bank-rate never varied more than one per cent (from 5 to 4) during the century and a half previous to 1844.

THE OLD SYSTEM.

For upwards of a century and a quarter, it was the invariable rule of the Bank of England to discount all commercial bills at 4 or 5 per cent. To us of the present day, who are accustomed to see the Bank-rate changed on the average every two months, sometimes every two weeks, and to range from 2 to 10 or 12 per cent, such a course of procedure appears strange. All the more so that, during the period when the Bank-rate was thus steady, our country and all its interests underwent changes and convulsions greater than any of which we have had experience, or than the country is likely again to undergo within a similar period of time. That century and a quarter witnessed the great war with France under Louis XIV.,—the dynastic troubles of 1715,—the formidable rebellion of 1745, which imperilled the existence of the Hanoverian dynasty,—the disas-

present time: along with the amount of bullion held by the Bank at the dates when those variations took place, from 1822 downwards.

trous war with our revolted American colonies, and with the allied powers of France and Spain,—and finally, the gigantic contest with France under the first Napoleon, when every Power in Europe, except England, was in turn beaten to the ground. There must have been some solid foundation for a practice which maintained itself steadily throughout so long and so trying a period. And if systems are to be judged by their fruits, we cannot boast that our new monetary system has worked with more advantage to the community than the old one. We have had no great wars, no rebellions or dynastic convulsions, yet the country has been more repeatedly in monetary difficulties since 1820 than it was during the whole century that closed with 1797. As regards the convertibility of the note, it was maintained with most perfect success during the whole of last century up to 1797,—under much greater difficulties than can now occur, seeing that the credit of the Bank was then not so fully established. And as regards the suspension of specie-payments in 1797, that was not a consequence of the Bank's rate of discount, but of the exports of specie which our Government had to make in the form of loans, and in a lesser degree for the support of our troops abroad.*

* On carefully considering the facts which led to the suspension of cash-payments in 1797, we see much reason to think that the suspension might have been wholly avoided, but for the panic

The questions naturally occur:—Why was the average rate of discount fixed at 4½ per cent? and why was the rate confined in its variations to one per cent? It was not the Usury Law which led the Bank to select four or five per cent as the fair rate of usage; for the 5 per cent Usury Law was not passed till 1712; and moreover, upon Government stock and good securities, the Bank used only to charge three or four per cent. What, then, is the explanation of the old rule? The principle upon which it was based is at least a very intelligible one. The Bank said,—"The average profit on money invested, at no small risk, in trade is 10 per cent,—hence 4 or 5 per cent is a fair profit upon money safely invested upon good securities. To charge more than that rate would check trade,—to charge less would needlessly diminish our profits: therefore we shall adhere to the fair rate." The rate of discount being thus fixed, the amount of the currency and of discounts was left to be regulated by the country itself—by the requirements of the community. "If we were greatly to lower the rate at

ITS PRINCIPLE.

occasioned by the refusal of the Bank to continue its discount-operations at the ordinary amount. For five weeks before the climax came, the Bank had been steadily diminishing its discounts (to the extent of £2,000,000—a serious amount in those days), while the private banks had to follow its example. A panic was the inevitable result: and the Bank had to shut its doors. But for that panic, we believe, the suspension of cash-payments might have been avoided.

one time and raise it at another," said the Bank Court, "we should virtually prescribe to the community the amount of trade which is to be carried on,—alternately expanding and contracting it. We should interfere with the natural action of trade, and at the same time we should endanger its legitimate profits. Our function is simply to provide the instrument of exchange, by which loans are made and capital transferred, at a fair rate (determined by the average rate of profits), and thereafter leave Trade to act free and untrammelled—to expand or contract according to its circumstances and opportunities." In short, they regarded the instrument of exchange as the handmaid of commerce; as a thing devised for the purpose of transferring capital and facilitating trade: and they regarded it as their function, as the national Bank of Issue, to maintain a supply of this commodity adequate to the fluctuating requirements of the community.

Recognising the disadvantages inflicted upon legitimate trade by frequent variations in the rate of discount, and seeing that 4½ per cent, as a rule, was the right rate to be charged, the Bank Court of those days preferred to adhere to that rate as closely as possible, rather than create embarrassments for trade, and for the community at large, by making the rate fluctuate. In this manner the Bank of England, for nearly a century and a half, adhered to the rule, and disregarded the exceptions. In recent times this policy has been reversed; and now we exalt the exceptions at the expense of the rule. Steadiness in the rate is obviously of great advantage to the community; and although the old rule need not be maintained, the principle upon which that rule was based ought not to be lost sight of. It ought never to be forgotten that all great changes in the rate of discount are inimical to legitimate trade. They introduce into trade the spirit of gambling. By a great fall in the rate of discount, a man may gain immensely by no merit on his part, and purely as a gambler wins in games of chance. And by a great rise in the Bank-rate, he may be made bankrupt equally by no fault of his. Fluctuations beyond the normal point, whether upwards or downwards, are *per se* undesirable. Variations in the rate of discount ought to be minimised, not exaggerated. The profit upon money employed in trade does not fluctuate in this manner: from year to year it remains pretty nearly the same: and as the value of money on loan naturally bears a relation to the amount of profit arising from the use of it, we are as much opposed to unnecessary reductions of the rate, as to avoidable elevations of it. Under our present monetary system, however, the natural relations between Capital ready to be loaned, and Industry willing to employ it, have been seriously deranged.

The fundamental elements which regulate the rate of interest are: the amount of loanable capital, and the demand for it—which demand is regulated by the profit which can be obtained from the employment of that capital in business. A third and subordinate element is, the instrument of exchange. In our present monetary system, this third element is made supreme. As we have shown, the changes in the rate of discount have no connection with the amount of capital in the country.* They are entirely occasioned by fluctuations in the available amount of currency. They are not caused by variations in the amount of capital deposited in the banks, but in the amount of currency which there is to represent and employ that capital.

CAUSE OF THE CHANGE.

In former times—during the century and a half which preceded 1844—little or no embarrassment arose from this cause. The currency in those times varied, by expansion or contraction, according to the varying requirements of the community. It was a self-acting system—regulated not by the banks, but by the community. It was only the wants of the community which took off an increase of notes from the banks, and when the want subsided, the note-circulation fell to its former amount. Now, it is equally a self-acting system—regulated not by the requirements of the country, but by the

THE NEW SYSTEM.

* See *supra*, pp. 219-227.

fortuitous scarcity or abundance of gold in the Bank of England. Under the former system, the value of money remained comparatively, and might have remained absolutely, steady; under the new system, it is subjected to ceaseless and excessive variations. Under the former system, prices were regulated by the scarcity or abundance of the articles to which they referred; under the new system, prices vary quite irrespective of that scarcity or abundance, and simply owing to changes in the value of money. Our measure of value—the standard by which all other things are measured—is now subjected to greater variations than any other commodity in the country. A merchant who gives his promise to pay £1000 three months after date, may find that, owing to a change in the value of money, he has to pay £1250; and it is quite a common case if he has to pay £1100 instead of £1000. For example, a merchant purchases a thousand pounds' worth of goods, and gives a bill at three months' date. In the interval, the Bank-rate is raised to 9 or 10 per cent; the markets are depressed to the extent of 20 or 25 per cent; so that, in order to get money to meet his bill, he must sell not only the thousand pounds' worth of goods which he received, but a fifth or a fourth part more, before he can realise the £1000 which he has to pay. This is not an imaginary illustration. Hundreds of our merchants had to do this in 1857; and a similar loss, to a lesser degree, is befalling them now.' Thus the value of money is made to change enormously in this country within a few weeks.

The theory of "variation" which now regulates our monetary system, and produces these extraordinary results, is briefly this :—If much gold happens to be brought into the country, the note-circulation is likewise to be increased to a corresponding extent; if gold is temporarily withdrawn from us, the note-circulation also is proportionately diminished. If, owing to a temporary cause, all the gold available for monetary purposes were sent abroad, all our paper-money would likewise disappear, and the country be left without currency of any kind. A more absurd theory never was propounded. If one kind of money fails us, we are upon no account to use any other. If metallic money fails us, we are not to use our paper-money. Nay, even as regards specie, we are restricted: for if gold fails us, we are not to use silver. This we are told to regard as a masterpiece of economical science; this is the great discovery which our advances in civilisation have revealed to us. Formerly, for generations, when the supply of specie became inadequate for their wants, our people had recourse to bank-notes to supplement the deficiency. Every other civilised nation has done the same. Every country in Europe or America has adopted bank-notes as an indispensable supplement to its stock of the precious metals.

Even Hamburg, where metallic money was the sole form of currency, had recourse to paper-money to meet the exceptional requirements of its citizens in 1857.* But a new light has at length dawned upon us. The gospel of monetary science now is: that when a country does not want paper-money, it ought to have a great supply of it,—and when it does require paper-money, it shall have none. When a country has enough of specie, it ought to double its currency by issuing an equal amount of bank-notes; and when there is no specie, there should likewise be *no* notes. Is it necessary to discuss such a theory? In order to be refuted, it only requires to be stated; in order to be rejected, it only needs to be understood. It is a theoretical monstrosity which common sense revolts against,—a burlesque of reason which even the present generation will live to laugh at.

The ebbs of gold which occasionally take place in our country as in others, are purely temporary. The gold returns to us, as it left us, in the ordinary course of trade. It does not leave us owing to any depreciation of the currency, and it will come back again without our taking measures artificially to enhance the value of money.† Under the present system, these transient ebbs of gold, instead of being neutralised,

* For a brief account of the remarkable monetary crisis in Hamburg in 1857, see Appendix C.

† See *supra*, pp. 235-38.

are so treated as to produce a serious derangement of our measure of value. Thus we violate the prime and sole object for which standard-measures are instituted.

STANDARD-MEASURES.

The first and indispensable requisite of standard-measures of all kinds is, that they shall at all times be free from variation. The material of which these measures are made is of no consequence, apart from the maintenance of the uniformity of the measure. It matters little—it is simply a question of convenience—whether the pound-weight be made of iron, lead, or stone; but it is indispensable that the material employed be always of the same weight. It matters nothing of what material or in what shape a pint-measure be made—whether of metal, glass, or earthenware, whether round or square or many-sided,—so that its cubic area remains always the same. Whatever it be made of, we cannot allow of the pint being enlarged by bulging, or diminished by indentation. Or take the case of our measures of length. The yard represents a scientifically-determined fraction of the earth's meridian—a certain portion of the arc which extends from pole to pole. But as the earth's surface happily is not marked off into yards for the convenience either of savans or shopmen, before this measure of length be applied to ordinary purposes it must be embodied and represented in a material form. And the indispensable requisite of this material yard is, that it shall not be subject to variations in length. We must make our standard-yard of the substance which is least liable to contract and expand in length; and if we cannot free that substance from variations, we must neutralise them. In our measures of time, likewise—in our chronometers,—we do not merely mark off a certain length of pendulum fitted to the latitude of the place, but we take means to neutralise the expansions and contractions to which the material of the pendulum is liable. For this purpose we employ two different materials, whose different action in expanding and contracting is made to neutralise the variations which would be unavoidable if only one material were used in constructing the measure. Look at the compensation-balance of a watch, and you will see that it is a combination of brass and steel, so constructed that the different contractile and expansive qualities of these metals are made to neutralise each other's effects, and maintain the balance in its standard form. The twin curves of brass and steel are so used that when the variation of the one tends to expand the balance, the variation of the other tends to contract it. And so the measure is kept true at all times.

The same principle applies to all measures—whether of weight or of time, whether of length or of value. It is of small consequence if the yard-measure of a shopman expand a little with the heat of summer, and contract a little with the cold of winter. But enlarge the process, and the result will assume a very different aspect. Let a faulty yard-wand (one liable to expansion and contraction) be applied as a basis of measurement to the whole country, and the evil will become of serious magnitude. Our distances would be all wrong,—the area of every field, the extent of every estate, would be falsified,—the heights of our mountains, the position of every rock and shoal on our coast, would be given erroneously. The extent of our islands would vary according as they were measured in summer or in winter; the area of each county would vary according as it was measured in a hot day or a cold one; and the skill of our chartographers would be totally foiled in their attempts to piece together the incongruous parts.

OUR MEASURE OF VALUE.

Far greater, and infinitely more injurious to the community, are the variations which at present take place in our measure of value. That measure is constantly expanding and contracting, in a manner that baffles all calculation. It varies sometimes even to the extent of a third or a fourth—to the extent of 20, 25, or even 30 per cent. This is as if the yard-measure, owing to contractions and expansions of the material of which it is made, were sometimes three feet in length, and sometimes four. A merchant who buys a thousand tons of coal, and gives a bill for £1000 at three months' date, sometimes finds that, owing to a change in the value of our currency, he must sell twelve hundred tons of the same coal before he can get the £1000 to meet his bill.

This, we repeat, is a violation of the prime and sole object for which measures of any kind—whether of weight, length, or value—are adapted. And there is no way of maintaining the accuracy of any standard-measure save by combining in it two different materials, the variations of which are made to neutralise each other. The principle of the compensation-balance is as indispensable in the measure of value as it is in other measures. We must combine with metallic money another form of currency by which its variations can be neutralised. A metallic currency is ceaselessly contracting and expanding; therefore another kind of money should be used along with it which can be made to expand and contract in inverse order. In this way alone can the measure of value be maintained, and the money-contracts of a country, the pecuniary engagements between man and man, be kept unaltered and inviolate.

Bank-notes are the means by which this may be effected. Combined with metallic money, they are like the steel curve in the compensation-balance which, applied to the larger brass one, keeps the measure unchanging. We cannot stop metallic contraction or expansion, but we can neutralise it. This is what science does in the measures of time and other standards which it employs: and this is what civilisation does in regard to the currency. Go where you will, in every civilised country you find paper-money. It is an infallible sign of advanced civilisation; and just in proportion as civilisation increases, paper-money is more extensively employed. And in every country it is used for the same purpose—namely, to supplement the use of metallic money, and to neutralise its occasional ebbs. In truth, for a country like ours to make its measure of value fluctuate with the ebb and flow of gold, is as absurd as if our yard-measure were to vary with the depth of the Thames at London Bridge.*

The value of money, like that of all other commodities, depends upon the amount of the supply, and the extent of the demand. If the amount of money in a country remains the same at a time when the monetary requirements of the community (owing to increase of population and trade, or any other cause) experience an increase, then the value of money will be altered,—all business will be deranged, and all contracts will be vitiated. In like manner, if the amount of money be diminished, while the requirements of the community continue as before, the same result will be produced. The value of the cur-

* We shall not here interrupt our exposition by an abstract discussion, but some remarks on "What is a Pound?" published by the author several years ago, will be found in Appendix D.

rency will be raised,—in consequence, prices will be lowered. The same quantity of goods or land, houses or labour, will no longer obtain for its owner the same amount of money. The trading-classes, and all others (constituting the bulk of the community) who hold their wealth in the form of goods and property, will undergo a serious loss; while the small class (forming not a ten-thousandth part of the population) who hold their wealth in the form of money, will reap immense gains. Every such change in the value of the currency sweeps away the profits of the trading and industrial classes into the pockets of the money-dealers. Nor is this loss confined to the trading-classes: the whole body of the working-classes suffer along with them. Owing to the losses inflicted upon their employers, the lower classes are in part thrown out of employment, and in part get less money for their work.

THE VARIATIONS WHICH VITIATE IT.

It is extraordinary to mark what a small variation in the amount of the currency suffices to produce the changes in our measure of value, and which equally would suffice to prevent them. The currency of the United Kingdom amounts to fully a hundred and fifty millions:* yet the variations which occasion our

* This is a conjectural estimate, but we do not think it can be above the mark. Twenty-five years ago (in 1839), our gold and silver coinage was probably upwards of fifty millions sterling. Since that time gold and silver coinage has been issued from the Mint to the amount of 120 millions. Assuming that fifty millions

calamities seldom exceed five or six millions. This seems a strange fact. It happens in this way. By far the greater portion of our currency (amounting to about 100 millions) is in constant use in carrying on the retail operations of daily life. It is fully occupied in effecting the exchanges between tradesmen and their customers, in the payment of wages, and the purchase of the necessaries and luxuries of life. It is constantly passing from hand to hand; and accordingly all this portion of our money, being fully employed in its own work, is not available for any other purpose. It is only the portion of our money which is kept in the banks (about 40 millions) that is available for the discount operations by which trade is carried on. Or rather it is only a portion of this money that is so available,—only the surplus portion which remains after the banks have made provision for the usual requirements of their depositors. It is this portion of our currency alone which is available to meet variations in the monetary requirements of the community,—and also which is acted upon by any variation in the amount of the

of metallic money (the amount existing in 1839) have been absorbed during the last twenty-five years in re-coinage, in wear and loss from casualties, or have been exported instead of bullion, there will remain 120 millions of metallic money in this country. To this have to be added nearly forty millions of bank-notes,—making the total currency fully 150 millions sterling. This estimate is exclusive of (say) ten millions of bullion, uncoined money, kept in the vaults of the Bank of England.

monetary supply. To withdraw five millions from a currency of a hundred and fifty millions is in itself a trifle; but when that diminution takes effect wholly upon this small portion of the currency, the effect produced is very great. Thus the occasional variations with which we have to deal are quite insignificant compared with the amount of our currency: and yet, our present monetary system causes these small variations to entirely vitiate our measure of value, and inflict both losses and wrongs upon the community. Instead of neutralising these variations, we greatly magnify them. An alteration of 5 per cent in the quantity of the currency is made to alter its value to five or six times that extent. When, owing either to a diminution of the supply, or to a temporary increase in the requirements of the community, the loanable portion of our currency is reduced to the extent of four or five millions below the ordinary amount, the value of money is raised some 20 or 25 per cent: although the currency itself is reduced only about a thirtieth or fortieth part, —or, it may be, not reduced at all.

The smallness of the variations which so vitiate our measure of value, show how easily these variations may be remedied. When the diminution below the ordinary amount which produces our monetary and commercial embarrassments is only a thirtieth part of our currency, it requires no great effort of science, or triumph of civilisation, to keep the standard-measure at its right length. In fact, it is legislation alone which makes the difficulty, by creating a dimunition of the currency which would not otherwise occur. Leave the community alone—leave to the public and the banks their natural freedom of action, and nearly the whole of the difficulty will at once disappear.

HOW TO CURE THEM.

The very fact that the deficiency of the circulating medium—the instrument of exchange by which payments are effected and loans made—occurs in the banks of a country, simplifies the matter. These establishments for the most part have a large capital of their own, and also large sums entrusted to them for the very purpose of being lent out; and if the community require and desire to take notes of these banks, it is an advantage to both parties that such notes should be issued. Not a single note can get into circulation unless the bank enjoys the confidence of the public,—for of what use would bank-notes be to any one if they were not accepted by others in payment? Nor would a single note be taken unless it were actually wanted,—for what trader would pay for discounts which he did not require? The banks, on their part, would take good care that they got ample security for their advances, and charged a fair price for the use of their capital thus loaned in the form of notes. And as the supply neither would nor could exceed the requirements of the community, the only effect of such issues would be to preserve our measure of value from sinking below its true level. It would be the duty (as it has always been) of the banks to maintain the convertibility of the notes which they issue. And in truth, at the seasons of which we speak—namely when the currency is from any cause inadequate for the wants of the country—people have even less desire than usual to exchange bank-notes for gold. The notes serve their purpose; and they want nothing else. There are at present upwards of two hundred banks of issue in the United Kingdom, and a mere fractional addition to the circulation of these banks would suffice to avert those variations in our measure of value which, under the present system, inflict such losses upon the community.

Actual experience, the safest of teachers, has demonstrated that the cause of all our crises is simply the fact of the currency becoming temporarily insufficient in amount for the requirements of the community; and that the moment this insufficiency is remedied, the crisis is at an end. We have shown this abundantly by reference to historical facts; and the calamities of 1847 and 1857 exemplified the same truth within the experience of the present generation. In every crisis, the moment the Bank of England has reversed its policy of contracting its discounts and circulation, and, to use the words of the Governor of the Bank in 1826, "made common cause with the country," the difficulty has come to an end. It was the notes of the Bank that were wanted by the public, and as soon as these were supplied the crisis terminated. Convertibility on these occasions is not endangered by a temporary increase of issues; on the contrary, by terminating the unreasoning panic in which a great crisis culminates, the issue of the notes actually stops the internal drain for gold.*

* This fact was exemplified in a remarkable manner in the American crisis of 1857, when the internal drain was owing to a contraction of discounts and note-issues on the part of the banks. At the time of the crisis there was no external drain of gold,—on the contrary, specie was then flowing into the country. The drain of gold was internal only, and was chiefly, if not wholly, occasioned by the mistaken policy of the banks. The *Times'* correspondent (writing from New York on the 20th October) remarks on the strangeness of a suspension of specie payments occurring at a time "when the Exchanges throughout the world gave a profit on the transmission of specie to New York." "It was absolutely impossible (he says) on the day of suspension that the specie of New York could find its way out of the town, except by some extraordinary operation unknown to trade. The European exchanges made remittances there impossible. The whole interior was largely indebted to New York. . . . But confidence was utterly gone here. . . . No man believed in anything or anybody this day week. . . . In the beginning of the panic, the banks commenced a contraction, which in a single week reduced their loans 4,000,000 dollars, and increased their specie as much. . . . They might have known that if they showed a want of confidence in the community, by contracting when increased accommodation was demanded, the want of confidence would react upon themselves, who were the depositaries of the floating wealth of the trading world. They, or rather enough of them to control the action of all, reasoned otherwise, and thought they could strengthen themselves at the expense of the merchants. . . . The banks con-

Now, why should not the Bank act in this manner at first, instead of waiting till disaster has overspread the country, and panic has endangered its own position? When gold leaves the country, the obvious remedy is to supply the temporary vacuum with bank-notes. No "depreciation" of the currency arises from such a procedure. No notes will go out unless

tinued to contract, until a very considerable portion of the mercantile community in despair agreed among themselves to withdraw their deposits in specie if relief was not afforded. The relief was denied, and the withdrawal began. There could of course be but one end to this. . . . The moment this game was begun, a suspension became inevitable."—*Times*, Nov. 2, 1857.

The cause of the panic, as the *Times* in its City article justly remarked (Nov. 3), was that "The banks, in their efforts to save themselves, had contracted their note-circulation far below the requirements of the country for its internal trade." And speaking of the result, the same journal observed:—"The entire suspension of specie payments by the New York and Boston banks is the most satisfactory announcement that could have been looked for. Had the step been taken a fortnight earlier, an immense amount of ruin might have been averted. The banks, after having by their mismanagement brought about the state of affairs which rendered the panic possible, sought to save themselves by the sacrifice of the whole mercantile community; but the public at last have taken the matter into their own hands, and forced them to a stoppage, which will place them in the same condition with their victims, and thus terminate the struggle. . . . Its effect was instantaneous. Every one, it is said, seemed to feel that the ordinary channels of business would forthwith be restored, and that from that moment the progress of recovery would commence. A postscript announces that everything was going on quietly, and that all excitement had passed away. This result was perfectly natural. The inconvertible paper of the banks would now circulate at a value in proportion to the discretion with which it might be issued; and supposing it to be kept within close limits, there is no reason that it should fall much, if at all, below par."—*Times*' City Article, October 27, 1857.

there be a demand for them; and the extra demand amply maintains the value of the extra issue. And when the temporary demand ceases, the notes are returned to the banks in the ordinary course of business. Even in the extreme case of a suspension of cash-payments by the banks of a country, the paper-money will preserve its full value, on the simple condition that the supply does not exceed the wants of the community. This is a self-evident proposition. As the *Times* observed, on the occasion of the suspension of cash-payments in America in 1857: "Supposing the paper-issues of the banks, which are based upon the security of State Stocks, to be kept—as there is little doubt they will be—within limits not exceeding the requirements for carrying on the internal trade of the country, this paper will be maintained at par: that is to say, it would be taken for its equivalent in English sovereigns or American eagles."* And the correctness of this opinion was amply established by the result. Nay, more: for "the extraordinary fact was exhibited, of the inconvertible currency of the New York suspended banks being actually at a premium compared with the specie currencies of other countries. That is to say, a bill on London would be purchased in the notes of the New York suspended banks at a price which, after allowing for interest and all charges, would bring back [from London to New

* *Times'* City Article, Oct. 29, 1857.

York] in gold a larger sum than had been paid for it." *

An extra issue of notes, when there is an extra demand for them, only suffices to preserve the measure of value unchanged. It simply prevents prices from being abnormally lowered, and serves to maintain the normal value of money, upon which all contracts are based, from being exceptionally altered. Nor does such an extension of discounts, to meet the requirements of the country, entail any difficulty or hardship upon the Bank of England. On the contrary, it is a source of profit to it. Every additional million's worth of bills discounted is so much additional profit to the Bank. In former times, when, owing to a temporary increase in the requirements of the country, the discount business of the Bank of England or of any other bank increased, it congratulated itself upon this extension of its business, and was well content to make the required advances at the usual rate of 4 or 5 per cent,—the profit on these advances being in greater part a pure gain. And as a basis of any permanent extension of their note-circulation, the banks added to their stock of specie, or of securities readily convertible into specie. In this way the requirements of the community were fully met, with benefit to both parties, and without any enhancement of the normal value of money. But all this is at an end. The natural expansion of the currency, as

* *Ibid.*, Oct. 31, 1857.

regulated by the requirements of the community, is now forbidden by legislative enactment. The great extension of banking, the increased use of cheques, and the enlargement of the "clearing-house" system, have happily sufficed to economise our currency,—so that the same amount now goes much further than it used to do. But in times of crisis, when an exceptional increase of the public requirements takes place, the effects of the new system are most disastrous. The exceptional increase of monetary requirements is always very brief,—and, as we have said, it may be caused by the action of the Bank itself. Yet, during the few weeks of its duration, the consequences to trade are so disastrous that the country is sometimes strewed with fallen firms. There is no longer any elasticity in our currency-system. It is no longer adequate to meet the occasional fluctuations in the demand for currency which are natural in every community. Nor is this evil confined to transient augmentations of the public requirements. If ever, owing to increase of trade and population, 24 millions of the Bank's notes should be permanently required by the wants of the community (instead of 21 as at present), 9 and 10 per cent would become the ordinary rate of discount—rising to 15 and 20 per cent whenever any little embarrassment occurred. Such a state of things—so artificial and so oppressive to trade—could not be tolerated: yet such is the monetary regime under which we now live.

At present the value of the currency, the rise and fall of prices, is regulated by the action of the Bank of England. The Bank has a monopoly of power. No other bank or banks can compete with it. If nine-tenths of all the corn in the country were in the hands of a single company, and if Parliament forbade the establishment of any new company, or any extension of business on the part of those already in existence, the whole community would protest against such an arrangement. Under such a system, the price of corn would not follow its natural course, but would be artificially influenced by the effects of the monopoly. There would be no competition, and accordingly we should have no means of knowing at any particular time what the natural price of grain really was. This is virtually the condition of the country under our present monetary system. If banks of issue had been left free, as they were in Scotland for the century and a half prior to 1844, the real value of money on loan would be at all times readily ascertained. For example, when, owing to an increase of trade or to any other cause, an increase of discounts was required by the community, if some banks were disposed to charge more than a fair rate, they would be kept in check by the others. The banks might fairly be trusted to look after their own interests, by not charging a rate too low to be remunerative: while mutual competition would tend to prevent

THE BANK'S MONOPOLY.

the exaction of rates unduly high. But no such check at present exists. The Bank of England has a virtual monopoly of the note-issues of the kingdom; and it is the only bank which can extend its issues on a sudden, so as to meet any exceptional increase in the demand for discounts. Hence it has a virtual monopoly at all times; and in exceptional times, as in a crisis, its monopoly is absolute. All the other banks of issue are such pigmies, compared to the Bank of England, that it is hopeless for them to enter into rivalry with it. Prior to 1844 the provincial banks of England used to extend their issues to meet the requirements of their locality,—doing so at 5 per cent with good profit to themselves. But they cannot so extend their issues now; and they compensate themselves for this contraction of business by readily following the example of the Bank by exacting the same high rates. To talk of the value of money in the "open market" in this country is simply to mislead. Owing to the great expenses of the Bank's establishment, the discount-houses, and many of the other banks, can afford to discount bills at a fraction below the Bank-rate. If the Bank discounts at 2 per cent, they can discount at $1\frac{3}{4}$. And whenever they see that the Bank's rate is likely to be lowered, they anticipate the fall. But so entirely dependent are they upon the Bank, that (except when there is an abnormal depression of trade) the Bank has only to raise its rate, and the whole banking and discount-houses raise theirs also. It is, of course, a source of profit for them to do so. They are not only dependent upon the Bank, but they have an interest in following it in every rise of the rate of discount. The note-circulation—the currency with which these banks and discount-houses carry on their business—is entirely under the control of the Bank of England. These banks and discount-houses have a vast amount of loanable capital deposited with them, but for the instrument by which this capital can be lent out, they are wholly dependent upon the Bank of England. They are but satellites, and can do nothing but follow suit.*

Before concluding this portion of our subject, we have one more remark to make :—

The Bank does not adhere to the "variation" theory at times when a drain of gold takes place; for it does not contract its note-circulation in proportion as its

* However the "market-rate" may occasionally vary from the Bank-rate, it is essentially dependent upon it. If the other banks and discount-houses see that the Bank's reserve is increasing, so that a fall in the Bank-rate is likely to take place soon, they anticipate this fall by at once reducing their own charges. But no such reduction of the "market-rate" takes place save as a simple forestalment of the expected fall of the Bank-rate. The truth of this is easily demonstrated. As we have shown, the Bank now charges 8 per cent under circumstances when formerly it charged only 4 per cent: and the essential dependence of the market-rate upon the Bank-rate is amply shown by the fact that the market-rate has risen in exact imitation of this arbitrary change in the practice of the Bank of England. The market-rate, we repeat, never sinks more than a fraction below the Bank-rate, unless as a simple forestalment of an expected fall in the Bank-rate.

stock of bullion decreases. The Bank's system, as we have stated, is to meet a drain of gold by greatly raising its rate of discount. Now, as a question between the Bank and the community, there is a vast difference between these two methods of procedure. If the Bank contracted its issues—as Sir R. Peel wished it to do, and also as the "variation" theory requires,—it would sell its Government securities in proportion as gold was withdrawn, and cancel the notes which it received in payment. This was the course which Sir R. Peel desired and expected it to take: and he anticipated that in some cases the Bank would, for this purpose, have to sell off the whole three millions of Government stock upon which it is allowed to issue notes. And if this did not suffice to produce an adequate contraction of its note-issues, the Bank would thereafter have to proceed by lessening the amount of its discount-operations. Such a method of procedure would diminish the profits of the Bank. The Bank would incur a loss (as other banks do) by selling its Government stock at a time of monetary pressure; and if it had at the same time to reduce the amount of its discount-business, it would lose in this way also. This, we repeat, was the course which Sir R. Peel expected the Bank to follow. He regarded a drain upon the Bank as one of those "hard times" which occasionally befall all

WHAT SIR R. PEEL DESIRED.

kinds of business, and which must be borne by those who carry on the business. He regarded it as an emergency for which the Bank itself must provide. Just as in hard times a merchant has to sell his reserve, whether kept in the form of goods or in financial stock, even though he must lose by selling at such times,—so Sir R. Peel expected and desired that the Bank should act in like manner, and provide for the requirements of its customers by realising a portion, or if need be the whole, of its reserved assets,—these reserves, in fact, being kept for no other purpose.

WHAT THE BANK DOES.

But the Bank does nothing of the kind. It does not sell its Government stock for the purpose of cancelling the notes received in payment —neither does it diminish its discount-business. Nor yet does it take means to provide itself with the gold which is requisite to carry on its business. It takes no loss upon itself at all. The loss which itself should incur it now throws entirely upon the community. Instead of selling its reserve of stock, and curtailing its business, it makes the mercantile classes sell *their* goods and contract *their* business. Indeed it does more than this. It not only throws upon the community the burden of replenishing its vaults with gold, but it makes a profit in addition. By charging very high rates of discount, it not only causes gold to be brought into the country at the expense of the mercantile classes (*i. e.*, in purchase of their artificially-depreciated goods), but, by the same process, it makes an addition to its ordinary profits, by wringing an extra sum out of these classes in the form of discounts.

It is important to note these facts. The Bank Directors do not work the Act of 1844 as its framer desired; they do not take the burden of their business upon themselves, as he expected them to do; they have shifted it on to the shoulders of the community, and, besides shirking a loss, make an actual profit in addition.

THE BANK NOW SUPPORTS THE ACT.

When such are the facts of the case, it is not surprising to know that the Bank Directors are unanimously in favour of our present monetary system. It would be strange if they were not. They have two separate reasons for upholding the Act of 1844. In the first place, it shields them from responsibility. Whatever measures they take, they appeal to the Act in justification. Whether they raise the rate of discount or lower it,—whether they expand the currency or contract it,—if they refuse to discount cotton bills or Exchequer bills, or decline to make advances upon personal assets and securities,—"the Act" is the answer which they make to all criticism and complaints. They prefer to cover themselves with this shield, rather than to have their management judged upon the merits. This is natural enough,—even though the provisions of the Act have frequently nothing to do with the policy which they adopt. In the second place, the Directors have another and more palpable interest in upholding the Act. Although the Act makes no regulations as to the rate of discount—although it enjoins a contraction of the currency which they do not put in force,—it affords them a ground for doubling the rates which they charge for money. It enables them to charge 8 per cent in circumstances where formerly they used to charge 4 per cent. They say—and it is not we who put the words into their mouth—"But for the Act of 1844 it would be impracticable for us to keep on hand so large a stock of gold, and at the same time charge the rates we now do: the commercial classes would rebel against such conduct on our part, if we could not fall back in defence upon this Act of the Legislature." They feel the weakness of their position, and answer all criticism by an appeal to the Bank Act.

This is natural. Every party supports the system which is most advantageous for it. But the fact that

WHY IT DOES SO.

the Bank Directors are now in favour of the Act is a very dubious argument in support of that measure. When the measures which have given freedom to Trade were under discussion, no one thought of leaving the merits of the Corn-laws to be decided by the opinion of farmers,—or the Navigation-laws to be judged by shipowners, —or the Silk-duties by the weavers of Coventry. Just as little are the merits of the Bank Act to be decided by the opinions of the Bank Directors. The Act is a convenient screen, which shields them from responsibility; and it is also a great source of gain to the Bank,—and to all banks. We do not say that it is from these motives alone that the Bank Directors so strenuously uphold the Act. Self-interest unconsciously biasses the judgment, and is fertile in suggesting arguments in its own favour. The Directors doubtless believe that the losses which their high rates impose upon the commercial classes are necessary to avoid worse evils. The farmers did not say, "We uphold the Corn-law because, though it occasions high prices and hardship to the community at large, it gives us high profits though the masses starve." They said, "The Corn-law ensures the growth of more wheat in this country than there would otherwise be, and thus acts as a provision against the effects of a widespread famine or of a blockade during times of war." In like manner the Directors say, "The Act keeps more gold in the Bank than there would be otherwise." The country ignored the arguments of the farmers, and there is still better ground for disregarding the opinion of the Bank Directors. The additional amount of wheat which would have been grown in this country if the Corn-law had been maintained, would, every bushel of it, have come into the market for the supply of the community; whereas the extra stock of gold kept by the Bank, under the Act of 1844, is as useless to the community, until the Act be suspended or annulled, as if it were at the bottom of the sea.

It is also to be observed that this unanimity on the part of the Bank Court in favour of the Act of 1844 is of recent date. For several years after the passing of the Act, the Bank Directors were by no means friendly to it. As long as the Act was worked according to the intentions of its framers, the Bank Court was unfavourable to it. And for this very intelligible reason, that it lessened their profits. As long as they adhered (which they never did fully) to the principle of the Act—namely, that whenever a drain of gold takes place, the Bank should contract its note-circulation—the only way of complying with the Act was for the Bank to sell a portion of its securities (of course at such times at a loss), and to contract its business by lending out less of its money. This imposed loss upon the Bank, and the Bank rebelled against the system. But now that they have adopted a new process—now that they have found that they can work the Act in a way which, instead of lessening their profits, greatly increases them,—the Directors have changed their opinion. The Act is now to them what the worship of Diana was to Demetrius and his fellow-silversmiths of Ephesus. Hence they uphold the Act most religiously.

There is another point which is deserving of attention. The Directors assert that they are quite ready to work the Act under all circumstances. They say that they have no desire, or need, to have the Act suspended. In their own words, they say, "Whatever may be the sufferings of the rest of the community, we can always save ourselves." It may be prudent for the Directors to feign this confidence, but we hope they do not feel it. If they do, they are cherishing what may prove a fatal delusion. They reckon that, though they have not another note to issue, they can go on discounting new bills as usual, as the old ones run off; and that, if the demand for discounts should increase beyond this means of meeting it, all they have to do is to raise their charge to more exorbitant heights. They reckon that a rate of "20 or 30 per cent" will lessen the demand as effectually as if they were frankly to decline discounting a portion of the bills; and this process, of course, would give them enormous gains upon the bills which they continued to discount. It is obvious, from the rates which they are at present charging, that they purpose to exact far higher rates should a really serious crisis occur. If they charge 9 per cent when their stock

AND THINKS IT CAN WORK IT.

of gold amounts to thirteen millions, what will they not charge when (as in 1857) their stock of gold is falling to seven millions? But this will not do. The Directors are reckoning without their host. They are counting the community as nothing. Their idea in this matter is like that of a general who arranges his tactics on the supposition that the other side will remain inactive, and simply allow themselves to be killed. The result never corresponds to such anticipations. If the Bank shows itself ready to sacrifice its customers, the commercial classes, it is not to be expected that the latter will tamely submit to the proposed immolation. The customers of the Bank at such a time need only to call up a million of their deposits, and then—instead of being able to carry out its programme of raising the rate of discount to 15, 20, or 30 per cent—the Bank is shut up at once, and becomes insolvent (not really, but, like many other firms which it had sacrificed) by Act of Parliament. Such a result, in such circumstances, would at once bring matters to their true level. Since the obstacle to the Bank's continuance of its ordinary discount-accommodation at such times is purely artificial, while the consequences to the commercial classes are disastrous in the extreme, the sooner the Bank is stopped in such a career of slaughter the better. Thereafter the real state of matters will be acknowledged: the artificial cause of all the mischief will be annulled,—and the artificial crisis and sacrifice of the mercantile classes will be at an end.

Whether we judge from the published sentiments of the more ardent supporters of the Bank Act, or from the recent and present conduct of the Bank, it seems evident that this game of enormously raising the rate of discount is the one which the Directors are resolved to play whenever another crisis like that of 1857 recurs. And it seems to us quite as certain that the game will fail. Surely, then, instead of the Directors awaiting, in ill-founded confidence, the deplorable conflict which may arise between the Bank and the commercial classes, when another monetary crisis occurs,—it were better for all parties to reconsider betimes the character of our monetary legislation, and to obtain the abolition of such enactments as have proved to be unworkable by the Bank and extremely injurious to the community.

WHAT SIR R. PEEL WOULD HAVE DONE.

We think we have now sufficiently, and with careful reference to facts, demonstrated that the Act of 1844 has failed in the object which it was designed to accomplish, and that it has subjected the country to new evils, of which its illustrious framer never dreamt, and which he would have been the first to deplore. If Sir Robert Peel had lived until now, and seen how completely his expectations have been falsified by the working of the Act, he would have been the first to acknowledge the failure, and to amend it. He was a statesman who never hesitated to change his opinions when he found them to be injurious to the country. A stanch opponent of Catholic Emancipation, he became its foremost supporter. The champion of the Corn-laws, he turned round and abolished them. The framer of the Act of 1844, he would—had he lived till now—have already tabled a Bill to amend it. He had made his reputation, and he was not afraid to risk it. At the present time, unfortunately, we have no Minister who enjoys the great reputation of Sir Robert Peel in questions of economical science. And our leading men, on both sides of the House, shrink from having the authority of so distinguished a statesman quoted against them: forgetful that if Sir Robert Peel had been still amongst us, his practical sagacity would not have delayed the work of amendment until now.

It is full time that the mistakes of the Bank Act should be recognised. It is time also that the Bank of England were restored to that freedom of action without which there can be no sense of responsibility on the part of the Directors,—no scope for real ability in the management,—and no adequate support to public credit in times of monetary and commercial difficulty. It is upon the sagacity of experienced men, not

GIVE FREEDOM TO THE BANK.

upon the dead formulism of a machine, that this country, and every country, must rely for an able and beneficial direction of so important a branch of the national resources. In England there has been far too much legislation for the welfare of banking. The Bank has been so swaddled and cramped, so favoured and fettered, so petted and plundered, by the State, that its natural growth was prevented, and its present condition is wholly artificial and anomalous. First Monopoly, and now Restriction, have exercised their baneful influence upon English banking. Both are pernicious in principle, injurious to the community, and incompatible with the due use and economy of capital.

We do not begrudge the Bank its actual amount of profits. Compared with those of other English banks, its profits are moderate. We simply object to the Bank making gains at the expense of the community by shirking its duty, and refusing to make proper provision for its banking requirements. If the State has imposed upon it undue burdens, that is a legitimate reason for its protesting against the legislation which has imposed those burdens. But it is too much that the Bank should lend its powerful support to the Act of 1844, simply because it has found a way to shirk its duty, and to throw upon the community in a tenfold degree the burden which under the Act (and indeed irrespective of the Act) should fall upon itself. In order to save itself from the ordinary losses incidental to banking, it covers the country with bankruptcies, sacrifices the mercantile classes, and throws thousands of the working-classes out of employment. Such a course of procedure becomes still more objectionable when the Bank actually makes an addition to its gains out of the calamities which it thus imposes on the country.

A HINT TO TRADE.

As to the commercial classes, a continuance of the present system is the worst evil that can possibly befall them. And if they cannot protect themselves—if the power which a long-continued monopoly has conferred upon the Bank is too strong for them,—we should advise them to lighten the burden thus thrown upon them by proposing a compromise. "Agree with thine adversary quickly whilst thou art in the way." Let the mercantile classes take the matter as philosophers, and make the best of a bad bargain. Let them "send round the hat" among themselves, and collect an annual sum which, whenever a drain of gold occurs, shall be employed in purchasing gold at a premium on the Continent, in order to replenish the Bullion vaults of the Bank. By paying this premium they will, of course, escape the black-mail levied upon them by the "Old Lady in Threadneedle Street" in the form of high rates of discount,—as well as the attendant depression of the home-market, and the depreciation of their goods to the extent of 20 or 25 per cent. In all earnestness—if the present system were to be maintained—the mercantile classes would make a gain by adopting such a course. At present the incubus under which they suffer is as firmly clasped upon them as was the Old Man of the Sea upon the back of poor Sinbad: and if they cannot shake it off, they had much better buy it off.

WHY THE BANK SHIRKS ITS DUTY.

When a powerful corporation like the Bank of England thus shirks the duty of providing for the legitimate demands upon it, it is well to examine whether there are not some special causes for such conduct. Now, one of these unquestionably is, the existence of the "variation" theory as the orthodox creed of monetary science. That creed holds that when gold leaves the country, it is incumbent to attract it back again *at once* (it would return in natural course of itself*), by depressing the home-market, and inducing foreigners to send over specie in purchase of the depreciated goods of our merchants and of the community in general. We have previously pointed out the demerits of this system, and need not recapitulate them. We allude to it now simply to explain the conduct of the Bank. When such is the established creed, the Bank naturally reasons thus:—"Our gold is leaving us. Losses, bankruptcies, and want of employment must be suffered by the country in

* See *supra*, pp. 235-238.

one way or other, in order to stop the drain. And since it can't much matter to the country in what manner we inflict upon it this suffering, it is best to do it in a way that is profitable to the Bank, instead of in a way that makes us as great sufferers as the country." This, no doubt, is the reasoning of the Bank Court. In accordance with the prevailing creed, the Bank regards the sacrifice of the community as an inevitable calamity; and, with that point settled, it sees no harm in doing the business in the manner most profitable for itself. If the Bank is to play the ungracious part of executioner, let it be well paid for its work. The "variation theory," as we have demonstrated, is essentially absurd. For the sake of the country, we hope soon to see it abandoned for a wiser and a better system. But as long as it remains the orthodox creed of the day, the only objection that can be taken to the Bank's view of the matter, as above described, is, that since the Bank finds this course so profitable to itself, it may be ready to play the part of executioner too often. If it shared the losses which it inflicts upon the community (as Sir R. Peel proposed), there would be an adequate guarantee against an unnecessary recourse to stringent measures. In that case, the Bank's losses would have to begin first. Moreover, in such circumstances we could rely upon the Bank Court giving an unbiassed opinion upon the merits of the Act which is the main cause of these recurrent national calamities. But, as long as the Bank is exempted from the general suffering occasioned by its present system—nay, makes an extra profit out of it,—its interests in this matter are directly at variance with those of the community.

There is another reason, or inducement, for the Bank pursuing its present system of action. The profits of the other leading banking establishments in England averaged last year 20 or 25 per cent; this year—judging from the last half-year, and from the fact that the rate of discount is now higher than before—the average will be 30 per cent. The Bank of England, on the other hand, is only making 12 per cent. Naturally the Bank Court is dissatisfied, and adopts every legal means of increasing the dividend. Twelve per cent, it is true, is a very good profit on banking business. The profits of every kind of business in the long-run are dependent upon the amenities of the business and upon its risks. The man who invests his capital in landed property does not get more than 3 per cent upon it: for the possession of land is a species of luxury,—it confers a greater social position than any other investment, and is attended with no risks. In like manner the farmer, whose avocation is healthy and agreeable, and attended by few risks, does not on the average make more than 8 per cent on his capital.

LARGER PROFITS OF OTHER BANKS.

The great merchants and manufacturers, on the other hand, who are exposed to serious vicissitudes of fortune, reckon upon getting 25 per cent profit on each year's transactions,—but, as a set-off to this, in some cases they get only 5 or 10 per cent, or none at all. And those tradesmen whose gains are in a great measure dependent upon the caprices of fashion, expect a similar high rate of profit. But banking belongs to the former rather than to the latter style of business. A banker is an influential man; his business gives him a good position in society; and it is not attended with much risk. Hence, we say, 10 per cent is a good rate of profit in banking. Nor is this a mere theoretical inference. In Scotland, where banking has been systematised to a greater extent than in England, and where certain fixed rules have been recognised and practised for at least a century,—we find that the profits of banking on the average do not amount to 10 per cent. Even in this year of very dear money, the profits will not reach 12 per cent. And the regularity of system pursued by the Scotch banks is evidenced by the fact that the percentage of profit of each and all of them is almost identical. We find the same fact evidenced by the dividends of the Bank of England and of the Bank of France. From 1823 up to 1854, the yearly dividends of the Bank of England varied from 7 to 8 per cent: it is only since 1854 that the dividends have risen to 9, 10, and this year to 12 per cent. For these several reasons, we think we are justified in regarding 10 per cent as a fair average profit in banking. The rate of profits, of course, will be higher in the case of banks which attract an exceptionally large amount of deposits in proportion to their paid-up capital: but still, on the average, 10 per cent is a fair profit on this kind of business. Nevertheless, when the fact is that the other leading English banks are at present reaping 25 or 30 per cent profit, it is natural for the Bank of England, the greatest establishment of the kind in the country, to do its best to lessen the disproportion between its own dividends and those of other great banking establishments.

Now, why is it that the profits of the Bank of England are so much less than those of the London joint-stock banks? A glance at their balance-sheets at once explains the matter. The capital of the Bank of England is enormously in excess of what is required to carry on its amount of business; the capital of the London joint-stock banks, on the other hand, is very much below the amount which in ordinary cases is deemed requisite for safe banking.* The paid-up capital of the Bank amounts to 14½ mil-

ITS CAPITAL TOO LARGE.

* We do not mean to say that the London joint-stock banks are carried on with inadequate capital: we hold no such opinion. Experience is the only guide in such a matter, and unquestionably the London joint-stock banks have worked exceedingly well. The smaller the amount of paid-up capital with which a bank can *safely*

lions, while that of the London joint-stock banks in no case exceeds one million. In the next place, the "Rest" (or fund set aside to supplement the dividend in years of low profits) amounts to 3 millions in the Bank of England, while in the new joint-stock banks it rarely exceeds a tenth of that amount. Now, putting out of view the "Rest"—which, though really a part of the paid-up capital, is reducible at pleasure to any amount which the Bank Court may think advisable,—it is manifest that an establishment which has a paid-up capital of 14½ millions is unduly weighted in a race with others whose paid-up capital does not in any case exceed one million. Its net profits would require to be about fourteen times larger than theirs to allow of its paying the same amount of dividend. The liabilities of the Bank (consisting in nearly equal proportions of its note-issues and of its deposits) amount to 40 millions. The Bank of France, with an identical amount of liabilities (three-fourths of which are note-issues, and the other fourth deposits), has a paid-up capital of less than 7¼ millions. A Scotch bank, if it had the same amount of liabilities (*i. e.*, 40 millions), would have a paid-up capital of five or six millions. An English joint-stock bank, with the same amount

carry on its operations, the better: for the larger will be its profits. In the text, we simply state the fact—namely, that the capital of these banks is very much less than has hitherto been found safe in ordinary banking.—For a synopsis of the position of these banks, and also of the Scotch banks, see Appendix A.

of liabilities, would have a paid-up capital of two millions. The Bank of France is a sufficiently exact parallel to the case of the Bank of England, yet the capital of the former is only one-half that of the latter bank; and nearly 2⅜ millions of it are withdrawn from banking purposes, being lent to the State. In fact, the Bank of France conducts its business with an available capital of five millions, which is just about what a Scotch bank would do if it had an equal amount of liabilities. From these facts it may safely be inferred that the capital of the Bank of England is at least double what is necessary for the safe prosecution of its business.

How comes it, it will be asked, that the Bank's capital is so needlessly large? No bank with the same amount of liabilities would ever think of calling up so great an amount of capital, and thereby needlessly, and to a most serious extent, diminishing its rate of profits. Why has the Bank of England done so? The explanation is simple. The calling up of these 14½ millions has been the chief means by which the Bank purchased its privileges from the State. Every expiry of its charter was made an occasion for new exactions on the part of the State, and for new privileges obtained in return by the Bank. It was in return for a loan of its capital that the State conferred upon it (in 1708) that monopoly which has worked so much mischief to the country; and it was

WHY IT IS SO.

by similar or analogous means that its charter was so often renewed, and its privileges extended. The large capital was not raised by the Bank as necessary to carry on its business, but in order to purchase a continuance or extension of privileges from the State. It is the price which it has paid for privileges obtained at the expense of the community. For the sake of getting certain loans on easy terms from the Bank, the Government in past times conferred upon that establishment a monopoly unfair to the other banks, and most detrimental to the country. That is the meaning of the largeness of the Bank's capital.

The age of monopoly is past; and gradually the monopoly of the Bank, already encroached upon, must be diminished till it disappear. But, in proportion as this end is to be attained, the State must give up the loans, &c., by which the Bank purchased its privileges. Thirty years ago one-fourth of the debt due by the Government to the Bank was paid off; and whenever the state of the finances permits, the process of repaying these loans ought to be resumed. The repayment of the eleven millions still due by the Government to the Bank is, in fact, the very best form in which the reductions of our national debt can be effected. The Government may fairly insist that the Bank shall accept repayment in the form of Consols, yielding an equal amount of interest to that which the Bank at present receives upon the loan.

Instead of receiving 3 per cent upon the loan, the Bank will be paid in Consols at par, yielding an equal amount of interest. Thus, suppose Consols stand at 91, ten millions will suffice to pay off the debt of eleven millions due to the Bank, without the Bank being a loser. Of course, such repayment would be spread over several years; so as not to embarrass the Government, nor unduly affect the value of Consols. Say the repayment were spread over ten or fifteen years, then about three-fourths of a million sterling would each year be invested by the Government in the purchase of Consols, which thereafter would be handed over to the Bank. As upwards of 200 millions of Consols change hands every year, the effect of these purchases by the Government would be quite imperceptible, even though they were very much larger. Thereafter (unless some limitation were imposed, inimical to the freedom which we desire for the Bank), the Bank would have full control over the Government Stock thus transferred to it; and might sell portions of it at its convenience,—employing the money thus received in the discount of bills, the purchase of gold, or in any other part of its business.

PAYMENT FOR ITS CHARTER.

Besides the undue magnitude of its capital, the Bank of England lies under another burden as compared with other banks, in the shape of the £120,000 a-year which it pays to the Government for the continuance of its

Charter. Such a payment is a relic of a bad and antiquated system. Like the loans which caused the Bank's capital to be unduly augmented, this payment is exacted by the Government in return for the privileges accorded to the Bank. The system of giving peculiar privileges to any company is now regarded as a most improper interference on the part of the State, injurious to the community, and unjust to other companies of a similar kind. Every one is now agreed on this point. Nevertheless, it does not necessarily follow that this annual impost upon the Bank should be abolished. This would be tantamount to increasing the Bank's profits to the extent of £120,000 a-year. The payment is levied as a means of compensating the country for the advantages acquired in former times by the Bank to the public detriment; and it is only in proportion as this detriment is removed that the Charter-money can be lessened. The evil to the community created by the Bank's long-continued monopoly cannot at once or easily be undone; and since the evil remains, the compensation-money may fairly be exacted. But, on principle, it is a highly objectionable arrangement. And moreover — as a practical question,— although it is true that the exaction of this sum tends to lessen the virtual monopoly of the Bank, by allowing other banks of issue to compete with it on less unequal terms, this plea cannot be adduced in support of the arrangement as long as Parliament actually forbids the establishment or development of banks of issue to compete with it at all.

The profits of the Issue Department of the Bank may be stated thus. On all note-issues above fourteen millions the Bank has no profit,—because it must hold gold to an equal amount (*minus* £650,000, on which the profits go to the Government). The profit on these fourteen millions of notes (if reckoned at 3 per cent) is £420,000 a-year. Deduct from this sum £117,000, being the cost to the Bank of making and managing a note-circulation of twenty millions; also £24,000 paid by the Bank to other banks which undertake to issue its notes on receiving one per cent of commission; also £60,000, being the composition paid to the Stamp-Office upon the note-issues; also £120,000, which the Bank pays for its Charter. Thus from £420,000 there is to be deducted £321,000,—leaving a balance of profit to the Bank upon its note-issues of £99,000. This was Sir R. Peel's estimate in 1844. But two other matters must be taken into account before the balance can be correctly struck. If the Bank were in a natural condition, instead of having a capital of fourteen millions (partly lent to the Government, and partly invested in Government stock), one half of that amount invested in Consols would suffice. The seven millions of capital that might thus be spared would, if invested in the Bank's business, yield a larger profit than the

PROFIT ON ITS NOTES.

3 per cent which it gets from them at present. On the other hand, in these times of dear money, the profit on the fourteen millions of the Bank's note-issues may be taken at a much higher rate than the 3 per cent at which it was estimated in 1844. Previous to that year, although the Bank's charge for discounting bills averaged 5 per cent, yet its advances on Consols, &c., were made at 3 or 4 per cent.; so that Sir R. Peel, dealing generously, was justified in estimating the profit on the notes at only 3 per cent.

The profit and loss account of the Issue Department, as reckoned by Sir R. Peel in 1844, was as follows:—

Profit on 14 millions of notes at 3 per cent,		£420,000
Cost of note-circulation,	£117,000	
Commission of 1 per cent to other banks,	24,000	
Composition with Stamp-Office,	60,000	
Payment for Charter,	120,000	
		321,000
Net profit to Bank on its note-issues,		£99,000

Owing to the higher rates of discount exacted by the Bank, the case is now greatly altered. For the last twelve months, the gross profit upon the Bank's note-issues, instead of 3 per cent, has been 8 per cent, —instead of £420,000, it is now £1,112,000: so that, after deducting the above-stated £321,000 of costs and charges, the net profit on the Issue Department has this year been £799,000,—eight times greater than in 1844, when the conditions of its Charter were last fixed by the State. If the Bank continues its present system of charging twice as much for its advances as it used to do, this fact will have to be taken into account whenever its Charter is renewed, and if the Government proceeds on the same principle as in 1844, the payment which the Bank makes for its privileges must be doubled.

Although the dividends of the Bank appear small compared with those of the London joint-stock banks, the amount of its profits, in relation to its deposits, is immensely larger than theirs. Take, for example, the case of the London and Westminister Bank. The amount of its deposits is fully 18½ millions; that of the Bank of England is rather more, say 21 millions. But the net profit of the London and Westminster Bank during the last half-year was only £234,000; while that of the Bank of England was £850,000, or more than 3½ times larger. This great excess of profit arises from the note-issues of the Bank: the profit upon which, during the last half-year, must have amounted to fully half a million *net*—*i. e.*, after deducting every cost connected with its note-issues, and also the sums paid to the State for Charter, &c. The profits of the Bank, in truth, are at present very great; and it is only the undue amount of its capital which makes its dividends appear small compared with those of the London joint-stock banks.

In the case of banks existing under natural conditions—that is to say, when the State confers no privileges upon any of them at the expense of the others, —the note-issues of each bank bear a general proportion to its amount of deposits. The instrument of exchange issued by a bank ought to have a certain relation to the loanable capital of the bank which it is designed to utilise and represent. In the case of the Scotch banks, for example, the proportion of note-issues to deposits is less than one-fifteenth. The Bank of England, on the contrary, has a note-circulation equal to the whole amount of the loanable capital entrusted to its keeping. After making every allowance for the influence of prestige, it may fairly be said that three-fourths of the note-circulation of the Bank of England are due to the effects of the monopoly conferred upon it by the State. And, whether reasoning from these premises or not, Sir R. Peel, in 1844, regulated the State's charge upon the Bank pretty nearly in this proportion. Assuming that the Bank made a profit of 3 per cent (£420,000) on the 14 millions of its note-issues for which it is not compelled to keep gold to an equal amount; and deducting from this sum £140,000 for the Bank's cost upon its note-issues, he charged upon the balance (£280,000) the sum of £180,000 as an impost which the State might fairly levy upon the Bank. If Sir R. Peel had foreseen that the Bank's profit upon its note-circulation would be greatly increased (as it has been in consequence of its increasing

REVISION OF ITS CHARTER.

the rate of discount), he would doubtless have raised in equal proportion the sum which the Bank pays for its Charter.

In truth the Bank of England now relies for its profits almost entirely upon its note-issues. While the joint-stock banks derive their whole profits from their deposits, and seek to increase the amount of these deposits by offering favourable terms to depositors, the Bank follows an entirely different course. It takes no measures to attract deposits,—it resolutely refuses to pay interest of any kind to those who bank with it. It stands still, while the rest of the world moves on. Compared with those of other banks, the amount of its deposits remains stationary. The loanable capital entrusted to its keeping hardly exceeds in amount that which is held by some of the leading joint-stock banks, —as, for example, the Union and the London and Westminster Banks. And yet, nearly a third of the Bank of England's deposits consist of Government money,—which it receives in consequence of its State privileges, and for the possession of which the other banks cannot compete. Deduct this amount of Treasury balances, and the Bank, judged by its deposits, would hold only a secondary position among the London banks. The effect of this policy (or rather stagnation) on the part of the Bank is, of course, to make it rely almost exclusively upon its note-issues for its gains. If it is to increase its gains—if it is in any measure to keep pace with the increase of profits which the other banks are obtaining from the yearly increase of their deposits,—the Bank must do so by working its note-issues in such a way as to make them more profitable. In other words, it must charge more for the use of its notes. The Bank must make the community pay more for the use of the paper-money which the State permits it to issue,—and in the making of which issues it has a virtual monopoly. In short, it must keep its rate of discount at a higher level than before. And, as we have shown,* this is the very course which it now follows.

As a renewal of the Bank's Charter is approaching, a revision of the agreement between the Bank and the State, and we trust of our whole monetary system likewise, will soon take place. As regards the position of the Bank, it is so anomalous that, as a practical affair, it is hardly possible to suggest a new arrangement based simply upon the natural principles of economical science. We cannot at once annul the past, and begin *de novo*. The position of the Bank, and its relations with the State, present a Gordian knot of entanglement. Only bit by bit can the knot be loosed: for it would be unwise to solve it by the summary process of the great Macedonian. But there are three leading points to be kept in view. The first of these is, that the present embargo laid upon six or seven millions

* See *supra*, p. 267.

of gold should be annulled, and the Bank should have the free use of all its resources. Secondly, its monopoly is injurious to the community, and may fairly be paid for,—the Bank's note-circulation being far above the amount it would have obtained but for the monopoly, and its power over the currency being proportionate. But thirdly, and most important of all, —it must be remembered that, as long as freedom of issues is prohibited, it is vain for the Government to seek compensation for the Bank's monopoly by levying upon it a proportionate charge; for, as long as the present monopoly of note-issues is maintained, whatever charge is laid on the Bank can be—as it at present is—transferred by the Bank to the shoulders of the community.

There is a source of profit of which the Bank might legitimately avail itself, and which would add to its gains in a less objectionable manner than its present course of charging abnormally high rates of discount upon inadequate grounds. When its stock of bullion is in excess of the usual amount, the Bank, instead of keeping a portion of its gold lying useless in its vaults, would do well to send it abroad,—by investing in foreign securities, ready to be sold and re-converted into gold when necessary. At present, when gold in unusual quantity flows into its vaults, the Bank reduces its rate to 2 per cent, and yet, even upon these terms, cannot get its surplus stock of notes taken off its hands. The Bank gains little or nothing by such a reduction of its rate, even though its discount-business be thereby greatly enlarged. If the Bank's weekly amount of discounts be seven millions at times when the Bank-rate is 4 per cent, then the weekly amount of its discount-business must be doubled, in order to be equally profitable when the rate is at 2 per cent. Would it not be better, then, for the Bank if, when it has a plethora of gold, it were to invest a portion of its surplus bullion in the purchase of foreign stocks,—say in New York, Paris, Calcutta, &c.? This investment, of course, to be in addition to its ordinary banking reserve of this kind which we have proposed.* When the Bank's stock of bullion is unusually large, the amount of notes which it is empowered to place in its banking department is greatly in excess of its requirements, either for issue or as a reserve. If it were to employ a portion of this surplus gold in the purchase of foreign securities, it would derive a profit from the investment, by obtaining interest on a large sum that would otherwise lie sterile in its vaults. When it has fourteen millions of bullion in its possession, it can issue £28,650,000 of notes—eight millions more than is required by the public in ordinary times. Every million of gold above this amount, therefore, might be invested in the manner we have described,

* See *supra*, p. 249.

not only with profit to the Bank, but with no loss to the public. For, as gold in its vaults began to sink below fourteen millions (or whatever were the point fixed), the Bank would sell out a corresponding portion of its foreign securities, and place specie to the same amount in its Issue department.* This would be a legitimate method of increasing the profits of the Bank. Such profits accruing to it would be a source of satisfaction to every one, and would be regarded in a very different light from the augmentation of its gains which it now makes in seasons of monetary difficulty, at the expense and suffering of the community, by raising its rate of discount to the exorbitant height of 9 or 10 per cent.

But why should there be any "excess" of gold at all in the Bank? This is occasioned by the peculiar provision of the Act of 1844, which enacts that the Bank shall buy all the gold that is brought to it, whether it desires to have it or not. It is compelled by the Act to receive deposits of bullion just as if they were deposits of money. If a man brings to it a certain sum in the form of a cheque upon another bank, or in the notes of another bank, the Bank is at liberty to decline opening an account with him, or to give him in exchange

BANK COMPELLED TO BUY GOLD.

* Or, instead of paying gold to customers who desire to export it, the Bank might let them draw upon its credits at New York, Calcutta, or other places: which would attain the same object by different means.

an equal sum in its own notes. But if he tenders to it a certain quantity of bullion, it is compelled to purchase that gold from him, either by giving him notes to an equal amount, or by placing that amount to his credit. No such necessity is imposed upon any other bank. The Bank of England is the only bank in the world which is placed under this compulsion. This is a great violation of the freedom of banking. Why should the Bank of England be subjected to it? The bullion which it is compelled to purchase from all comers, is not money. Take one of those glittering ingots which are ceaselessly being brought to the Bullion Office, and taken away again, and see if it will anywhere pass as money. Will any tradesman accept it in payment of his account? Will any bank receive it in payment of a bill, or as a sum to be placed to the account of the bringer? Or will the Government accept it in payment of taxes? Not a bit of it. Even cut it up into small pieces, and let each of those pieces be of the exact weight and purity of a sovereign or half-sovereign, and the result will still be the same. It will not circulate: no one will receive it as money. Why, then, should the Bank of England be compelled to receive it as money? If the Government will not receive bullion as money, why should it compel the Bank to do so?

The bullion which the Bank is thus compelled to purchase is not only not currency, but the greater part of it is not meant to be turned into currency. Nearly the whole of it is kept in the Bullion Office in the form of ingots. The Bank does not turn it into money: to do so in fact would be a disadvantage. It is not kept by the Bank in the form of sovereigns; and it is not wanted in the form of sovereigns by those who withdraw it from the Bank. It is kept simply as bullion, which is not meant to be converted into English money, but to be exported (as it was imported) simply as a valuable commodity,—as an article which is in general request over one-half of the world, and which therefore may be employed for settling international accounts. Bales of cotton, cargoes of iron, or coal, or corn, will serve the same purpose, but gold (at least in the Western world) will do it better. Bullion is only brought to the Bank when there are no foreign buyers for it: and there it remains, as in a place of temporary deposit, until it is wanted for export. It is simply as a commodity of widely-acknowledged value that gold is brought to the Bank of England,—it is in the same character that it is kept in the Bullion Office,—and it is in the same character that it is taken away. It is not money—it is not currency at all: why, then, should the Bank be compelled to treat it as if it were money? Why should the Bank be compelled to purchase bullion whether it wants it or not? The consequence of the present arrangement is, that the Bank at times has to overload itself with gold in the form of bullion when it does not want gold in any shape.

This arrangement, under the system pursued by the Bank, occasions many unnecessary and unnatural fluctuations in the value and amount of the national currency. Upon these points we have already spoken. At present we regard the arrangement in a different light,—simply as one of those needless and injurious interferences with the freedom of banking which are so numerous under the Act of 1844. Let the Bank buy bullion or not as it pleases. It knows its own requirements, and will purchase bullion in accordance with its wants. To compel it to buy bullion which it does not require, and which it does not desire to have, is an objectionable infraction of its freedom. Instead of compelling it to buy the bullion, let the Bank, when it has enough of gold, make advances upon the bullion brought to it, just as it does upon other assets and securities. Bullion, in fact, ought to be dealt with in the light of a first-class bill,—upon which the Bank is always ready to make advances. This would entail no hardship upon the holder of the bullion. There is already an establishment, maintained by the State, for the very purpose of converting bullion into British money. Any man who wishes to convert his bullion into money, has only to take it to the Mint, and this will be done for him gratis. On the other hand, if he does not do this—if he chooses to keep his gold in the form of bullion, he must expect it to be dealt with accordingly,—namely, as a valuable commodity, upon which the Bank of England or any other bank will readily advance money, but which neither our banks nor the Government, nor any other party, can be expected to accept as if it were money of the realm.

We come now to the last portion of the monetary system established by the Act of 1844—namely, that which relates to the general paper-currency of the kingdom. Having already discussed fully, and we believe fairly—certainly, in an honest spirit—the various theories and principles relating to monetary science, this concluding section of the subject can be treated with comparative brevity.

RESTRICTION OF BANK-ISSUES.

The Act of 1844 enacted that no new banks of issue should be established in any part of the kingdom. The notes which the existing banks of issue were allowed to continue were fixed at their average amount at the time when the Act was introduced. The banks of Scotland and Ireland were allowed to issue notes beyond that amount, on condition that for such extra issues these banks should keep on hand an equal amount of gold. Such issues accordingly yield no profit. Moreover, no provision was made for the lapse of issues arising from any of these banks discontinuing business:

so that any vacuum in the Scotch or Irish currency arising from this cause can only be filled up by the other banks extending their issues and correspondingly increasing their stock of gold. The provincial banks of England (*i.e.*, all the English banks of issue except the Bank of England) were placed on a somewhat different footing. They were not allowed to extend their "fixed issues" (*i.e.*, the average amount of their note-circulation at the end of 1843) upon any terms,—not even on the condition of holding gold to an equal amount. If any addition to the English note-circulation became necessary, it was to be supplied by means of the notes of the Bank of England. It was also enacted that, in the event of any of the English banks of issue discontinuing business, the vacuum thereby occasioned in the currency should be supplied by the Bank of England to the extent of two-thirds of the lapsed issues. And this only on two conditions: namely, that the Bank of England should be empowered to do so by an Order in Council; and also, that the profit upon these additional issues of the Bank (for which it was not required to keep an equal amount of gold) should go to the State.

The effect of these regulations has been greatly to reduce the number of the banks of issue, and to some extent to reduce the amount of currency. When the Act of 1844 was passed, the number of banks of issue in England (exclusive of the Bank of England) was 275,—it is now 202; in 1844 the authorised issue of those banks was £8,648,853,—it is now £7,535,080. Thus, since 1844, the banks of issue in England have been reduced in number by 73, or considerably more than one-fourth; and their authorised circulation has been diminished to the extent of nearly one-seventh. In lieu of the £1,113,773 of lapsed English issues, the Bank of England has been authorised to issue notes of its own to the extent of £650,000,—leaving a deficiency to the amount of nearly half a million (£463,773). And as a lapse of the authorised note-issues of Scotland has taken place to the extent of £337,938, the total diminution of the currency from this cause at present amounts to rather more than £800,000.

During the twenty years which have elapsed since the passing of the Bank Act, the English banks of issue have been diminishing in number almost at the rate of four every year. Already one-fourth of them have discontinued business; and if the same process continues, as it is likely enough to do, they will be nearly all extinct before the end of the present century. Thus, under the Act of 1844, we are steadily marching on to a time when the Bank of England will be almost the only bank of issue in the country. The virtual monopoly of the circulation which the Bank already possesses will then become absolute.

There is another feature of the Act of 1844 in its relation to the general note-issues of the country which merits attention. This is the enactment that upon all the additional issues made by the Bank of England in partial replacement of the lapsed issues of the English banks, the profits shall go to the State. This is another interference of the State with the freedom of banking. If the State, in return for receiving the profit upon these note-issues, were to become security for them—if it were to take upon itself the duty of ensuring their convertibility,—the arrangement would at least be intelligible. There would be a *quid pro quo.* But the State does nothing of the kind. It does not in any way guarantee the convertibility of these note-issues. What, then, is the meaning of this arrangement? Upon what grounds is this interference with banking business made? It is important to have a definite answer to this question, because in many quarters the provision of the Act of 1844 in this respect seems to be regarded as a precedent which is to be accepted without discussion. Last spring the Chancellor of the Exchequer, in his Bill for replacing the lapsed issues of Scotch notes, proposed to extend the same principle to Scotland,—doing so, not on the ground that the principle was a right one, but simply because it had been adopted in the Act of 1844. This is a very erroneous way of proceeding. In every case, and especially when the proposal is not merely to maintain a principle but to extend its operation, a question of this

THE STATE AND NOTE-ISSUES.

kind should be discussed upon its merits. The real question is, not whether such a principle was adopted in the Act of 1844, but whether it is a right one.

The motive which led to the adoption of this principle in the Act of 1844 was twofold. In the first place, it was a natural consequence of the system of monopoly which was embodied in that measure. The Act of 1844 extended the monopoly of the Bank of England. It enacted that whatever extension might take place in the English note-issues should be made exclusively by the Bank of England; and that whatever diminution might take place in these issues should likewise, so far as it was replaced at all, be replaced by Bank of England notes. In return for this extension of the Bank's monopoly, the Act required that the profit upon these issues should be paid to the State. It is the old story over again. More monopoly to the Bank, and more payment exacted from the Bank by the State. In 1844 this vicious game was resumed. The State extended the privileges conferred upon the Bank to the detriment of the community, and in return exacted a larger payment from the Bank. The profit upon the £650,000 of the Bank's issues in partial replacement of the lapsed issues of other banks (if reckoned at 3 per cent), is just £20,000 added to the annual sum which the Bank pays for its Charter—*i.e.*, for the monopoly conferred upon it.

As a similar monopoly, in a less concentrated and injurious form, was conferred in 1845 upon the Scotch banks, it follows, of course, that they also may be made to pay for their monopoly. The vicious principle of the State selling privileges to private establishments, which has been the bane of English banking, is now to be introduced into Scotland. It is true that the Scotch banking system was so fully developed in a natural form prior to the introduction of the principle of monopoly in 1844, that less evil can be done in Scotland with her dozen of independent and co-equal banks, than in England, where the monopoly of the Bank began so early, and was made so stringent, that no rival banks of issue have ever been able to establish themselves. Nevertheless, it is deplorable to see so vicious, and we should have thought so antiquated, a system actually receiving fresh extension at the present day. We boast of "free-trade"—any one who insinuates a word against the doctrine is regarded as an antiquated imbecile: yet the system of monopoly, of restriction, of "protection"—or by whatever name it may be called—which we have abolished in all other forms of trade and industry, has been revived and is daily being extended in regard to banking. It is a startling anomaly. It is a fact so anomalous—so diametrically opposed to the spirit of the times, and so injurious to the community, that the only difficulty is to account for its existence. Instead of proposing to extend this deplorable system to Scotland, the only thought of an enlightened statesman ought to be, how it can be most speedily, and for ever, eradicated from the banking laws of England.

This appropriation of the profit on note-issues, we repeat, is simply the price which the State exacts from banks upon which it has conferred privileges injurious to the community. The right course is, not to continue or extend this impost upon the banks, but to remove the occasion for it,—by abolishing the monopoly of which it is the price. Even as a matter of compensation, it is useless. Every tax which the State lays upon the banks, can be (and is) shifted by them on to the shoulders of the community, by the simple process of exacting higher rates of discount. Under the present system of monopoly, no other result is possible. Availing themselves of their command over the currency, the banks of issue can nullify every impost laid upon them by the State, by simply transferring the loss to the community. What does the community gain by the State making these banks pay for their monopoly, when for every thousand pounds thereby added to the revenue, the community have to pay a like sum to the banks in the form of increased charges? The whole arrangement is illusory, antiquated, vicious. Sweep it away,—by removing the evil which it is vainly designed to meet. Instead of seeking to make banks of issue pay for their monopoly, abolish the monopoly.

There is another motive which may induce a State to appropriate the profit on bank-notes. And that is when the Government desires gradually to extinguish the existing note-issues with a view to establish a State Bank. We see this process at present going on in the Federal States of America. There the State has issued a new currency of its own (not convertible into gold, but receivable in payment of taxes); and it has imposed a confiscatory tax upon the note-issues of the old banks in order gradually to annihilate them, and leave the ground clear for the new National banks which are being established. And as these National banks issue only State notes (greenbacks), which they purchase from the Treasury, they are in reality nothing else than branch-banks of the great Issue Office of the Government.

A STATE BANK.

The idea of a State Bank seems to have floated, perhaps not in a very distinct form, in the minds of the framers of the Act of 1844. And, beyond all question, Sir Robert Peel, adopting the views of Lord Overstone, was in favour of the establishment of a single Bank of Issue for the whole country,—either in the form of a State bank, or of the Bank of England. A State bank would unquestionably have certain advantages. Its notes, being receivable in payment of taxes, and being issued on the security of Government, would be made a legal tender throughout the kingdom. They would furnish an adequate currency for the whole internal trade and domestic requirements of the country. And thus, in great emergencies and exceptional times, these State notes would supply an adequate currency for the country, even if, owing to an absence of gold, they were temporarily inconvertible. Nay more. By means of such a State currency, the precious metals, and the fluctuation inseparable from them, could be dissociated from the currency, and their value would be measured in it like that of all other commodities. With such a currency, in fact, gold and silver would be bought and sold just like corn or coal, iron or cotton.

OBJECTIONS TO A STATE BANK.

Attractive as such a currency-system is, it is open to what we regard as a fatal objection. It is in the form of a State-currency alone that the paper-money of a country can be depreciated. The note-issues of banks never cause the currency to become redundant. Indeed, if the rate of discount be maintained at the just level, it is doubtful if the measure of value can be depreciated by the note-issues of banks, even though cash-payments were suspended. The banks of a country have no motive to diminish their profits by unduly lowering the rate of discount; and if there be no undue lowering of the rate of discount, there can be no undue expansion of the currency. The trading and industrial classes will not pay for more discounts than they want; and it is only by means of discount-operations and suchlike advances that a bank can get its notes into circulation. But with a Government the case is widely different. A Government expends many millions of money every year, and all these payments can be made in its own notes. Any amount of paper-money may thus be forced into circulation, whether there is a demand for it or not. It is true that a State bank may be conducted on perfectly sound principles; but the temptation to do otherwise, in exceptional times, is very great. By issuing, in the form of Government expenditure, an excessive amount of paper-money, the Government virtually raises a forced loan from the community, without becoming liable to repayment either of capital or interest. The depreciation of the currency which ensues is an index of the profit (the amount of the forced loan) obtained upon these issues by the Government. All great depreciations of paper-money have been occasioned by State-issues. The assignats of revolutionary France, the greenbacks of America, and the many other kinds of paper-money which have sustained a great depreciation, have all been State-issues. Such issues are conducted on a totally different principle from the note-issues of banks. They can be forced out whether the community want them or not; whereas bank-notes cannot be so forced out, nor, if got out, could they remain out. Banks will not issue their notes save upon ample security, and at a fair profit; and the public, on their part, will not pay for borrowing money on such terms if they do not want it; nor will the notes remain in circulation a day longer than they are needed, —neither will they circulate at all unless the public have confidence in the bank which issues them.

A State bank, therefore, seems to us, of all others, the most dangerous source of a national currency. A community best knows its own wants, and a currency will always be regulated by those wants if it be supplied by banks, and if the State does not interfere by means of legislation. But a community has no such check upon a State bank, whose notes are issued in the form of Government expenditure.

MONOPOLY OF A SINGLE BANK OF ISSUE.

The same objections do not apply to the establishment of a single bank of issue. Such a bank has no motive to depreciate the currency, and, what is more, no power to do so—unless by unduly lowering the rate of discount, which no bank, if left in its natural condition, will be willing to do. The danger, in fact, lies in exactly the opposite direction. A State bank is apt to make money too cheap,—a single bank of issue is disposed to make it too dear. A restriction of note-issues to a single bank confers upon that bank a monopoly of the currency, and thereby enables it to raise the value of money at its pleasure. And the higher a bank can raise its rate of discount, the greater are its profits. This is especially true of an establishment like the Bank of England, which pays no interest on its deposits. With Scotch banks, and in a lesser degree with the English joint-stock banks, a rise of the rate of discount is not pure gain, because they have in some measure to raise also the rate of interest which they pay on deposits. But, weak and utterly inadequate as this preventive to over-charges is, it is wholly inoperative as regards the Bank of England. Every rise in the Bank-rate is pure gain to that establishment. And if it were made the sole bank of issue, the country would be subjected to a despotism which would be intolerable. Unlike a State bank, the Bank of England is conducted simply on the principle of making the largest possible profit on its money. A State bank, from self-interest, would give all due aid to trade and commerce; for by so doing it would increase the revenue, and also promote the welfare of the people. But the Bank of England has nothing to do with such considerations. It simply looks to its own interests. It has simply to consider by what means it can obtain the largest amount of profit. In this respect, to confer a monopoly of note-issues upon the Bank of England would be infinitely worse for the community than if the right of issue were confined to a State bank. Trade and industry would be placed in permanent bondage; and the moneyed interest, the Plutocracy, would be rendered omnipotent. This would be the worst kind of "protection,"—it would be class-legislation in its most obnoxious form. It would be a greater violation of the freedom of trade, and a worse oppression of industry, than any which has figured in our Statute-book.

THE GOAL OF THE BANK ACT.

Such, then, is the goal to which the Act of 1844 is gradually but surely conducting us. It is undesirable in two respects. Firstly, inasmuch as the operation of the Act will ere long produce a serious diminution of the currency. Secondly, because it is gradually extending the monopoly of the Bank of England. Let us consider these two results separately.

REDUCTION OF THE CURRENCY.

Already one million and a half (£1,451,711) of the note-issues of our banks has lapsed, producing a diminution of the available currency to the extent of nearly a million. And even supposing that all the Scotch and Irish banks of issue continue in existence, a steady decrease is certain to occur in the English banks of issue. As we have shown, these banks are discontinuing business at the average rate of four every year. And as even the largest of them all, the National Provincial Bank of England, with an authorised issue of nearly half a million, is said to contemplate resigning its right of issue for the sake of being allowed to establish an office in London, we may safely infer that, unless the law be changed, all or nearly all of these banks will either drop business, or at least resign their right of issue. This would cause a further lapse of upwards of seven and a half millions of notes, which could be replaced by Bank of England notes only to the extent of two-thirds. In other words, in addition to £801,711 of note-issues already lapsed, there would be a further lapse of £2,535,630 : making a reduction of the available currency to the extent of nearly three and a half millions. Either this vacuum would remain unfilled, or else the Bank of England would require to keep three and a half millions more gold than at present to maintain the note-circulation of the country at its present amount. The effect of this is obvious. The amount of gold which the Bank Directors think sufficient would have to be raised, and the Bank-rate would be raised in proportion. Since the Directors at present think it necessary to charge 9 per cent for their discounts when there are thirteen millions of gold in the Bank, they would, when the above-mentioned lapse of notes is accomplished, charge the same rate when their stock of gold is upwards of sixteen millions. This is the state of things to which, under the Bank Act, we are advancing. A still larger amount of gold would be nullified in the Bank,—ten millions instead of six or seven: and a corresponding rise would take place in the Bank-rate, raising still further the rate of usage throughout the country. We do not believe that this result will take place, because we do not believe that the country will submit to it. But the result is sufficiently certain if the Bank Act be allowed to remain in operation.

GROWTH OF THE BANK'S MONOPOLY.

Secondly, along with this evil of a diminished currency, will come an extension of the monopoly of the Bank of England. As a lapse of issues on the part of other banks occurs, it is the Bank of England alone that is permitted, in part, to replace these issues. Thus the whole currency of England will by-and-by be in the hands of the Bank. Great as is the power of the Bank Court at present, it will become still more omnipotent as time rolls on. The other banks may discount as they please, but the Bank has a power to regulate their operations in this respect at its will. The currency is wholly in its hands; and by contracting that substratum—that fundamental basis of credit,—it can compel the other banks to contract their operations in proportion. Or rather, as we have said, the other banks, feeling their helplessness, will be ready, as now, to co-operate with the Bank, and increase their profits by adopting its high rates. Already we see that every bank which allies itself with the interests of Trade ere long comes to grief, or has to reverse its policy, and imitate that of the Bank. It either breaks down, or, learning its helplessness by bitter experience, chimes in with the Bank,—disregards the claims of Trade, and thinks only how to make money at the expense of the commercial classes by charging high rates of discount. The cause of the fall or embarrassment which successively overtakes these banks is, that they think mainly of the legitimate requirements of their customers. They say, "Here is an excellent firm, carrying on a sound business; it is a good customer, and we have no doubt as to its solvency,—therefore it is only right that we should assist it." But they forget that in so doing they are at the mercy of the Bank of England, and that a change in the value of money, owing to the action of the Bank, may at any time turn good business into bad. A rise of the Bank-rate, by depressing the markets, may bring ruin upon firms who have conducted their business alike with prudence and ability. Hence it is that all banks which endeavour to make common cause with the commercial classes, get into difficulties, and soon cease to struggle against the overwhelming power of the Bank of England. *Its* rates determine the fate of Trade. Its power is a despotism against which it is in vain to struggle. If our leading joint-stock banks had a right to issue notes of their own, and were to use this power when occasion required, they would to some extent be independent of the Bank. They would have a means of lending their deposits—of making advances of their loanable capital—which at present they have not; and thereby they could support solvent firms when temporarily embarrassed. Their action also would lessen at times the depression of the markets produced by the high rates of the Bank of England. But at present rivalry is vain. The other banks have to carry on their business with the Bank's notes: it is the only means they have of carrying on their business. They have a vast amount of loanable capital, it is true, but they have not, of themselves, the means of lending it. Hence it is vain for them to follow a different system from that pursued by the Bank. They must act as it acts, or suffer the consequences. Surely this is not a state of things to be desired. Monopoly is as evil a thing in banking as in any other business. Yet, if the Act of 1844 be maintained, we shall year by year see this despotism of the Bank rendered still more absolute.

It has frequently been suggested that Bank of England notes should be made a legal tender in Scotland as well as in England. Such a proposal is objectionable, theoretically; as a practical measure, it would fail to realise the object which its advocates desire to attain; and also, in its character, it is essentially reactionary. The principle of making the notes of any private bank a legal tender is an erroneous one. No paper-money should be made a legal tender unless it be issued by the State: and such State-issues we have no desire to see. The circulation of the notes of every bank of issue should be a voluntary act on the part of the community, or of the locality in which such banks exist. In this matter, however, as in all the others which we have discussed, we lay little stress upon abstract principles. The worship of theories is the idolatry of the young. The real question, when considering the merits of a system, is, how does it work? We have no desire to see the State recall from the Bank of England the legislative privilege which makes its notes a legal tender in England. We think it was a mistake to give such a privilege to any private bank; but the privilege has been enjoyed for thirty years, and there is no adequate motive for cancelling it. The notes of the Bank of England had been accepted as a valid tender by the community for generations before the privilege was conferred upon them; and it would be unadvisable to affect their present prestige in any way by an act of legislation which is not indispensably called for. But to extend the operation of this State privilege in favour of the Bank's notes to Scotland is a very different affair. Such a proceeding would be most objectionable; it would be directly at variance with the wishes of the Scotch; and, moreover, it would not accomplish the object of those who advocate it.

The practical object sought by those who desire to

see Bank of England notes made a legal tender in Scotland, is to obviate the drain of gold upon the Bank, which occurs in times of monetary pressure, in consequence of the Scotch banks selling their securities, and withdrawing the amount in coin from the Bank of England. No one can object to the Scotch banks adopting this course: they merely do as every individual in the community has a right to do. And, moreover, this is precisely the course which Sir Robert Peel wished that all provincial banks should take when it became necessary for them to extend their circulation. He stated that whenever an English bank of issue required more money than the amount of the notes which it was permitted to issue, it should sell a portion of its securities, and thus obtain a supply of notes of the Bank of England. And to withdraw notes from the Bank has precisely the same effect, under the Act of 1844, as to withdraw an equal amount of gold. But the real point to be observed is this. The drain upon the Bank of England which the advocates of this proposal desire to obviate, is wholly occasioned by the Act of 1845. Previous to the passing of that Act, there never was any drain upon the Bank of England to meet the requirements of Scotland. Neither would there be now, but for the Act. The cause of the drain is simply this. In periods of crisis or panic, the monetary requirements of the community are exceptionally increased; and as the Act of 1845 forbids the Scotch banks to issue additional notes unless they at the same time provide themselves with an equal amount of gold; they have no choice but to cash their securities and provide themselves with an extra stock of gold. If the Scotch banks were let alone,—if they were allowed to conduct their business in their own way, and simply with reference to the wants of the community,—there would be no such drain on the Bank of England. Let the Scotch banks issue their own notes, and that is all that is wanted. But as long as they are prohibited from extending their issues, except on the condition of providing themselves with an extra stock of gold, this drain upon the Bank of England is the necessary and natural consequence. The real remedy for this occasional withdrawal of gold from the Bank, therefore, is to annul the legislative enactment which is the cause of it.

To make Bank of England notes a legal tender in Scotland, would be an extension of the vicious system of State interference and banking monopoly, of which the country has already had far too much. Alike the banks and the community of Scotland would have a right to complain,—and certainly would complain. They are quite content with their own notes and banking-system, and would strenuously, and we think most justly, oppose any attempt to subvert these by a further extension of the State privileges of the Bank of England.

Moreover, in what way would the proposed innovation obviate a drain on the Bank of England in times of monetary pressure? At present the Scotch banks have to provide themselves with an extra stock of gold, in order that they may issue an extra amount of their own notes, to meet the increased monetary requirements of the community. Under the proposed system, they must equally add to their stock of money, by obtaining a supply of Bank of England notes. Such a change would make no difference in the drain on the Bank of England. To withdraw notes from the Bank has precisely the same effect, under the Act of 1844, as to withdraw gold.* The same amount of gold would have to be kept in bank under the one system as under the other. The only difference is, that under the new system the gold would be in the Bank of England,—whereas, at present, it is kept (where it ought to be) in the Scotch banks. Accordingly, the Scotch would be well entitled to object to a change which would not only damage their own banks, and extend the vicious monopoly of the Bank of England, but which, as a measure of detail, would simply transfer from the Scotch banks a certain amount of gold, and place it in the keeping of the Bank of England.

The right of a community to the free use of bank-notes is, or ought to be, undoubted. The recent violation of this right—the prohibition of such issues

* See footnote to p. 239.

by the Acts of 1844-5—is an interference on the part of the State with a matter in which it has no concern.

RESTORE FREEDOM TO BANKING.

Bank-notes circulate by the free will of the community. They cannot be issued save in accordance with the wants of the public. The State may refuse to receive these notes in payment of taxes and other dues: but it has no right to forbid their use among the people. Indeed, as we have said, no notes of any private bank ought to be made legal tender. Bank-notes should circulate simply by the free will of the community. The condition of their existence is a voluntary act on the part of the public.

NO DANGER FROM FREEDOM OF ISSUE.

The right of the community in this matter should be restored. The freedom of banking which existed for a century and a half prior to the Bank Act should be re-established. And it would be re-established in a better form. Private banks of issue are things of the past. No new ones would be established, any more than private banks of any kind. In truth, few private banks would ever have existed but for the monopoly of the Bank of England, which for more than a century prevented the establishment of joint-stock banks. The system which grew up under the regime of freedom in Scotland is the one which would now be followed. If any joint-stock bank wishes to issue notes, let it do so. We do not know that any condition should be attached to that right. For its own sake, a bank may be trusted to secure its notes just as it secures its other liabilities. Nevertheless, in the case of new banks, it might be enacted that for all notes issued they shall keep an equal amount of Consols, valued at par. These notes, too, might be ear-marked, so to speak,—might be placed apart from the other assets, and kept for the note-holders. But, in truth, the banks would naturally take good means to meet the wishes of the public in this matter. Their only chance of success would lie in making their notes acceptable as a circulating medium. If they failed in that, their notes would not circulate. Therefore we are in favour of perfect freedom. The action of the community ought to regulate the matter.

There would be no danger, under such a system, of the country being flooded with bank-notes. No over-issues have ever taken place in Scotland, where the right of issue was fully established for a century and a half. For a bank to make over-issues is simply to spoil its own trade. Every bank desires to lend its money upon the highest terms it can get. Who ever heard of a mercantile company selling its goods too cheap? and why should it be otherwise with banks of issue? Moreover, English banks now set comparatively little value upon their note-issues.* These issues form but a very small portion of a bank's business;

* As in England there are no notes of less value than £5, cheques in ordinary circumstances answer all the purposes of bank-notes.

and it is only in exceptional times that there would be any call for an extension of them. But it is precisely at these times that such issues become of immense importance to the community. It is precisely because there is no means of meeting these exceptional cases, under the present system, that our disasters are so frequent. Let banks be free to issue notes when a demand for them arises. Our monetary system has been deprived of its natural elasticity. It can expand, it is true, when nobody wants it to expand; but it also contracts at the very time when contraction is fatal. It is no longer elastic,—it no longer answers to the demands made upon it; and in lieu thereof it is subjected to rigid expansions and contractions which have no more to do with the requirements of the public than with the changes of the moon. The wants of the community necessarily fluctuate at intervals; but there is no provision to meet those fluctuations. On the contrary, the means of remedy which formerly existed have been taken away by Act of Parliament. Serious as the difficulty is in its consequences, it is purely artificial in its origin. It is simply owing to a legislative enactment, which was passed under misapprehension, and the practical working of which has wholly falsified the intentions of its well-meaning framers.

The period is approaching when the whole question of banking and currency will, doubtless, be discussed anew. And the great point to be desired is, that the monetary system of the country be then freed from the influence of baseless theories and revised by the light of that best of teachers,—practical experience.

HISTORICAL REVIEW.

There were errors (of monopoly) in the monetary legislation of England previous to 1844; and since then there have been still greater legislative errors affecting the whole kingdom. Passing over the crisis in 1696, when the Bank of England was struggling with the difficulties natural to a new establishment, and when a too hasty calling in of the metallic money of the country for the purpose of re-coinage produced a crisis of a peculiar kind not likely to recur,—we find that the difficulties which arose under the old system were of three kinds. There was, first, the partial loss of faith in the Bank, which produced a run upon it in 1745, when both the dynasty and the form of Government were imperilled by the rebellion in favour of the House of Stuart. That crisis in the Bank's history was not due in any degree to the currency-system. Secondly, and posterior to that crisis, difficulties were occasionally experienced in consequence of the multiplication of private banks of issue,—some of which were improperly conducted, and many of which were deficient in the amount of capital requisite for safe banking. This defect was mainly, if not wholly, due to legislation. It was the necessary consequence of the monopoly conferred upon the Bank of England, which forbade the formation of joint-stock banks, such as (under the free system) were successfully established in Scotland. Thirdly, there was the mistaken policy of the Bank in reducing its discounts and the amount of the currency at times when a drain of specie for export took place. This was the chief cause of the crises of 1793, 1795, and 1826. This contraction of discounts in 1793 and 1795 was condemned even by the Bullion Committee of 1810; nevertheless, it was repeated in 1826 with the same results—namely, a general panic, and a run upon the Bank. We say, deliberately, that each and all of these three crises might have been obviated, or at least greatly lessened in severity, if the Bank had not adopted the mistaken policy of reducing its discounts and the amount of the currency. And each and all of these crises were at once terminated as soon as the Bank reversed its policy, and began to discount as before.

Since 1844 new elements of difficulty have been imported into our currency-system. By nullifying nearly seven millions of gold, the Bank Act produces artificial crises,—crises which would not arise at all if the Bank had the use of these seven millions of specie; and also, in consequence of the same arrangement, the rate of discount, and with it the rate of usage throughout the country, has been artificially enhanced. Moreover, under the Act of 1844, our measure of value has been vitiated, and now fluctuates to and fro in a manner that baffles all calculation. And finally, the rights of the community have been violated by the prohibition against the establishment of new banks of issue, —and by the monopoly thereby conferred upon existing banks of issue, and especially upon the Bank of England, in whose favour this restrictive policy was purposely framed.

ITS LESSONS.

Profiting by the lessons of experience, it is time that our monetary system were now freed from the difficulties and defects which, whether under the old system or the new, have beset it. It is to be hoped that the Directors of the Bank of England, and of all our banks of issue, will now see clearly that to contract their discounts in a time of monetary difficulty is the very way to aggravate the crisis and produce a panic. If the facts which we have adduced on this point, in various parts of this volume, do not demonstrate this truth, we know not what demonstration is. As to the rest, the country's difficulties arise wholly from legislation. The multiplication of private banks under the old system was owing to this cause; and the difficulties which arise under the new system from the inadequacy of our currency-system to meet temporary fluctuations in the requirements of the public, are likewise wholly due to legislative enactment. So also is the absurd nullification of nearly seven millions of gold in the Bank of England. A difficulty occasioned by legislation is of all others the most easily remedied. And it is time the remedy were applied. Our currency-system ought to be remodelled in such a way as to remove the embargo on these seven millions, and restore the Bank of England to its full freedom. We must also restore to the community the right of freedom of issues,—but in a better form than under the old system; namely, by allowing any joint-stock bank to issue its own notes, if the public desires to have them. Let freedom be the order of the day—in banking as in all the other departments of business. Leave the banks and the community free to act for themselves, and three-fourths of our present difficulties will at once be at an end. In banking, as in other matters, let us have done with monopoly,—let us have an end of legislative interference and fetters. The community best knows its own wants. Let it act for itself. And then, rely upon it, it will soon find a remedy for the evils which, under a well-meant but most mistaken legislation, have of late years pressed upon the country so heavily.

CONCLUSION.

We do not want "cheap" money any more than we want dear money. Our views may be summed up in a few words. We desire that there should be no waste of the national capital, and no artificial calamities inflicted upon trade by Act of

Parliament. We desire that the loanable value of capital should be regulated by its normal causes—namely, the amount of the supply and the extent of the demand,—and not, as at present, by fluctuations in the instrument of exchange, which have been created by erroneous legislation. Finally, we desire that the national measure of value, in which all contracts are made, should be preserved. We maintain that the State has no right, by means of legislation and of the monopoly which it has conferred upon one great bank of issue, to subject the measure of value to variations amounting at times to one-third or one-fourth,—variations which periodically rob industry of its legitimate profits, which subject commerce to "tremendous sacrifices," and which throw thousands and tens of thousands of our working-classes out of employment.

We object to the nullification of seven millions of gold in the Bank of England, because it is not only an uncalled-for waste of capital, but, still more, because, owing to our currency-laws, it is a means of artificially enhancing the rate of usage throughout the country. And we object to the prohibition against banks issuing their own notes, as a violation of commercial and industrial freedom,—as an interference with the legitimate rights alike of the banks and of the community. We object to the existing legislation as a whole, because it establishes a system of monopoly vicious in principle and injurious in its working. And we object also to that legislation in its details, which have been so erroneously framed that they inflict upon the community evils which the framers of the Bank Act never contemplated, and which might to a great extent have been avoided, even though the evil principle of monopoly were maintained.

England is at present the opprobrium of the world in the matter of monetary convulsions. Our country suffers greater and more frequent disasters from this cause than any other. We suffer more than America,—reckless and impetuous as is the temper of the people there. We suffer more than all Europe put together. England is the peculiar seat of monetary crises: and we have told the reason why. As ingenious as the *Boy's own Book*, which shows how to make artificial earthquakes and volcanoes by burying a fulminating mixture which in due time explodes—our legislators have imparted to our currency a volcanic organism, the alternate expansions and contractions of which periodically shake down our fabric of Trade and strew the country with ruins. Surely it is time to mend this. Again and again have the commercial classes been subjected to "tremendous sacrifices" by the working of the present system. Again and again has Trade been prostrated, paralysed; and again and again have the working-classes, owing to this cause, been deprived of their

TRADE IN BONDAGE.

means of support,—have been willing to work, and yet could get no work. Thousands, whose only capital is their labour—whose only wealth is in the work of their hands—suffer during those artificial monetary crises as much, in proportion, as the wealthy merchant who has cargoes on every sea. And at this moment —as if the evil of the cotton-dearth were not enough —our great seats of industry are paralysed anew. As we now write, there is many a fireless home, and many a starving family, in Lancashire, simply because seven millions of gold lie useless in the Bank of England, and because our whole banking system is cramped by a policy of monopoly and restriction.* England, which

* In consequence of the depression of the cotton-market, caused by the rise in the Bank-rate, upwards of a hundred manufacturers, employing more than 20,000 operatives, have already been forced to suspend payment. And this represents only a small portion of the increased distress which prevails in the manufacturing districts; because many of the employers who remain solvent have closed their mills, or put their workpeople upon short time. At present (Nov. 8) the number of cotton-operatives out of work is nearly twice as great as it was at the end of July (when the rise of the Bank-rate began), and the number of operatives upon short time has more than doubled. The following table shows the number of operatives on short time, and out of work, in the last week of each month,—and also the changes of the Bank-rate:—

	Short time.	Out of Work.	Bank-rate raised to		
July,	67,660	101,568	7	per cent on	July 25
August,	59,074	102,090	8	,,	Aug. 4
September,	102,047	135,821	9	,,	Sept. 8
October,	125,296	171,568	9	,,	

Thus, during the three months in which the Bank-rate has been

boasts of her freedom of trade, and of free popular action in all matters—which boasts that she is a self-governing country, in which Industry thrives unshackled by legislation—nevertheless has thrown over

raised from 6 to 9 per cent, about a hundred manufacturers have been forced to suspend,—65,000 operatives have been placed upon short time, —and 70,000 more have been thrown entirely out of work. Nearly the whole of this increase of the Lancashire distress has taken place during the last two months, when the Bank-rate has stood at the minimum of 9 per cent.

The operation of the Bank-rate in producing this lamentable increase of distress in the manufacturing districts is shown by the following comparison of the prices of cotton in the second week of August with those at the beginning of the present month. We take the prices from the Commercial List given in the *Economist* of Aug. 13 and Nov. 5 :—

	Aug. 13.	Nov. 5.	Depreciation.
Sea Island,	44d.	41d.	7 per cent.
Upland, .	30d.	23d.	23 ,,
Mobile, .	30¼d.	23¼d.	23 ,,
New Orleans,	30¾d.	23⅛d.	23 ,,
Egyptian, .	28¼d.	21d.	24 ,,
West Indian,	29d.	22d.	24½ ,,
Surat, .	19d.	13d.	31½ ,,
Bengal, .	15d.	8½d.	43½ ,,

As is generally known, the price of "middling Orleans" regulates the cotton-market; and hence the fall of prices (as shown in the table) between the middle of August and the beginning of November has been 23 per cent. And this is a minimum estimate. So that every cotton importer or manufacturer, besides having to pay 9 per cent. of discount on his bills, has seen his stock of goods reduced in value to the extent of nearly one-fourth. It is estimated that the stock of cotton goods has in this way been reduced in value to the amount of £8,000,000. And as long as the Bank-rate is maintained at 9 per cent, the depreciation will continue to increase, and with it the number of bankruptcies, and of operatives thrown out of employment.

all that trade, over every branch of her manifold industry, the meshes of a golden net, which envelops and fetters, and periodically strangles the industrious classes, robbing Labour of its wages and Commerce of its profits.

COMPLETE FREE TRADE.

Trade has been set free in each separate branch; but over it all there has been established a virtual Despotism — a monopoly which weighs upon and fetters every part of the national industry, and which at times confiscates its gains to an extent which no autocrat would venture upon. Who is the Minister who will undo these fetters? Which of our statesmen will complete the work of Free-trade, by annulling the artificial restrictions and the injurious monopoly which weigh upon our national industry as a whole? It is a great work that has yet to be done,—but it is a simple one, and one also which would entail no loss upon the State. All that is needed is to abolish legislative restrictions which ought never to have been imposed. All that is needed is to leave to the community freedom of action in this matter as in others. When a community is left free to act for itself, the Government at least is no longer chargeable with responsibility. But in the present case, it is the very legislation of the Government that has done the mischief. All that is needed is to annul that legislation, and leave the community to attend to its own interests.

We trust, then, that the time is not distant when some one of our leading statesmen will take in hand this great but simple work,—will undo the legislation which produces a waste of the national capital, which vitiates our measure of value, which perpetuates a system of restriction and monopoly, and which ever and anon sacrifices Trade and impoverishes the working-classes. All that is to be desired is, that such a statesman should act in the spirit of the late Sir Robert Peel, and seek to ensure, as far as legislation can, to Labour its wages, and to Commerce its legitimate profits.

OUR TRADE

WHEN Crœsus made a display of all his treasures and good fortune to Solon, the Athenian sage is said to have hastened his departure from the Lydian Court, feeling assured that such great and uninterrupted prosperity would ere long be overtaken by disaster. If Solon, or some other ancient Greek, were amongst us at present, he would probably experience a similar foreboding.* The gods, in old times, were thought to be jealous of the unbroken prosperity of mortals; and it was regarded as a tempting of the gods when men thus happily circumstanced openly boasted of their good fortune. England is not only remarkably prosperous, but we all boast loudly of our prosperity. The Ministers of the Crown lead the jubilant chorus of self-congratulation. Doubtless they are desirous to make us forget the political humiliation to which England has been subjected under their rule, by extol-

* This exposition of the state of our Trade was written in September, and it appears unadvisable to alter the text of it, as the subsequent changes have been alluded to in the preceding chapter.

ling in an unusual manner our material prosperity. But the jubilant spirit has become infectious; and amid the lull of politics, and the stillness of the Parliamentary recess, the only voices which catch the ear are those which are uplifted in praise and admiration of the wonderful increase of our trade and commerce.

As we listen, in our study, to this apotheosis of Trade, our tight little island seems to rise into the shape and proportions of a magnificent Temple, thronged with busy crowds swarming out and in,—making ample use of the sanctuary, but seldom even touching their hat, as they pass, to the golden statue of the goddess Fortuna which stands in the midst. There they are ceaselessly storing up the wealth that flows to them from the rest of the world. Men in strange climes, and in strange dresses, and speaking all manner of tongues, are seen preparing produce and luxuries of all kinds for the Temple, which flow thither in long streams across both land and sea. And still the work of storing goes on: gold, silver, and all precious things, the delights of life, the cream of the earth's good things, accumulate higher and higher in the chambers of the temple. And ever and anon, as the recorders announce the increasing tale, there rises a great shout from the busy throng, which sounds in our ears like that which St Paul heard of old when the people cried out with one voice, "Great is Diana of the Ephesians, whom the world worshippeth!"

ITS INFLUENCE ON THE WORLD.

It is a remarkable position which England occupies in the world. A little spot amidst the northern seas almost invisible to the schoolboy as he seeks for it on his globe, and which inadvertently he may hide with his finger-point as he turns round the coloured sphere, the British Isles are nevertheless the heart of the world, the centre to which the thoughts and acts of men most generally tend, and to and from which the streams of material life are ever flowing. If we draw on a map the great lines of commerce, we will see what a large proportion of them converge to our shores. It was once a proverb that "all roads lead to Rome;" and England, commercially, now holds in the world at large the same predominant position which the Eternal City held in the lesser area of the Roman empire. Our country is the chief goal of the highways of commerce. Caravans, with their long strings of laden camels and horses, are ceaselessly crossing the plains and deserts of Asia,—railway-trains, drawn by the rapid fire-car, rush across Europe and America with their freight of goods,—and ships in thousands bring to us from all parts of the world the staple supplies of our food and industry.

The sun never sets on the dominions of England: in one part or other of the globe his rays still shine on the red-cross banner of St George. But is not England herself a sun—diffusing civilisation, while adding to the material comforts of mankind? She furnishes employment to tens of millions of people in the uttermost parts of the earth. The Chinaman in his tea-plantations and mulberry-gardens—the Hindoo in his rice and cotton fields—the poor Indian miner on the Andes—the Gaucho as he follows his herds on the Pampas,—even the Negro of Africa, and the native of the far and fair islands of the Pacific—are stirred to industry and kept in comfort by the employment which we in our little island give to them. If—as has been in the æons of the Past—the British Isles were to sink slowly until they were submerged beneath the surrounding seas, their disappearance would be like the setting of a sun, and the world of commerce would suffer an eclipse. Why, then, should we not boast of our Trade, seeing that it not only increases our wealth, but confers benefits on mankind at large?

True, commerce does not always appear as a benefactor. With equal indifference we send forth the clothing which preserves, and the arms which destroy, life. We not only give employment, but we occasion and facilitate wars. Our skill is as conspicuous in the manufacture of the enginery of war as in the fabrics and machinery of peace. True, also, we fight for markets. If a people will not accept the blessings of trade, we force them upon them at the point of the bayonet, or at the mouth of the cannon. This is indefensible,—it is a reproach to civilisation; but it is natural. There is no unmixed good—but evil itself is made to develop good. The action of self-interest has been made by Providence the regulating force of human progress; and self-interest—low motive as it may seem to those who fancy they could have made the world better than its Maker has done—when rightly understood, through experience of life, ever propels us in the end towards the good.

The first result of the contact of civilisation with barbarism is uniformly war. Yet slowly and surely Peace is winning her triumphs. Broader and broader expands the area of commerce — wider and wider extends civilisation,—and more and more prevail the doctrines of peace and the principle of international brotherhood. The Elysian time, the golden age of the world, when there shall be universal peace, is too far off to be discernible at the present day. Wars probably will never cease out of the earth. Like the poor, they will be always with us. Nevertheless they will grow fewer and milder. The heart of the world will rest at peace, and wars will only fringe its borders —in the outlying countries not yet brought within the pale. And in effecting this happy change, the influence of commerce—the operations of self-interest—will accomplish more than all the moralising of sages or the preachings of philanthropy. Have we not felt, during this present year, how firmly the golden meshes of trade have wound themselves round the heart of the nation? Unfelt, unnoticed, in ordinary times, it is only when England raises her right arm in anger to strike that she becomes sensible of the golden meshes that have slowly encircled her. We are bound over to peace by chains which are not unpleasant to us. This, too, may have its bad side,—but that is a question beyond our subject. Let it suffice that other nations also, our neighbours and rivals, are gradually coming into the same golden bondage, and that the more potent that bondage becomes, the less need will there be for "a policeman" in Europe.

We send forth the material comforts of civilisation, and we rouse to industry and give employment to millions of human beings who would otherwise stagnate or starve. But, more valuable than all the rest, we export men also—our own countrymen. Led by the potent agency of self-interest, they invade the solitudes and attack the barbarism of the world,—peopling with a higher race the waste places, and, as conquerors or masters, leading the natives of other countries into a higher life than they could have reached of themselves. A new race has repeopled America,—a new population has grown up in Australia,—as lords of India, we are rejuvenating the effete world of the East,—a kindred destiny awaits the gigantic empire of China,—and soon Egypt, Syria, Asia Minor, and the African shores of the Mediterranean will likewise come under European tutelage.

Where commerce goes, influence follows. And the

commerce of England is gradually overspreading the world. It widens and pours along like a rising flood,—whose outer edges indeed are gross with sand, and whose waves as they advance sweep away much and devastate not a little, but which nevertheless enrich the soil and produce new and better forms of fertility, making the world more beautiful and man more happy. In the old theology of Persia, the disciples of the Good Spirit, Ormuzd, were bound to wage ceaseless war with the works of the evil Ahriman,—not only by crusading against alien religions, but by warring against all that obstructs the beauty and fertility of the earth. To keep clear and pure the water-courses, to plant fruit-trees, to extirpate weeds, to extend cultivation—these were parts of that old religion, and were regarded as not the least worthy service which man could render to his Maker. We no longer call such acts religion: yet is it not a carrying out the beneficent work of Providence in the world,—a work which is left to human hands to accomplish—which must be done by man or not at all? And thus Trade has a religion of a very practical kind—invisible in and unfelt by her votaries, yet appearing in the result of their labours, and aiding most powerfully the onward progress of the world.

We are pre-eminently a trading nation, and the dry figures of the Board of Trade returns are the index of our commercial prosperity. They are the most palpable sign of our material greatness. Like the Nilometer which has stood for ages in Egypt, recording upon its column the height of the annual inundation which regulates the prosperity of the land of Misraim, these returns show the ebb and flow of trade which regulate the profits of our merchants and the employment of our people. As the Nile on each overflow deposits a new layer of alluvium, increasing the soil, the parent of future crops,—so each annual rise of our commerce brings a deposit of profits, an addition to the capital and productive power of the country. The ebbs shown in the returns mark the bad years, while the increase is a sure sign of contemporaneous comfort and prosperity. Happily the ebbs are but occasional, while the increase in the main is steady and astonishingly great. It is marvellous to mark the increase of British commerce in recent times, especially from the epoch when the discovery of the gold-mines of California and Australia began to add new and immense supplies to the metallic currency of the world. We desire to eschew tables of figures, but in this case we make an exception. The subjoined column represents the Nilometer of the British Isles, and records upon its face the steady rise, with occasional ebbs, of the stream of trade which annually enriches our country. The exports and imports are given in round numbers, and the figures represent millions sterling:—

OUR NILOMETER.

OUR NILOMETER.

Year.	Exports.	TOTAL.	Imports.
1863	146½	£395,470,700	249
	124	349,709,200	225¾
	125	342,600,200	217½
1860	136	346,422,100	210½
	130½	309,593,800	179
	116½	281,192,500	164½
	122	309,910,500	188
	116	288,371,100	172½
	95½	239,230,900	143½
	97	249,573,700	152
	99	257,210,300	158 *
	78	218,692,300	140
	74½	216,745,300	142
1850	71⅓	200,502,700	129
	63½	199,741,400	136
	53	173,086,500	120
	59	175,744,300	117
	57¾	155,417,100	97
	60	173,636,400	113
	58½	155,540,900	97
	52	142,482,780	90
	47¾	131,182,200	84
	51½	133,404,100	83
1840	51⅓	138,085,000	86

This year our exports are likely to amount to 160 millions sterling, and our imports to 270. Between 1839 and 1849 our trade increased rather more than 25 per cent; but in the next ten years, aided by the

* Previous to 1854, the official returns are of no use as showing the real value of our Imports; for the scale of prices by which the official value was determined was fixed so far back as 1698, and has long ceased to represent the true value of the articles. But the official value serves to show the fluctuations in *quantity*. And as for several years after 1854, both the "official" and the "real" value of the Imports was published, we are

gold-discoveries, it increased 100 per cent. During the last twenty-five years our trade has trebled in amount,—the exports having risen from 52 millions to 160 millions, and our imports from 86 millions to about 270.

OUR SOURCES OF WEALTH.

The increase of our national wealth arises in the main from three different sources. It arises (1) from an increase in the produce of our soil and our rocks (*i.e.*, grain, animals, weaving materials, and fruits, and of coal, iron, and other metals), or from a diminution in the cost of production thereof; (2) from an increase in the amount of foreign goods which we manufacture and export, or in a diminished cost in the manufacture of them; and (3) from a profitable investment of our spare capital in the construction of railways and suchlike enterprises abroad.

The *Economist* reckons that our annual *savings* amount to £130,000,000, and the lowest computation is £100,000,000. The contribution made to the income of the country by the profits on our foreign trade are rapidly on the increase. It is true, the returns of our export trade do not indicate with accuracy the amount of profits arising from it. There may

enabled to observe the difference between these (the real value being about 2-7ths greater than the official); and by applying this ratio to the returns for the fourteen years previous to 1854, we have presented (in the prefixed table) our Imports for these years at their real value—or at least an approximation to it sufficiently correct for our purpose.

be over-production, causing a glut in the foreign markets, and consequently a fall of prices, and less profit to our exporting merchants. Such was the case in 1860,—although by good-luck, it was quickly righted by the dearth of cotton goods that followed. It is also to be noted, that during the last two and a half years, the profits of our exporting manufacturers have not been in the same proportion to the value of goods exported as formerly. The great increase in the cost of the raw materials must be taken into account. It is only upon the manufacture of these materials that we derive a profit; and as the declared value of our exports includes the cost of the raw material, as well as the cost and profit of manufacture, it is obvious that when the raw material rises in price, the proportion of our profits to the total value of the goods exported becomes reduced. Cotton is now fourfold the price it was in 1860; so that, although the value of exported cotton goods last year was only 10 per cent less than in 1860, the diminution in the profits of our manufacturers must greatly exceed this proportion. The *quantity* of the goods exported is a better criterion of the profits of our manufacturers than the value of the goods,—the value being largely affected by fluctuations in the cost of the raw material. It is the quantity of their manufacture (in other words, the amount of work which they get to do) that chiefly regulates the profits of the millowners; and, we need hardly say, it is likewise the quantity of our manufactures which indicates the amount of employment furnished to our people. Although the value of cotton exports this year promises even to exceed that of 1860, neither the profits of our manufacturers, nor the amount of employment for our operatives, will be nearly so great as they were four years ago.

Let us analyse the Board of Trade returns, and show in detail of what our traffic with foreign countries consists,

OUR IMPORTS.

The Imports are what we buy,—the Exports are what we sell. Of our Imports last year, two-fifths (103 millions) consisted of materials for our manufactures; of which amount fully one-half consisted of cotton, and rather less than one-half of wool, silk, flax, and hemp, hides, oil and tallow, metals, indigo, and saltpetre. The other great branch of our imports consists of food and stimulants, or luxuries, for the subsistence of our people, and forms nearly one-third (75 millions) of our whole imports. Of this amount one-half consists of the necessaries of life,—grain and flour, bacon, butter, cheese, and rice; the other half of what may be called luxuries,—sugar, tea, coffee, wine and spirits, tobacco, and fruit. The remaining portion of our imports consists of wood, for house and ship building and furniture, manufactured articles of dress, &c. We import twice as much cotton as corn, and twice as much corn as wool.

Next as to Exports. Of the goods which we sold to other countries last year, fully two-thirds (100 millions) consisted of articles manufactured by us out of foreign materials,—the cotton goods alone amounting in value to 47½ millions; and less than one-third of materials of our own production (raw or manufactured), chiefly metals and coal. Cotton goods form the largest portion of our exports, and next to them metals and metal goods,—the former constituting one-third, and the latter one-fourth, of the whole of our exports. We export twice as much cotton as woollen goods, and twice as much woollen as linen. The total value of the metals and metal goods exported last year was 33 millions; but we cannot claim all this as the produce of our own mines, seeing that we imported four millions' worth of metals (chiefly copper) from other countries.

OUR EXPORTS.

As we import about ninety millions' worth of cotton, wool, silk, flax, hemp, and hides, while we only export articles manufactured from these materials to an equal value,—and as the value of the manufactured article may (even with the present high prices of the raw material) be stated at almost double that of the raw material,—we may infer that nearly one-half of these textile imports are employed for our own use—consumed in the manufacture of clothing for our own people. If this be correct, about 40 millions' worth of the textile fabrics

OUR CONSUMPTION.

imported are required by us for clothing. Thus, in addition to the produce of our own country, we import 75 millions' worth of food, and 40 millions' worth of the raw materials of clothing; besides nearly 20 millions' worth of other goods, consisting of articles of dress and for household use, and wood for building and furniture. In all, 135 millions' worth of foreign goods are consumed by us annually, simply in maintaining our present highly comfortable existence.*

The two largest items in our imports—namely, cotton and corn—are also the most variable, alike as

* The following is a list of the chief articles imported and exported by this country in 1863, arranged under descriptive heads:—

IMPORTS.

For Food—		
Corn & Flour,	£26,000,000	
Bacon, Butter, Cheese, .	8,800,000	
Rice, . .	1,866,000	
Sugar, . .	12,367,000	
Tea, . .	10,666,000	
Coffee, . .	4,155,000	
Wine, . .	4,900,000	
Spirits, .	1,700,000	
Tobacco, .	3,000,000	
Fruit, . .	1,562,000	
		£74,616,000
For Household Use—		
Oil and Tallow (say), .	£4,000,000	
Paper, . .	342,000	
		4,342,000
Articles of Dress—		
Broadstuffs, Ribbons, &c.,		5,600,000
For Building and Furniture—		
Wood, ...		10,760,000

For Manufactures—		
Cotton, .	£57,300,000	
Wool, . .	13,900,000	
Silk, . .	9,870,000	
Flax and Hemp,	6,150,000	
Metals, . .	4,000,000	
Hides, . .	2,780,000	
Indigo, . .	2,400,000	
Oil and Tallow (say), .	2,500,000	
Seeds, Flax and Linseed, .	3,370,000	
Saltpetre, .	1,100,000	
		102,870,000
For the Farm—		
Guano, . .	2,660,000	
Oilseed Cake,	660,000	
		3,320,000
		201,508,000

Articles not included, £47,474,942. Total, £248,982,942

regards quantity and price. The variations of the one are due to natural, and of the other to political causes.

CORN.

The state of the weather, the favourable or unfavourable nature of the season, determines whether our harvest is a good or bad one; and the difference in value between a very good and a very bad harvest is at least twenty millions sterling. In other words, in a very bad year we have to buy of our neighbours twenty millions more corn than when our harvest is decidedly good. This makes an enormous difference in the national balance-sheet. The outlay of the farmer is the same in a bad year as in a good one: the expenses of cultivation are a fixed charge, but the return depends on the skies and the weather. A very fine summer is worth twenty millions in hard cash to this country, besides the many other less direct benefits which it brings.

EXPORTS.

Manufactured from Foreign Material—		*Of our own Materials—*	
Cotton Goods of all kinds,	£47,400,000	Metals, Cutlery, Machinery, &c.,	£25,000,000
Woollen do.,	21,000,000	Coal, . .	3,700,000
Linen do.,	9,000,000	Earthenware,	1,334,000
Metals (say),	8,100,000	Soda, . .	807,000
Haberdashery,	4,360,000	Glass, . .	750,000
Apparel & Slops,	2,800,000	Soap, . .	250,000
Silk do.,	3,000,000	Beer, . .	1,776,000
Leather do.,	2,230,000	Spirits, . .	454,000
Jute do.,	400,000	Stationery & Paper,	900,000
Hats, . .	440,000	Books, . .	457,000
Furniture, .	300,000	Bags, . .	550,000
Gunpowder,	460,000		36,038,000
Sugar, refined,	500,000		
	£99,990,000		£136,028,000
Articles not included, £10,461,768.		Total,	£146,489,768

Father Sol is a very potent deity, whose favours we cannot afford to slight. His rays are a veritable shower of gold. He is fickle, it is true, though not quite so fickle as of yore; and we may hope for some slight improvement still, when by draining and planting or clearing we have rendered our Isles a more pleasant spot for him to look upon. Of late years the variations in the amount of corn imported have been unusually great. In 1859 the amount imported was not quite £18,000,000; in the two following years it rose to 31½ and 34¾ millions; in 1862 to 37¾ millions—more than double what it was in '59; last year it was £26,000,000, and this year it promises to be as much.*

COTTON.

The variations in the import of cotton during the same years have been still more remarkable. Indeed the changes connected with the late cotton-crisis are the most astounding of their kind that could well be imagined. A civil war in America suddenly sealed up the region from which we derived five-sixths of our supply of cotton; by far the most important branch of our manufacturing industry was smitten with paralysis; a large portion of the cloth-

* The great increase which has taken place of late years in our dependence upon foreign countries for corn, is shown by the following facts given in a recent Parliamentary return of our imports of grain, flour, and meal, for the last twenty-three years. In the ten years 1841-50, the quantity averaged 5,810,470 quarters a-year; in the ten years 1851-60, 9,629,425 quarters; since then it has been larger than was ever known before—namely, in 1861, 16,094,914 quarters; in 1862, 18,441,791 quarters; and in 1863, 15,352,559 quarters.

ing of mankind became suddenly very scarce and dear; and a great alteration took place in the channels of commerce. The old cotton-fields being blocked up, new areas of cultivation were opened. Instead of drawing our supplies from, and sending our money to, the West, we have been drawing our cotton from, and sending our money to, the East. India, Egypt, and Turkey are now fertilised by the golden stream which previously poured into the United States.

THE COTTON DEARTH.

We need not speak of the manner in which the great calamity of the cotton famine has been borne by this country. We need not describe the admirable patience of the suffering operatives, nor the magnificent charity displayed by the nation at large on their behalf. But it may truly be said that the manner in which the calamity has been met and surmounted has astonished even ourselves. A branch of industry which employs half-a-million of operatives, and whose products constitute one-third of our export trade,* was suddenly paralysed; yet the general prosperity of the country hardly experienced a check, and already our export trade is rushing ahead again at its former rate of increase. Let any one study

* Mr Arnold, in his *History of the Cotton Famine*, states that in 1860, the *annus mirabilis* of the cotton-trade, there were 2650 factories, worked by about 440,000 operatives, whose wages amounted to £11,500,000 a-year. And the capital invested in this branch of our manufacturing industry was £65,000,000. This amount, of course, is exclusive of the capital of the cotton-merchants who trade in the raw material.

the following brief statistics of our cotton trade during the last four years, and he will discern how vast have been the changes produced by the blockade of the American ports:—

Imported.	1860.	1861.	1862.	1863.
Quantity, . . cwts.,	12,419,096	11,223,078	4,678,333	5,973,422
Price.	£35,756,889	£38,453,398	£31,093,045	£56,277,953
From United States,	£30,069,306	£26,570,399	£1,221,277	£644,138
From other countries,	5,687,583	12,082,999	29,871,768	55,633,815

The startling change in the channels of commerce is here visible at a glance. In 1860, the United States sent us five-sixths of our supply of cotton, and now they send us next to none—only one-sixtieth of their former amount. On the other hand, the rest of the world has increased its rate of supply tenfold,—sending us 55½ millions' worth of cotton, in place of the 5½ which it sent in 1860. Another change which is strikingly shown in the above figures is that of price. Although the quantity of cotton imported fell from 12½ million cwts. in 1860 to only 4½ in 1862, the price which we paid for cotton in the latter year was almost as great as in the former. And last year, although the quantity imported was less than one-half what we imported in 1860, we paid upwards of one-half more for it!* So enormous has been the increase

* If we compare the present prices with those in 1859 (the year before the exceptional period of the cotton-trade began), we find the following results. First, as regards the raw material. In 1859 the average price of "middling Orleans" was 7d. per lb.—this year the average has been 28d. per lb.; or four times greater than before

in the price of cotton, caused by the dearth on the one hand, and on the other by the general prosperity of the nations, which seems* to admit of their buying cotton clothing freely, even at unusually high prices.

Peculiar circumstances connected with the late cotton crisis have sufficed greatly to moderate its bad effects. In 1860 and beginning of '61, the Southern States, seeing a blockade approaching, hurried out every bale of cotton which they had on hand; this enormous amount was as speedily worked up by our manufacturers; and the consequence was, that a great glut ensued in the markets of the world.† In ordi-

the outbreak of the civil war in America. And as regards "fair Dhollerah," the price per pound has similarly increased—namely from 5¼d. to 21½d. Secondly, as regards the manufactured article, since 1859, the price of "40's mule-yarn" has risen from 12½ to 33d.—or more than 2½ times the price before the exceptional period began. And "8 lb. 4 oz. shirting" has increased from 9s. 7d. to 21s. 2d.—*i. e.*, nearly 2¼ times. As the cost of manufacture remains the same as before, the change in price is occasioned simply by the rise in the price of the raw material. And on this account the rise in the price of the finer kinds of manufactured goods is less than in the coarser kinds,—and in both of these is less than in the raw material.

* We say "seems," because the Eastern markets are still heavy; and although the old cheap stocks of 1860-61 have been cleared off, it is doubtful how far the new and dear stocks will be taken into general consumption.

† The exports of cotton goods from this country during the last seven years have been, in round numbers, as follows:—

1857,	£39,000,000	1861,	£46,600,000
1858,	43,000,000	1862,	36,134,000
1859,	48,000,000	1863,	47,000,000
1860,	51,960,000		

nary circumstances this glut would have produced a severe crisis in our cotton-trade, and extensive failures would certainly have occurred. But, as events turned out, the over-production of 1860 proved a fortunate thing for our manufacturers; for a considerable portion of the goods manufactured at low prices in that year, afterwards sold at very high prices in 1862-63.

The cotton-trade is still in a transition state, and fresh changes will assuredly take place whenever peace is re-established in the United States. But these changes will be on the side of plenty; and, however injurious they may perhaps be to India and the other cotton-fields recently opened, they cannot fail to be highly advantageous to this country. This at least ought to be the result. But any great fall in the value of the raw material, if it take place suddenly,* must have an injurious effect upon merchants or manufacturers who have laid in a large stock at the present high prices. Moreover, it behoves our manufacturers to bear in mind that a comparatively small amount of production when prices are at their present exorbitant height will produce a glut as certainly as a much larger production will do in ordinary times. An

* We have no doubt that, whenever the civil war in America comes to an end, a customs-duty will be imposed upon the export of cotton,—which may be so high as to yield a large return to the American Government, and yet allow of the Southern States being again, what they used to be, the cheapest market from which we can supply ourselves with cotton.

amount of production which may be healthy when prices are low, becomes excessive if carried on when prices are high. In 1860-61 the glut was caused by cotton goods being too plentiful; but, let it be remembered, a similar glut may be produced simply from the goods being too dear. In 1860-61, the quantity of goods manufactured was greater than people required, —now, we fear, the price of the goods is greater than our customers at large can afford to pay.

OUR CUSTOMERS.

Let us now see the kind of produce which each country sends us, and the commodities which each takes from us. China sends raw silk and tea; India sends cotton, indigo, and rice. We get our spices from the Philippine Islands, and almost all our coffee from Ceylon. We get a portion of our cotton from Egypt; hides chiefly from the Pampas of Buenos Ayres; wool chiefly from Australia and the Cape; wood from the northern countries of America and Europe; flax and tallow from Russia; corn chiefly from the United States and Russia; and the precious metals from Australia, California, Mexico, and the Andes of Peru. Of our exports, we send beer to India and Australia; coal to many places to supply coaling-stations for steam-vessels, but chiefly to France. We send cotton-yarn for manufacture to India, Holland, and Germany; and cotton piece-goods to India and China, Turkey, Egypt, the United States, and Brazil. Our hardwares and cutlery go chiefly to Australia, India, and the United States; and our woollen and worsted goods to the United States, India and China, Germany, British North America, and Australia. The material of war—cannon, rifles, and gunpowder—we send to any country which, unhappily for itself, may stand in need of them.

As the amount of our imports shows, we are good customers to the world at large. Having seen the kind of goods which each country takes from or sends to us, let us indicate the countries with which the greatest amount of our trade is carried on. Of the 249 millions' worth of goods which we imported last year, 84½ came from our own possessions (*i. e.*, our colonies and India)—from France, 24,—United States, 19½,—Egypt, 16½,—Germany, 13½,—China, 13,—Russia, 12½ millions. Thus our own possessions send us fully one-third of our imports; France, the United States, Egypt, Germany, and China, send rather more than another third; and of the remaining 77½ millions, Russia and Holland send us fully 27 per cent. Arabia and Persia figure lowest in the list. In 1862, Persia sent us £5 worth of goods,—Arabia nothing; in 1863 Arabia sent us £2 worth of goods, and Persia nothing. Japan sends a million.

The same countries which sell to us the greatest amount of goods are also (though not quite in the same order) those which buy from us the most. Of the 146 millions of our exports last year, our own possessions purchased 51 millions' worth,—the United States, 15,—Germany, $13\frac{1}{4}$,—France, $8\frac{2}{3}$,—Turkey (exclusive of Egypt), nearly 7,—and Holland, $6\frac{1}{3}$. Arabia and Persia again figure lowest in the list; in some years taking nothing at all, in others a thousand pounds or so,—less than the amount of goods sent to our consuls and embassy. These two countries, doubtless, take very little from us; but the infinitesimal appearance which they make in the Board of Trade returns is greatly owing to their want of good and accessible seaports, in consequence of which the goods which they take from us are conveyed to them overland, and figure in the imports of other countries.

OUR COLONIES.

Our own possessions, it will be seen, are as good customers to us in the buying as in the selling. They take from us fully one-third of our exports; the United States, Germany, France, Turkey, and Holland take another third; and the remaining third is taken in various proportions by the other countries of the world. These facts bring out in a very clear light the importance to us of our colonies and possessions. The whole cost of our colonies to the British exchequer is barely three and a quarter millions sterling,—of which sum about a million is absorbed by our military stations of Malta and Gibraltar; while India costs us nothing at all, and moreover furnishes a profitable sphere of action for our adventurous youth, who in due time bring home with them their gains. India at present buys annually 20 millions' worth of goods from us, and Australia 12½.

OUR SHIPS AT SEA.

We are the great carriers of the world. Thirty thousand ships sailing under the flag, or bearing the cargoes of England, says Mr Cobden, are ever on the seas, going and coming from all parts of the globe. The once solitary and unnavigated surface of ocean is now whitened with the sails and tossed by the paddles of countless vessels. Not promiscuously do these white-winged ships dot the expanse of ocean, but following and crossing and meeting one another on regular highways, which men have found, not made, on the deep. We make roads with vast labour on land,—we find them made for us at sea, in the great currents which wind through the deep, and in the steady-blowing gales which traverse in similar fashion the realms of air. From the Thames, the Mersey, the Tyne, the Humber, and the Clyde, argosies and commercial armadas are ever leaving, and jostle in our estuaries with similar squadrons making to port.* The shores of these estuaries, lined with miles of docks and building-yards, ring with the clang of hammers; and vast ribs of wood and iron,

* The amount of the export trade from the twelve chief ports of the United Kingdom in 1862 was as follows:—Liverpool, £50,297,135; London, £31,523,812; Hull, £11,916,375; Glasgow and Greenock, £6,096,228; Southampton, £3,379,503; Newcastle, £1,968,118; Leith, £1,298,099; Bristol, £298,260; Cork, £132,130; Dublin, £48,777; Belfast, £4188.

curving upwards from still vaster keels, show where leviathan vessels are being got ready for their adventurous career. As we watch the launch of these vessels,—still more as we see them setting off, with full-spread sails or smoking funnels, for all parts of the world—to China or the Cape, to the St Lawrence or La Plata, to the North Sea or the Mexican Gulf, or to double the wintry promontory of Cape Horn on their way to the guano islands of Peru or the golden shores of California,—we think of icebergs and sunken reefs, of typhoons and tornadoes, as well as of fair winds and sunny seas. All the year round, a ceaseless stream of ocean-traffic is flowing to and from our shores. Last year 90,310 vessels with cargoes entered or left our ports, carrying on the foreign trade of the country.* Of this shipping, British and colonial vessels exceeded the foreign in number by one-fourth, and in tonnage (our ships being a half larger) by nearly two to one.

In regard to the amount of British shipping, we find accurate information in the official register. In the home trade,† employed on our coasts in conveying goods and passengers from port to port, we have

* This statement shows clearly the vast amount of shipping employed in our trade; but it is not a guide to the number of separate ships employed—seeing that many of them make double or treble voyages, and are entered anew each time.

† The "home trade" includes our own coasts, together with the ports between Brest and the mouth of the Elbe.

11,000 sailing-vessels, averaging 75 tons burden each, and employing 40,000 men; besides 450 steam-vessels, averaging 240 tons burden each, and employing 7000 men. Engaged partly in home and partly in foreign trade, we have 1500 sailing-vessels, averaging 160 tons each, and employing 10,000 men; besides 90 steamers, averaging 330 tons burden, and employing 1700 men. In the purely foreign trade, we have upwards of 7000 sailing-vessels, averaging 430 tons each, and employing 100,000 men; also upwards of 500 steam-ships, of the average burden of 645 tons, and employing 20,000 men. Thus, in our home and foreign trade, taken together, we have fully 20,000 ships, with a tonnage of 4½ millions, and employing 175,000 men. Both classes of our ships, both steamers and sailing-vessels, are regularly increasing in numbers, but much the greater ratio of increase is in the number of steamers. In both kinds of vessels, too, there is a steady increase in size. Comparing the present amount of our shipping with what it was in 1850, we find that we have eleven per cent more ships, forty-four per cent more tonnage, and fifteen per cent more men. Moreover, a great economy has of late been effected in the working of the vessels. Since 1850, there has been a reduction of one-fifth in the number of men required for a certain amount of tonnage; so that our 175,000 seamen now work an amount of shipping which in 1850 would have required 220,000 men.

The last feature of our trade which remains to be noticed is the traffic in the precious metals. It is a curious, and at first sight a puzzling one. It is so, at least, to those who fancy that the receipt or export of the precious metals is an indication of a country's gains or losses. Gold and silver in large quantities are constantly pouring into this country, and flying off again. The native countries of the precious metals—Australia, Mexico, and California (through the United States)—send us a large portion of their annual produce; and we send it off again, chiefly to Turkey, Egypt, and India. There is also a constant flux and reflux of the precious metals between England and the other countries of Europe, especially between this country and France. During the last five years we received 18 millions of gold and silver from France, and we sent thither nearly 40 millions. But of the balance of 22 millions thus apparently acquired by France, a considerable portion simply took its way through that country, *viâ* Marseilles, to the East. No less than 140½ millions sterling of the precious metals were imported into England during the last five years, and 138 millions were exported; so that of the enormous quantity which we received, only two and a half millions remained with us.

THE PRECIOUS METALS.

How was this? What became of the 138 millions of gold and silver which no sooner reached our shores than they went off again? We made the best possible use of this bullion. We sent it abroad, chiefly to purchase materials for our industry; and the goods manufactured from those materials we in turn sent abroad, selling them to other countries. Thus we send away our gold in order that we may make a profit on the materials which the gold purchases. It is a fair exchange. The foreign country gets the value of its goods in gold, and we get the value of our gold in goods. But these goods, by being manufactured and re-exported, not only give employment to our people, but enable us to make a profit which we could not do by keeping the gold.

MOVEMENTS OF BULLION.

There are some countries which export more goods and less bullion than they import; and there is another class of countries which regularly export less goods and more bullion than they import. India is an example of the one class,—the gold and silver producing countries, Australia, California, and Mexico, of the other. The goods which we get from the former are taken from us by the latter; the bullion which we get from the latter is taken from us by the former. Each exports what it best can spare; and, dealing with both, we pay the one by sending to it the produce of the other.

A drain of gold from any country may be occasioned simply by a change in the channels of trade. For example, as long as we drew our cotton supplies from the United States, gold was hardly needed in the trade, because the United States took from us goods of equal value; whereas now, when we get our cotton from India, Egypt, and other countries which take less goods from us than we buy from them, we have to pay away a very large amount of bullion every year. Yet there is not a loss in the one case any more than in the other. The influx or efflux of bullion is no sign of a country's gain or loss. Australia is constantly sending away her gold, and is growing rich by the process. Her whole prosperity depends on her parting with the gold: it would be the worst evil that could befall her if she were compelled to keep it. As we have said, the annual savings of the United Kingdom are reckoned at the astounding sum of £130,000,000. What is there in the flow of bullion to show for this? In one year our national wealth increases by a sum which is nearly equal to the whole amount of the precious metals which came to our shores during the last five years; yet of that amount all that remained with us was only two millions and a half,—only equal to the amount of the gold and silver which in a single year we consume in ornaments and the arts.

NO INDEX OF GAIN OR LOSS.

If the import and accumulation of the precious metals were a test of national progress in wealth, then India should be making greater gains every year than England and all Europe put together. But the ebb and flow of the precious metals is no indication whatever of the amount of a nation's gains or losses. It is an event which indicates nothing but itself,—namely, that payments in bullion are being made: and nothing can be predicated therefrom as to the relative condition of the sender or receiver.

An influx of bullion may be equally a sign of gain or a sign of indebtedness. Suppose the Government of any country—say Russia—raises a foreign loan of ten or twenty milions; then to that extent, or nearly so, the precious metals are drawn from other countries and poured into Russia. Is that any sign that Russia is increasing in wealth, or that the balance of *trade* is in her favour? No, certainly: it is a sign of neither of these things. The indebtedness of Russia is only increased thereby. Or again,—of the immense savings which we make annually, suppose our capitalists resolve to devote ten or twenty millions to the construction of railways or suchlike enterprises in foreign countries, which will yield a good profit. Thereupon the precious metals leave our shores in great quantity; but are we losers thereby? Would the money be sent abroad if it were not to get larger profits than the senders can get at home?—and does not the annual interest, or dividends, on the sums thus invested abroad come back to us regularly, to increase the profits or income of our people?

Finally, the coming and going of the precious

metals may be a sign neither of gain nor of loss, but simply of the amount of trade which a country is carrying on.

THE USE OF BULLION IN COMMERCE.

The precious metals pass through this country as through a sieve; and the immense quantities that thus come and go are simply one of the consequences of our extensive trade. To a large extent our merchants act as intermediaries between countries which have little commercial relation with one another. For example, Australian and Mexican merchants order goods from China or India, between which countries and their own there is little or no direct trade, and consequently no bills of exchange in which payment can be made; moreover, gold is not money in China, neither is it yet a legal tender in India. Therefore these Australian or Mexican merchants give the China or Indian exporters bills upon some well-known firm in London, and send bullion to London to meet these bills when due. The exporters on their part at once get these bills discounted at their banks in Calcutta or Shanghai, where the amount is placed to their credit; and the bills themselves are sent by post to London to the parties on whom they are drawn, and who thereupon have to make payment. Now, as these bills on London are always in excess of our bills on India and China, the balance has to be sent out from this country in the precious metals: and thus the bullion which comes to us from the gold and silver producing countries for the most part simply rests here as at an entrepôt, and is quickly sent off to the East. Only, the gold must first be exchanged for silver in Europe,—since it is silver only that is current money in India and China.

It is only in making such payments that the precious metals are of any use to trade. Their use is to effect purchases or payments which cannot be accomplished by the ordinary means of bills of exchange. In such cases only are the precious metals needed. Indeed, the use of the precious metals is even more restricted than this. When there is a want of bills of exchange, goods may be sent abroad instead of bills or of gold. These goods are then sold in the foreign market, and with the proceeds the English merchant pays his foreign creditor, without a single sovereign having left this country. Instead of sending specie from this country he buys it abroad with goods,—paying his creditor out of the stock of specie held in the creditor's own country. Any merchant can get these precious metals, whether for export or import, in the same way as he gets cotton or iron. He may order gold from Australia just as he orders cotton from India. Or, with less trouble, he can buy bills on any place he likes, and order the proceeds of the bills to be sent home to him in specie: and he will only have to pay freightage on this specie in the same manner as he pays it on other commodities. So much elaborate nonsense is talked on this subject and on "the exchanges" that one is apt to think that the precious metals ought to be styled the "mysterious metals." Yet there is no mystery either in their influence or their movements. They can be dealt in like other commodities,—bought and sold in the same way as sugar, soap, or tea.

Gold is sent abroad only when it suits the interests of the sender to do so. Hence, to place restrictions on the export of gold, is simply to compel traders to send goods at a bad bargain when they could send gold at a good one. It is an antiquated system, incompatible with the liberty of trade. For example, in November last, the Bank refused to discount the bills of cotton-merchants simply because the proceeds of those bills were meant to be sent abroad in the shape of specie. Lancashire was idle for want of cotton. The most important branch of our national industry, next to the cultivation of the land, had been for two years almost at a standstill for want of the raw material; an immense national subscription had been requisite to keep half a million of our working-classes from absolute starvation. Cotton means employment for these suffering myriads. It means also profits for the master-manufacturers. To obtain a supply of cotton, therefore, has become a matter of great importance, even in a national point of view; yet our monetary system creates obstacles to our obtaining it. For the last twelve months the Bank of England has regarded the importers of cotton as its peculiar enemies. "In November last it refused discounts to purchasers of cotton, not because their bills were doubtful, but because of the dread of a drain of gold."* The Bank thus checks the imports of cotton, and thereby prevents the revival of our cotton-trade, and the employment of our manufacturing population.

In fact, to talk of "free trade" under our present monetary system, is a mockery. Instead of being "free," trade is restricted alike in whole and in every part, and to an extent far greater than could be effected by customs-duties. In antiquated times, it was thought that a country's prosperity depended upon its exports being greater than its imports,—because it was imagined that an accumulation of specie was the only proof of an increase of national wealth. This theory is now scouted in every quarter. In fact the principle is now reversed. "Take care of the imports, and the exports will take care of themselves," is now recognised as the true principle of legislation as regards Trade. But it is wholly neutralised by the adoption of the very opposite principle in our monetary legislation. The Bank Act revived the old, and we should have thought, antiquated system, and seeks to restrict the import of goods, in order that specie may be sent

* *Banker's Magazine*, Feb. 1863, p. 92.

hither instead. Under our recent legislation, the country has gone back two hundred years. While the legislation as regards Trade has been wondrously improved and almost perfected, our monetary legislation has become retrograde. While freedom and full liberty of expansion have been given to Trade, monopoly and restriction have imposed new fetters upon Banking. It is like tying the living face to face with the dead. It is like placing a growing child within an ever-contracting cradle. What can be expected of such a system but misery and disaster? What can follow from so discordant a union but a constant antagonism of interests between active and ever-expanding Trade and the soulless despotism of Money which keeps it in fetters?

OUR DEPENDENCE FOR FOOD.

The statistics of our trade which have now been passed in review, exhibit in a startling manner our dependence upon other countries. We are dependent upon them to a large extent alike for food, for clothing, and for employment. Our dependence for clothing may seem a small matter, though it is not; but our dependence for food and employment is unquestionably a very serious affair. If Mr Caird is right in estimating the consumption of our people at 20 million quarters of wheat, then, during the last three years (when the annual importation of corn and flour has averaged 16 million quarters) twenty-four millions of our population—four-fifths of the nation—have been dependent for grain-food upon foreign countries! Even taking the most favourable estimate that can be formed, it appears, on the average of years, that fully one-third of our population is dependent upon grain-supplies from abroad,*—and our dependence in this respect is yearly increasing. This

* As, unfortunately, there are no agricultural returns for England and Scotland, a reasonable conjecture is the only approximation to correctness which can be made in estimating the amount of wheat consumed by our people. Twenty years ago it was assumed that, on an average, one quarter of wheat was consumed per head,—which would give a total consumption of 30 million quarters. Mr Caird estimates our consumption of wheat at only two-thirds of that amount,—namely, at 20 million quarters. The truth may lie between these different estimates. There can be no doubt that wheaten bread is more in use by the lower classes than it formerly was; the consumption of wheat in manufactures in the form of starch must likewise have largely increased (individual manufacturers in Manchester are known to use 5000 quarters of wheat per annum): and looking to these facts, as well as to the enormous quantity of wheat now annually imported into this country, we cannot but think that Mr Caird's estimate of the consumption of wheat is too low.

Mr Caird's estimate of the amount of wheat produced in this country also appears to us too low. It appears from the returns obtained by the Highland and Agricultural Society that in 1856-7 the extent of land under wheat in Scotland amounted, on the average of these two years, to 243,240 acres,—yielding an average produce of rather more than 27 bushels to the acre. If we take this rate of produce as an average for the whole kingdom, and also accept the common (but purely conjectural) estimate that there are (or used to be) 5 million acres under wheat in the kingdom, it would follow that the total produce of wheat in the country is 17 million quarters,—instead of 12, as estimated by Mr Caird.

But both in Scotland and in Ireland the acreage under wheat is steadily decreasing, owing to the present unremunerative price of wheat, which compels farmers to devote more of their fields to grass and turnips, for the purpose of rearing sheep and cattle, is irrespective of the nine millions' worth of animal food which we import, and two millions' worth of rice,—necessaries of life. And, over and above, there are thirty-six millions' worth of sugar, tea, coffee, wines, &c.,—which were luxuries in former times, but which have now become part of the ordinary diet of the people.

FOR EMPLOYMENT.

Next, as to our dependence upon other countries for Employment. We annually import about 120 millions' worth of materials, the working up of which, in factories and other workshops, gives employment to probably a million and a half of operatives, many of whom have families dependent on them. This is a startling picture, but it has two sides. In one aspect, it is the greatest eulogy which could be pronounced upon our enterprise and greatness. Our little islands no longer suffice for us. Our energies have far overpassed their limits. There is room for us to live and work here,—that is all. These Islands are our house and garden, but our farm is detached. Or rather, we have no farm of our own, but draw our supplies from the farms of all our neighbours. We live upon the world. We have made so much money by

which pay better. The same cause (namely, the present unremunerative price of grain) is also leading to an increased culture of flax: a result which is being accelerated by the cotton-dearth and the great rise in the price of all textile materials. The growth of flax is extending in Ireland, and is also being introduced to an important extent into England. This autumn the traveller by the Great Northern Railway could see many large fields of flax standing in sheaves, where no such sight was to be witnessed in former years.

generations of industry, and we employ our capital so well in trade and in profitable investments abroad, that we can command supplies of what we want from all parts of the world. On the other hand, what would be the consequences of a blockade? Would it not wither us up at once, as if the national life had been smitten by paralysis? Would not our greatness fare like Jonah's gourd, which perished in a night by the gnawing of a little worm?

We say these things not in alarm or despondency. But it is well that a consideration of these things should incite us to renewed zeal in projects which are at present too little regarded. England, if she preserve her greatness, must always be dependent upon other countries; and, so far as regards trade and employment, that dependence must continue to increase. But at least let us strive to lessen our dependence upon foreign countries for food. Large tracts of ground, now lying waste, may yet be cultivated. Even between London and Southampton, in the finest part of England, there are wide expanses of level moorland, such as in the lowlands of Scotland would quickly be brought into profitable cultivation. The waste of sewage, which is a disgrace to our civilisation, will ere long, we trust, give place to an economy which will work wonders, and make many a blade of corn grow where none ever grew before. The steam-plough, also, will do something,—partly by lessening the

REMEDIES.

cost of working the soil, but still more by working it deeper than is possible with horses. Finally, we ought to take measures to stock all our rivers and lakes amply with fish. A very large portion of the food of China consists of fresh-water fish,—yet in this country it is as rare as if it were a costly luxury, and by millions of our people is not tasted once in the year. Let us hope, then, that the future—among the other good things it may have in store—will see the sewage of our great towns, instead of being wasted in poisoning our rivers, applied in fertilising streams to the soil, —the steam-plough in general use,—our level waste-lands reclaimed,—our lakes and rivers amply stocked with fish,—and the luxury of oyster-beds plentifully established on our coasts. We might even with advantage enact a "close time" for our coasts as well as for our rivers,—the destruction of female mackerel and herring while in roe being a most wasteful practice. Such measures are called for by the necessities of our position. They are urgently needed to lessen, or at least to arrest the progress of, our perilous dependence upon other countries for food,—a dependence which every year is increasing, and which, if the proper measures be not taken, must continue to increase with the spread of luxury and the growth of the population.

These are considerations for the Government and for the general community. All that our trading classes have to think of is to extend their operations, and to do so in as profitable a manner as they can. But they have apprehensions of their own—perils which primarily affect themselves, although the whole community ultimately suffers along with them. The present year has been commercially prosperous almost beyond example: yet shadows, as if of coming calamity, have ever and anon flitted across the sunny scene, and ever and anon our commercial classes have been filled with forebodings. The City of Gold has been troubled. In Tennysonian phrase, "its dreams are bad." The ease with which evil reports find currency is symptomatic of the prevailing nervousness. Only a week or two ago—in the beginning of September—just before the Bank-rate was raised to 9 per cent, there was a panic on 'Change. The failure of several extensive firms was said to be impending, and the money-market was seriously affected. The panic which occurred serves to show that the trading community is by no means at its ease. Nor can it be so when the Bank-rate is rising, and threatens to cause a depression of the markets. Evil which all men expect, says the proverb, never comes,—all men being on the alert to prevent it. Let us hope that such will be the issue in the present case. But at the same time let us see what are the dangers to which our trade is exposed.

THE CITY IN TROUBLE.

It is a common saying, in some quarters, that the commercial classes in this country go mad every ten years. The great crisis of 1826 was followed by the minor crises of 1837 and '39; these by the crisis of 1847; and that in turn by the grand crash in 1857. Periodical insanity is alleged to be the cause of these calamities. An ever-recurring mania for over-trading is believed to seize upon the commercial classes, and hurry them into ruin. This is a very bold assumption. A theory which supposes insanity on the part of the shrewdest and most practical portion of the community certainly lacks, *a priori*, the air of probability. That, to the parties who hold this theory, our commercial classes seem to perform acts of insanity periodically, may be true; but does not the appearance of insanity arise from the acts being viewed through a wrong medium? Suppose a person, walking up and down in front of our windows, always as he passed a particular pane of glass appeared to be grimacing; would it not be sane on our part, before questioning his sanity, to look whether there were not a flaw in the glass which made him appear to be grimacing, when in truth he was walking as soberly as usual? The first question, then, which naturally suggests itself is,—Is it the fact that the commercial classes of the United Kingdom do actually, and in a manner suicidal for themselves, go mad every ten years? Or is there not something, in the circumstances of the country, which at certain periods gives to their operations a semblance of recklessness, when in reality

PERIODICAL INSANITY.

they have no such character? Before charging the whole commercial and manufacturing classes with fits of insanity in over-trading, it is right to ascertain whether there be not some element in the case which their libellers have overlooked, and a consideration of which may place the matter in a different light.

OVER-TRADING.

"Over-trading" is a charge of recent date. The crisis of 1857 was the first occasion on which it was heard. Previous to that time, another cry had been in vogue to account for the recurrence of commercial crises. They were attributed to "over-issues." That was the current theory from the beginning of the century down to 1844. Even in 1847 the old cry was heard in certain quarters, and the Bank was blamed for not having "contracted its issues"—*i.e.*, reduced the amount of its notes in circulation. But that was the last of it. The theory would not hold water, and it was abandoned. Facts were too strong for it, and it was exploded.

It came to be seen that the importance which had been attached to fluctuations in the amount of the Bank's circulation was groundless. The old cry was abandoned before 1857, and no one dreamt of reviving it when the great monetary crisis of that year occurred. But if the Bank Act had rendered our monetary system perfect, what explanation was to be given of this new calamity? Then it was that the theory of "over-trading" was propounded; and it became as current as the cry of "over-issues" used to be. The old cry has been given up,—has the new one any better basis of support? It does not matter with what parties the cry originated—we need not speculate whether it was the result of an honest belief, or whether it was adopted as a convenient means of shielding from scrutiny our present monetary system. All that we have to concern ourselves with is,—Is it true?

What has been may, and, if not guarded against, will occur again. If over-trading were the cause of the terrible calamity of 1857, the more fully the fact is investigated and exposed the better. If it were not, then the sooner we disabuse ourselves of the idea, the sooner we shall be in a position to discover the real cause of our commercial disasters. We must get off the wrong scent before we can find the right one. The question is of momentous importance to the welfare of our trade, and should be put beyond the influence of haphazard conjectures. In so matter-of-fact a department as trade and commerce, it behoves one to eschew mere assertions and vague generalities. In commercial matters, above all things, let us have precision. Now, if over-trading were the cause of the disasters of 1857, what was the amount of it, and when did it begin? In the summer of that year—as every one will remember who gives attention to commercial matters—all parties were agreed as to the soundness and prosperous condition of our trade; and not a whisper was heard of credit being overstrained to support it. Not only the mercantile classes, but our most cool and observant economists, held and expressed this opinion. How was it, then, that the trade which was not felt to be excessive in the summer, broke down so suddenly at the end of autumn? How was it that the credit-system of the country, which supported that trade buoyantly and prosperously in July and August, proved utterly unable to sustain it in November? Manifestly, in that short interval, there must have been a great change: either Trade must have experienced a great expansion, or Credit must have become grievously enfeebled. Which of these things was it which happened? In the altered relations between Trade and Credit, which caused trading to become or appear over-trading, was it on the side of Trade or on the side of Credit that the alteration took place? In the brief period that intervened between the height of our prosperity and the depth of our adversity, was it Trade that extended itself, or Credit that became crippled?

SOUNDNESS OF TRADE IN 1857.

The storm came upon us from America: but when it was seen raging on the other side of the Atlantic, the journals which are the most observant critics of commercial affairs—the *Times* and *Economist*—were unhesitating in their assertions that a similar disaster would not extend to this country, so firm and healthy was the condition of our trade. So late as the 7th November, after several large failures had occurred—including the exceptionally bad ones of Macdonald and Monteith in Glasgow,—the *Economist* continued to reiterate unhesitatingly its testimony to the sound and prosperous character of British trade. "That this country is intrinsically better off, as regards its obligations and financial position," it said, "than any other, there can be no doubt." In another editorial article in the same number upon our Imports, it was remarked, that "one of the great sources of loss which have attended former periods of commercial pressure, has been the large accumulation of foreign products in our warehouses,—the consequence of extensive and improvident importations, stimulated by high prices, and the necessary reaction which took place at such times;" but that "this cannot be said, at the present time, of any of the chief raw materials, if we except the single one of silk." Again, in a leader upon our Exports, in the same number, the editor put and answered the following decisive questions:—"Is there any evidence that the export-trade of this country during the last year has been of a forced character? Has there been any glut in the home market, either of raw materials or of manufactured goods, which could have led to such a trade? Has there not, on the contrary, been a great scarcity of raw materials and a continually rising price, caused by an extending demand?

The mere fact that failures have taken place in the United States, which have led to heavy losses in this country, in no way affects the general argument,—unless it can be shown that those failures have been caused by losses directly resulting from the imports from this country. *No such proof exists.* On the contrary," &c. And in the same article, as if the real soundness of our trade could not be too often or too explicitly stated, it was said :—" Unlike the crisis of 1847, we have in the present year, in common with all Europe and the United States, instead of scarcity and famine, one of the most abundant harvests ever known; and, unlike the crisis of 1847, when we had obligations to the extent of more than £150,000,000 in the shape of railway-calls impending over the country, our commercial classes are now more free from such demands upon their resources than they have been for many years."

These are weighty statements. Here is a writer—a recognised authority—carefully considering the whole subject, and speaking with all the official returns and private trade-circulars before him. Here is a man who, in the presence of a great danger, anxiously scans all parts of our position, to see if there be any weak points, and can find none. Again and again the *Times* expressed a similar opinion. For example, on the 9th October, when the Bank began to raise the rate of discount, the leading journal in its City article remarked: "As regards the broad trade of the empire, it is impossible to discern the cause of fear. Month by month our commercial payments increase in magnitude, and yet are met with a punctuality never surpassed. All the leading bankers will testify, that thus far there is an absence even of those premonitory symptoms which invariably warn *them* of the possibility of a coming struggle, long before the community at large have become awakened to it. Hence the belief may be confidently indulged that, although with our universally diffused transactions we must necessarily participate in every shock that occurs elsewhere, our commercial prosperity is destined still to continue a marvel to the world."

WHAT CAUSED THE CRISIS?

The *Times* and *Economist* were right in these statements as to the soundness of our trade. What, then, caused their anticipations to be so lamentably falsified by the issue? Instead of remaining "a marvel to the world," what caused our trade to break down utterly, covering the country with wrecks and misery? The *Times* and *Economist* erred in their calculations because they looked simply to the state of Trade, and overlooked the effect which the American panic would produce upon our Monetary System. It was the failure of the latter which occasioned the failure of the former. The cause of the crisis of 1857 was not bad trade, but a defective currency-law. It was not the fault of our commerce, but of our monetary system. *After* the crisis had done its work, indeed, the impression became general that our commerce had been running wild; and the numerous bankruptcies and suspensions were appealed to as showing that such must have been the case. This was an *ex post facto* argument of a most inconsequential kind. That thirty thousand soldiers died in a week's time—that week having witnessed a battle—is certainly no proof that the army to which they belonged was in a frightfully bad sanitary condition. Doubtless the ailing soldiers of an army are sure to be knocked over in a hand-to-hand fight, but the proportion of such cases is insignificant; and thousands more perish who, but for the battle, might have lived in health and strength for the natural term of existence. The country knows to its cost that the failures and suspensions in 1857 were disastrously numerous; but the question remains, What was the cause of them?

The supporters of the cry of overtrading founded their charge against the commercial classes on the fact that the export-trade in 1857 was greater than it had ever been before. It had increased six millions above the highest amount in any previous year. True, in some of the previous years, there had been an increase not only as great, but three times greater. That was undeniable; but, said the supporters of the overtrading theory, that does not matter: it is now obvious that our merchants and manufacturers have carried trade beyond the limits which the capital of the country can support. The amount of the increase on the year may have been only six millions, but these six millions have been an excess. An export-trade of 122 millions, they said, is a forced and inflated trade, beyond the requirements of the world, and greater than our accumulated wealth can support. And when the exports fell—in consequence of the crisis, and of the stagnation of trade which followed—they appealed to this fact as a proof of the justice of their opinion, and said that this reduction in the amount of exports was simply owing to the country having returned to its normal amount of trade and of production. For the time, they had it all their own way. No one could bring positive proof that they were wrong. It might be—though it was not probable—that British trade had reached and temporarily exceeded the maximum which the requirements of the world permitted. But even if this had been the case, it was certainly unfair and ungenerous so bitterly to taunt the commercial classes, in the midst of their disasters, with recklessness and insanity, merely because they had exceeded a limit which—supposing it had existence—could not possibly be discovered save by actual experience.

But what is to be thought of such an allegation now? Actual experience has been acquired, and what does it show? Look back at the column of "our Nilometer," given on a previous page, and see how insignificant was the increase of trade which was thought to be "reckless overtrading," and the cause of all our calamities, seven years ago. Such an increase appears a bagatelle; and the ill-fated year, as figured in the returns of its trade, is passed over by the eye as a very ordinary one. Despite the limit which theorisers assigned to it as its *ne plus ultra,* British trade has continued to increase, and to an extent which throws all former years into the shade. No sooner was the year of stagnation, which naturally followed the crisis of 1857, at an end, than trade not only resumed its old rate of progression, but began to exceed it. In 1859 the exports were eight and a half millions greater than those of 1857; in 1860, they were fourteen millions greater; and last year they exceeded those of 1857 by twenty-four millions and a half. Yet no crisis came: the country was prosperous, and every one rejoiced in the marvellous expansion of our industry and enterprise. Even the terrible cotton-dearth in 1861 failed to reduce our exports to their amount in 1857; and if any such reduction were to take place, it would justly be regarded as one of the greatest calamities which could befall us. A steady increase of trade on the part of this country is what may naturally be expected, and is much to be desired. In truth, if we consider the annual increase of our wealth and of our population, and the increasing facilities for trade with other countries, it will be evident that when the Board of Trade returns are no greater for one year than for its predecessor, such a fact indicates not merely that we are not gaining ground, but that we are losing it. When the amount of labour and capital in this country is annually increasing, and better markets are being opened for the produce of that labour, it is alike unnatural and unfortunate if our exports do not likewise show an annual increment.

Although the "excess" of exports shown by the Board of Trade returns was the chief ground upon which the charge of overtrading was brought against the commercial classes in 1857, another circumstance, peculiar to the times, contributed notably to make the charge popular with the general public. This was the publicity then for the first time given to the examination of bankrupts. Failures which previously would have passed unnoticed by the public, then began to be reported in full detail in the newspapers, and became the subject of conversation in every city and market-place in the kingdom. Scandal-lovers delighted to recount the extravagance of the bankrupt in his wines, furniture, and housekeeping,—how much went to keep up his dog-cart, and how much was lavished on his mistress; while men of business dilated upon the nature and extent of the "accommodation-system," by which this speculation and extravagance were carried on. It was the revelation of these cases that was new in 1857—not their occurrence. Such exceptional cases are, have been, and will continue to occur in every large and active commercial community. One may as well hope to sever shadow from sunshine, or evil from good in this world, as to find a condition of trade in which many cases of recklessness and mismanagement do not coexist with legitimate and profitable enterprise. *Cæteris paribus,* the more numerous a population is, the greater the amount of poverty, folly, and crime; and in like manner, and from the same cause, the brisker trade is, the more numerous will be the cases of bad trading. We may regret this, as we deplore the other imperfections of human nature, but we cannot help it. It is a clog upon prosperity, but not a barrier to progress. The population of these Islands has doubled since this century began, and we are afraid to say how much more numerous are the cases of crime and poverty amongst us now than they were sixty years ago; but, despite these drawbacks, the nation has advanced immensely in its social condition and prosperity. Progress in Trade is just like progress in anything else. There may be, and doubtless are, a greater number of bad failures now than in former times, but certainly there are not more in proportion to the amount of trade carried on.*

* In 1862 the number of bankruptcies in England was nearly ten thousand (9663), of which upwards of nine thousand (9113) paid no dividend at all! In 1863 the returns are a little better,—the number of bankruptcies being 8470, of which 996 paid a dividend of some kind, and 20 paid in full.

The *Times,* in a leader on these returns of the Bankruptcy Court,

And if, in 1857, among the scores of bankruptcy cases revealed in detail to the public, there were some of more than usual shamelessness and recklessness, it must be also remembered that there were dozens of cases of suspensions—probably representing in value one-half of all the failures that then occurred—in

observes:—"Tradesmen must run tradesmen's risks. Bankruptcy is an ominous word, but it means, or ought to mean, nothing but the proportion borne by misfortune to fortune under fair conditions of management. Trade, in the grand sense of the term, always involves a certain element of speculation. In old times merchants were commonly called 'adventurers,' and their transactions were styled 'ventures' without any implication of reproach. In these days we use the word 'enterprise' to express a similar idea,—the meaning in each case being that the merchant or tradesman runs a certain risk for the chance of a certain profit. 'Nothing venture, nothing have,' says an old commercial adage. It would be possible, no doubt, to make trade a certainty instead of a speculation, but in that case we may depend upon it that we should not have sold goods, as we did, to the amount of £195,000,000 in the year 1863. All those exports show a considerable proportion of 'adventures;' and adventures must now and then turn out unluckily, or they would cease to be what they are. The point to be ascertained is, whether these miscarriages exceed or not a certain reasonable ratio —whether trade, in short, is 'sound,' or otherwise; whether the bankruptcies of a year represent a natural percentage of misfortunes or a reckless system of business; and, further, as a more practical question, whether the laws affecting proceedings in such cases are operating satisfactorily.

"Now, should as many as 7000 traders 'smash' so completely in one single year as to leave not a penny for their creditors? Is this a fair average? Is it the actual average? Do 10,000 bankruptcies, of which 7000 are without assets, speak of good times or bad? Do they represent a *maximum* or a *minimum*? It would be hard, perhaps, to answer these questions accurately, but the figures are rather surprising to ordinary people. More than half these failures, it is true, were for small sums, but that does not affect

which the assets of the firms not only covered their liabilities, but exceeded them.*

It may well be asked, how came this to be? In these cases, at least, there was no "overtrading." The fault must have lain not in trade, but in something else. And that thing is the very element of the question which the supporters of the "over-trading" theory desire to overlook. It is that "something in the circumstances of the country" which, as we have previously suggested interrogatively, on certain occasions makes our commercial classes *appear* to be over-trading when in truth they are not. This element is the operation of the Bank Act: and this it is, and not periodical insanity on the part of the trading community, which is the fundamental and originating cause of our recurrent crises. They are not "commercial,"

the principle of the matter. The bankruptcy, without a sixpence to show for it, still remains. Are we to suppose that this very fact explains the bankruptcy, and that if there had been anything divisible among creditors the bankrupt would have been kept out of court? If so, it is certainly not unreasonable that inquiry should be made into the operation of the Bankruptcy Act."

These questions are important ones, but they cannot be answered until we have similar returns from the Bankruptcy Court for the last twenty years. The publication of annual returns only commenced in 1862; but we hope that similar statistics—so far as relates to the number of bankruptcies, the total amount of gross receipts, and the amount of dividend—will be obtained from 1840 downwards.

* See a list of some of these cases, *supra*, pp. 110-11. They form an extraordinary contrast to the ordinary bankruptcy returns just given, and demonstrate in a most striking manner the artificial character of the disastrous crisis of 1857.

but monetary crises. It is commerce indeed that suffers, but it is our monetary system which deals the blow. The commercial community is the *vile corpus* in which the disease chiefly operates, producing misery and ruin; but it is the system pursued by the Bank, under Act of Parliament, which is the primal source and efficient cause of the calamity.

NATURE OF THE DIFFICULTY.

Apart from the operation of the Bank Act, what was the nature of the difficulty which our traders had to encounter? We cannot answer this question better than in the words of the *Times*. Commenting on the large failures that were taking place, it said: "Messrs Dennistoun have houses in New York and New Orleans, and the almost total cessation of remittances from those points has rendered the stoppage unavoidable. . . . What has caused Messrs Naylor, Vickers, & Co., and Messrs Dennistoun to stop? The simple fact that each succeeding mail from America arrived without bringing them remittances of bills to enable them to apply for discount. *Their capitals were ample.*" * "Any firm with fair capital and credit is always prepared to meet a short strain; but few can be expected for weeks and weeks to discharge the cost of wages, raw material, and all the other items in the manufacture of the goods they have shipped, when the returns for these goods are stopped by a convulsion so violent and so

* *Times*, November 9, 1857.

little foreseen that it is likened on the spot to an attack of epilepsy."* Such was the embarrassment which our traders had to meet,—sudden, unforeseeable, and neither arising from nor revealing any fault on their part. The embarrassment, also, was as temporary in its nature as it was artificial. "In America," said the *Times*, on the 13th of October, "the arrears now due to England and the Continent are enormous, and are accumulating every week: and the moment the panic there subsides, and the influence of the fortnightly gold arrivals again begins to be felt, the scarcity of bills upon us may be as remarkable as their present abundance. There is, consequently, nothing to excite apprehension that the disturbance will be protracted." †

This, then, was the whole difficulty,—perfectly artificial in its character, and temporary in its duration.‡ Any man of common sense will wonder that so slight a difficulty should have led to so tremendous a crisis. Our traders had Capital enough, but they could not get Money. Their credit was unquestioned, but our credit-system had wholly given way. Again we ask, Why was this?

A word will explain the matter. A drain of gold—though, as we have shown, a merely superficial event,

* *Times*, October 26, 1857. † *Ibid.*, October 13, 1857.

‡ In truth, so ephemeral was the difficulty, that within two months after the crisis reached its height, we had not only got from America all the gold that we had sent thither, but nearly three times as much,—namely £3,200,000.

in no way necessarily connected with national loss, or expressive of national indebtedness—under our present system, is the grand cause of the recurrent "crises" which inflict vast losses upon our commercial classes. But the same result may be produced by an internal drain (whether of gold or of notes), owing to panic or some other cause temporarily increasing the monetary requirements of the community. And such a panic and drain naturally arise whenever the banks refuse to continue their usual advances to Trade. In 1857, in consequence of the panic and temporary suspension of cash-payments by the banks in the United States, there was a delay in the usual remittances from thence; and also, a million and a quarter of gold was sent thither from this country, —partly for the purpose of purchasing American stocks, then unduly depreciated. Such investments, made by our capitalists, were as legitimate, and at least as profitable, as if iron or cotton goods had been exported to an equal value. But the export of property in the form of specie has a very different effect, under our present system, from the export of property of other kinds. Merely temporary as was this diminution of our usual reserve stock of specie, the operation of the Bank Act was such as to occasion an internal drain likewise, and ultimately, and very rapidly, to shake down our fabric of trade altogether.

The operation of the Bank Act, when a drain of

gold takes place, is threefold—viz., 1, To raise the rate of discount even for first-class commercial bills to an exorbitant height; 2, To render many bills (*i.e.*, the form of currency by which our larger monetary transactions are carried on) unnegotiable, which in other circumstances would have been esteemed perfectly good; and 3, at the culmination of the crisis, so to reduce the *available* resources of the Bank as to render that establishment incapable of lending the customary assistance to firms upon any terms,—even though the solvency of these firms be as unquestioned as that of the Bank itself, and though their suspension should cause a panic which would endanger the position of every bank in the kingdom. For example, in November 1857, the great house of Peabody & Co., temporarily embarrassed by the suspension of payments in America, applied to the Bank for the loan of nearly a million sterling, which the Bank, with its power of issue restricted by the Act of 1844, refused to give; and all London tottered,—for it was known that if that great firm went down, dozens more would fall with it, and the panic would become universal. The suspension of the Bank Act alone prevented this catastrophe, by relaxing the arbitrary fetters on the Bank's issues, and thereby enabling it to advance the sum required. We may add, so thoroughly solvent, indeed excessively wealthy, was this temporarily embarrassed firm, that the private property

AGGRAVATED BY THE BANK ACT.

of the chief partner was of itself held by the Bank to furnish sufficient security for this enormous, but urgently-needed, loan.* But if Peabody & Co. were saved—and we rejoice that they were so,—why were the Dennistouns, Naylor, Vickers, & Co., and many others, sacrificed? The circumstances of all these firms were alike,—why was their fate different? Each had an ample capital—each, from no fault of its own, was temporarily embarrassed; why, then, was not the required assistance given equally to all? Simply because we have an unworkable Bank Act, which it is a point of honour with some theorists, and a point of self-interest with all money-dealers, to uphold to the last, although trade and industry go to wreck and ruin.

The originating cause of the crisis of 1857 in this country, as the *Times* correctly stated, was a delay in the usual remittances of bills from America,—these bills being the chief instruments by which all our trade is carried on. It is upon these bills that the banks make their usual advances to trade; but such advances may be, and often are, made irrespective of bills, upon the securities and assets of mercantile and other firms. But when this temporary want of bills took place in 1857, owing to the crisis in America, the

* For some interesting incidents connected with the threatened failure of this great firm, and of the eminent philanthropist who was at the head of it, see the recently published *Notes on Speculation*, by that veteran City man, Mr Morier Evans.

temporarily embarrassed firms in this country were refused advances upon other securities. There was no adequate reason for this. There was a large supply of loanable capital in the banks; and many of the embarrassed firms—such as the Dennistouns, Naylor, Vickers, & Co., and others—had ample securities to offer for the accommodation which they required. But, under our present system, there is no adequate means of making those advances. There are two difficulties in the way. There is (1) a monopoly of the instrument of exchange; and (2), besides that monopoly, there are artificial restrictions imposed upon the amount of currency. And when the Bank of England refused to assist the temporarily embarrassed firms, there was no help for them. The Bank of England, as we have shown in the previous chapter, is the only bank of issue which, under the present law, can greatly extend its issues. Our other banks of issue are so weak that hardly any one of them would venture to make advances to the extent of half a million in aid of an embarrassed firm, however ample might be the securities which the firm had to offer. Moreover, all our banks of issue are so insignificant compared with the Bank of England, that they now simply follow its example—willing to profit by the high rates of discount which the Bank's policy at such times establishes.

Hence when the Bank of England refused to aid the Dennistouns and others, these perfectly solvent firms were brought to a stop, and had to suspend payments. Thereupon each of these suspended firms became a centre and fountain of fresh embarrassments. Many of the lesser firms commercially connected with them had likewise to stop payment. Distrust overspread the country. Every trader doubted his neighbour's bill; and cash was demanded where a bill would have been accepted in ordinary times. More currency being thus required, a drain commenced upon the Bank. Many persons also, seeing the Bank's reserve declining, and knowing that the rate would soon be raised still higher, hastened to provide themselves with even more money than they required. They could not tell what might happen, and they prepared themselves for still greater emergencies. Up and up went the Bank's rate,—lower and lower fell prices. The markets were so depressed that merchants could not sell their goods save at a loss of 25 per cent. Failures, of course, multiplied,—and each fallen firm brought down with it some of its customers. Distrust swelled into panic. The discount-houses stopped discounting,—the joint-stock and other banks did likewise, or at least greatly contracted their discount-operations. There was plenty of capital to lend, but, for the means of lending it, the other establishments were all dependent upon the Bank, the great fountain of our domestic currency. Accordingly, nearly the whole burden and profit of discounting was thrown upon the Bank. It made its own terms; it exacted 10 per cent. Nevertheless, its resources (restricted by the Bank Act) were insufficient to meet the demand upon it. In other two hours, the failure of Peabody & Co. and other firms would have created such a panic in London, that a tremendous run upon the Bank for deposits would have arisen. Then, at last, the Government did for the Bank what it would not do for the equally legitimate interests of Trade, and suspended the Act of 1844.

No crisis could more clearly demonstrate the defects of our present monetary system. It proved how entirely all the other banks are dependent upon the Bank of England, and how fatal are the artificial restrictions placed upon the bank-issues of the country. There is not only a monopoly, but even the banks which enjoy the monopoly have not, under the present system, the means of supplying the wants of the community. True, for our own part, we believe that if the Bank had at the outset freely employed its "reserve" (that portion of its resources which it is allowed to use) in the support of all solvent though embarrassed firms, like the Dennistouns, the crisis might have been prevented,—the evil might have been nipped in the bud; and no panic would have arisen to occasion the heavy internal drain which at length proved fatal to the Bank—or at least to the Bank Act. But if the Bank Court be exonerated, only the greater blame must fall upon the Act. And the heavy charge substantiated against our monetary system in 1857 is this: that, by its operation, it *imported* the American crisis into this country. A transient embarrassment, in no way affecting the solvency of British trade, instead of being met by the proper means, was aggravated into the severest crisis which this country has yet undergone. Trade was robbed of its wealth, through a depression of the markets to the extent of 25 per cent, and scores of firms, as solvent as the Bank itself, were forced into the Gazette.

And all this was caused by an unwise interference of the Legislature with our old freedom of banking; and especially by the legislative embargo placed upon nearly seven millions of gold in the Bank of England,—in consequence of which monetary crises are now produced under circumstances in which (but for this embargo) no embarrassment at all would be experienced. Under the existing system, the ordinary monetary accommodation is withdrawn from Trade at the very times when it is most urgently required. The Bank turns its back upon Trade: the Act says, "No—you cannot have your bills discounted upon any terms," even while there are six or seven millions of gold in the Bank. When the Bank has exhausted its powers of issue as restricted by the Act, it has still these millions of gold on hand,—yet not one sovereign of that immense sum can be used by the Bank, either for discounting purposes, or in discharge of its banking liabilities. The reserve, in fact, as established by the Act, is useless. Yet for the sake of keeping up an inert deposit, these millions are withdrawn from banking purposes, and the whole commerce of the country is periodically sacrificed. It is not Trade that periodically becomes insane,—it is our Monetary System that ever and anon becomes inadequate. A drain of gold occurs—or, it may be, a crisis in some other country temporarily embarrasses our traders: thereupon the Bank of England refuses to assist these firms—raises its rate,—depresses the markets,—aggravates the difficulty; the other establishments stop discounting, and Trade is brought to the ground. This, in brief, is the position. How long is it to last?

APPENDIX A.

No. I.

SYNOPSIS OF THE POSITION OF THE PRINCIPAL LONDON JOINT-STOCK BANKS, January 1 to June 30, 1864, drawn up by the Author from the Balance-sheets exhibited, Reports rendered, and Speeches made at the recent Half-yearly Meetings.

	Established.	Subscribed Capital.	Paid-up Capital.	*Present* amount of Reserved Fund.	Deposits and Acceptances.	Net Profits on last Half-year.	Percentage of Profit on Paid-up Capital.	Interest paid or due to Customers.	Current Expenses and Bad Debts.	Cash in hand, at Bank of England, or at call.	Government and Guaranteed Stock.
		£	£	£	£	£	6 Mo. Per An.	£	£	£	£
London and Westminster	1834	5,000,000	1,000,000	282,852	18,516,083	234,032	23·4 = 46·8	No return	50,693	1,516,695	2,492,412
London Joint-Stock . .	1836	3,000,000	600,000	276,301	14,959,649	124,476	20·75 = 41·5	No return	27,972	No return	1,025,070
Union Bank	1839	3,000,000	780,000	187,000	19,517,675	154,370	19·8 = 39·6	149,520	...	2,566,889	1,266,000
London and County . .	1839	1,500,000	692,913	192,913	12,167,884	109,501	15·8 = 31·6	76,354	72,315	2,461,386	951,312
City Bank	1855	1,000,000	500,000	140,000	4,781,633	57,970	11·6 = 23·2	No return	14,214	706,482	309,224
Bank of London	1855	600,000	339,000	130,000	4,890,280	59,321	17·5 = 35·	44,010	16,590	750,821	227,822
Metropolitan & Provincial	1861	1,000,000	295,000	40,000	1,060,688	27,000	9· = 18·	No return	8,115	146,019	58,191
Alliance Bank	1862	3,000,000	692,725	84,000	6,065,889	62,397	9· = 18·	47,837	23,457	555,232	54,489
Imperial Bank	1862	2,250,000	344,520	51,288	1,017,223	63,437	18·4 = 36·8	9,7[illegible]7	7,131	178,027	37,320
Consolidated	1863	1,494,670	597,628	38,500	4,284,581	71,012	11·88 = 23·76	No return	20,791	905,236	130,922
London & South-Western	1863	387,500	110,060	14,500	291,526	4,168	3·8 = 7·6	No return	No return	76,394	No return

There is no uniform method adopted in these Balance-sheets, as some banks give information which is not given by others. Under the head of "Deposits," the banks generally include the amount of their liabilities on Acceptances—which are not Deposits in the sense which the Public attaches to the term. The London and County and the Consolidated Bank state the amount of their Deposits and of their Acceptances separately; and it is to be hoped that the other banks will adopt the same course. § The Reserved Fund, or "Rest," consists of a portion of the profits of past years which have not been divided among the shareholders, and which are kept in hand to supplement the amount of dividend in years when the profits of the Bank may fall below the average. *Pro temp.*, they are really an addition to the Paid-up Capital of the Bank, although it is not usual to take them into account when calculating the percentage of the Bank's profit upon its capital. § It is to be borne in mind that the amount of the "current expenses" depends very much on whether or not the bank has branches. § The figures in the 10th column in some cases include the cash which the bank keeps "at notice." § In the 11th column, the amount set down to the London and County Bank under the head of Government and guaranteed stock, includes £105,000 of other kinds of stock; and the amounts set down in the same column to the City and the Union Banks likewise include a certain portion of "other debentures." § "No return" means no separate return. For example, in the balance-sheet of the London Joint-Stock, the "cash in hand" is classed with the amount of "bills discounted and other securities;" and in the London and South-Western, the amount of "interest" paid is classed with the "current expenses."

No. II.

English and Scotch Banking.

In making this Table, we have to confine our list of the London Banks to those whose balance-sheets state the amount of interest paid. As specimens of Scotch banking, we give the British Linen Co. Bank, the Union Bank, and the Clydesdale—these being the only ones which as yet publish balance-sheets.

	Liabilities: Deposits and Acceptances.	I. Cash in hand, at Bank of England, and at call. II. Government Stock.		Total Banking Reserve.	Reserved Fund or "Rest" on 30th June.	Proportion of Banking Reserve to Liabilities.	Average Rate of Interest paid to Depositors.*	Percentage of Profits per annum. I. On Capital. II. On Capital & "Rest."	
		I.	II.			per cent.	per cent.	I.	II.
London and County	12,167,884	2,461,386	951,312	3,412,698	192,913	28·04	·82	31·6	24·72
Bank of London	4,890,280	750,821	227,822	978,643	112,460	20·01	·92 or 1·17	35·	26·28
Alliance Bank	6,065,889	555,232	54,489	609,721	54,000	10·05	·77 or 1·03	18·	17·54
Imperial Bank	1,017,223	178,027	37,320	215,347	3,000	21·17	·96 or 1·02	36·8	36·44
British Linen Co. Bank (established 1746):—									
Deposits, notes in circulation, and all other liabilities to the public,				£7,318,545					
Government Stocks and balance at credit with London correspondents			£1,082,769						
Bank of England stock, and other stocks, bonds, debentures, &c.			1,183,386		300,000	38·6	3·75	11·82	9·1
Gold and silver coin, notes of Bank of England and of other banks			563,761	2,829,916					
Union Bank of Scotland (established 1830):—									
Deposits, notes in circulation, and all other liabilities to the public,				£8,178,130					
Consols and other Government Securities			£1,064,065						
Other Securities			326,508		78,156	29·71	3·75	11·8	10·96
Coin, notes of other banks, and cash-balances in hands of London and country bankers			1,039,334	2,420,907					
Clydesdale Bank (established 1838)					200,000	32·2	3·75	11·13	9·44

* In the first half of this column the interest is calculated on the total sum given as "deposits" in the balance-sheets. But, as a considerable portion of this sum consists of acceptances and circular notes, which bear no interest,—in the second half of the column, the rate of interest is calculated on the so-called "deposits" after deducting from their amount 23¼ per cent—which is the proportion which the Acceptances, &c., bear to the true Deposits, or customers' balances, in the case of the London and County Bank.

As a general rule, the London joint-stock banks pay interest at the rate of 2 per cent on the minimum monthly balance of Current-accounts which do not at any time fall below £500 during the half-year; and 1 per cent on such accounts when they fall below £500 but not below £200. On Deposit-accounts, which cannot be withdrawn without a week's notice, the joint-stock banks pay interest at the current rate of the day—*i. e.*, at the minimum rate of the Bank of England,—provided that the rate do not exceed 5 per cent.

Of the banks whose balance-sheets show the amount of interest paid to customers, only one (the London and County) gives also the true amount of its customers' balances (as distinguished from Acceptances, &c.); therefore there are no adequate data for ascertaining the exact percentage of interest paid by these banks on the money intrusted to their keeping. In the case of the London and County Bank, where the requisite data are given, the rate of interest paid to customers amounts to only ⅘ths of a per cent. In the case of the three other London banks given in Table II., the rate of interest which we have conjecturally assigned to them is greater—varying from 1 to 1⅛ per cent: but our calculation is made on the supposition that the amount of "Acceptances" held by these banks is as large, in proportion to their total so-called "Deposits," as that held by the London and County Bank,—should it be less, then the rate of interest which we have assigned to them is too high. One per cent, or at most 1¼, appears to be a safe estimate of the average rate of interest paid by the London joint-stock banks upon the aggregate money of their customers, during the last half-year.

The Scotch banks, on the other hand, pay interest on every sum intrusted to their keeping, whether large or small. They now divide their Deposits into two classes: in one of which the interest is calculated on the daily balances, in the other, on the minimum monthly balances,—a higher rate, of course, being allowed upon the latter than upon the former. In one bank (which has obligingly favoured us with statistics) the latter class comprises rather more than one-half of the whole deposits in the Bank; and it is also found that a current-account calculated on the minimum monthly balance shows one-twentieth part less than if calculated by the daily balances. In other words, suppose the daily balances show a customer's account to have averaged £200 throughout a month, the minimum balance for that month would be £190.

During the last half-year, the Scotch banks have paid a fixed rate of 3 per cent interest on current-accounts calculated on the daily balances,—and 4½ on deposit-receipts and current-accounts calculated on the minimum monthly balances. And as it is found that the sums deposited with the banks are divided between the two classes in nearly equal proportions, it follows that the average rate of interest paid by the Scotch banks during the past half-year has been 3¾ per cent.

The results of the comparison between the English and Scotch systems of banking, as shown in Table II., may be summed up thus:—

I. The Scotch banks pay to their customers a greatly higher rate of interest upon the money deposited with them than the English banks do: the Scotch banks at present paying at the average rate of 3¾ per cent, and the English banks about 1 per cent.

II. The Scotch banks keep larger banking reserves than the London banks do: the average proportion of reserves to liabilities kept by the four London banks being 20 per cent; while that of the three Scotch banks averages 33½ per cent.

III. The profit of the Scotch banks amounts to 11½ per cent on their paid-up capital, while that of the English banks amounts to 30 per cent.

Hence it is manifest that the Scotch system of banking gives much greater advantages to the public than the English system does. And, as a natural consequence, the English system yields larger profits to bank-proprietors than the Scotch system.

APPENDIX B.

No. I.

TABLE showing the changes in the Bank of England's rate of discount from 1695 down to the passing of the Bank Act in the autumn of 1844; and also the amount of coin and bullion simultaneously held by the Bank subsequent to 1822.

Year.	Bank-rate.	Bullion.	Year.	Bank-rate.	Bullion.
	per cent	£		per cent	£
From 1695 to 1762	4 & 5		1836 June	4 & 4½	7,888,700
From 1762 to 1822	5		,, Aug.	4½ & 5	6,325,000
1822		10,600,000*	,, Sept.	5	5,719,000
1823		11,500,000*	1837	...	5,400,000
1824	4	12,800,000*	1838 Feb.	4 & 5	9,543,000
1825		6,200,900*	,, Mar.	4	10,015,000
1826 Jan.	4 & 5	3,000,000†	1839 May	4 & 5	5,119,000
1827 Feb.	5	2,459,510*	,, June	5 & 5½	4,344,000
1827 Aug.	4	10,159,020*	,, July	5½	3,785,000
1828		10,400,000*	,, Aug.	6	3,265,000
1829		6,800,000*	1840 Jan.	5 & 6	3,454,000
1830		10,000,000*	,, Feb.	5	3,964,000
1831		7,300,000*	1841	...	6,590,000
1832	4	6,400,000*	1842 Apr.	4 & 5	7,032,000
1833		9,700,000*	,, May	4	11,700,000*
1834		7,500,000*	1843	...	16,213,950
1835		6,200,000*	1844 Feb.	...	15,314,540

—Compiled from statistics given in the Appendix to the Report of the Parliamentary Committee on Commercial Distress in 1848 (see App. Nos. 4, 7, and 13). And also from Francis's *History of the Bank of England*, vol. ii. pp. 267-274.

* The sums in the bullion column which are marked by an asterisk represent the approximate amount, in most cases calculated upon the amount of bullion in the Bank on the 28th February and 31st August of each year.

† The amount of bullion in the Bank in January 1826 we have estimated from the amount held at the end of the following month, making allowance for the rapid decline which was then taking place.

No. II.

TABLE showing the changes in the Bank of England's *minimum* rate of discount subsequent to the passing of the Act of 1844; and also the amount of coin and bullion held by the Bank at the date of each of these changes.

Date of Change.	Rate.	Bullion.
	per cent	£
1844 Sept. 5.	2½	14,351,295
1845 Mar. 13.	2½	15,148,060
,, Oct. 16.	3	13,778,955
,, Nov. 6.	3½	13,202,365
1846 Aug. 27.	3	15,867,890
1847 Jan. 14.	3½	13,225,335
,, ,, 21.	4	12,766,260
,, Apr. 8.	5	9,236,340
,, Aug. 5.	5½	8,634,645
,, Oct. 25.	8	7,865,445
,, Nov. 27.	7	9,525,845
,, Dec. 2.	6	10,366,085
,, ,, 23.	5	11,609,075
1848 Jan. 27.	4	12,782,235
,, June 15.	3½	13,352,845
,, Nov. 2.	3	12,796,660
1849 Nov. 22.	2½	15,570,425
1850 Dec. 26.	3	14,351,730
1852 Jan. 1.	2½	16,992,450
,, Apr. 22.	2	19,099,150
1853 Jan. 6.	2½	19,170,165
,, ,, 20.	3	18,918,040
,, June 2.	3½	17,790,405
,, Sept. 1.	4	
,, ,, 15.	4½	15,399,075
,, ,, 20.	5	15,065,880
1854 May 11.	5½	11,857,270
,, Aug. 3.	5	12,593,700
1855 Apr. 5.	4½	14,392,500
,, May 3.	4	14,911,030
,, June 14.	3½	17,350,395
,, Sept. 6.	4	13,668,005
,, ,, 13.	4½	13,110,270
,, ,, 27.	5	12,368,255
,, Oct. 4.	5½	11,765,025
,, ,, 18.	6* 7†	10,682,230
1856 May 22.	6	9,938,875
,, ,, 29.	5	10,766,040
,, June 26.	4½	12,428,970
,, Oct. 1.	5	10,226,745
,, ,, 6.	6	9,589,400
,, ,, ,,	7	
,, Nov. 13.	7	9,061,235
,, Dec. 4.	6½	9,871,520
,, ,, 18.	6	10,050,995
1857 Apr. 2.	6½	9,342,720
,, June 8.	6	10,909,255
,, July 16.	5½	11,840,652
,, Oct. 8.	6	10,109,943
,, ,, 12.	7	9,369,704
,, ,, 19.	8	8,731,553
,, Nov. 5.	9	6,666,065
,, ,, 9.	10	6,079,595
1858 Jan. 7.	6	12,112,925
,, ,, 14.	5	13,746,475
,, ,, 28.	4	14,970,165
,, Feb. 4.	3½	15,745,760

Date of Chapge.	Rate.	Bullion.
	per cent	£
1858 Feb. 11.	3	16,542,675
,, Dec. 9.	2½	18,377,470
1859 Apr. 28.	3½	16,960,270
,, May 5.	4½	16,382,765
,, June 2.	3½	17,266,890
,, ,, 9.	3	17,266,185
,, July 14.	2½	17,338,055
1860 Jan. 19.	3	14,867,620
,, ,, 31.	4	14,277,710
,, Mar. 29.	4½	14,212,415
,, Apr. 12.	5	13,890,225
,, May 10.	4½	14,752,655
,, ,, 24.	4	15,145,550
,, Nov. 8.	4½	12,522,655
,, ,, 13.	5	12,535,995
,, ,, 15.	6	12,725,079
,, ,, 28.	5	12,419,043
,, Dec. 31.	6	10,292,300
1861 Jan. 7.	7	9,869,817
,, Feb. 4.	8	9,744,970
,, Mar. 21.	7	10,981,258
,, Apr. 4.	6	11,525,338
,, ,, 11.	5	11,520,488
,, May 6.	6	11,302,248
,, Aug. 1.	5	11,481,675
,, ,, 15.	4½	11,741,980
,, ,, 29.	4	12,241,955
,, Sept. 19.	3½	13,173,445
,, Nov. 7.	3	13,566,675
1862 Jan. 9.	2½	15,473,420
,, May 22.	3	15,317,890
,, July 10.	2½	16,187,635
,, ,, 24.	2	17,565,130
,, Oct. 30.	3	17,011,715
1863 Jan. 15.	4	13,238,175
,, ,, 28.	5	12,737,475
,, Feb. 19.	4	13,651,255
,, Apr. 23.	3½	14,531,830
,, ,, 30.	3	14,491,405
,, May 16.	3½	
,, ,, 21.	4	13,694,505
,, Nov. 2.	5	
,, ,, 5.	6	13,194,575
,, Dec. 2.	7	12,484,390
,, ,, 3.	8	
,, ,, 24.	7	13,503,160
1864 Jan. 20.	8	12,305,490
,, Feb. 11.	7	12,753,185
,, ,, 25.	6	13,053,080
,, Apr. 16.	7	12,056,520
,, May 2.	8	11,778,430
,, ,, 5.	9	
,, ,, 19.	8	12,601,165
,, ,, 26.	7	13,041,305
,, June 16.	6	13,553,835
,, July 25.	7	12,304,525
,, Aug. 4.	8	12,171,725
,, Sept. 8.	9	12,226,895

* For 60 days' bills. † For 95 days' bills.

The high rates of discount charged by the Bank of England during the last twelve months, call for a parting word of comment.

Loud complaints are made at present in regard to the costly armaments maintained by the Great Powers of Europe, which burden Industry by means of the heavy taxation which they occasion. But does it never occur to our economists and reformers, and to all who have the welfare of industry at heart, that there is a belligerent monetary policy established in this country, hardly less detrimental to the interests of industry and to the welfare of the masses, and which could be more easily dispensed with than the defensive armaments of war?

Ever and anon the Bank of England makes war upon all other countries, either in defence of its own stock of gold, or in order to gain possession of theirs. It makes war upon them by exorbitantly raising its rate of discount. How far such a procedure is called for, we have discussed in the body of this work: we here allude to this belligerent policy for the sake of pointing out its results from an international point of view.

Its only result is to raise the value of money throughout Europe, and thereby to oppress the industry and check the commerce of other countries as well as of our own. The Bank of England does not now obtain its object. Whenever it tries to rob other countries of their gold, the banks of those countries retaliate, and effectually defend themselves by raising their rates in proportion. Then up goes the Bank of England's charge still higher,—and up in turn go theirs. And so the position, *quoad* the possession of gold, remains unchanged. But a great change is thereby made in the profits of banking, and in the condition of Trade.

This policy of war, howsoever the banks may profitably play at it, is most detrimental to Industry. It abnormally raises the rate of discount throughout Europe,—the banks get increased profits—and the commercial classes are plundered.

"Quicquid delirant reges, plectuntur Achivi."

However mad, in a monetary point of view, may be this war of the banks, the commercial classes of each country have to pay the cost of it. The international conflict is carried on—the Bank of England ever acting on the offensive, and charging the highest rates,—until Trade in this country fairly breaks down. And then the money which the Bank could not get from other countries, accumulates in its coffers simply because our own industry has been paralysed, and no longer needs so much money to carry it on.

Surely it is time to put a stop to such a policy—so needless and so injurious—which obtains no advantage for any country, but which inflicts injury upon them all,—and which simply profits the banks of Europe at the cost of the commercial and working classes.

APPENDIX C.

THE CRISIS AT HAMBURG IN 1857.

The following account of the remarkable monetary crisis at Hamburg in 1857, is taken from Fenn's *British Funds* (eighth edition), pp. 266-267 :—

"The commercial embarrassments in the United States, the suspension of several London houses closely connected with Hamburg houses in the Swedish trade, brought down in November and December most of the houses engaged in the Swedish, Norwegian, and Danish trade. A state of things now ensued never before known in Hamburg; confidence was entirely destroyed, and it was thought imperative that the State should interfere.

"The Burgerschaft empowered the Senate to advance Government bonds, to the amount of £1,200,000, against the deposit of goods; and passed a law suspending, until April 1, 1858, the bankruptcy laws in favour of such houses as could show that on the day of suspending they had sufficient means to justify the belief that they could, if time were allowed, meet all their engagements, and allowing them to wind up their affairs under administration, with the consent of the majority of their creditors. But these measures of relief were found quite inadequate; the panic was so great that the Government bonds thus issued could not be discounted; and on no security whatever would capitalists part with their money.

"At last, after many discussions, on the 6th of December, the Senate finally proposed that a silver loan of £1,125,000 should be contracted for; and that, in the mean time, a deposit of Government bonds and railway shares, to the amount of £375,000, should be placed in the public Giro Bank, and the sum so represented employed by the State in discounting good mercantile bills. The proposal of the Senate was acceded to by the Burgerschaft; and shortly afterwards the Austrian Government agreed to advance the loan wanted by the Hamburg Senate, which the Prussian Government had peremptorily refused to do.

"But even this measure of relief did not restore confidence, though there were large stocks of silver in the hands of capitalists, owing to the dread generally entertained that some of the leading houses in Hamburg and Altona would not be able to meet their engagements. When, therefore, 10,000,000 of marcs Banco in silver—part of the 17,000,000 marcs loan advanced by the Austrian Government—arrived from Vienna, the Senate, to whom the houses thought to be in difficulties in the mean time had applied for assistance, called another meeting of the Burgerschaft, and proposed that the latter sum should be intrusted to a secret committee, which should be empowered to lend the same to the houses in question on good security. This proposition was agreed to; and on the 12th of December, immediately that it was made known that the assistance of the State would enable the leading houses to fulfil their engagements, the panic ceased,—and money became so abundant that in the last week of December, the Government bonds issued as the first measure of relief, which in the beginning of that month could not be discounted at 15 per cent, were readily taken at a discount of 2 to 3 per cent, and bills on houses of undoubted credit were discounted at the same rate.

"Altogether about 220 Hamburg and Altona houses suspended payment in the months of November and December 1857. Of this number 176 houses (nearly three-fourths of the whole number) availed themselves of the law of the 2d of December passed to aid the winding up of the affairs of suspended firms under administration. About 50 were declared bankrupt, and the rest made private arrangements with their creditors. The bill liabilities of the suspended firms were better met than was at first expected."

APPENDIX D.

What is a Pound? *

"The main object" of our present currency system, as regulated by the Act of 1844, says the recent Report of the Select Committee, "was undoubtedly to secure the *variation* of the paper-currency of the kingdom according to the same laws by which a metallic circulation would *vary*." Variation! what a strange principle whereon to base a currency. Is not the prime requisite of a currency stability of value? And, in the face of this truth, how is it that our statesmen adhere to a legislation the avowed object of which is to base the whole currency of the kingdom upon the principle not of stability in value, but of fluctuation? At first sight there seems a great mystery here,—namely, as to how men of good sense in other respects can be found supporting so pernicious an absurdity. But this proceeds from a mistake often witnessed in the history of nations, especially at times when the progress of society is becoming fettered by institutions which once promoted its growth. Our statesmen now err by mistaking a means for the end. Gold, which is but *one* form of money, they have come to regard as the sole form: and hence, believing that nothing but gold *can* constitute a currency, they are forced to accept it with all its defects,—or indeed even regard these defects as worthy of respect, because necessary parts of what they conceive to be an indispensable system.

If those statesmen would either cast their eyes back into history, or lift them to view the world as it is, they would discover their mistake. Let them, for example, turn back to the origin of Money, and consider the state of things when gold was first adopted as a form of that most useful handmaid of commerce. Was there not as much controversy then in regard to gold-money as there is now with respect to paper-money? Most assuredly there was, and must have been. Gold-money has been so long recognised in this and the other countries of the Occi-

* Reprinted from the *Edinburgh Advertiser* of July and August 1858.

dental world, that no one questions its validity as a medium of exchange; but when it was first introduced, the difficulty of getting it accepted was doubtless far greater than that which was experienced on the introduction of paper-money amongst us a century and a half ago.

In Greece and elsewhere, the earliest coinage is said to have been instituted to represent the value of cattle;—just as in their State of Utah the Mormons, from a dearth of the precious metals, lately established a paper-currency based upon a like standard. Of old, as thus in Utah, an ox or a sheep was the measure of value,—because these animals formed the chief wealth of the community, and were the most common form of payment when trade was conducted on the principle of barter. But assuredly, in that primitive age, when a purchaser appeared in the market for the first time offering these coins in exchange for goods, he would find few men ready to strike a bargain with him. We can easily conceive some bucolic possessor of fat beeves turning with angry contempt from the proffered bits of yellow metal, and thinking himself as much a fool if he were to part with his stock for such glittering dross as the mother of Jack the Giantkiller thought her hopeful son when he sold her cow for a hatful of beans. "It is of no use to me," he would say, "of itself,—I can neither eat it nor drink it, nor turn it in any way to use; and as to what you say about other people being ready and willing to give me goods for it the same as if this gold-piece were an ox, that's all nonsense, and you had better not try to 'come over' me in that style." The Lord Overstone of those times, with his wealth all in sheep and cattle, would have resisted any proposal to assign an independent value to those gold-pieces,—just as the great capitalist of the present time refuses to accord the slightest independent value to pound-notes. Sir Robert Peel, in answer to "What is a Pound?" pulled out of his pocket a sovereign; the Peel of ancient times, in answer to an analogous question, must have lugged into the Senate-house an ox! The Bullionist maintains that a note ought not to be allowed to circulate unless there is an equal amount of gold in the bank which issues the note; his prototype in early times would have treated the gold-pieces in similar fashion whenever they could not instantly be converted into oxen. The former, when war or panic temporarily drains away our gold, insists that our paper-money shall be diminished in like proportion; and the latter (had there been such a being) must have in like spirit demanded the destruction of the gold-money whenever there was a murrain amongst the cattle.

It was only by a slow process at first that gold-pieces came to be recognised as a medium of exchange, in supplement to barter. Even when fully established in one city or community, other cities or states would for long refuse to have anything to do with it. Commerce and civilisation in time did the work,—inducing one city or tribe or nation after another to give up barter, or at least to supplement it by means of gold-money. Nowadays gold-money is established in credit all over the greater part of the civilised world, yet the process is far from complete: for, besides barbarous regions, in civilised China one-third of the entire population of the globe refuse to acknowledge gold as money; and in India gold-money is not a legal tender, and has comparatively little place in the circulation. Whether, therefore, we look back into history, or abroad upon the world as it is, the truth is forced upon us that gold has no claim to be regarded as the only real form of Money,—that it is not recognised as money at all amongst nearly one-half of the civilised population of the earth,—that it circulates as money solely by force of social agreement, and that the same force may demonetise it at pleasure, or create other forms of money to supplement its deficiency or compensate its fluctuations.

Paper-money, the chief of the forms of currency which have been devised to supplement the defects of metallic money, is now going through the same course as gold and silver had to do in early times, and is as surely winning its way to general acceptance. Paper-money is beyond all question infinitely cheaper, as well as more portable, than metallic money; and, by a due regulation of its issue, the measure of value in any country can also be kept more steady in value than if the currency were solely based upon the precious metals. As a mere matter of cost (which is but a trifle compared with the weightier points involved), the gold-money in circulation in the United Kingdom, amounting to about £80,000,000, costs the country, by loss of interest and wear and tear, fully five millions a-year,—a sum which, if saved, would prove a great alleviation of the national burdens, and an important agent in diminishing the National Debt. But a still more important advantage from an improved use of paper-money would be the means thereby afforded of obviating the extraordinary fluctuations to which our currency is subjected from being based entirely on gold-money. Paper-money has already established itself as a *representative* of gold-money; what it must next do is to establish itself as a *substitute* for gold-money,—just as the gold coins of old, from being representative of oxen, became by-and-by a substitute for them in commercial transactions, and invested with a recognised value of their own.

No one questions that paper-money would do perfectly well for the internal circulation of the kingdom. Bank of England notes lowered to £1 would serve all the purposes of the 80,000,000 sovereigns circulating amongst us, besides possessing many great advantages. But then, say the objectors, if the domestic circulation be permitted to become one of paper-money, how are we to meet the foreign exchanges? Our paper-money will not circulate abroad, and if we keep no gold in our own circulation (say they), how are we to get it when we want to send money to other countries? Now—even putting out of view the fact that, whatever amount of sovereigns be circulating in this country, they are quite unavailable for sending abroad unless we issue one-pound notes to fill their place and allow the domestic trade to be carried on,—there are two sufficient answers to this question. One of these may be made in Scotch fashion, by asking another, —namely, how this country managed from 1797 to 1815, when there was hardly a guinea in circulation? That period was the most perilous and trying which the British empire ever came through—it was a period, too, remarkable for a great expansion of our trade and commerce,—nevertheless, although gold-money had almost disappeared from circulation, no difficulty was found in settling the foreign exchanges, and the Government was even able besides to obtain large sums of metallic money to pay and feed our armies abroad and to subsidise those of other States. Where, then, is the difficulty of procuring gold, though the domestic circulation consist of paper-money? It is merely imaginary. Gold may be bought in the market like any other commodity. Indeed the "difficulty" anticipated by the Bullionists in regard to gold already exists, without producing harm, in regard to silver. With no two countries in the world are the exchanges so perpetually against us as with India and China,—and with both of those countries we must settle the exchanges not in gold but in silver. Yet we find no difficulty in getting the silver,—and there would be just as little in getting gold, though not a sovereign were in circulation in this country. In fact, by dispensing with the use of gold in our domestic currency, there would just be so many millions more of the precious metals thrown into the markets of the world.

The other answer is, that if a system of paper-money possessed (*de jure* as well as *de facto*) of an independent value were fully established in this country, that very fact would tend to make our notes acceptable to a considerable degree even in foreign countries; and that acceptability would go on increasing year by year, as the international bonds of commerce are drawn closer. At present, by Act of Parliament, we expressly take away *de jure* from our paper-money the value which it has *de facto;* and foreigners would be fools indeed if they were to attach to our paper-money a value which we ourselves (or at least our Acts of Parliament) repudiate. Nevertheless, if any one go to Paris with his whole money in Bank of England notes, he will find not the least difficulty in getting French coins for them at the money-changers,—just as he requires to do with our shillings and half-crowns and sovereigns, which he has to commute into francs and the other coins of the country. In fact, in process of time, as the various European States are drawn into still closer commercial relationship, we have no doubt that a "Bank of Europe" will be established, whose notes will pass current as a means of settling the exchanges, just as bills of exchange do now.

"What is a Pound sterling?" was the question which puzzled our legislators in 1844, and which seems to puzzle them yet. After long consideration, Sir R. Peel declared that he could see no answer to the question except that "a pound was a sovereign, and *nothing but* a sovereign." The answer is an intelligible one, inasmuch as the idea is expressed most plainly; and it has also a very practical look about it, which doubtless did much to win for it the ready acceptance it met with from the Senate of the most practical-minded people in the world. But the idea itself is only half-true, and in many important respects is calculated to mislead. The sovereign unquestionably is a pound sterling, but we deny altogether that a pound is and can be nothing but a sovereign. Common folks, who are not so uplifted by theory as to be blind to the facts around them, have an idea that twenty shillings are quite as much a pound sterling as a sovereign is; and so they are, although payment in silver cannot now be forced upon any one save to the extent of forty shillings. Nevertheless, with this arbitrarily and recently imposed restriction, twenty shillings are quite as much a pound sterling as a sovereign is. We have also the idea that a pound-note is a pound sterling; and as long as the bank that issues it is solvent (*i. e.*, has the right to issue it), that piece of engraved paper will buy quite as much corn, or coal, or labour, as either a sovereign or twenty shillings.

If a sovereign be a pound sterling, it is only because the will of the nation has made it so. The pound has existed for centuries,—the sovereign is a thing of yesterday. Our fathers, or at least our grandfathers, knew of no such coin. Twenty shillings, or a guinea minus a shilling, was their pound. And in the previous generation, silver was the standard-money quite as much as gold was,—or more so. That was the case a century ago. In earlier times the case was still more different from what it is now. The pound sterling was originally a pound of silver. If that standard had been retained, the pound would now have been worth four sovereigns,—for, according to the present relative value of gold and silver in Europe and America, it takes £4 to buy a pound of the latter metal. By making a sovereign to represent the pound sterling, therefore, a great change has been made—gradually and almost imperceptibly as our monetary wants required, but still a very great change. The ancient money-standard of France, the *livre*, underwent a similar change. In fact, it is the commonest thing in the world to find that though the money-standard of a country preserves its ancient name, it has entirely lost its original value. In Classic ages the money-pieces which at first got their name from being equivalent in value to an ox or a sheep, in process of time entirely departed from that standard. So invariable is this process, and so characteristic of all monetary systems, from the most developed down to those but little removed from the system of barter, that we find it illustrated even among the Negro communities of Central Africa. In Kukawa (the capital of Bornou) and surrounding district, the same thing has happened to the pound of copper that with us has happened to the pound of silver. "The ancient standard of the country—viz., the pound of copper," says Dr Barth, "has long since fallen into disuse, though the name (*rotl*) still remains." The price of commodities is still reckoned in the *rotl*, or pound, although the pound has disappeared from the currency. He tells us that as copper became inadequate to the wants of trade in that not very civilised but manifestly sensible community, cotton-strips of a certain size, and cotton shirts of various quality, came into use as a supplementary medium of exchange; and of late another form or species of currency has been added to these—namely, cowries (shells), which were introduced by a foreign tribe which now constitutes the ruling race in Bornou. Still further, European commerce has introduced also the Austrian and the Spanish dollars,—and, what may seem strange, yet has its parallel in other parts of the world, the former of these coins, though of less intrinsic value, is better liked in Bornou than the latter.* Here, then, let it be observed, we have an original standard of copper, the name of which is preserved (just as our pound is) though the thing itself has disappeared from the currency; and in lieu of this extinct form of money, we find cotton-strips and cotton shirts, shells, and silver coins, all adopted by the people. Startlingly various as are these forms of currency, they all agree

* In the ports of China the reverse is the case,—the Spanish dollar, from being better known, bringing a higher price in proportion to the amount of silver which it contains than any other of our European forms of silver-money.

in this, that they are recognised by the people as mediums of exchange. And *this is the sole indispensable requisite of any form of Money.* Doubtless, the cotton-strips at first circulated simply as representatives of the pound of copper, and the cowrie-shells as representatives of the cotton-strips; but, by-and-by, as the strips and the shells became fully acknowledged as measures of value and mediums of exchange, they acquired a perfectly independent value of their own (as pound-notes have *de facto* with us). And mark this. The cotton is useful—the shells are useless: demonetise the former, and it will still possess a value,—demonetise the latter, and they will be wholly worthless. Yet both circulate on equal terms. Why? Precisely because each, though widely different in intrinsic value, is *equally acknowledged as currency* by the people. Now, cowrie-shells are just our paper-money in another form, though a much less perfect one. And thus, in this little State of Central Africa—in one of the most barbarous regions of the world—we find, firstly, an extinct and now merely nominal standard of value, precisely analogous to our pound sterling. Secondly, we find there, as in a lesser but not more reasonable form in this country, that the acknowledged representatives of that standard are modified from age to age by the wants of trade and the circumstances of the people. And, thirdly, we find that currency to comprise various elements—viz., (1) the precious metals, and (2) the principle of paper-money, blended with (3) a form of barter which is very convenient to that African community,—just as silk-pieces form an established medium of exchange in the civilised and highly commercial empire of China. Principles express themselves by different names and in different forms in the various parts of the world, but the principles themselves (whether commercial or political) are wondrously akin.

What do these things teach us? What do the widely different forms of currency existing in the world, and the various changes from age to age in the currency of every country, suggest if not this:—First, that *anything* may be made currency, if the people agree to acknowledge it as such; and that many very different things may coexist as currency, and be equally valuable as such, if the people decree or agree to accord to them equal recognition as mediums of exchange. Secondly, a review of the monetary systems of different countries shows that all nations modify, and introduce new elements into, their currency from age to age, in accordance with the commercial wants and altered circumstances of the community; and also that those States will thrive best who act intelligently upon this principle, and avoid the folly of allowing the swaddling-clothes of their infancy to become fetters upon their advancing growth.

If we now repeat the question, What is a Pound? we think the reader will hesitate to affirm the dogma of Sir R. PEEL that it is and can be nothing but a sovereign. Some generations hence, owing to the progressive expansion of commerce and greater enlightenment on the part of our community, the pound sterling may be manufactured out of something much less costly than the present sovereign, though holding an equal recognised value, and, we doubt not, subject to fewer fluctuations. The pound sterling, in truth, is just a measure of value, as the yard is a measure of length, and the pound avoirdupois of weight. A pound sterling is no more merely a piece of gold, than a yard is a piece of wood. A certain length of wood, and a certain weight of gold minted in a certain form, may be representatives of those measures, and the medium through which they are applied to the uses of life; but other things may represent those measures as well. A yard will be a yard whether it be represented by three feet of wood, of iron, or of cotton tape; and a pound sterling will be a pound sterling whether it be represented by gold, silver, or paper. As Length is an abstract thing, and its measures possess little or no value apart from the things measured; so Value is likewise an abstract thing, and its measures also need not possess any value apart from the things which they serve to measure. This is the true statement of the case.

Commerce is a game which all the world is playing at, and Money is the counters by which the game is carried on. Different nations use different kinds of counters; and it matters not of what those counters consist, so that they possess a recognised value in the sphere within which they are meant to circulate. The business of the world is to buy and sell, and our relative position is determined by the number of counters we hold: the more counters, the more land or labour or luxuries may be purchased. And, manifestly, the less costly those counters are, the better. If a set of men were to insist upon playing whist with pearl counters, what better would they be? Would the costly pearls better show the relative success of the players than if they used counters of paper or bone? Certainly not. And we trust the British nation will speedily learn to apply this principle as a means of improving its currency,—which is at present not only most costly in material, but, what is far worse, liable to such sudden and excessive fluctuations in value as to violate the very first requisite of a currency—namely, stability of value.

If we calmly review the circumstances of the late crisis (of 1857), from its origin in the railway panic of the United States (greatly caused by the organised *bearing* operations of certain journals and speculators), which quickly extended to the whole commerce and banking of the Union, producing not only a suspension of payments to, but also a drain of specie from, this country, and thereby, under our antiquated currency-system, creating a similar but still more disastrous crisis in Great Britain, which thereafter extended into France, Northern Germany, Denmark, and the Scandinavian kingdoms, besides sending a lessening wave of disaster to far California, Rio Janeiro, and Australia,—we think it will plainly appear that the "overtrading," upon which so much stress has been laid, was merely the driblet of powder forming the train, that the panic in the United States was the spark which fired it, but that *it was the defective currency-system of the times that formed the combustible mass which blew the commerce of one-half of the civilised world into the air*, and has paralysed the scared survivors ever since. Is it not a remarkable fact that it was precisely amongst the most civilised nations that the shock was most felt and the disaster greatest? What does this mean? It was the States most advanced in commercial enterprise and civilisation—Great Britain, the United States, and Hamburg,—which proved most signally unequal to the emergency. How was this? It was because *in our commercial progress, all parts of the fabric have not advanced abreast. While Commerce has been advancing rapidly, our monetary system has lagged behind.* While Trade has been extending immensely, its supports are restricted by principles suited only to a past and less developed state of things. This is the fundamental cause of the constantly-recurring crises of the last five-and-thirty years; and the increased severity of each new catastrophe is just because every ten years our fettered monetary system is proving more and more inadequate to our expanding trade. The evil is not confined to our own shores—other nations likewise feel it,—but we suffer oftenest and most severely; and this for two reasons—(1) because our currency-system is more fettered than that of any other country, and (2) because, even if it were not, our commercial system is so much more developed than theirs, that it suffers more from the shackles of an antiquated system.

What, then, is to be done? Are we to attempt to shut our eyes, and abide by an impracticable system? Or shall we not rather revise our opinions, and review the whole question, in order to bring our monetary system abreast of the new era of developed trade and commerce in which we find ourselves? A century and a half has elapsed since banks and paper-money were established amongst us. That was a great step. Only a few able heads foresaw the wisdom of that measure,—the majority of would-be authorities were against it, foreboding from it disaster; and nothing but the necessities of the State sufficed to secure its adoption. A similar advance is needed by the nation now, though doubtless it will encounter similar opposition. A century and a half ago, we had arrived at a point when the supplies of gold-money no longer sufficed to permit of the further expansion of commerce; and the alternative was, either that the nation, though increasing in population, should remain nearly stationary in trade (the greatest calamity that can befall a people), or else that some means be devised for supplementing the supplies of gold in such a manner as to permit of further expansions on the part of trade, and of increased employment for the people. The institution of banks and paper-money accomplished that end.

The problem now is an infinitely easier but not less urgently needed one. We have outgrown the currency-system that sufficed a century ago; and at the same time, misled by false theories, we have abandoned the principles of common-sense and statesmanlike wisdom by which our fathers adapted that system to most trying circumstances and exceptional times. We have gone backwards. The Act of 1844 places us in a worse condition, as regards the currency, than we were a century ago. Commerce grows as well as population, and monetary institutions need revision from age to age not less than political ones. Even if the Bank Act had not been passed, a time would have come when the currency-system of last century would have proved inadequate to the altered circumstances and expansion of trade. But that retrograde Act—the principles of which might have been suitable in the 17th century, but were repudiated as antiquated by our grandsires of the 18th, and which are still more out of place in the middle of the 19th century—is the grand error which we must first remove.

Paper-money during the last century served the purpose of supplementing the inadequate supply of gold-money in ordinary times: what it must be made to do now is, to supplement also that deficit in extraordinary times—or rather in times which, though once extraordinary, have now become common, or at least of steady recurrence. It was only in times of war that our fathers, the men of the past generation, found their currency-system inadequate; and at such times they boldly altered it, as they did not choose to be strangled for the sake of a theory. But commerce has so greatly extended in our day, so many nations now eagerly engage in it, that a drain of gold-money, which formerly used only to occur in times of war, has become a steadily recurrent feature of our commercial history even in times of peace. Every ten years such drains are becoming more certain in their occurrence, and more terribly severe in their consequences. They have become ordinary occurrences, and must be provided for in our ordinary legislation. *To equalise those temporary fluctuations—to supplement the sudden ebbs of gold-money from our shores until it have time to return—is the prime and most urgent want of our monetary and commercial systems.* There are various ways in which this may be done, and it is of comparatively little moment which of these be adopted. But let it be done. It required a great war, and serious necessities on the part of the State, before the founders of the Bank of England could carry their point, and introduce amongst us the blessings of banking and paper-money, to which our wondrous subsequent prosperity has been mainly owing. In like manner, we believe that another great war, and the pressure of State necessities, will be needed before the errors of the Bullionist-theory will be fully recognised, and the monetary reform which we advocate be introduced. But as to the ultimate triumph of these views, we entertain not the slightest doubt. It will come as certainly as the end of the present century,—and we trust more speedily.

THE END.

CPSIA information can be obtained
at www.ICGtesting.com
Printed in the USA
LVHW101339160422
716387LV00003B/98